F
Miller

Miller, Linda Lael
  Pirates

DATE DUE

OCT 27 '08			
DEC 0 1 '08			
MAY 1 3 '09			
MAY 1 2 '10			
JUN 0 8 '10			
7/16 WC			
SVHH 4/18			
JU			

#47-0108 Peel Off Pressure Sensitive

PIRATES

Linda Lael Miller

PIRATES

WHEELER
PUBLISHING, INC.
ROCKLAND, MA

★ AN AMERICAN COMPANY ★

Published in Large Print by arrangement with
Pocket Books, a division of Simon & Schuster, Inc.,
in the United States and Canada.

Wheeler Large Print Book Series.

Set in 16 pt. Plantin.

Library of Congress Cataloging-in-Publication Data

Miller, Linda Lael.
    Pirates / Linda Lael Miller.—Large print ed.
        p.   cm.—(Wheeler large print book series)
    ISBN 1-56895-249-X (large print : hard)
    1. Large type print.   I. Title.   II. Series.
[PS3563.I41373P57   1995b]
813'.54—dc20   95-34858
                                                                    CIP

For Diane Kirk and Anita Battershell.

Thanks for your confidence in the romance
genre and your commitment to the
empowerment of women.
You are two terrific females!

1

When the dog deserted her and moved in with Jeffrey and his new bride, it was, for Phoebe Turlow, the proverbial last straw.

She had weathered the divorce well enough, considering how many of her dreams had come crashing down in the process. She'd even been philosophical about losing her job as a research assistant to Professor Benning, at a time when finding a comparable position was virtually impossible, given recent government budget cuts. After all, the professor had been writing and lecturing on the subject of American History at Seattle College for forty-five fruitful and illustrious years; he was ready, by his own admission, to spend his days reading, fishing, and playing chess.

Phoebe had held herself together, through it all. And now even Murphy, whom she'd rescued from the pound as a mangy, slat-ribbed mongrel and carefully nursed back to health, had turned on her.

She lowered the telephone receiver slowly back into its cradle, gazing at the dismal Seattle rain sheeting the window of her rented house. The glass reflected a hazy, pixielike image of a woman with short chestnut hair, large blue eyes, high cheekbones, and fair skin.

But Phoebe was looking through herself, mentally reliving the phone call she'd just received. Heather, Wife Number Two and widely proclaimed light of Jeffrey's life, hadn't been able—she probably hadn't even tried—to suppress the smug note in her voice when she called to relay the news that the hound of hell was "safe and sound" in their kitchen. To hear Heather tell it, that furry ingrate had crossed a continent, fording icy rivers and surmounting insurmountable obstacles, enduring desperate privations of all sorts—Phoebe could almost hear the theme music of a new movie, rated G, of course. *Murphy, Come Home.*

Muttering to herself, Phoebe crossed the worn linoleum floor, picked up the dog's red plastic bowl, and dumped it into the trash, kibbles and all. She emptied the water dish and tossed that away as well. Then, running her hands down the worn legs of her blue jeans and feeling more alone than ever before, Phoebe wandered into her small, uncarpeted living room and stared despondently out the front window.

Mel, the postman, was just pulling up to her mailbox in his blue and white jeep. He tooted the horn and waved, and Phoebe waved back with a dispirited smile. Her unemployment check was due, but the prospect didn't cheer her up. If it hadn't been for her savings and the small amount of insurance money she'd received when

2

her mother and stepfather were killed in a car accident years ago, Phoebe figured she would have been sitting on a rain-slicked sidewalk down by the Pike Place Market, with a cigar box in front of her to catch coins.

Okay, she thought, maybe that was a bit of an exaggeration. She could last for about six months, if she didn't get a new job soon, and *then* she would join the ranks of Seattle's panhandlers. An inspiring prospect, for somebody who was all of twenty-six years old.

Snatching her blue hooded rain slicker from the peg beside the door and tossing it over her shoulders, Phoebe dashed out into the chilly drizzle to fetch her mail. She'd sent out over fifty résumés since losing her job with Professor Benning—maybe there would be a positive response, or one of the rare, brightly colored cards her half brother, Eliott, sometimes sent from Europe or South America or Africa, or wherever he happened to be. Or a letter from a friend . . .

Except that all their friends were really Jeffrey's, not hers.

And that Eliott didn't give a damn about her, and never had. To him, she was a trifle, an unfortunate postscript to their mother's life. She wished she could stop caring what he thought.

Phoebe brought herself up short; she was feeling sorry for herself, and that was against her personal code. Resolutely, she wrenched open the door of her rural mailbox, which was affixed to a rusted metal post by the front gate, and reached inside. There was nothing but a sales circular, and she would have crumpled it up and tossed it into the nearest mud puddle, but she couldn't bring herself to litter.

She walked slowly back up the cracked walk to her sagging porch and the open door beyond it. The bright yellow envelope, now sodden and limp from the rain, was addressed to "Occupant," and the street numbers were off by two blocks. *Damn*, she thought, with a wry grimace. Even her junk mail belonged to somebody else.

The letter was about to join Murphy's kibbles and tooth-marked bowls when an impulse—maybe it was desperation, maybe it was some kind of weird premonition—made Phoebe stop. She carried it to her kitchen table, sat down—wondering all the while why she hadn't just chucked the thing—opened it, and smoothed the single page inside with as much care as if it were an ancient scroll, unearthed only moments before.

SUNSHINE! screamed the cheaply printed block letters at the top of the paper, which had been designed to resemble a telegram. SPARKLING, CRYSTAL BLUE SEAS! VISIT PARADISE ISLAND ABSOLUTELY FREE! WALK IN THE FABLED FOOTSTEPS OF DUNCAN ROURKE, THE PIRATE PATRIOT!

Phoebe was an intelligent adult. She'd gone

through college with zero emotional support from her family and had worked at a responsible job from the day she graduated until two months ago, when the academic roof had fallen in. She had voted in every election, and she was by no means naive—even if she had married Jeffrey Brewster with her eyes wide open. She knew a tacky advertising scheme when she saw one.

All the same, the prospects of "sunshine" and "crystal blue seas" prodded at something slumbering deep in her heart, behind a bruise and a stack of dusty, broken hopes.

She frowned. And there was that name, too—Duncan Rourke. She'd seen it before—probably while doing research for Professor Benning.

Phoebe rose from the table, leaving the sales flyer spread out on the shiny surface, and took herself to the stove to make a cup of herbal tea. Knowing that the promise of a free trip to Paradise Island—wherever that might be—was a scam of some kind did nothing to quell the odd, excited sense of impending adventure tingling in the pit of her stomach.

The kettle gave a shrill whistle, and Phoebe poured boiling water over a tea bag and carried her cup back to the table. She read the flyer again, this time very slowly and carefully, one eyebrow raised in skepticism, the fingers of her right hand buried in her short, tousled hair.

To take advantage of the "vacation all her friends would envy," Phoebe had only to inspect a "glamorous beachfront condominium guaranteed to increase in value" and listen to a sales pitch. In return, her generous benefactors would fly her to the small Caribbean island "justly named Paradise," put her up in the "distinctive Eden Hotel for two fun-filled days and nights," and provide one "gala affair, followed by a truly festive dinner."

The whole thing was one big rip-off, Phoebe insisted to herself, and yet she was intrigued, and perhaps just a little frantic. So what if she had to look at a condo made of ticky-tacky, watch a few promotional slides, and listen to a spiel from a schmaltzy, fast-talking salesman or two? She needed to get away, if only for a weekend, and here was her chance to soak up some tropical sunshine without doing damage to her rapidly dwindling bank account.

Phoebe's conscience, always overactive, pricked a little. Okay, suppose she *did* call the toll-free number and book herself on the next flight to Paradise. She'd be making the trip under false pretenses, since she had no intention of buying a condominium. Her credit was fine, but she was divorced, female, and unemployed, and there was no way she'd ever qualify for a mortgage.

Still, there was nothing in the flyer specifying that buyers had to be preapproved for a loan. It was an invitation, pure and simple.

Phoebe closed her eyes and imagined the warmth of the sun on her face, in her hair, settling deep into her muscles and veins and organs, nourishing her very spirit. The yearning she felt was almost mystical, and wholly irresistible.

She told herself that she who hesitates is lost, and that it couldn't hurt to call, and then she walked over to the phone and punched in the number.

Four hectic days later, Phoebe found herself on board a small chartered airplane, aimed in the general direction of the Caribbean, with her one bag tucked neatly under the seat. The man across the aisle wore plaid polyester pants and a sweater emblazoned with tiny golf clubs, and the woman sitting behind her sported white pedal pushers, copious varicose veins, a T-shirt showing two silhouettes engaged in either mortal combat or coitus, and a baseball cap adorned with tiny flashing Christmas tree lights. The seven other passengers were equally eccentric.

Phoebe settled against the back of her seat with a sigh and closed her eyes, feeling like a freak in her brown loafers, jeans, and blue cashmere turtleneck, all purchased at Nordstrom with a credit card and a great deal of optimism. She might have been on a cut-rate night flight to Reno, she thought with rueful humor, judging by the costumes of her fellow travelers.

The plane lifted off at seven o'clock in the morning, rising into the foggy skies over Seattle, and presently a flight attendant appeared. Since the aisle was too narrow for a cart, the slender young man carried a yellow plastic basket in one hand, dispensing peanuts and cola and other refreshments as he moved through the cabin.

The woman in the battery-powered hat ordered a Bloody Mary and received a censuring stare and a generic beer for her trouble.

Phoebe, who had planned to ask for mineral water, merely shook her head and smiled. She was making the trip under false pretenses, after all, and the less she accepted from these people in the way of amenities, the less guilt she would feel afterward.

She tried to sleep and failed, even though she'd lain awake all night worrying, then pulled an ancient thin volume, purloined from Professor Benning's extensive personal book collection, from her bag. The book, published years and years ago, was entitled *Duncan Rourke, Pirate or Patriot?*

Phoebe opened it to the first page, frowning a little, and began to read.

Mr. Rourke, according to the biographer, had been born in Charles Town, in the colony of Carolina, to gentle and aristocratic people. His education was impeccable—he spoke French, Italian, and Spanish fluently and had a penchant for the work of poets, those of his own time, and those of antiquity. He was also known to be proficient with the harpsichord and the mandolin, as well as the sword and musket, and, the writer hinted, he'd been no slouch in the boudoir, either.

Phoebe yawned. Duncan Rourke, it seemed, had qualified as a Renaissance man. She read on.

Until the very day of his death, no one had known for certain whether Rourke had been a cutthroat or a hero. Speculation abounded, of course.

For her part, Phoebe wondered why he couldn't have been both rascal and paragon? No one, after all, was entirely good or bad—a human being, particularly a complex one, as Rourke must have been, could hardly be reduced to one dimension.

Presently, Phoebe closed her eyes—and the musty pages of the old book—and a faint smile trembled on her lips. Pondering Mr. Rourke's morality, or lack of same, she slept at long last.

1780
Paradise Island, the Caribbean

Duncan Rourke sat at the table in his study, full of consternation, affection, and a vast, roiling uneasiness.

The precious letter, penned by Duncan's sister, Phillippa, and dispatched to him months before by devious and complex means, lay before him, slightly crumpled.

"Come home . . ." the diabolical angel had written, in her ornate and flowing script.

Please, Duncan, I implore you to act for our sakes, Mama's and Papa's and Lucas's and mine, if not for your own. You must return to the bosom of your family. Surely nothing more would be required to prove your loyalty to His Majesty than this. Papa might then cease his endless pacing— he traverses the length of his study, over and over again, night after night, from moonrise until the sun's awakening—if only he knew you could be counted among the King's men, like himself and our esteemed elder brother, Lucas . . . Papa fears, dear Duncan, as we all do, that your escapades in those southerly seas you so love will be misunderstood, that you will be arrested or even hanged . . .

Duncan sighed and reached for the glass of port a serving girl had set within reach only moments before.

"Troublesome news?" inquired his friend and first mate, Alex Maxwell, from his post before the terrace doors. A cool, faintly salty breeze ruffled the gauzy curtains and eased the otherwise relentless heat of a summer afternoon in the Caribbean.

"Only the usual rhetoric and prattle," Duncan replied, after taking a sip of his wine, swallowing a good many contradictory feelings along with it. "My sister pleads with me to return to the fold and take up my place among His Majesty's devoted adherents. She implies that, should I fail to heed this warning, our sorrowing and much-tormented sire shall wear out either the soles of his boots or my mother's rugs, in his eternal and evidently ambulatory ruminations."

Alex grimaced. "Good God, man," he said with some impatience, turning at last from his vigil at the window overlooking the sultry blue and gold waters of a sun-splashed, temperamental sea. "Can't you speak in simple English for once in your bloody life?"

Duncan arched one dark eyebrow. Language was, to him, a toy as well as a tool. He loved to explore its every nuance and corner, to exercise various words and combinations of words, to savor them upon his tongue, as he would a fine brandy or an exquisite wine. Although he liked and admired Maxwell—indeed, Duncan had entrusted Alex with his very life on more than one occasion—he would not have forsworn linguistic indulgence even for him. "Tell me, my friend— are you liverish today, or simply obstreperous in the extreme?"

Alex shoved the fingers of both hands into his butternut hair in a dramatic show of frustration. Like Duncan, Alex had lived one score and ten years; they had been tutored together from the time they could toddle out of their separate nurseries. Both loved fast horses, witty women with sinful inclinations, and good rum, and their political views were, in the opinion of the Crown at least, equally subversive. Physically and emotionally, however, the two men were quite different— Alex being small and slightly built, with the ingenuous brown eyes of a fawn and, when vexed, all the subtlety of a bear batting at a swarm of wasps with both paws. Duncan's temperament was cool and somewhat detached, and he stood tall enough, as his father said, to be hanged from a high branch without a scaffold. He prided himself on his self-control, whereas his enemies, no less than his friends, credited him with the tenacity and cunning of a winter-starved wolf. His hair was dark as jet, tied back at the nape of his neck with a narrow ribbon, and his eyes a deep and, so he'd been told by grand ladies and whores alike, patently disturbing blue. His features, aristocratic from birth, had been hardened by the injustices he had both witnessed and suffered.

These, given the troubled nature of the times, were many.

"I'm sorry," Alex said with a weariness that disturbed Duncan greatly, turning at last to face his friend. "I don't deny that I've been foul-tempered in recent days."

"I trust there is a reason," Duncan ventured in a quiet voice, folding Phillippa's letter and placing it, with more tenderness than he would have confessed aloud, in the top drawer of his desk. "Or are your moods, like those of the delicate gender, governed by the waxing and waning of the moon?"

"Oh, good Christ," Alex bit out. "Sometimes you drive me mad."

"Be that as it may," Duncan replied moderately, "I should still like to know what troubles you. We are yet friends, are we not? Besides, a distracted man makes a poor leader, prone to grave errors of judgment." He paused to utter a philosophical sigh. "If some comely wrench has addled your wits, the only prudent course of action, in my view, would be to relieve you of your duties straightaway, before someone in your command suffers the consequences of your preoccupation."

Alex's fine-boned face seemed strained and shadowed as he met Duncan's searching gaze, and his eyes reflected annoyance and something very like despair. "How long?" he asked, in a rasping whisper. "How long must we endure this interminable war?"

Duncan stood, but did not round the desk to approach Alex. There were times, he knew too well, when an ill-chosen word, intended to comfort, could be a man's undoing instead. "Until it has been won," he said tautly.

The vast, sprawling house, dating back to the mid sixteen hundreds, seemed to breathe like a living creature, drawing in the first cool breezes since dawn and then expelling them in soft sighs. A goddess of white stone, with the sapphire sea writhing in unceasing worship at her feet, the palatial structure was a haven to Duncan, like the welcoming embrace of a tenderhearted woman. And it gave him solace, that place, as well as shelter.

Alas, he was wedded to his ship, the *Francesca*, a swift and agile vessel brazenly named for his first lover, the disenchanted wife of a British infantry officer named Sheffield. While the lady had been spurned and sent back to England years ago, where she languished yet in a state of seedy disgrace, the gossips would have it, her husband remained in the colonies, waiting, taking each opportunity for revenge as it presented itself.

Duncan tightened his jaw, remembering even though he had schooled himself, through the years, to forget. He rotated his shoulders once, twice, as the tangle of old scars came alive on the flesh of his back, a searing tracery mapping another man's hatred. He'd been fifteen when Sheffield had ordered him bound to a post in a public square and whipped into blessed unconsciousness.

"Sometimes I wonder," Alex said, startling Duncan out of his bitter reverie, "whether's it's Mother England you're at war with, or the lovely Francesca's jealous husband."

It was by no means new, Alex's propensity for divining the thoughts of others, and neither was Duncan's reaction. "If you will be so kind," he said curtly, "as to keep your fatuous and sentimental attempts at mystical wisdom to yourself, I shall be most appreciative."

Alex rolled his eyes. "I have it," he said in the next instant, feigning a rapture of revelation. "We'll capture Major Sheffield, truss him up like a Christmas goose so he can't cover his ears, and force him to endure the full range of your vocabulary! He'll be screaming for mercy inside half an hour."

Despite the memories that had overtaken him, Duncan clasped his friend's slightly stooped shoulder and laughed. "Suppose I recited the whole of Dante's *Divine Comedy*," he said.

"In Italian, of course," Alex agreed. "With footnotes."

Duncan withdrew his hand, and he knew his expression was as solemn as his voice. "If you want to beat your sword into a plowshare and spend the rest of your life tilling the earth," he said, "I'll understand, and not think less of you for it."

"I know," Alex said. "And I am weary to the soul from this blasted war. I long to settle down, take a wife, father a houseful of children. But if I don't fight, the sons and daughters I hope to sire will stand mute before Parliament, as we do now." He stopped and thrust his fingers through his hair, which was, as always, hopelessly mussed. "No, my friend, to paraphrase Mr. Franklin, if we don't hang together, we shall surely hang separately. I will see the conflict through, to its end or mine, as God wills."

Duncan smiled just as the supper bell chimed, muffled and far off. "You are right, and so is Mr. Franklin. But I must take exception to one of your remarks—we rebels can hardly be accused of 'standing mute before Parliament.' Our musket balls and cannon have been eloquent, I think."

Alex nodded and smiled.

Again, the supper bell sounded. Insistently this time.

Without speaking, the two men moved through the great house together, mindful now of their empty stomachs. They sat at the long table in the dining room, with its ten arched windows overlooking the sea, watching as the sun spilled over the dancing waters, melting in a dazzling spectacle of liquid light. A premonition touched Duncan's spirit in that moment of terrible beauty, a warning or a promise, or perhaps both.

For good or ill, he thought with resignation, something of significance was about to happen.

"Welcome to Paradise!" boomed a plump, middle-aged man with a crew cut and a Jack Nicholson smile, scrambling out of the van to greet each member of the small party of potential investors with a handshake. They stood on the grass-buckled tarmac, numb with exhaustion. "Don't make any snap judgments, now," he warned, before anyone could express a misgiving. "After all, it's late and you've had a long trip. Tomorrow, in the bright light of day, you'll get a good look at the place, and, trust me, you'll be impressed."

Phoebe didn't want to think about tomorrow, didn't want to do anything but take a quick shower and fall into bed. Jack was certainly right about one thing: It *had* been a long trip. After leaving Seattle, the plane had landed in Los Angeles, Houston, Kansas City, and Miami to

16

pick up a dozen other weird characters, before proceeding to Condo Heaven.

The motley crew boarded the minibus, yawning and murmuring, and despite her decision not to think, Phoebe found herself studying the others, each in their turn, out of the corner of her eye. She'd eat every postcard in the hotel gift shop, she thought, if a single one of them could land a mortgage to buy a fancy island hideaway, let alone scrape up the cash to buy one outright.

The young couple who'd boarded the plane in Kansas City were newlyweds, Phoebe figured, because they'd been necking and staring into each other's eyes for most of the flight. Some honeymoon. The man in the plaid pants and golf-club sweater had come along strictly for the ride, providing his own liquor, and the Human Beacon, whose batteries had finally run down, appeared to be the sort who'd try anything as long as it was free.

So what's your excuse? Phoebe asked herself.

The hotel appeared suddenly out of the night, looming like smoke from some underground volcano or an enormous genie rising out of a lamp. Phoebe's breath caught on a small, sharp gasp, and she sat bolt upright on the bus seat. A strange progression of emotions unfolded in her heart.

Recognition, for one. And that was impossible, because she'd never seen the building before. Nostalgia, for another. And a strange, sweet joy,

17

as if she were coming home after a long and difficult journey. Underlying these emotions was a sense of poignant and wrenching loss, threaded through with sorrow.

Tears sprang to Phoebe's eyes.

"Here's the Eden Hotel now, folks," the bus driver announced, with relentless goodwill. "It's a grand old place. Belonged to a pirate once, during the Revolutionary War, name of Rourke, and before that, to a Dutch planter who raised indigo." The minivan's brakes squealed as it came to a sprightly stop under an ugly pink and green neon palm tree affixed to the wall. Two of the fronds were burned out. "Near as we could find out, the house was built in 1675, or thereabouts."

Phoebe sniffled, dried her eyes with the back of one grubby hand, and got off the bus, staring at the shoddy hotel in mute grief. She'd read a brief description of the place in Professor Benning's book about Duncan Rourke; that explained her complicated and overwrought reactions. The odd sensations lingered, though— Phoebe felt certain that she had known every nook and corner of this house once, had loved it when it was grand and elegant, and taken refuge within its walls when storms swept in from the sea. She had come home to a place she had never seen before, and she had arrived too late.

Like the foul brew in a witch's cauldron, the storm roiled and grumbled on the horizon, shrouding the rolling waves of the deep and blotting out the light of the moon and stars. Duncan stood on the balcony outside his room, the wild wind playing in his hair and catching at the loose fabric of his shirt. The *Francesca*, always his first concern, was safe at anchor, in a sheltered cove some two miles down the shore. He would go to her all the same, and had no explanation to offer for delaying even this long, save the eerie certainty, imprinted in the marrow of his bones like a seal pressed into warm wax, that his life was about to change for all of time and eternity.

Behind him, in the shadows, stood Old Woman. If she had any other name, Duncan had never heard it, though he considered her a friend of sorts and had heeded her advice on more than one occasion. The servants and other islanders feared and revered her, believing she had magical powers, a notion Duncan privately scorned.

"Come inside, Mr. Duncan," she said. Although she spoke in a tranquil voice, he heard her distinctly over the noise. Beyond the terrace, earth and air and water met to spawn the tempest, and the birthing shrieks rode the wind. "It's dangerous out there."

Still unsettled, and with regret, Duncan turned and obeyed Old Woman's summons, closing the

heavy shutters and then the French doors themselves.

She stood in her regal robe, a seamless garment
woven of some fabric Duncan did not recognize,
holding a candelabra high, so that it shed a thin,
shadow-streaked mantle of light over the both of
them.

"She's on her way," Old Woman said. "At
last, she is coming to us."

"Who?" Duncan demanded impatiently,
taking the candelabra from the strong, wrinkled
hand and starting toward the inner doors.
"Mother England? She won't be an amicable
guest, I fear. No need to brew tea and bake sugar
cakes."

Old Woman caught at his arm and stopped
him with easy strength, even though she weighed
no more than a bird and the top of her grizzled
head barely reached his breastbone. "Not the
soldiers, with a whip for your back and noose for
your neck," she said firmly. "The woman. She
comes from a world very far away and yet"—
with ancient, withered fingers, she reached out
and plucked at nothing—"so close that you might
touch her."

Duncan felt a chill trickle down his spine, like
a droplet from a northerly sea, but he was not a
fanciful man, despite the strange, glorious, and
unnamed fear stirring in the pit of his belly, and
he put no stock in spells and enchantments and
invisible worlds near enough to touch or otherwise. "Superstitious rot," he grumbled. Then,

somewhat unchivalrously, he shoved the cande-labra into her grasp and muttered, "Here. Take this and go on about your business, whatever it is."

She thrust the exquisitely wrought piece of ster-ling silver, candles wavering, back into Duncan's hand with an insolence none of the men under his command would have dared employ. It was no accident, either, he thought, when hot wax dripped onto his wrist in stinging splotches. "Old Woman see fine," she said. "It is Mr. Duncan who has empty eyes."

In silence, he watched her move away into the shadows with sure and unhesitating steps.

"Poppycock and bilge water," Duncan said under his breath, but he found himself thinking, as he made his way down the wide, curving stair-case, carrying the candelabra in one hand, of the odd, inexplicable noises he had heard in that house on rare occasions. Music, sounds he did not recognize from instruments he had never seen. Footsteps where no one walked. The muted laughter of invisible men and women, and the melodic chime of glass striking glass.

He supposed he was going mad. He considered confiding his terrible secret to Alex but, after long and hard deliberation, decided against the idea. He wasn't sure his friend could be trusted, if confronted with such a confession, to show the proper degree of surprise.

★　★　★

Phoebe's room was roughly the size of a phone booth, and the bed looked as though it had been designed for a doll's house, but she could hear and smell the sea, singing softly in the night. When the sun came up, she would have an ocean view, and the promise of that lifted her spirits.

She took a shower under a spindly trickle of cool water, causing a rusty rumble in the pipes, brushed her teeth, pulled on an old T-shirt and a pair of cotton boxer shorts, and crawled into bed. Her last conscious thought was that the sheets were clean; she sank into the depths of her mind and slept without dreaming.

It was still dark when the music awakened her, its sad and beautiful strains twisting and turning through the profound silence like ribbons.

A tiny muscle leaped, somewhere deep in Phoebe's middle, and then subsided into a steady quiver. She listened harder, groping for sounds she had heard earlier and barely noticed—the clamor of the old-fashioned elevator, creaking and rattling along its shaft, the shrill, metallic moan from the plumbing, the ponderous drip-drip-drip of the faucet in the bathroom—and heard only the swelling, heartbreaking eloquence of the music.

Phoebe bit her lower lip and settled into her pillows, listening, reaching for memories that eluded her, but just barely. Her face was wet with tears she could not have explained, even to herself, and she wondered fancifully if the hotel might be haunted. The notes of the harpsichord surrounded her, caressed her, and finally lulled her back to sleep.

The next time she woke up, tropical sunlight was spilling in through the window, full of dancing diamonds snatched from the sea, bathing her in a dazzle of gold and platinum. But the music had stopped.

Phoebe stood on her bed, grasping the windowsill in both hands, and gazed out at the blue-green sea and the white sand, stricken to the heart by their splendor. It was worth it, she thought, as her soul stirred, painfully at first, like something long frozen. Here and there, in the uncharted regions within, a dream trembled into wakefulness and reached for the light.

Someone hammered at the door of her room, startling Phoebe so thoroughly that she nearly toppled off the bed.

"What?" she demanded, annoyed.

"I got your costume," answered an unfamiliar adolescent voice.

"What costume?" Phoebe asked, after wrenching open the door to find a teenage girl standing in the hallway, chewing gum and holding out a pile of cheap muslin.

"There's a party tonight," the young woman said, orchestrating the words with a series of crisp snaps. "After you've seen the condos and stuff, I mean." She smiled, revealing enough braces to set off the metal detector in an airport. "My name's Andrea," she said wistfully. "I wore that outfit last time we had a batch of investors out from the mainland. It was kinda fun to dress up."

Phoebe frowned. This, she thought, must be the "gala affair" the brochure had mentioned.

She decided to feign a headache that night and sneak out to walk on the beach. "Great," she said without conviction.

Andrea waggled her fingers. "Don't worry," she said. "You'll make a great wench."

Phoebe stepped out into the hall, not caring, at that point, that she was wearing a T-shirt and boxer shorts. "Wait a second," she called. "I'll make a great *what*?"

"Wench," Andrea replied blithely, without slowing her steps or looking back. "You know, one of those chicks who served rum and grog and sat on pirates' laps."

Phoebe closed the door and leaned against it, holding the muslin dress against her bosom and gazing into the murky mirror on the opposite wall. "You deserve whatever happens to you," she told her reflection.

2

Phoebe sincerely tried to be philosophical.

Breakfast consisted of two wilted croissants and a cup of strong coffee. The condominiums faced the sea, and they were nice enough, though cheaply built and alike down to the last carpet tack. An extensive sales pitch followed the tour, involving slides and brochures and flip charts and overhead projections, and seemed to go on forever. Lunch—fruit salad on a wilted lettuce leaf, strawberry gelatin, and hard rolls—was brought in by tanned and slender young women in shorts and the standard Paradise Island T-shirts. Once the meal had been served, the Amazons took up their posts beside the door again, arms folded, expressions impassive, clearly prepared to foil any attempt at escape.

It was three o'clock when the captive audience was finally released, though the reprieve was only temporary, of course. Everyone was expected to attend the costume party that night, the man Phoebe had privately dubbed Jack announced, explaining that anybody who skipped the festivities would be required to find his or her own way back to the States.

Phoebe accepted the fact that she would have to dress up as a pirate's main squeeze and listen to another lecture on real estate, and made a dash for the nearest exit. Her only other option, she figured, was to swim across the Bermuda Triangle and hope she washed up in Florida. In the meantime, she was free to enjoy the sun and sand, and she meant to make the most of the opportunity.

After purchasing sunscreen and a big straw hat in the hotel's dusty gift shop, Phoebe headed for the beach.

The tide was warm enough for a bath, and the water so clear that she could see the thin reeds and jewel-like shells wavering on the bottom. The sand was as fine and white as sugar, and Phoebe kicked off her sandals and waded in to her knees, exultant with the pure joy of being exactly where she was.

Within the hour, despite the sunscreen she'd lathered on every inch of exposed skin, Phoebe was forced to cease communing with the sea and go inside. She bought a tall pink drink with a cherry in it at the bar and sipped the concoction as the old elevator wheezed its way to the third floor.

In the privacy of her room, Phoebe gingerly removed her red polkadot sundress, smeared herself with burn cream, and stretched out on her bed, imagining that she was lying in a hidden cove, naked except for the shade of a palm tree. She smiled, perfectly content, the sea murmured a lullaby from beyond her window, and sleep stole over her, soft as the shadow of a phantom.

Her dreams were erotic, mysterious, interwoven with the music of a harpsichord.

She was lying in the sand, shaded by the fronds of a palm tree. A man came and knelt beside her, and, although she could not see his face or find his name on her tongue, her heart knew him well. He stroked her bare thighs with a minstrel's light, deft fingers until she quivered and whimpered beneath him, and then he weighed her breasts, first one and then the other, in a reverent,

26

calloused hand. Phoebe felt as beautiful and magical as a mermaid, or a princess waking to her prince's touch after a century of slumber in a castle encompassed by thistles, and she longed for the familiar stranger to make her completely his own.

He bent his head, and she caught just the hint of a smile on his well-shaped lips just before he kissed her.

An exquisite instrument played by a master, Phoebe's body arched, bowlike, in response, and there followed a surge of passion so strong that it flung her spiraling upward, out of the sleeping rhapsody and into the real world. She lay despairing on her lumpy hotel bed, soaked in perspiration and still trembling from the violence of the imagined release. And she grieved, because she was alone, after all, and because her lover had vanished with the dream.

Since the divorce from Jeffrey, Phoebe had been telling herself that celibacy wasn't so bad, but now the very essence of her femininity was saying something quite different. She was still young and vibrantly healthy, and she wanted the emotional and physical satisfaction of total intimacy with a man.

Well and good, she thought, wincing as her sunburn made itself known. She was ready for another relationship, ready to trust a guy, to let him touch her heart and her body. Now all she had to do was find one who met her standards, which were much stricter than they had been when she'd met and fallen in love with Jeffrey, back in college.

It wouldn't be easy to make a new start, Phoebe knew, but she resolved to try. Maybe the best thing was to leave Seattle entirely, with all its memories, and look for work in San Francisco, or New York, or even somewhere in Europe. London or Paris, for instance, or somewhere smaller, like Florence or Lyon. In time, if she didn't creep back into her shell to keep from getting hurt again, and if she was very, very lucky, she might just meet a terrific man.

Feeling better just for having made a decision, Phoebe took her watch from the nightstand and squinted at its sand-coated face. "Damn," she murmured. It was almost time for that dratted costume party.

Phoebe dressed carefully in the cheesy gown, with its lace-up bodice and low-cut neckline, brushed her hair, and applied a touch of makeup. A headache was just pulsing to life beneath her right temple, but she didn't pause to gulp down an aspirin because she didn't want to be late. It wasn't that Phoebe was afraid of missing the flight back to the mainland—if it hadn't been for the condominium people, she might have decided to stay forever, swinging from jungle vines, wearing fig leaves, and living on coconut milk. No, she only wanted to get through the evening, return to her room, and listen for the faint strains of a harpsichord.

Phoebe's headache intensified as she stepped

into the elevator, alone, and pushed the button for the basement level. Odd place for a ballroom, she thought, opening her purse and rummaging for the small, dented tin of aspirin she'd glimpsed a few weeks ago among the debris.

"Hell," she said, doggedly plundering the mysterious depths of her bag as the metal cage lurched on its no-doubt rusty cables and settled, with a clatter, to the floor. There was no sign of the wonder drug, and by now Phoebe knew she wasn't going to survive the evening without anesthesia. No sooner had she left the elevator, her attention still fixed on her purse, when she decided to risk going back to her room to swallow two tablets from the bottle in her cosmetic case.

She turned, hoping to get back inside before the elevator doors closed.

A blank wall confronted her.

For a moment, Phoebe just stood there stunned, staring in disbelief. The elevator was gone, grillwork, rattle and all, and furthermore, the light had changed, dimming from a hard fluorescent glare to a faint and flickering glow. She could no longer hear the laughter and talk coming from the ballroom.

Phoebe took a deep breath and shut her eyes for a moment. It was the headache that was making her see things, she reasoned. Maybe she was suffering from sunstroke. Or it might be that she'd simply gotten off on the wrong floor while she was looking through her purse for the aspirin.

She raised her eyelids again and was discouraged to see that the elevator had not reappeared. Some time had passed before she realized that her head no longer ached, and under the circumstances, she wasn't sure whether that was good news or bad.

She stood still, waiting, but the wall where the elevator should have been was just that—the wall where the elevator should have been. And most definitely wasn't.

Phoebe had decided to look for another way out of the basement when she heard whistling, decidedly masculine and unconcerned, from somewhere farther along the passage. She peered into the shadows.

"Hello?" she called. "Who's there?"

He rounded a corner just then, carrying an old-fashioned brass lantern in one hand, and something slammed into Phoebe's heart, like a mallet laid hard to a great brass gong. For a moment, she couldn't breathe, let alone speak, and simply stood there trembling with the reverberations.

The man was tall, with dark hair worn long and tied back at the nape of his neck with a thin ribbon or a thong. Fawn-colored breeches of some soft material like chamois clung to his finely muscled thighs, and his black boots reached, cavalier style, to his knees. He wore a loose shirt, probably made of linen, and carried a dagger in a scabbard on his belt.

Phoebe found her voice at last. "Wow," she said, a little too brightly, "you certainly got a better costume than I did."

He raised one eyebrow, and the corner of his mouth twitched slightly, though whether from amusement or impatience, or something else entirely, Phoebe could not determine. "Who are you?" he demanded, his gaze moving over her in an imperious sweep of assessment before swinging back to her face.

Phoebe was flushed, and she hoped he couldn't see that in the dim light of the lantern. "My name is Phoebe Turlow," she said. "And I'm lost. I'm also late. Could you just show me the way out of here, please?"

He ignored her request, stooping a little and peering at her as though she were some sort of curiosity. Her breath caught in her throat, though not from anything so sensible as fear, when he reached out and touched her hair. What she felt, to her everlasting chagrin, was the same erotic heat that had made her cry out in her dream that afternoon. "Have you suffered a head injury?" he asked. "Or been taken by a fever? Or perhaps you've fallen upon hard times and sold your hair to a wigmaker?"

"A *wigmaker*?" Phoebe retreated a step. The man was obviously eccentric, or even crazy. There was little harm in his wanting to dress up like a pirate, she supposed, but it was just plain irresponsible to let him wander through the bowels of the hotel, carrying a kerosene lantern and armed with a knife. Someone should have a word with whoever was supposed to watch him. "I like my hair short," she added, patting it self-

31

consciously, only too aware that she sounded hysterical and still unable to help herself. "I have good bone structure, and this style accentuates it."

"Speak plain, wench," commanded the handsome maniac. "Who are you, and what are you doing prowling about my house in the dead of night?"

Careful, Phoebe told herself, easing her way backward along the very wall that had swallowed the elevator. She summoned up a shaky and, she hoped, reassuring smile. "Have you taken your medication today?" she countered.

"God's blood," the pirate muttered. "You are a lunatic."

Phoebe wasn't foolish enough to point up the irony of a full-grown man in a pirate suit calling *her* crazy. By then, all she wanted was to escape before he decided to shiver her timbers, or hoist her on her own petard, or whatever it was people suffering from pirate delusions liked to do to their victims.

She turned and ran wildly into the darkness, wondering what the hell had happened to the lights, not to mention the elevator and the ballroom and the people who had been trying to sell her a condominium all day. Just then, she would have been glad to see them, even if it meant sitting through another sales pitch.

Fate, alas, is not always kind. Phoebe tripped over the hem of her wench's costume and plunged headfirst onto the cold stone floor of the passageway. She was dazed, but when a powerful arm encircled her waist and wrenched her onto her feet, she struggled like a wildcat, clawing and kicking and, when she could find a place to sink her teeth, biting.

Her captor cursed roundly, but his grip did not slacken. He hauled her easily through the dark labyrinth beneath the hotel and up a set of stairs lighted on either side by candles in wall sconces. Phoebe stopped fighting for a few moments, saving her breath to scream for help as soon as she thought the lobby might be within earshot.

A second man loomed at the top of the steps, dressed for the eighteenth century in breeches, a tailored shirt, and a bottle-green waistcoat. There were large, shining buckles on his shoes.

Wonderful, Phoebe thought from that calm place in the center of the storm of delirium swirling around her. The pirate has a friend who likes to play dress-up, too.

"Great Apollo, Duncan," growled said companion, "what in *hell* are you doing?"

No sense in calling for help, Phoebe reasoned prosaically in her state of shock. Then her eyes widened as the name struck home, and she turned to stare into the hard, ruthless face of the man who carried her as easily as if she weighed no more than his pocket watch.

"Did he just call you Duncan?"

"Yes," he replied, pushing past his friend, who looked sane, in spite of his odd clothes, and very concerned.

"Why?"

"Most likely because that is my name." He flung her onto a settee in a billow of cheap muslin, and Phoebe, always a quick thinker, came up with a new theory. This was a part of the hotel she had never been in before, reserved, perhaps, for the bizarre and decadent pleasures of the rich. She should probably be grateful that the theme for the evening was pirates and not the Arabian Nights—in which case she might have been issued a veil and harem pants and ordered to dance for the sultan's entertainment.

Phoebe folded her hands in her lap and smiled winningly, first at one man and then the other. "I'm afraid there's been some kind of mix-up, fellas. You've obviously mistaken me for part of the entertainment, but the fact is that I'm a guest in the hotel, too. I'm here to look at condominiums—not that I can afford to buy one—while you two are obviously with the deluxe tour . . ."

"Is she mad, poor creature?" Alex said, color climbing his neck. "By God, Duncan, if you've been keeping this woman hidden away somewhere, like a bird in a cage . . ."

The man who called himself Duncan paled beneath his tan. It was a relief to know he probably wasn't a crackpot at all, but simply an overworked professional man from California or some other sunny, progressive state, enjoying a unique vacation from the real world. "And if you were anyone but who you are, Alex," he countered, "I would call you out for insulting my honor."

Phoebe tried to stand, intending to make herself scarce, but Duncan extended a hand and stopped her without so much as glancing in her direction.

Alex gave a great sigh. "Who is this girl, and where did you get her?" he demanded evenly.

"I found her skulking about in the cellars," Duncan replied, and though his voice was soft, it was plain that he was seething.

"I'm not a girl," Phoebe said with admirable restraint. "I'm a woman." She paused, making a real effort to be diplomatic. "You guys are really good at this," she said. "I'm sure dressing up and playing games is very relaxing for executive types with stressful jobs. However, I definitely do not appreciate being dragged into the act, and if you don't let me leave this room, right now, I will scream until the chandeliers rattle. And when the police come, I will have you both arrested."

Both men turned their heads to stare at her, Alex in bewilderment, Duncan in cold, speculative irritation.

"You are and shall remain a prisoner," said the latter flatly, "until your identity and your reasons for being here are brought to light." Phoebe caught a glimpse of fire in his eyes and knew, despite undeniable evidence to the contrary, that this man was not mad. The vitality he exuded came not just from physical strength, but from a formidable intellect, sharper than his tongue and more deadly than the dagger worn so carelessly at his side. "In the meantime, you will be given comfortable quarters, food, and something fitting to wear."

Phoebe bolted for the double doors at the other end of the room, which were at least twelve feet high and trimmed in gilt, and this time no one gave chase. "Help!" she screamed, bursting into a foyer with marble floors and exquisite paintings on the walls. "Somebody help—" The cry died in her throat as she stopped at the base of the great curved staircase—the same one that graced the lobby of the Eden Hotel—and turned slowly around in a circle, staring, as yet another revelation struck her. "Oh, my God," she whispered hoarsely. Somehow, impossibly, this *was* that place, in an earlier and still-glorious incarnation.

With a little gasp of protest and unutterable confusion, Phoebe Turlow fainted for the first time in her life.

When she awakened, disoriented and sick, she was being carried up the staircase, Scarlett O'Hara style, and the hard arms supporting her were Duncan Rourke's.

He proceeded along a darkened hallway, refusing to look at Phoebe even though she sensed that he felt her gaze. The long muscles on either side of his neck were corded, and a muscle pulsed in his jaw.

"Please put me down," she said in a reedy voice. All her theories about the disappearing elevator and businessmen in silly costumes had vanished; the unfortunate and frightening truth was that Phoebe didn't have the vaguest idea what was happening to her. Still, it was probably easier to be brave when standing up.

"Your merest wish, madam, is my creed and my philosophy," Rourke replied, and, passing through an open doorway on the right, he hurled her unceremoniously onto a waiting feather bed. "It would behoove you to mind your manners," he added in parting. "For if you don't, I promise you I shall take drastic measures."

Phoebe watched, trembling, as her host, be he pirate, patriot, hallucination, or ghost, turned and left the room. She heard a key grate in the lock, and started to scramble off the bed, but the strong brown hand of a native woman touched her shoulder. Phoebe had thought herself alone until then.

"Here, now, child," her companion said, in a soft and soothing voice. "You drink this medicine tea Old Woman made for you, and sleep. You came a long way to find us, I think, and you be tired."

Phoebe sat up and accepted a steaming cup with both hands. The woman's motherly manner and kind words calmed her a little. "Something strange is happening to me," she confided. "I think I'm having a nervous breakdown." The tea tasted of honey and sweet herbs and probably contained a drug, but Phoebe drank it anyway.

Old Woman smiled as she reached out and smoothed Phoebe's ruffled hair. "No, child,

37

you're not sick," she said. "It's good magic afoot here, so don't you fret. Old Woman, she been expecting you oh so long a time. She made ready. You finish tea, and you sleep. Tomorrow, just like always, the sun he shine bright to warm the heart."

Phoebe was beyond trying to make sense of anything; she, like Alice, had gone through the looking glass into another world. She set the cup aside, sorry that it was empty, and settled back onto the pillows. "What did you mean, when you said you've been expecting me?"

"Old Woman sees things, that's all. Sees them in smoke and in the mists that rise from the waters to dance for the moon."

"Well," Phoebe said, with weary wryness and no little resignation, "that certainly clears things up." She sighed as a light, soft blanket settled over her, seemingly in slow motion. Her words were childlike, and she knew it, but they were out before she could polish them to an adult shine. "Good night, Old Woman. I probably won't see you again, because when I wake up, I'll be back where I belong, and all of this will be nothing but a dream."

Phoebe's self-appointed guardian shook her head. "That other place is the dream, child, not this one. You belong right here, with Mr. Duncan and me. You was lost before, maybe, but now you be found."

"Right," Phoebe agreed, as her eyelids fluttered and closed. She heard the music again then, as delicately wrought as ever, but full of restrained passion and fury now, instead of the old, aching sorrow. She didn't open her eyes, lest the dream end before she was ready to let it go. "That's Duncan playing—isn't it?"

"Yes," Old Woman said tenderly. "He be talking to you. You listen, and try to understand."

Phoebe smiled, turned onto her side, and nestled deep into the feather bed. The subconscious mind, she reflected just before she drifted off, is a marvelous thing, full of magic and mystery.

Duncan played until he'd purged his spirit of the music, taking no note of the compositions he chose, for he knew countless tunes and could execute any one of them without thinking. That night, like many before it, had its own unique melody, however, complicated and original and never to be heard again. When he had exhausted the terrible restlessness, the sense of seeking that had tormented him all his life, he covered the well-worn keys of the harpsichord and strode out of the drawing room.

The great house was quiet, settled, and yet it fairly vibrated with her presence—the lunatic or crafty spy, who called herself Phoebe Turlow. She looked like a lad, with that close-cropped hair, and he might have checked to make sure she wasn't one, if there hadn't been a tantalizing swell of cleavage visible above her laced bodice.

He smiled slightly. In truth, he'd been sorely

39

tempted to look anyway, or at least untie the laces.

He needed a woman, plainly, and copious amounts of smuggled rum. Or better yet, a rousing fifth.

It was this damnable waiting that was driving Duncan insane, and vexing Alex and the others as well. They were warriors, seldom idle; men who sailed the seas, and marking time until a message arrived was pure torment.

To keep from mounting the stairs, shaking his houseguest awake and subjecting her to a relentless interrogation—Old Woman would surely put a hex on him if he did—Duncan lit a lantern and returned to the cellar with its maze of passages, retracing his steps to the spot where he'd found the intruder.

Searching the stone floor, he discovered an oddly shaped leather pouch. Farther along, in the place where Phoebe had fallen, a small metal object caught the light. It was a bracelet of a type he'd never seen before, with a tiny pocket watch affixed.

Duncan frowned, pondering the clever gadget and its curious, though admittedly delectable, owner. In the sacrosanct province of his mind, he wondered if Mistress Turlow was the "she" whose imminent arrival Old Woman had predicted on the night of the storm and before that, and promptly discarded the notion as pap and whimsy. Phoebe, with her lad's hair, bow-shaped mouth, and "good bone structure," was no mystical creature from another world. More likely she was an agent of the British, come to get the goods, once and for all, on Duncan Rourke, enemy of the Crown, and the two dozen skilled fighting men who followed him.

He'd known, of course, that the English would eventually locate the island, hidden though it was among a hundred unpopulated places like it, and surrounded by rocks and reefs so treacherous that only an expert captain could navigate them. Van Ruben, the Dutchman who had settled Paradise and built the mansion, with its secret channels leading to the sea, had not been a sociable sort. He'd wanted, according to legend, simply to live in refinement and peace, raising indigo, transporting and selling it himself. After the house was finished and most of the workers had gone back to Europe, Van Ruben had lived on in happy isolation, with a rich wife and a native mistress and children by both. In time, no one save the crews of the planter's two small ships even remembered the island, let alone traveled there.

Discovery had been inevitable, of course, for the English were intrepid explorers, among other things, and they were deft seamen. Duncan had hoped for a little more time, but the arrival of Phoebe Turlow was a clear indication that Paradise was no longer a secret from the rest of the world.

He frowned, carrying the bracelet and the bag in one hand and the lamp in the other, as he moved back along the passageway to the stairs.

41

There was another possibility, too, one even less appealing than the prospect of a full-scale British invasion. Phoebe might not be an English spy at all, but an associate of yet another enemy, the pirate Jacques Mornault.

Mornault knew where the island was, though he'd stayed away for two years, having been thoroughly disgraced by rounds from Duncan's well-placed cannon, which were hidden in the lush tropical growth on the high ridge overlooking the main harbor. Sending a woman to scout the area and prepare the way for fresh attack would be like Jacques; the Frenchman was meaner than the devil's cross-eyed stepfather, and cunning along with it. To underestimate such a man would be a foolish blunder and shortsighted.

Duncan reached the main floor, extinguished the lantern, and set it aside, moving without hesitation through the darkened house. By God, he'd have the truth out of that woman come the morning, and if she was Mornault's mistress, he would make a point of seducing her before sending her back to her lover.

He met Old Woman on the main staircase, and her wise, night-shadowed gaze fell immediately on the trinket and pouch he'd recovered from the cellar floor.

"She sleeps," said the beloved witch. "You will not disturb her."

"I am the master of this house," Duncan pointed out blandly. He had learned, long since, that a wise leader never relinquishes authority, even in the smallest matters—to do so is to invite chaos. "Should I wish to awaken our lovely visitor, I will do so."

Old Woman smiled, but not, this time, with fondness. "Look inside her medicine bag. You will see that the things she carries are unknown to us."

Duncan shivered inwardly, but his jaw was set. "I fully intend to examine Mistress Turlow's belongings," he said. "If she's not an English spy, I'll no doubt find some ribbon or bauble, a remembrance of her lover, Mornault."

"You go far," Old Woman said, not unkindly, "to avoid the truth. Phoebe was sent here to give you joy, to bear your children, to teach you and to be taught. Without her, you cannot be the man the gods meant you to be, and she needs you, also, to become herself."

He sighed. He'd never met anyone who spoke with the convoluted grace that Old Woman did. She was often astonishingly articulate, though at other times it seemed she could barely shape a comprehensible sentence. He suspected her of playing roles, choosing the one that best suited her purposes at the moment, and was absolutely certain that her mind was, in some ways, quicker than his own.

"Enough of your riddles," he said, suffering an insight into how Alex must feel when he, Duncan, performed his own verbal acrobatics. "Mistress Turlow is a prisoner, though of course she will be treated with courtesy as long as she behaves.

In the morning, however, I intend to question her until she tells me what I want to know."

"Take care," Old Woman warned gently, moving past him, as slight and boneless as a breeze, to proceed down the stairs. "You are too certain of the answers, and the questions have yet to be asked. A man already convinced is deaf and blind to proof that he is wrong."

With that, she was gone, disappearing into the darkness of the foyer like a haunt.

Duncan proceeded to the second floor and stopped outside the locked door of Phoebe's room, her odd belongings in his hands. He imagined her thrashing, nubile and eager, in Mornault's bed, and the image enraged him so profoundly that he muttered a curse and went, in long strides, to his own chamber.

There, where a silvery wash of moonlight streamed in through the great windows, twins to those below in the long dining room, Duncan opened the catch of Phoebe's bag and dumped the contents onto the polished library table where he did most of his reading.

A tubular object of some sort, half out of its wrapping of thin white paper, with a string dangling. A small mirror. A book, strangely bound in stock hardly thicker than its pages, rather than the usual cloth or leather. He scanned the first page, which described a gruesome murder in odd terms and meters, much like Phoebe's speech. A leather folder, filled with photographs, little squares made of a hard, slick substance he had never seen before, and currency.

Puzzled, Duncan struck a match and lit the candles on his desk, holding one of the ornate green bills to the light. The phrase "The United States of America" leaped out at him, making his heart pound with an excitement the likes of which he had never felt before. Inside an oval, couched in what appeared to be wheat fronds, was the likeness of a homely and somber-looking man with a beard. "Lincoln," read the tiny print beneath the engraving.

He laid the bit of paper down with the other things, blew out the candles, and began to undress. Though mystified and distinctly worried, Duncan Rourke was smiling as he stretched out between the smooth sheets of his bed, savoring five magnificent words he, and many others, were willing to die for.

The United States of America.

3

Phoebe opened her eyes, fully expecting the Duncan Rourke fantasy to be over, leaving reality swirling in its backwash. Instead, she saw Old Woman standing beside her bed—which wasn't the one in her hotel room—beaming with benevolent triumph and gesturing toward the row of windows on the other side of the room. "There," she said. "The sun's been waiting for you to look at him."

Phoebe covered her face with both hands and groaned. "This isn't real," she said. "I'm hallucinating."

Old Woman laughed, her voice mellow, polished, and resonant. "No, miss. You was doing that before, in that other world. Like I told you last night, what you see around you is what's true."

Even though Phoebe was more inclined toward wild hysteria than anything else, she forced herself to concentrate, focus, keep her internal balance. "My name is Phoebe Turlow," she recited in determined if moderate tones, speaking to herself alone. "I live in Seattle, Washington. I was born in 1969, and I have a bachelor of arts degree in English Literature. I was married—"

"Yes, yes," interrupted Old Woman indulgently, prodding Phoebe into an upright position and setting a breakfast tray in her lap. "All that's over and done. Here. You eat. You need your strength to make a match with the likes of Mr. Duncan."

Phoebe's appetite proved unhampered by the situation. She reached for a piece of toasted bread, thick and buttery, and took a bite. "I really don't think I imagined Seattle," she said, musing aloud rather than talking to Old Woman and chewing as she spoke. She frowned at her companion. "I'll bet you're a subconscious archetype. Yes—it's all very Jungian. You're some sort of mother-figure—both nurturing and controlling . . ."

Old Woman rolled her luminous brown eyes. "Such strange talk," she scolded, but with affection. Then she sighed and sat down in a chair drawn close to the bed. "You be careful what you say outside this room, miss. There be some who would call you witch, hearing such wild talk. And these folks here, they don't much take to magic and the like."

Overwhelmed and hungry, Phoebe swallowed the arguments that rose in her throat, along with a sip of strong tea, and said nothing. After that, she consumed an egg and a portion of stewed apples, flavored with cinnamon and nutmeg.

Then, emboldened, Phoebe reiterated her original theory. " 'Old Woman.' Even your name is straight out of a textbook. You symbolize wisdom, I think, and compassion, and—"

"I am flesh and blood, miss, just like you," said the archetype. "I just myself, that's all."

Phoebe shook her head, waggling her fork for emphasis. "No," she said. "You're a remarkably detailed projection of my deeper mind, which is obviously troubled. If you were real, you would have a name."

"I have," came the quiet reply. "I am called 'Old Woman' because I have lived so long. My true name is a secret—to say it aloud is to make a powerful spell."

Phoebe gave up, for the moment, and was just

setting the tray aside to get out of bed and look for the bathroom when a brisk rap sounded at the door. Before she could say "come in" or "stay out," Duncan stepped over the threshold, looking even more authentic in the daylight than he had by the glow of oil lamps and candles.

The loose laces at the neck of his shirt and the dark stubble of a beard added to his roguish charm, and Phoebe pondered his role in her personal mythology. Like Old Woman, he was surely an illusion, signifying some facet of her psyche.

Embarrassing though it was, Phoebe finally concluded that Duncan represented the deepest yearnings of her libido. Freud would have a heyday with this, she reflected. But underlying all her tidy, though alarming, psychological speculations was something else: an absolute certainty, evidence to the contrary notwithstanding, that her sanity was still very much intact.

Her instincts told her that Old Woman really was flesh and blood, just as she appeared to be, and so was Duncan Rourke. He stood at the foot of her bed by then, looking imperious and, though he was clearly trying to hide the fact, every bit as confused as Phoebe herself. He took a small object from the pocket of his breeches and tossed it into her lap.

Her watch.

"A clever application of an old principle," he said, grudgingly, as if by commenting on a modern gadget he must also give Phoebe the credit for inventing it.

Grateful for this small proof that she hadn't imagined her other life in the late twentieth century, Phoebe pulled the watch onto her wrist and checked the time—not that the hour mattered. It was, after all, the year that was in question.

"Thanks," she said. "For a while there, I thought I'd gone crazy. By the way, what year is this?"

Duncan raised one dark eyebrow, silently indicating that he had yet to discard the possibility of lunacy. Old Woman, whose true name could not be uttered because it was magic, stood by, not speaking, protective, and bristling with dignity.

"It is 1780, of course," said the master of the house. Then, after a lengthy and thunderous silence, he demanded, "Who are you?"

Phoebe, though still reeling from the announcement that more than two hundred years had just fallen off the celestial calendar, recalled Old Woman's warning about the eighteenth-century attitude toward witches, self-proclaimed or otherwise, and thought carefully before answering. "My name is Phoebe Turlow," she said. "I believe I've told you that already. In fact, I'm thinking of changing it, out of pure boredom. Do I look like an Elisabeth to you, or a Helen?"

A muscle leaped in Duncan's cheek, and was promptly stilled—by force of will, no doubt.

49

"The truth, madam," he intoned. "I have had enough of your nonsense."

"That *is* the truth," Phoebe insisted, swinging her legs over the side of the bed and standing up. She was not ill, not physically anyway, and talking to Duncan while lying almost prone disquieted her in a way that was not entirely unpleasant. It also gave him the psychological advantage. "I know you're wondering how I got here," she went on, trying in vain to smooth her crumpled wench's costume and at the same time lend herself some shred of credibility. "Well, as it happens, I have no idea."

Duncan muttered a pithy exclamation, then said, "The articles found in your possession, madam, are hardly commonplace." His blue eyes pierced her, warmed her in places where their gaze should not have reached.

He had found her purse, then, and rifled through it. She was annoyed on the one hand and relieved on the other. No two ways about it: To go through a woman's handbag was an invasion of privacy. Still, her driver's license, her credit cards, the wallet photos—all were irrefutable proof, if only to Phoebe herself, that she was still firmly rooted in her own identity. The odd restlessness that possessed her now, however, was nothing she wanted to claim as a part of her personality.

Phoebe drew a deep breath and squared her shoulders. "I would like my things back, please," she said.

"Regrettably," Duncan retorted immediately, though his expression indicated that he felt no remorse for anything he'd said or done so far, that his authority was unassailable, in this room and far beyond its boundaries, "I cannot grant your request until you've answered my questions satisfactorily."

The excitement Phoebe felt was not voluntary, nor did it seem to have much of anything to do with finding herself in the wrong century, but she kept her composure. "Then we are both defeated," she replied, "because you don't believe a word I say. You've already made up your mind about me, so why not just go ahead and hang me for a witch and be done with it?"

He glared at her, his eyes glinting with the hard shine of gemstones, while their pure, dark blue color, that of summer seas mirroring the sky, presented, in contrast, a sense of softness and great, fiery depths. "Perhaps you are a sorceress," he said at last, and Phoebe wished she could tell for sure whether he was serious or not. "Mayhap I should send you to the mainland, with your odd belongings and your babbling, and let a magistrate sort the matter out."

"You wouldn't blow your cover that way," Phoebe challenged, hoping against hope that her guess was right, and he was only bluffing, trying to scare her into confessing a litany of sins he had already ascribed to her. Though he was opinionated, she did not believe Duncan Rourke was superstitious.

Duncan put his hands on his hips and tilted his head to one side. "Blow my cover?" he drawled. "Damn it all to perdition, woman, what *are* you talking about?"

Phoebe sighed. "I'm sorry," she said. "I keep forgetting that things need to be translated. What I meant was, you won't send me to the States— er, the colonies—because you don't want the British to know you're here."

He gave a long, measured, and downright lethal sigh. Then, ignoring Old Woman, he clasped Phoebe's upper arm in a hard but painless grip and shuffled her across the room and out into the hallway. Before a protest could be raised, Duncan had thrust his unwanted houseguest over another threshold and into a chamber that was plainly his own.

He dragged her to the desk, a beautifully carved piece that would probably bring a fortune at an antiques auction in a couple of centuries, and pressed her into the matching chair. Her purse was there, and some of its contents, including Phoebe's pitiful store of cash, were arrayed on the shining surface.

He thumped the currency, which he'd laid out in a neat fan shape, with one index finger. "Where did you get these notes?" he asked, and this time there was wonder in his voice instead of anger.

Looking at her belongings and then at Duncan, Phoebe realized, in a moment of blinding revelation, that the impossible had happened.

To her.

Somehow, she had indeed found an opening in time, and she had slipped through it.

"I'm afraid to tell you," she confessed fretfully at long last.

Duncan crouched beside her, looking up into her face, gripping the back of her chair with one hand and the edge of the desk with the other. He drew unseen lightning down from the skies, like a human divining rod, and it crackled through Phoebe.

"Please," he said.

Phoebe bit her lower lip and raised her eyes to Old Woman for a moment in silent question, and her guardian nodded slowly.

"I came from the future," Phoebe blurted in a rush of words.

"I don't understand," Duncan admitted, brushing her face lightly with the backs of his knuckles, leaving prongs of fire in their wake. At least he hadn't said, *I don't believe you.*

"Neither do I," said Phoebe, barely able to keep from crying. "I was minding my business, in my own time, and suddenly the elevator was gone and I was here and there you were . . ."

He took one of the bills, a crisp twenty, and held it up. "It says 'The United States of America' on this paper. What does that mean?"

"That you won the war," she told him, speaking impatiently because she was still trying to comprehend that she had slipped through a crack in time and found herself in another century. There was no sense in asking herself how it had happened—that was a mystery she might never solve, though she certainly meant to try. All Phoebe could do for the moment, as far as she could tell, was accept her circumstances and make the best of them.

And try to make some sense of the things this man made her feel.

Duncan rose gracefully to his full height, still holding the twenty-dollar bill and gazing at it in quiet amazement. "He is a clever man, the printer who made this," he said, and the wistful note in his voice wrenched at something hidden far back in Phoebe's heart. "Some Tory trick, without doubt, calculated to mock our efforts to win liberty."

"You asked for the truth," Phoebe pointed out. "And just as I predicted, you think I'm lying."

"How can I even imagine otherwise?" he asked, meeting her eyes at last. Sadly. "It is a wild tale you tell. And an impossible one in the bargain."

"Is it?" Phoebe asked, putting the question to herself as well as to Duncan. She was still trying to deal with matters herself, still speculating, wondering, marveling. "We don't know much about such things, in my century or yours. For all any of us can say for sure, time is merely a state of mind, a matter of perception. Maybe, instead of being sequential, unfolding minute by minute, year by year, century by century, eternity exists as a whole, complete in and of itself."

"Gibberish," Duncan said, but she saw,

distracted by the many ramifications of her predicament though she was, that he found her theory intriguing, if not entirely likely.

"The question is," Phoebe muttered, running the tip of her index finger over the raised lettering on one of her credit cards, "what do I do now? Can I go back, or is the way closed forever?" She looked, as she spoke, not at Duncan, who had stepped back, but at Old Woman. "If I guessed your name," she asked, whimsical in her state of polite shock, "and dared to say it out loud, would the magic take me home?"

Old Woman laid one hand on Phoebe's shoulder, warm and heavy and reassuring. "You already be home, child. And you got here by a magic all your own. You're with us because that's what you wanted in the deepest part of your heart."

Duncan sighed, drew near again, and picked up a small photograph of Eliott, Phoebe's half brother. "This miniature is remarkable," he said, a frown of confusion creasing his forehead. "I cannot see the brushstrokes."

"That's because there are none," Phoebe said, quite gently, considering that she was both irritated and scared. And something else that was harder to define. "This is a photograph—sort of a reflection, captured on paper."

Her handsome host looked up, his eyes narrowed in wariness and suspicion and something Phoebe hoped was the beginning of belief. "And when was—will—this be invented?"

55

"Sometime in the nineteenth century, I think. There are a great many pictures of the Civil War, which began in 1860, so even though the process was still pretty cumbersome, they'd mastered the fundamentals by then."

Duncan looked pale and, again, a muscle flexed at the edge of his jaw. "What Civil War is this?" he asked, in a reasonable but otherwise utterly expressionless tone of voice.

"You're not ready to hear about that just yet," Phoebe told him. "You've got your hands full with the Revolution, and, well, let's just say that the War Between the States wasn't one of our country's finer moments. And then there was Vietnam, but that would *really* depress you—"

"Enough," Duncan interrupted. "Are you telling me that our nation will go to war against itself?"

Phoebe sighed, wishing, of course, that she hadn't mentioned that particular period in American history. "Yes," she said.

"For what cause?"

"It was very complicated, but I suppose it had more to do with slavery than anything else."

Duncan appeared to be developing a headache of monumental proportions. "Even now," he mused, "that question makes for bitter division among the staunchest patriots."

"If you guys had only outlawed it when you drew up the Declaration of Independence, everyone—especially black people—would have been spared a lot of grief. But it isn't going to happen: The planters from the southern colonies, among others, will maintain that slavery is necessary to economic survival, and, in the long run, they'll get their way."

Old Woman interceded quietly. "That's enough of such talk, child," she said, laying her hands lightly on Phoebe's cramped shoulders. The tense muscles relaxed with dizzying suddenness, as if some powerful drug had been injected. "Come away with me now. You got to have some sunshine and fresh air if you want to mend yourself proper."

Phoebe didn't protest that she wasn't in need of mending, because she wasn't entirely sure, given all that had happened to her since the night before. Besides, she felt a deep and elemental craving for the sea and the sky and the tropical breezes that roared and whispered between the two. She rose slowly, her gaze locked with Duncan's for a long moment. Then, conquered in some subliminal and utterly delicious way, she lowered her eyes and turned to follow Old Woman out of the room.

After the women had gone, Duncan gathered up Phoebe's uncanny possessions, one at a time, and tucked them back into the bag. All except for the likeness she had called a "photograph," that is—he kept that, gazing into the masculine face and wondering if this was the man Phoebe loved.

In the deeper regions of his mind, of course, he was considering the evidence he'd seen with his own eyes, touched with his own fingers. He wanted to believe Phoebe's story, despite the unsettling prediction of a war between the colonies themselves, because it meant the Continental Army would prevail. Despite the terrible odds, the deprivations, betrayals, and disappointments.

Tucking Phoebe's bag into a deep drawer in his desk, Duncan turned and resolutely left the room. That night, he and Alex would ride to the opposite side of the island, where a watch was posted, in case the long-awaited signal of a ship's approach should come from that direction. The vessel in question, christened the *India Queen*, was rumored to be all but sinking with the weight of its cargo: gunpowder, barrels of the stuff, along with crates of muskets and balls. General George Washington's militia was in dire need of all the munitions that could be begged, borrowed, or stolen.

Now, there were plans to be laid. The British ship would, without question, be well defended, her course set for Boston Harbor. The task of intercepting the vessel and confiscating the weaponry required flawless timing, and the slightest mistake might well result in disaster for Duncan and every member of his crew. According to his information, the man at the helm of the *India Queen* was a seasoned captain, with an understanding of the sea and its ways that seemed imprinted on his spirit like some unseen tattoo.

To get the better of such an adversary was not easy.

Duncan descended the main staircase and left the house by a side door, looking neither to left nor right but straight ahead, lest his gaze fall by accident on Mistress Turlow, who was surely somewhere nearby. He did not wish to be distracted from the business at hand—securing arms for General Washington's army.

He walked through the gardens, lushly scented and flamboyant with color, even after the ravages of the recent storm, past Italian statues and marble ponds and elaborately carved stone benches. Van Ruben, the Dutch merchant and planter, had come to this island seeking solitude, but he had brought the beauty of the Old World with him, to savor in private moments.

Duncan passed through an opening in a hedge taller than he was, and descended a steep, pebble-strewn path snaking down the verdant hillside to the beach. The cove where his ship rode at anchor was down the shore, fairly wreathed by trees and foliage.

He was pleased to see members of his crew on deck, preparing the vessel for a swift journey. Apparently, he thought, he wasn't the only one who expected the signal; Alex, as first mate, had already given orders that the *Francesca* was to be made ready for a voyage.

Seeing their captain standing on the beach, two of the men lowered a skiff to the water, fully rigged, and one climbed down a rope ladder to take up the oars.

Duncan waded out into the cove without troubling to remove his boots—they were of sturdy leather, after all, and expected to hold up under hard use. When the small boat drew near enough, he climbed deftly aboard, barely rocking her even though he was a man of considerable size.

"She's a fine sight, isn't she, Captain?" boasted the sailor, whose name was Kelsey, as proudly as if it were his own.

That sense of pride and personal interest was a trait Duncan valued in a crew member. He smiled, looking up at the *Francesca*'s sturdy masts and trim sails. "Aye," he agreed, with affection. "She is that and more."

Reaching the ship, where the ladder dangled in wait, Duncan and Kelsey made the skiff fast to her side and then climbed aboard.

Alex was waiting on deck, hands caught behind his back, ruddy of complexion and bright of eye. He plainly relished the prospect of a mission, just as Duncan did, and there was reason to hope, from his happy countenance, that he'd left his dark mood behind, like a ship outrunning a sea squall.

"You're expecting the signal tonight," Alex said.

Duncan nodded, taking in the bustle of preparation with a glance. "Aye. And you are in agreement, it would seem."

"Yes." Alex paused and cleared his throat

60

diplomatically, but he couldn't help grinning. "What of the mysterious Mistress Turlow?" He pretended to search the shore, tilting his head to peer around one of Duncan's shoulders. "I half expected you to bring her along, poor chit, and hang her from the yardarm for a traitor and a spy."

Duncan did not appreciate the reminder; he'd put forth a considerable effort, after all, to set aside all thought of that troublesome personage. He scowled and moved past his friend to descend the steps and proceed along the passageway toward his quarters. His desk was there, with his charts and logbooks and navigational tools. "We have more important matters to discuss," he said, for Alex was practically on his heels. "The *India Queen* may well have an escort, given the cargo she carries, and in any case, the British can be counted upon for a respectable flight."

Alex sighed, closing the cabin door while Duncan opened the portholes to air and light.

"We've been planning this raid for weeks," the first mate reminded his captain. "What else is there to say?"

Duncan took a chart from a cabinet affixed to the wall and unrolled it on the surface of his desk. "Plenty," he replied. "Should our first strategy fail, we must have another at hand. And still another after that."

Alex's jaw tightened, then relaxed again. He could manage any weapon, from a slingshot to a cannon, with uncanny accuracy, and he was a

61

fine horseman as well as an able sailor and swordsman. There could be no question of his courage, and his skills as a commander were also above reproach. For all of it, he was sometimes hasty, due to an impatient nature, and had been known to take rash and therefore, to Duncan's way of thinking, foolhardy risks.

"The British won't be expecting us while they're still so far from the coast," Alex said after a moment's pause, used, no doubt, to regroup.

"The British," Duncan answered, frowning thoughtfully as he studied the chart, measuring distances with his eyes and probabilities with his mind, "are always expecting us. They did not assemble the greatest navy on earth by leaving the security of vital supply ships to chance." He looked up, at last, and saw that Alex's neck had reddened, probably with suppressed irritation. "Have you any suggestions," asked the captain, "or must I labor over the problem alone?"

Alex had been offered an opportunity to salvage his dignity, and he did not refuse it. He bent over the chart, examining it thoroughly, and then offered an idea . . .

The signal came as soon as darkness had settled over the long and tangled chain of islands, a bonfire blazing on a distant shore, and Duncan saw it from the terrace outside his room. The *India Queen* would be within their grasp, if they sailed with the next tide and the winds were favorable. Once they'd boarded her, and subdued the captain and crew, the vessel would be diverted to a harbor just south of Charles Town, where a band of patriots waited to claim the muskets and gunpowder for use against the King's men.

Duncan turned to go back inside the house just as the bells in the small chapel Van Ruben had built for his wife began to toll. He smiled, grimly pleased that the watchman on duty had been paying attention. The crewmen, who had huts and houses of their own all over the island, would converge on the cove where the *Francesca* bobbed on the rising tide, ready to set sail for the colder waters to the north.

Candles and oil lamps filled the hall and the foyer with a pleasant glow, and Duncan felt a twinge of sadness because he had to leave. He was, he told himself silently, getting too attached to his comforts. Ten days or a fortnight at sea would be good discipline.

He had not seen Phoebe, there in the warm shadows of the drawing room doorway, and when she stepped into the light, he was arrested by the surprise of her presence. She was wearing an ill-fitting frock that Old Woman had probably salvaged from the bottom of some trunk, and her strange hair gave her a fey look, like a nymph or a pixie strayed from the musty pages of some ancient folktale. There was a fragility about her, a bereft air, that tugged at Duncan's heretofore invulnerable heart.

"I haven't managed to go back to the twentieth

century yet, as you can see," she said. "I take it those bells are some sort of rallying call?"

Duncan was in a hurry, and he could not have said why he was tarrying in the foyer. His thoughts, usually so orderly, tumbled over each other like apples spilled from a cart, and several moments passed before he managed a reply. "Yes," he said. He didn't move.

"You still think I am a spy, don't you?" she asked, and there was a bruised expression in her enormous blue eyes, as though it did her injury to think he didn't trust her.

"I do not know what you are," he replied succinctly and in all honesty, as his wits returned at last. "Mind that you cause no trouble in this household while I'm away, and do not attempt to flee the island. You shall be watched, be assured of that."

Phoebe flushed. "I didn't plan on trying to swim to Florida," she said. Her eyes seemed to shimmer with tears, but perhaps that was merely a trick of the candlelight, for she blinked and the effect was gone. "I wonder if anybody has even noticed that I'm not there."

Duncan resisted a foolhardy impulse to take her into his arms and shelter her against his chest for a few moments. The chapel bells were still pealing, more insistently now, and he was conscious of the fact that most of his men would reach the ship before he did, and wonder at his delay. They might begin to doubt his resolve, or

64

question his authority, and no good could come of either.

"Old Woman will look after you," he said. He left Phoebe then, but he knew she stood in the doorway, watching him go, for he felt her gaze upon his back.

Phoebe closed the door and leaned against it, worried. She wished she'd read all of Professor Bennings's book about Duncan before tumbling through the time warp; suddenly it was important to know, for instance, how he would die, and when.

It wasn't hard to guess his mission—he was off to bedevil a British ship and probably seize its cargo. According to Chapter Three of his biography, Duncan made a career of that, and Phoebe recalled that he'd been wounded once, rather badly, in a sword fight with an English sea captain who'd refused to surrender.

A knot formed in the pit of Phoebe's stomach, threatening to expel the supper she'd taken by the kitchen fire with Old Woman, just an hour before. She was not in love with Duncan Rourke—she hadn't known him long enough for that—but she had begun to care what happened to him. She would have liked to believe it was because he was to play such an important part in American history, but Phoebe wasn't very good at fooling herself. Or others, for that matter.

She was attracted to Duncan, not just physically, but emotionally. Of course, she reflected a little sorrowfully, pushing away from the door, it was probably only because she was afraid. Something very weird was happening to her, and Duncan, despite his suspicions and brusque manner, was like a lighthouse, towering in the dark heart of a storm. He was a touchstone—the only person she knew to be real, besides herself.

Wishing she could stow away on Duncan's ship, like the heroine of a book, and be part of the action, Phoebe took herself slowly up the main stairway. She wasn't clever enough to pull off such a feat, she thought. He'd discover her, for sure, hiding behind a barrel or face-down underneath his berth, and either toss her overboard or lock her up in the brig.

She moved like a wraith along the upper passageway, which was only dimly lit, and, examining her mind and heart, marveled at the lack of panic she found there. Sure, she'd been terrified when she'd first realized that she had accidentally wandered into another time, as easily as if the eighteenth century were one room in some great, rambling museum, and the twentieth another. Now that she'd had a day to assimilate things, however, she had a feeling of rightness. Just as Old Woman had predicted, the other world, the world of Seattle, and condominiums, and Jeffrey, already seemed unreal.

There was a fire burning low on the hearth in her room, intended to give light rather than heat, for the night was balmy. Phoebe removed her dress—Old Woman had told her it was part of a trunkful of goods salvaged long ago from a shipwreck—and looked around her.

The bed dominated the room, a gilt and tapestry-draped affair fit for Marie Antoinette's boudoir, along with an exquisite writing desk and a settee upholstered in embroidered velvet. The carpets were Persian, the draperies scallops of intricate lace. A fabulous lacquered armoire, with a bureau to match, completed the decor.

"I could get to like this," Phoebe told her reflection in the looking glass above the bureau. "In fact, I already have."

There was a soft rap at the door, and in answer to Phoebe's summons, Old Woman entered the room, carrying a pitcher of steaming water and a towel.

"That's a poor dress for the mistress of such a grand house," the dark-skinned fairy godmother remarked. "Mr. Duncan has money, though. He'll see that you have gowns befitting his wife and the mother of his children . . ."

Weary color surged into Phoebe's cheeks. She had just come to terms with the fact that she was there, in 1780. It was an accomplishment she could be proud of—undergoing such an experience without losing her mind. She wasn't quite ready, however, for a husband, be he Duncan Rourke or not, much less children. Not even if that husband was a handsome pirate/patriot, and the children had dark hair and eyes as blue as indigo.

"I am not a wife," she said. "Or a mother. I'm

simply a wayfarer, thought to be a spy or a pirate's mistress."

Old Woman smiled complacently. "You not a wife yet, neither a mother. But you will be. No telling, though, which will come first."

4

There seemed to be no point in questioning her fate, or resisting it—Phoebe had already concluded that this new life she'd been thrust into was more interesting, if more dangerous, than the one she'd left behind. Then Old Woman took her to the laundry room, which occupied a vast and mildewy chamber in the cellar—Phoebe glanced about furtively for any sign of the vanished elevator—and pointed to a vat of steaming water and a pile of cotton shirts.

"If you going to manage this house," she told Phoebe, "you got to know its ways. Mr. Duncan, he like to be clean all the time, and his clothes has to be washed and pressed real regular-like."

Half a dozen other women were working in that unbearably hot place: Three were old, greeting Phoebe with toothless smiles, but the others were closer to her own age or younger, and they looked at her with curiosity but no visible trace of friendliness. One, a tall, lithe creature with the sandalwood skin and black hair of a native, contrasted by wide hazel eyes, tossed the pair of breeches she'd been scrubbing into a tub of soapy water and crossed the room to face the new arrival. She smiled, obviously aware that she was beautiful, but her expression was hostile as she took in Phoebe's short hair and ill-fitting, borrowed clothes.

"You go on back to your washing, Simone," Old Woman said.

Simone didn't move, except to put her hands on her hips. She was exotic in her bright yellow sarong, and Phoebe felt somehow fraudulent, like an insecure actress ad-libbing a part, or a little girl dressed up in her mother's clothes.

"This be the witch-woman," Simone said, in a speculative drawl. "The one that came out of nowhere."

Phoebe opened her mouth, then closed it again.

Old Woman gave Phoebe a subtle shove toward the washtubs, though her words, like before, were directed to Simone. "No more than you are," she retorted. "Don't you be devilin' this child, either, girl. I hear of such a thing, I'll take off some of your hide with a switch."

How to win friends and influence people, Phoebe thought, and offered a faltering smile before stealing a swift glance at the other women in the laundry. They were all concentrating pointedly on their various tasks—pressing, sorting, scrubbing, and mending—but most likely every ear

69

was tuned to the unfolding drama in the center of the room.

Simone curled her lip, turned with a flourish, and went back to her tub, where she snatched another pair of breeches out of the water and pounded it against the washboard with a vengeance.

Old Woman ignored the girl and whispered to Phoebe, "You can keep me company in the kitchen if you'd rather."

Phoebe shuddered. She was not a cook. "I'll earn my keep like everyone else," she said, with some bravado, and approached the untended tub. There was a small mound of dirty stockings on the floor beside it.

Moments later, Old Woman was gone, and Phoebe was alone with the others. Biting her lower lip, she turned and saw that except for Simone, they were all watching her, some with wary interest, some with indifference. It didn't take a nuclear physicist to guess that Simone cared for Duncan, and that she probably saw the mysterious newcomer as a rival for his attentions. He, as lord of the manor in particular and no doubt of all he surveyed in general, might well have given the beautiful laundress reason to believe he returned her devotion.

Maybe he did.

Phoebe's shoulders slumped a little at the thought. With a sigh, she gathered up the small mountain of stockings and dumped them into the assigned tub. She owed a debt to Old Woman and, indirectly, to Duncan, and if she could offset it by washing socks, that was fine with her.

She did not wish to be obliged to either of them. Besides, if Simone could do this work, so could she.

Scrubbing, rinsing, and wringing, Phoebe occupied her hands with menial labor while her mind reeled from one wild, unworkable plan to another. The past had become her future, while she wasn't looking, and until further notice, she had to make her way in a strange, antiquated environment. Whatever Old Woman's fancies might be, and Simone's suspicions, Phoebe had no intention of living out her days as a prisoner on Paradise Island, laundering the master's socks.

As much as she wanted to be near Duncan, she was neither his mistress nor his servant, and she would not be at his beck and call. Furthermore, being a history buff, she wanted a look at the outside world. It wasn't every day that a person stumbled into another century.

Phoebe racked her brain for a plan to get off the island. After twenty minutes or so, she was soaked with steam and sweat, her hair plastered to her cheeks and neck and forehead, and no closer to a sensible escape scheme than before. Then something cold and wet struck her across the back.

Even before she turned to face her adversary, Phoebe knew who it was, and she armed herself with a sodden stocking. Furious, she swung it at Simone, who was still holding the drenched shirt she'd just wielded; striking the other woman's right cheek, it made a satisfying *thwack* sound.

Simone retaliated, and Phoebe, her pride stinging, snatched another piece of laundry from a tub and hurled it with all her strength.

Both Simone and Phoebe were in deadly earnest, but the others shrieked with laughter as they joined the skirmish, and soon shirts and sheets and stockings and breeches were flying in every direction. Pandemonium reigned for a time—washtubs were overturned, and the combatants slipped in spilled water and tangled their feet in spent ammunition, and finally everyone was breathless, and there was nothing left to throw.

Simone was wet to the skin, and so was Phoebe. They stood staring at each other for a long moment, gasping in the midst of soapy carnage, and then, at one and the same time, they began to laugh.

Old Woman swept in, drawn by the shrieking ruckus, and was plainly not amused. Phoebe was ordered from the room in disgrace—"What will Mr. Duncan say if you catch a chill and die? You just tell me that!"—while Simone and the others were roundly scolded in the swift, musical dialect of the island.

In her room, Phoebe stripped to her skimpy chemise—recovered from the same shipwreck as the dress, no doubt—and dried her hair with a rough towel taken from the washstand. Presently, there was a light knock at the door and, at Phoebe's invitation, Old Woman entered.

"Simone loves Duncan, doesn't she?" Phoebe asked, before her fairy godmother could tell her what she already knew—that she'd behaved like an adolescent in the laundry room.

"Yes," came the succinct reply. A somber black skirt, plain cotton blouse, and the accompanying antique undergarments were produced from the armoire and extended to Phoebe.

Obediently she accepted the dry clothes and stepped behind the changing screen to put them on. "Is she his mistress?" The answer was ridiculously important to Phoebe, though she intended to go away, and she would have given anything not to feel the way she did.

"You'd best ask Mr. Duncan about that."

Phoebe was glad she was out of sight, because the mere suggestion of bringing up such a topic turned her cheeks scarlet. "It would be simpler to ask Simone," she ventured, wriggling into lace-trimmed drawers and a petticoat, then reaching for a camisole.

"You won't get the truth from that one," Old Woman said flatly. "She's like you—she don't have the first idea what's inside her own heart."

Phoebe peered around the edge of the screen, fastening the tiny buttons of her blouse as she spoke. "You're not fooling me, you know. By the way you talk, I mean. It's colorful, and all that, but I can tell when somebody is putting me on."

Amusement sparkled in Old Woman's liquid

eyes, along with the keen and kindly intelligence she couldn't hide. "Reckon I'll set you to hoeing and weeding, since you're not good at washing clothes."

"You changed the subject," Phoebe pointed out.

"So did you," Old Woman replied.

Phoebe spent the remainder of the day in the vegetable garden, wearing a broad-brimmed straw hat given her by Old Woman, and when she was finally called to supper, she was so tired that she couldn't eat. She climbed the stairs laboriously, every muscle aching in concert, stripped off her skirt and blouse, and collapsed onto the bed with a piteous groan. Even her eyelids throbbed, and she lowered them, wanting to lose herself in the painless oblivion of sleep.

"Everything hurts," Phoebe said when she heard the door of her room open and then close again. She wanted Old Woman to know she was suffering and feel guilty for it. "Has horse liniment been invented yet?"

Silence.

Phoebe opened her eyes. Simone, not Old Woman, was standing beside the bed, and she was frowning. This time, however, her expression was one of puzzlement, rather than poisonous dislike.

"Let me see your hand," she said.

Phoebe sat up, but made no move to comply with Simone's request. "I'd appreciate it if you'd knock, next time you stop by," she remarked.

Simone reached out and closed strong brown fingers around Phoebe's callused ones, bent, and peered into her palm. She murmured something, and tears brimmed in her strange, pale eyes.

Phoebe pulled free, but not because she was afraid. Instead of fear, she felt sympathy. And the beginnings of friendship. "Short lifeline, huh?"

Simone covered her mouth with one hand and turned away. She did not leave the room, but instead went to stand gazing out the windows, toward the sea. Phoebe knew without asking that the other woman was watching for Duncan and wondering if he was safe; she wondered, too, and missed him, though she had no right.

She stood, but did not approach Simone. "He'll be back," she said.

"Yes," Simone responded after a pause, without turning to face Phoebe. "And you will be here, waiting for him."

Phoebe's heart was soft, had always been so, and it ached just then. Not for herself, but for this woman who was, by tacit agreement, no longer an enemy. "Duncan doesn't even like me," she felt compelled to say. "He thinks I'm a spy."

At last, Simone left the windows, and though she kept her distance, she looked Phoebe in the face. "He will take you for a wife," Simone said, with dignity and pride, but no rancor. "Many children wait to be born. But he'll come to my bed, too, and I shall give him sons and daughters as well—as many as you."

Phoebe was a misplaced person, on a cosmic

scale. She had no reason to think she would stay in the eighteenth century, or in her delusion, if that was what it was. She was attracted to Duncan, but she did not love him, and she had no claim on his loyalties. In fact, it seemed he could barely tolerate her.

The sensible thing to do was leave.

But for all that, Phoebe was certain of one thing: If she ever married again, no husband of hers, be he Duncan Rourke or anyone else, would ever go to another woman's bed. She'd had enough of that kind of humiliation and hurt with Jeffrey.

"No," she replied with a shake of her head, and though she did not elaborate, it was plain that Simone understood and saw the assertion as a challenge. With a smile and a shrug of one elegant shoulder, Phoebe's guest left the room.

In the morning, Phoebe returned to the garden.

By noon, she was hoping to make a quantum leap back to the future, just so she could escape the hot sun and that wretched hoe, but nothing happened. Weeds grew and flourished before her very eyes, it seemed, and Old Woman assigned her the same task the next day, and the next, and the one after that.

And Phoebe worked, because anything was better than sitting around, waiting. Wondering what would happen.

Two full weeks passed, during which Phoebe hoed and watered and weeded and, for purposes of personal entertainment as much as anything else, plotted her escape from Paradise. At night, she waited to be beamed up—*there's no place like home, there's no place like home*, she repeated over and over again like a litany—but evidently, the time wizard wasn't paying attention. She awakened each morning in 1780, and mingled with her disappointment, always, was a touch of relief.

One day, she was bent double, pulling quack grass out of the turnip patch, when her heart gave a sudden flutter of warning. She rose, holding her bonnet in place with one hand, and saw Duncan standing at the edge of the garden, watching her. A smile crooked the corner of his mouth and flickered in his eyes.

Phoebe felt a tug, deep down in a part of herself she'd never explored, never been conscious of before, and barely kept from running across the rows of carrots and potatoes and string beans to fling her arms around his neck and sob for joy merely because he was alive. On some level, she realized, she'd feared that he would not return.

"I started in the laundry room," she said, knowing the words were ridiculous even as she uttered them and speaking anyway because she couldn't endure the silence. "That didn't work out, so I was transferred to the veggie detail."

Duncan laughed and shook his head. He was impossibly attractive, tall and sun-bronzed, with broad shoulders and the clean, briny smell of the sea about him. "I have yet to discern which language you speak," he said. "Not the King's English, to be sure."

Phoebe smiled, but she was already counting the nights Duncan had been at sea, and picturing him in Simone's arms, making up for lost time. The image turned the pit of her stomach ice-cold, and her heartbeat outran itself and skittered painfully. "No," she said. "I speak the American version, circa 1995."

Duncan looked solemn, all of the sudden, and bone-weary. Certainly her presence was as much a mystery to him as it was to her, and he plainly did not like unsolvable riddles. It was a pity he couldn't simply write her off as crazy and go on about his business, but of course her watch and driver's license and other wondrous possessions complicated matters.

"You are well?" he asked, at last. It meant something, she supposed, that he lingered,but she couldn't guess what. Maybe he was still trying to come up with a rational explanation.

"Yes," she answered, too proud to tell him the truth—that her arms and legs and back ached from hard work, and that she would have traded her right kidney for a couple of aspirin and a hot-water bottle. "I guess your mission must have succeeded."

It was a mistake to mention the recent foray against the British, but the damage had been done before Phoebe realized as much. Duncan visibly withdrew from her; his eyes were narrowed, and he folded his arms across his chest, unconsciously erecting a barrier between them. "That it did," he said distantly, as if Phoebe had taken up arms against him and his men herself. "But at great cost."

With that, he strode away toward the house, leaving her standing there in the turnips, dirty and sunburned and full of pain. She understood why her body hurt, but what ailed her heart?

Duncan reached his room to find the big copper bathtub on the hearth. Simone and another servant were pouring buckets full of hot water into it.

He did not speak, but instead went to his desk, where a decanter of fine brandy waited, and splashed a quantity of amber liquid into a snifter. The captain and crew of the British ship, the *India Queen*, had put up a valiant fight, and the decks of that vessel had been awash in the blood of both sides before the battle was over. He had lost three men—he'd forgotten that, for a few blessed minutes, watching Phoebe in the garden—but the memory would live in his dreams for months, or even years, beside the other recollections that haunted his sleep.

And Alex, his closest friend. Dear God, Alex had taken a lead ball in the knee. He lay at that moment in another room, on the opposite end of the house, with Old Woman for his physician, delirious with fever and with pain. Even if Alex survived—a miracle, should it happen—he would be a cripple, unable to ride and fight. Perhaps unable to walk.

Bile rushed into the back of Duncan's throat.

He had forgotten about that, too, talking with Phoebe. *Forgotten.* Sweet Jesu, what was wrong with him?

Simone touched his arm, and he started, for he hadn't realized that she'd crossed the room to stand before him. "I will stay and give you comfort," she offered softly. The other servant had gone, he noticed, for it was no secret that he had already taken solace in Simone's embrace on innumerable occasions.

Duncan yearned for what she would so willingly give him, ached for the release, both mental and physical, that such a union could provide. The problem was, he wanted someone else lying beside and beneath him, someone he dared not trust.

Phoebe.

"Be gone," he said with gentle cruelty. "My bath grows cold."

Simone's splendid hazel eyes blazed with passion and some lesser emotion that he did not trouble himself to identify. "You want her," she accused in a fierce, bitter whisper. "Look at her hair—she is like a boy! Perhaps your tastes have changed, Captain?"

Rage seized Duncan's weary mind, blinding and white-hot, and only by a supreme act of will did he restrain himself from slapping Simone. He, who had never laid a hand to a woman in anger. "Get out," he muttered, "I will not tell you again."

She searched his face, and he saw regret in her

80

eyes and a great suffering, and although he did not stir, or utter so much as a breath, he was not unmoved. There had been no promises between them, but she had given him pleasure, and the sweet, fiery distraction he'd believed he could not live without.

Simone started to speak, then stopped herself. With a small sob, she turned and hurried out.

Duncan locked the door behind her, lest she suffer a change of heart, finished his brandy, poured another, and stripped off his clothes. His bathwater was only lukewarm by that time, but he sank gratefully into it. Although he was tired to the very center of his soul, he dared not close his eyes, for if he did, he would see his men fall, Alex bleeding on the deck of the vanquished *India Queen*. He had been silent, Alex had, but Duncan, who knew him well, had heard the agonized screams his friend withheld and had wanted to cry out himself.

Presently, Duncan downed the last of his drink, washed, dried himself off, and took a triple portion from the decanter. He was mildly drunk by the time he'd donned fresh clothes, and grateful for that anesthetic state, rather than repentant. His father had been right, he reflected, sitting on the edge of his bed to pull on his boots. If there was such a place as hell, Duncan Rourke would find his way there presently and make a name for himself.

To any casual observer, Duncan would have looked quite normal as he made his way along the hallway toward the back of the house and the quiet room where Alex lay. He knew, however, that he was unsteady, and if called upon to fight, he'd get his throat cut.

He hesitated outside Alex's door, wishing he could offer a prayer. But he was, alas, a pagan and a rebel, and although he did not disbelieve, neither could he profess an honest faith. He did not make a petition because he did not expect to be heard.

His surprise, when he stepped over the threshold and found Phoebe in that room, instead of his aged servant, was profound. She had drawn up a chair and was holding Alex's corpse-gray hand and biting her lip as she watched over him.

"You didn't tell me," she said, her voice hardly above a whisper.

Duncan closed the door gently and went to stand on the opposite side of the bed, looking down at Alex's still face. He could not bring himself to admit that he had forgotten about the battle, about the men who had died, about his best friend, while standing at the edge of the garden watching her. Wanting her.

"There are a great many things you don't need to know," he replied, without sparing her so much as a glance. In truth, he feared he might be caught in her enchantment, lose himself in her again, if he took that risk.

"Will he die?" Her voice was small, mirroring all the terror Duncan felt but could not reveal.

"Probably," Duncan answered.

"Why haven't you sent for a doctor?"

At last he met her eyes, but only because he had no choice. Her gaze had drawn his, somehow, the way the warmth of the sun finds seeds nestled in the earth and causes them to stir and struggle and seek the light. "This is an island," he reminded her grimly. "We are miles from anywhere. And even if that were not so, I would not permit the bloodletters who call themselves physicians to lay one filthy hand to my friend."

Phoebe was pale, and shadows had appeared under her eyes in the short time since he'd encountered her outside, in the fresh air and sunshine. She seemed to be wilting, like some exotic blossom taken from its natural element. "Yes—I had forgotten what medicine was—is—like in the eighteenth century. I guess there isn't much we can do for him, is there?"

Duncan waited a few moments to answer, for he was on the verge of weeping, and would have died before showing such weakness in the presence of another person—most notably this one. He had given way to his emotions before, of course, but only in private; he generally grieved— and celebrated—through his music. "No," he said at last. "There isn't much we can do to ease him. What brings you here, Phoebe?"

She smoothed Alex's sweat-soaked hair back from his forehead, as if soothing a fretful child after an ugly dream. "I don't know," she replied, without looking at Duncan. "He was kind to me the night I came to this house."

"Unlike myself," Duncan said. He touched Alex's hand with the tips of his fingers and hoped his friend knew he wasn't alone, that someone, however helpless and guilty, was keeping a vigil.

"You were a complete bastard," Phoebe said, almost as an aside. "I thought I'd wandered into some kind of role-playing weekend for perverts."

Duncan grasped enough of her convoluted English to be chagrined, but his attention, like hers, was focused on the patient. "Alex was furious with me that night. Sometimes I wonder how we ever became friends—I've always been a libertine, while he is the most decent of men, living by standards I don't even aspire to reach."

"Maybe he thought he could save you," Phoebe said.

"Maybe," Duncan agreed and smiled ruefully. "He should have known it was an impossible task."

"Are you so terrible as all that?" Phoebe asked. Alex was stirring, and she soaked a cloth in cool water and bathed his forehead as she spoke. "Granted, you are an extremely moody individual, and you're not entirely sober at the moment, I think, but you obviously care for your friend and for your cause. You are a gifted musician, and you must love beauty or you wouldn't live in this wonderful house."

He was touched by her matter-of-fact assessment and supposed that what had happened to Alex was making him unusually sentimental. "Do you think the devil doesn't love music, as much or more than any angel in heaven could?" he asked quietly. "I should think he makes angry tunes sometimes, and more often sad ones. Perhaps he plays because he cannot weep."

She watched him in silence for a time, then asked in a reasonable voice, "Is that why you play, Duncan? Because you can't cry?"

He stood and left Alex to stand at the small window, which Phoebe or perhaps Old Woman had opened to a salt-scented breeze. He gazed, unseeing, at the sea, which had been his soul's lover, his life's blood, his sanctuary, throughout his adult life. This time, it did not soothe him.

"Alex is dying," he murmured. "Because of me." He turned and knew by the expression in Phoebe's eyes that his face was terrible to look upon, but silence, however prudent it might have been, was beyond him by then. Something in her made him want to confess the deepest, most wretched secrets of his soul. "God in heaven, *look at him*! Do you think Alex needed a devil to cause this suffering, this waste? No. All that was required to bring a good man to his end was to call Duncan Rourke his friend!"

He had said all those things in whispers, but he might have shouted, for the room fairly quaked with the force of his fury and his pain.

Phoebe rose to her feet and rounded the bed to stand glaring up at him, her eyes glistening with tears of outrage. "Stop it! Alex wasn't forced to fight with you, he chose that life for himself." She sniffled ingloriously, wiped her face with the back of one hand, and went on. "If you want to salve your bruised conscience and wallow in the singular tragedy of your existence, then at least have the decency to do it somewhere else. This time belongs to Alex, not you."

Duncan retreated a step, aware that she was right. Before he could think of an answer, Alex stirred again and murmured something.

He'd asked for water, and Phoebe went back to his bedside and, using a spoon, gave him one sip and then another. He opened his eyes briefly and looked at Duncan. That one glance held a plea that struck Duncan like the point of a lance.

Alex wanted to die.

"No," Duncan told him, hoarsely. "No, damn you."

All that night, Duncan sat beside Alex's bed, waiting, watching, willing his friend to live. At some point Phoebe left the room, and Old Woman took her place, bringing poultices and muttering odd, reverent incantations. She did not speak to Duncan, and he did not speak to her, and yet they were in perfect accord.

At dawn, she gathered her medicines and went out, and Duncan got up to stand at the window and watch the sunrise fling shards of crimson and gold and fiery orange over the waters.

"Duncan."

He turned and saw that he had not imagined the sound; Alex was indeed conscious, though deathly pale, and Duncan's relief was so great that, for the moment, he could not utter a sound.

"What kind of soldier will I make now?" Alex asked in quiet despair.

Duncan found his voice and sat down again, after drawing his chair up close to the bed. "There are other callings besides soldiering," he said gruffly. "You could go into business, or read the law. You could marry and sire a flock of children . . ."

Alex's lips moved in a parody of a smile. "A woman wants a whole man for a husband, not a remnant."

"You are whole," Duncan insisted. "Or you will be, once you've had time to heal. Give yourself a chance."

"The leg is worthless," Alex said. "I felt it die."

Duncan squeezed the bridge of his nose between his thumb and forefinger. It was a struggle to keep his tone of voice level, to hide his own sorrows and misgivings. "You will be strong again," he said. "In six months, a year—"

There were tears on Alex's face, and the sight of them silenced Duncan.

"I will try," Alex murmured. "But I must have your word on one thing, or there will be no such bargain."

"What are you saying?" Duncan asked. "What bargain is this?"

"If I could do as I wish at this moment," Alex said, "I would put a pistol to my head. Because you believe I can recover, I shall make every attempt to do so. If, six months hence, I still want to end my life, you must help me to die."

Duncan's stomach rolled. "Great Zeus—"

"Promise me," Alex insisted. He was weak, drifting toward sleep.

"I cannot!"

"Duncan."

"Damn you—how can you ask me to do murder, to kill my closest friend?"

"For exactly that reason. Because you are my closest friend. 'Tis a hard journey that lies before me, Duncan. I haven't the strength to try, knowing I might be condemning myself to a lifetime in a broken body that is, nonetheless, too strong to perish."

"Are you telling me that you will give up the ghost if I refuse to make this vow? But you cannot make yourself die simply by willing it so." Even as he made this desperate speech, Duncan knew he was wrong. He'd seen other men embrace death, men far less grievously wounded than Alex. It was often a simple matter of turning one's mind toward the grave, and the peace that waited there, offering an end to pain and fear and regret.

Alex did not reply; there was no need. He simply looked at Duncan and waited.

"Do not ask this of me!"

"I can ask it of no one else," Alex said.

Duncan was silent for a long time. "Very well, then," he spat at last in an agonized whisper. "You have my promise, damn you. But I do not give it willingly."

Alex smiled, closed his eyes, and rested.

Duncan strode out of the room, along the hallway, down the broad staircase. He moved swiftly, though blinded by his thoughts, and made his way to the drawing room, where the harpsichord stood, innocent, inanimate, vulnerable to the violence of his emotions. He could not think, he dared not speak.

He sat down before the exquisite instrument and spread his fingers over the familiar keys. He was not aware of what he played, could not hear the music, did not know its character. He lost track of time.

Presently, Duncan raised his eyes from the keyboard, though the notes continued to flow from him, like a river of thunder, stemming from the loneliest, most barren regions of his soul. Phoebe stood close by, watching him, listening. Weeping.

He saw her mouth shape the word "stop," but he shook his head. She didn't understand; he couldn't control the music because he was not its master, it was his. He lowered his gaze again and went on pounding at the keys, and the furious concerto filled the room, the house, the universe with its pulsing chords.

Phoebe touched him then, something no one else had ever dared to do while he was in such a state. She stepped behind him and laid her hands on his shoulders, and the shock of that struck him with the impact of a storm-tossed ship splintering upon the shoals.

He stood and whirled, oversetting the stool.

She did not retreat, though he must have looked like a demon in his anguish, but rested her light, cool hands upon him again, this time on his upper arms, then his face.

"Duncan," she said. "Oh, Duncan."

It was more than he could bear, her tenderness. He wanted nothing so much as to lift her into his arms and carry her to his bed, there to lose himself in her sweet fire and be consumed by it, but he would not seduce her, much less use force. He left the drawing room by way of the French doors that opened onto the main garden and did not return to the house until darkness had descended over the island and lamps had been lighted in the windows.

5

Duncan's terrible, beautiful, and singularly anguished music echoed in Phoebe's ears and trembled in the very marrow of her bones, long after he had hurled himself from the keyboard, overturning the bench in the explosive violence of that motion, and stormed out of the drawing room. The wires of the harpsichord still hummed a feeble lament when a door slammed soundly in the distance.

Phoebe did not stop to set the stool upright

90

again; even that would be a presumption, and she had done enough meddling for one day. Instead, she ran the fingers of her right hand over the pristine ivory keys, gently, as if to soothe the instrument, and a tinkling spray of forlorn and fragile notes rose in the wake. Out of the corner of her eye, she saw Old Woman, brown hands folded, face as serene as an angel's, keeping her silent vigil.

"If only I had left him alone," Phoebe mused with quiet misery.

"You wanted to help," Old Woman responded benignly. "Still, his is a wound of the spirit, and even you cannot heal it. That is a task only Mr. Duncan himself can manage, with the help of his Maker."

Phoebe turned to meet her friend's placid gaze. "You are a marvel," she said with affection, though she was still too sad to smile. "How did you get so smart?"

"I have lived a long time," was the answer. "I have watched and listened."

Phoebe nodded and sighed, pondering. She announced the conclusion she had long since reached but had been unable to voice. "I can't stay here," she said.

Old Woman did not react verbally, but drew near and took Phoebe's hand, as Simone had done, studying her palm at length. This time, Phoebe made no attempt to pull away, and in those moments she felt her very soul being examined, weighed, explored.

At last, a smile fluttered upon Old Woman's full lips, like a bird lighting softly on a branch. "Yes," she said. "You will go from this place. It is necessary."

"You'll help me?"

Old Woman gazed deeply into her eyes, and it seemed she saw visions and portents there, things Phoebe herself did not know. A shiver trickled down her spine, but the sensation was born of mystery, not fear. "Tonight a boat will take you away, to an island far north of this one. You must determine to be strong, though, for this will not be an easy journey."

Phoebe had already learned that nothing about life in the eighteenth century was easy—it took all a person's energy just to meet the most basic needs. Even simple things, like going to the bathroom, required strategic planning, and taking a bath was a monumental undertaking. "I'm not surprised," she said reasonably.

She spent the remainder of the day sitting beside Alex's bed, though he was unconscious again, reading aloud from a volume of Chaucer she had found in the drawing room. Although she was intelligent, Middle English was not Phoebe's forte, and she understood little of what she read. Still, the task kept her mind off her own troubles and, she hoped, served as a thread, however tenuous, to link Alex with the world of the living.

At sunset, she ate in a dim corner of the kitchen, a place separate from the main house, and when night had settled over the island, a young native man came to collect her. He led the way along a tropical path to the shore without speaking at all, and once there, motioned her toward a sleek, canoelike craft resting upon the white sand.

After swallowing hard, Phoebe climbed aboard, clutching to her bosom a pitiful bundle containing a spare dress, underthings, some salt for cleaning her teeth, and a bar of soap, and sat down on a narrow bench. Coppery muscles rippling, the boy waded into the dark turquoise water, pushed the boat off expertly, and was soon rowing along the shivering, silver cone of moonlight spilling over the sea.

Old Woman had been right; the journey was hard.

First, there were mosquitoes. Then a bout of seasickness that had Phoebe retching over the side. They wove between dark islands, with the stars for a guide, and slipped into a sheltered cove at sunrise, where they slept, sprawled in the sand. Phoebe used her bag for a pillow.

For three days they traveled in just that way, gliding silently over the waters by night, resting on land by day, when there was a danger of being seen. Phoebe kept quiet most of the time, but once in a while she felt compelled to chatter, out of sheer loneliness. She told her mute companion about Jeffrey, and Professor Benning, about cars and airplanes and shopping malls, fast food and fat grams. He listened, smiling occasionally, and offered not a single word in reply.

At last, early the fourth morning, they arrived on an island, not isolated and uninhabited, like previous ones, but full of sound and fury, hustle and bustle. There were ships in the harbor, flying the British flag, and the shore was lined with wharves and barrels, slaves and freemen, wagons and carts and buildings. Phoebe thanked her escort and waded bravely ashore, with her heavy skirts practically pulling her under.

She had absolutely no idea where to go, except forward. So she did that.

Phoebe wandered up and down the muddy, manure-littered streets until her dress and shoes had dried, a tourist from another century. She passed a candlemaker's shop, a weaver's, a shipping office, and a general store. The most prominent structure by far, though, was the Crown and Lily, an obviously popular tavern.

After summoning up all her remaining courage, Phoebe stepped over the threshold and into the rollicking dimness beyond. She smelled malt and sweat, tobacco smoke and treason within those humble walls and proceeded directly to the bar, where a stout man in a stained shirt and cheap powdered wig dispensed pewter mugs spilling over with ale.

"To the rear with you, wench," he said, before Phoebe could say a word. "There's ample work for you here, I dare say, if you can serve up a mug and keep your thoughts to yourself. Speak to Mistress Bell—she'll give you a pallet and a bite to eat."

Cheeks burning, Phoebe restrained from telling the bartender off in vivid Anglo-Saxon terms for daring to talk to her like that and proceeded between the trestle tables to the back of the tavern. She needed to find work, if she was going to survive this strange cosmic odyssey, and serving drinks at the Crown and Lily was a beginning.

She couldn't expect to advance to management, of course, but that was something she would think about later. For now, she only wanted a clean bed and food to eat.

Mistress Bell was an ample, unself-conscious woman in a coarsely woven gown. With her abundance of gray hair and gruff, good-natured manner, she reminded Phoebe of one of her favorite characters from the movies of the 1940s—Ma Kettle, as portrayed by Margery Main.

"My name is Phoebe Turlow," Phoebe announced, hoping she sounded like a regular eighteenth-century woman and knowing she didn't. Mistress Bell's astute gaze had gone straight to her short hair. "I'm looking for a job. Work. A position."

The older woman narrowed her eyes. "I don't know you," she said in her rough, booming voice. "Be you a bondwoman, run off from your master? Where did you come from?"

Phoebe swallowed. "I'm no one's servant," she said in a steady voice. "And I come from a place called Seattle." It might have been better to lie, but she wasn't good at impromptu prevarications; that had always been Jeffrey's specialty. "I'm a very hard worker," she added. "I waited tables in college."

Mistress Bell gave a low, snorting hoot. "College, is it?" she mocked derisively, as though such a thing were impossible. Which, of course, it was, that being 1780. "You can sweep and wash pots and kettles and make a hearty stew with what comes to hand?"

"If pressed," Phoebe agreed.

Mistress Bell chuckled, and the sound was deep and rich and utterly benign. "Suppose a man should invite you to share his bed, be he King's man or rebel?"

"I would refuse," Phoebe said.

"Aye," replied Mistress Bell. "I think you would. Follow me, lass, and I'll show you your room. There's a pot of boiled venison in the kitchen, too—you may help yourself to that. No ale, though. Not until you've finished the tasks of the day. Are you agreed?"

Phoebe never considered refusing. She nodded, grateful that she'd fallen into a job so quickly, and followed Mistress Bell up a rear stairway of rough-hewn planks, then up another. Her room, it turned out, was a sweltering cubicle in the rafters, only a little larger than the average twentieth-century closet, graced with a rough wooden cot, one tattered quilt, and a bowl and pitcher teetering on a rickety wash table. There was a chamberpot under the bed, and a single peg in the wall to accommodate her wardrobe. Which consisted of exactly two dresses.

"Thank you," Phoebe said sincerely. Although she missed Duncan sorely, and Old Woman, this humble cell was at least her own. The door was heavy, and there was a bolt on it, and whatever the hardship, she could cross this threshold each night knowing that she'd paid her own way.

"You're an odd lass," Mistress Bell observed, one bristly gray eyebrow raised. "From whence do you hail? Since this place you call See-attle, I mean?"

"Boston," said Phoebe, finding that she could lie promptly after all, if the situation called for it. She hoped the reply didn't automatically mark her as a patriot, though, of course, she was just that. There were just as many Tories about, if her recollections served her correctly, as rebels against the Crown. Both groups, as a general rule, were following the dictates of their consciences, and both factions considered themselves loyal citizens. It was a matter of semantics.

"You know Samuel Adams, then? And those other troublemakers?"

"Only by reputation," Phoebe answered cautiously, laying her bundle on the cot by way of laying a claim on that humble chamber. *American History 101,* she thought, with weary wryness. *Samuel Adams, known for the egg stains on his lapels as well as for his leadership skills, recalcitrant nature, and formidable intelligence.* "Are you a Tory, Mistress Bell?"

"Are you?" retorted that august personage.

"No," said Phoebe, who had a lot invested, by that point, in personal honesty. Perhaps, in fact, her very life, for she had just declared her true loyalties, and the political climate was perilous indeed. "I'm backing the winning side. The Continental Army will triumph, in the end."

Mistress Bell smiled the barest of smiles and revealed nothing of her own allegiance. "Some say so. Others disagree. You'll serve this night, miss," she said. "But first, you must wash, and rest a while, and take proper sustenance."

Phoebe's gratitude knew no bounds. She was an alien, a sojourner in a strange time and place, and thus in no position to expect more than the simplest concessions to survival, let alone comfort. She nodded acquiescently and would have turned to unpack her bundle, if Mistress Bell hadn't spoken again.

"What became of your hair, child?" she asked.

"I suffered a fever," Phoebe said. It was, for better or for worse, getting easier and easier to bend the truth. She could not, after all, tell this woman that she had come from another time, more than two centuries in the future, where people wore their hair any way they wanted. "But don't worry. I'm not contagious."

"Odd," said Mistress Bell, still pondering Phoebe's abbreviated tresses. "There's more than just that that's peculiar about you, but I suppose it's of no moment. Work hard, miss, and bed Tories or rebels, if you will, but not both. That can only bring trouble."

"I wouldn't think of disagreeing," said Phoebe. Without Duncan, the experience seemed less real somehow, for all its colorful authenticity. More like a very vivid dream. "All I want is a place to sleep, food to eat, and a few—shillings?—to call my own."

The mistress of the Crown and Lily harrumphed. "Shillings, is it? It's ha'pennies that'll find their way into your purse, miss, and then only if you prove diligent and behave in a seemly manner."

Phoebe couldn't resist a curtsy, though she did not mean it as a mockery. It was more a reflex, suggested by the environment and by Mistress Bell's quaint manner of speech.

Mistress Bell was grudgingly pleased and instructed the new wench to wash the dust of the road from her person and present herself in the scullery immediately afterward. Phoebe obeyed, pouring tepid water from the pitcher to the basin when her new employer had gone, and splashing herself industriously. She used her fingers to comb her hair, tucked her bundle underneath the washstand, and hurried downstairs, her stomach grumbling.

The kitchen of the Crown and Lily was a crowded, steamy place, full of smells both pleasant and foul. Phoebe accepted a trencher of thick stew, too hungry to question its preparation, and sat on a bench near the slop bucket, eating purposefully. During the journey from Paradise Island, with her silent guide, she had subsisted on hard bread packed by Old Woman, accompanied by whatever fish, roots, coconuts, or berries her escort had been able to scare up along the way.

No one spoke to her, though she was subjected to a number of curious, speculative stares, just as she had been after being consigned to the laundry room at Duncan's house. Phoebe was not timid, though she avoided trouble when possible, and she returned the gazes of the other women unflinchingly. Any sign of fear or subservience, she suspected, would doom her to being bullied and ostracized.

She washed her hands after her meal was done, the injunction to rest apparently forgotten, and was given a spotted apron and sent summarily among the customers.

They made a colorful bunch, the clientele of the Crown and Lily—there were British soldiers, in buff breeches, Hessian boots, and the famous crimson coats, along with plain men in homespun or buckskin—craftsmen and apprentices and farmers and tradespeople. Some of the latter, Phoebe thought, as she hurried to serve pewter mugs spilling over with ale, were rebels. Others were Tories, of course. Who was who was anybody's guess, though King George's supporters did tend to be more vociferous in offering their opinions.

The brew had been flowing from the taps in

the keys behind the crude plank bar for some time when one of the redcoats, who'd been addressed as Major Lawrence, suddenly grasped Phoebe by the apron strings and pulled her onto his lap. She struggled, but he only laughed, his strong hands almost encompassing her waist and subduing her easily.

Even in her extremity, Phoebe did not fail to notice that some of the other men lining the long trestle table, all English, were uncomfortable with the turn matters had taken.

"Let the baggage go, Major," said a cultured voice from somewhere down the line. "It's plain she's ailing—look at her hair. All but gone."

The major, bleary with drink and an overabundance of testosterone, pushed the furious Phoebe to the bony ends of his knees and studied her. "I'd think her a bloody boy, if it weren't that there are curves and swells in all the proper places."

Phoebe squirmed, flushed and sputtering with indignation.

"Let her go," repeated Phoebe's champion, but he didn't stir himself to effect a physical rescue or even lean forward far enough that she could see his face and get some fleeting measure of his character.

"Mayhap the major fancies the lads," observed some intrepid soul, punctuating the remark with a belch and a resounding fart. "Have a care, men, and keep your bums covered when *he's* about."

The major put Phoebe away from him with such haste and vigor that she nearly tumbled onto

101

the filthy floor. In the next instant, Lawrence sprang to his feet, ruddy from the ale and the indignity of it all, and fumbling for his sword. "Who said that?" he demanded.

Phoebe might have laughed, if it hadn't been for the gravity of the situation in general and the sword in particular. One man sat alone at the end of the bench, while the other members of the party were scrunched together at the other, wearing expressions of cheerful disgust.

Process of elimination, Phoebe thought, and no pun intended.

"Cheers," said the digestive miscreant, raising his mug to the major. He was a small, sturdy person, with a bald head and a florid complexion, and one of the brass buttons sprang from his coat when he stood, clattering across the tabletop.

The major withdrew his hand from the hilt of his weapon and retreated a step, his long, aristocratic nose wrinkled. "God in heaven, Sergeant, you are a disgrace to the Crown," he muttered. "I'd kill you where you stand, as a service to His Majesty, if it weren't for the deuced legalities of the thing!"

The sergeant's eyes twinkled as he groped for his button and dropped it into his pocket. "There is that," agreed the bumbler in a merry tone. "The documents and such, I mean." He donned a dusty tricorne, after fanning the air with it in a show of personal consideration, and winked at Phoebe as he turned to take his leave. "Farewell, good mistress," he said.

Phoebe nodded in response and took herself well out of the major's reach, just in case the party got rowdy again, but things were not the same after the sergeant had gone. One by one, the bored soldiers pushed away their mugs, rose from the benches, and left the tavern. Their leader lingered, brooding, refilling his cup, with an unsteady hand, from the wooden pitcher in the center of the table.

"I'd suggest coffee," Phoebe whispered to another servant, a young girl wearing a shapeless dress of butternut muslin, a mobcap, and a dirty apron, "but caffeine might be worse for his disposition than alcohol."

Her colleague—Phoebe had heard her addressed as Molly, over the course of her illustrious half-day career at the Crown and Lily—looked utterly baffled, and nearly dropped the trencher of roasted meat she carried. But then she gave a wobbly smile, and Phoebe hoped she might have made a friend. Besides the sergeant, that is, who had saved her from the unwanted attentions of the major with remarkable finesse, all things considered. Now all she had to do was stay out of Lawrence's path; he might be an officer, but he was no gentleman.

Molly served the meat to the ravenous craftsmen gathered at a corner table and gave the solitary Brit a wide berth when she returned to the bar with an empty pitcher.

The place had emptied out completely, and Phoebe was industriously scrubbing a table, as instructed by Mistress Bell, who prided herself, she claimed, on her worthy reputation, when the woman came to stand at her elbow.

"He'll have a flogging for insulting Major Lawrence the way he did," she said in low and matter-of-fact tones. "I hope you prove to be worth that kind of suffering."

Phoebe thought she would be sick. Her knees went slack, and she sank onto a bench beside the trestle she'd been scouring. Terrible images of a man bound to a whipping post and savagely beaten filled her head. "The sergeant?" she asked weakly and rested her head on her folded arms with a groan when Mistress Bell nodded.

The tavern keeper laid a gentle hand on Phoebe's shoulder, in rough sympathy.

"Was I hired to be a whore?" Phoebe asked, looking up at Mistress Bell's weathered, careworn face. "Is that why Lawrence felt free to manhandle me? Is all this happening because I was too witless to understand what I'd agreed to do here?"

The older woman shook her head, and the leathery skin over her cheekbones glowed with brief, faint color. "No, lass—you needn't share any man's bed unless you wish it so. I've told you that already. Lawrence is a coward and a rogue—and mark me, there are those like him in the Continental Army as well. He'll not soon forgive you—much less one of his own sergeants—for showing him up for a fool."

"Isn't there something I can do—someone I can talk to?"

"If you don't want to make matters worse for that poor blighter, you'll stand back and let things fall out as they will."

"But a decent man is about to be whipped because of me—"

"And there's naught to be done to stop it," Mistress Bell interrupted. "Finish your scrubbing, miss, and take yourself off to bed. Tomorrow will come almost as soon as you've closed your eyes."

Despondently, missing Duncan and Old Woman's wise, reassuring advice, Phoebe completed her chore and, carrying the candle Mistress Bell had given her, climbed the steep, narrow steps to her room. There, after stripping to her petticoats, splashing her face with cool water from the pitcher on the washstand, and using a salted fingertip for a toothbrush, she collapsed onto her bed and cried.

Morning came all too quickly, just as the boss had predicted, and Phoebe washed, dressed, and hurried outside to use the stinking latrine behind the tavern. She scrubbed her hands again, in a basin beside the back door, using hard yellow soap that made no lather, and then went into the inn's kitchen.

"He fair perished from the beating you got him, did Jessup Billington," said a red-haired woman who would have been beautiful if not for the pockmarks fanned over one cheek.

"Hush yourself, Ellie Ryan. It's not Phoebe's fault that Major Lawrence is a pig," Molly interceded, with a spirit surprising in someone who presented such a frail and mild appearance. "He's the one that wants a proper hiding, if you ask me."

Phoebe put out both hands in a bid for peace. She had never meant to get poor Billington into trouble, and she certainly didn't want to be the cause of strife between Molly and the redhead. "Please don't argue," she said, squeezing her eyes shut against the terrible headache that suddenly pulsed in both temples. "It won't do the sergeant any good, will it?"

Half an hour later, while serving a breakfast of sausage and ale to two merchants, Phoebe's worst fears were confirmed. Sergeant Billington had indeed been tied to a post in the town square and soundly punished for insubordination. Lawrence had wielded the whip personally, one shopkeeper told the other, and there had been plenty of blood. They'd flung the poor bastard into a room in the back of the blacksmith's place to recover as he might, and it had all come about because of some chit working in that very inn.

Who cared, they concluded in the end. Wasn't he British, and hadn't those rotters destroyed a lot of good men with their ruinous taxes and their war? Why, it was all an honest fellow could do to put food on the table, in these terrible times. There was precious little pity to spare for a lobsterback.

Phoebe, who felt sick again, might have been invisible for all the notice they paid her; she was only there to serve, like a footstool or a faithful dog. She suspected, too, that even if they *had* known she was the "chit" who'd earned a British soldier a whipping, they probably wouldn't have given a rip.

She brought their ale and somehow kept from pouring it over their heads, and when Mistress Bell sent her out with a basket to buy eggs to be hard-boiled for the evening trade, she made her way to the blacksmith's instead of the market. There was no one about—it was midday by then, and the tropical sun was hot—so she slipped inside, moving quickly past the forge and the horses nickering in their stalls, and found the room where Jessup Billington lay. He'd been stripped to the waist for his beating, and the skin on his back was not only lacerated, but bruised as well, and hideously swollen. He lay on his belly, his trousers crimson with dried blood, and cursed when Phoebe touched him.

"I'm so sorry," she said.

"Bugger that," said Billington. "Get me some good stout whisky, lass, and be quick about it. The smithy keeps a flask on one of these shelves."

Phoebe withheld the observation that water would be better for a man in his condition and went looking for the whisky. It was, given her involvement in the matter, the least she could do.

Billington raised himself onto one red-crusted elbow with a groan when she knelt to offer the flask, and the effort was agonizing to watch. He took a long, thirsty draught of liquor before sinking into the straw again. "I don't know why you came, miss," he said, "but I would beg you, as one Christian soul to another, to leave me be from now until Judgment Day."

"I want to help you, if I can," Phoebe said.

"You've helped me quite enough already," Billington replied, groping for the flask, which Phoebe placed in his hand. "Do be so kind as to get out of here before Lawrence sees you and hangs me for a traitor and you for a spy."

Phoebe rose to her feet. "Why would he do that?"

"Because he's a spiteful snake," Billington said, with excruciating patience, "and because I am indeed a traitor, and you might well be a spy. Give my sympathies to Rourke when he comes to collect you, the damn fool. And now, if you have a merciful bone in your body, get yourself gone."

Phoebe felt herself turn pale. "What do you know of Duncan Rourke's and my association?"

Billington laughed hoarsely. "Nothing I'm willing to confide in a devil-blessed bit of baggage like yourself," he said. "Word gets round, and that's all I'll say."

With that, he passed out, though whether from the pain or the whisky or both, Phoebe could not guess.

She found a pail of water on a bench near the forge and lugged it back to the dark, dirty chamber where her rescuer lay. Tearing off a part of her one and only petticoat, she soaked the cloth and began, ever so gently, to bathe the mutilated flesh of Billington's back. Every once in a while, she was seized by a bout of deep retching and had to stop the careful washing, but eventually the worst of the blood had been removed, revealing the true extent of the wounds. Phoebe closed her eyes for a long moment, preparing herself for what she had to do, then opened the flask and poured its contents over Billington's raw flesh.

He shot screaming and cursing from his stupor, like a man set afire, and Phoebe scrambled out of his reach, certain he would have killed her if he could.

"Damn your black soul, wench!" he bellowed. "What witchery is this?"

Phoebe was crying, though she was barely conscious of the fact. "It wasn't witchery, it was common sense," she said. "You might have gotten an infection if I hadn't done something to prevent it, and your precious whisky was the only antiseptic on hand." She paused, lip quivering. "You might still die, but at least you have a chance to recover."

"Get out," Billington seethed, through his clenched teeth, "before I rise and find a pitchfork and run you through for the pure pleasure of it!"

Phoebe got out and returned to the Crown and Lily, where Mistress Bell was waiting to blister her ears with a lecture for tarrying too long and not bringing back the eggs, but she endured it without protest.

Phoebe had been gone more than ten days when word reached Duncan, via the usual complicated, clandestine route, that she was in Queen's Town, a British-held settlement on the northernmost island, working in Sally Bell's tavern. He was respectfully advised by his contact to fetch her before her good intentions got them all hanged, it being common knowledge that she hadn't the sense God gave a pot handle.

Fiercely angry and, at the same time, wildly relieved to learn that that exasperating woman was still alive and making trouble, Duncan crushed the missive in one hand and then held it to the candle in the middle of the table until it blazed between his fingers. When it had been consumed, he glared at the ashes, as if to ignite them, too, by the heat of his gaze.

"What is it?" asked Alex, who had been moved downstairs to the drawing room, where he had a view of the sea. Physically he was mending, but there was no light in his eyes, and his state of mind worried Duncan deeply, though he was careful to hide the fact. "From the look of you, that dispatch might have been penned by the devil himself."

Duncan deliberately stilled a muscle leaping in his jaw. He did not believe in striking women, children, dogs, or horses, but at that moment, if he could have gotten his hands on Phoebe

Turlow, he'd have throttled her with a smile on his face and a melody in his heart.

"I must go to Queen's Town," he said. "Immediately."

Alex, already pale, turned a grayish white. "*Queen's Town?* Good God, Duncan, why don't you just sail to London and present yourself at Court? The effect will be the same, either way—they'll hang you, and put your head on a pike!"

Duncan left the table, where he had taken a light meal before the message had arrived, hand-delivered by one of Old Woman's native lads. "I have no choice," he said. "Phoebe is there."

Alex cursed roundly. "Well, if she's a blasted British spy, she's told them about Paradise Island, and we're *all* about to be fitted for the noose!"

"They'd have been here by now, if she'd told them anything," Duncan said. His instincts, on which his life and those of his men so often depended, assured him that Phoebe was as loyal to the rebel cause as General Washington himself. But she was also a creature of impulse, with a degree of courage unwarranted by her survival skills, and she could easily trust the wrong person. "Don't worry, my friend—I'll see to Phoebe."

By the time the tides changed, a little after ten o'clock that night, Duncan had assembled a minimal crew and was sailing steadily toward the settlement of Queen's Town, where there was a price on his head. At dawn, they dropped anchor, a few miles south of the harbor, and Duncan and two of his men rowed for shore.

Phoebe was still in Mistress Bell's bad graces more than a week after her failure to buy eggs, but at least she hadn't been fired and sent from the Crown and Lily in disgrace. If that happened, she would be left with only two choices—turning tricks or starving. No one else would hire her— word had gotten around about her propensity for causing grief—and she couldn't have found her way back to Paradise Island even if she had the faintest idea where it was. So she kept her opinions to herself and steered clear of Major Lawrence whenever he came into the tavern, which he did on a regular basis, and resigned herself to emptying spittoons and slop jars and washing all the mugs and pitchers every night. One day soon, if there was a God in heaven, Mistress Bell would get over being miffed and stop assigning all the nasty jobs to Phoebe.

She was comforting herself with this thought and making her way along the moonlit path to the privy, when a shape loomed suddenly before her like a demon's shadow. She tried to scream and was wrenched against a hard chest for her trouble. It was little consolation that the chest in question, like the hand over her mouth, was Duncan's. This was not a friendly visit.

Phoebe struggled, on principle, though a part of her wanted to be captured and carried off to the eighteenth-century equivalent of the Casbah, whatever it might be.

"Silence," he breathed, close to her ear, stilling her with the sheer power of his grasp. "If we're caught, I won't be the only one dangling from a high branch. You'll be right beside me."

He had a point. No one would believe Duncan had taken her by surprise; instead, they'd say it was a tryst, that she was his lover and his accomplice, every bit as guilty of treason as he was.

Because she didn't want to die—and for a few less urgent reasons, too—Phoebe stopped fighting.

6

"I could lose my job over this," Phoebe complained, when Duncan had dragged her through shadowy alleyways and down some worn wooden steps into what smelled like a cellar. "I'm still in trouble for visiting Mr. Billington when I should have been buying eggs."

He struck a flame, using a flint and steel taken from a small tinder-box, and the glow of a single squat candle smoked and wavered in the gloom. "You have already lost your position at the Crown and Lily," Duncan said flatly, his face craggy in a shifting pattern of darkness and light.

"And Sally Bell won't miss you overmuch, I'll wager."

Phoebe hugged herself, because the cramped, musty space was chilly and dank, and because a large, lonely, and very unpredictable world lay beyond those cellar doors slanting at the top of the steps. A person could be riding peacefully in an elevator one moment, and find herself flung into another century in the next. Having read about Mr. Einstein's theories concerning parallel dimensions was one thing, but experiencing them firsthand was something else. She felt like a cosmic guinea pig.

"You should have left me alone," she said, as Duncan removed his dark, tailored waistcoat and laid it gently round her shoulders. "I was doing fine."

"Oh, wonderfully well," Duncan responded. His expression was unreadable in that wretched light, but his tone was wry. "So well that you've already gotten one man beaten half to death."

Phoebe stiffened. Whether she spent the rest of her life in this century or returned to her own, she would never forget what had happened to Sergeant Billington, nor ever completely forgive herself for it. "It was an accident," she said, after taking a moment to swallow the lump in her throat. "What should I have done? Let Major Lawrence have his way with me? I struggled, and the sergeant came to my rescue, and I'm very grateful that he did. However, I didn't ask him to do it, and I'll thank you to keep that in mind."

Duncan rose from the overturned crate on which he'd been sitting—Phoebe's seat seemed to be a three-legged milking stool—and plundered a cabinet, stirring a cloud of dust. Phoebe sneezed loudly.

"Do be quiet," Duncan enjoined, returning with a corked bottle and two wooden cups. "We're supposed to be hiding, in case you haven't deduced that. But perhaps you wish to signal some British compatriot?"

Phoebe sniffled. "Are we back to that? I'm no spy, Duncan Rourke."

"Then why did you leave Paradise Island without my permission?"

"Because . . ." She paused, watching him pour wine into the cups, which he had wiped out hastily with the tail of his finely stitched linen shirt, and accepted one when he held it out to her. "Because I was developing codependent behavior patterns. Toward you."

" 'Codependent'?"

"I wanted to take care of you."

He hesitated, taking a long, elegant swallow from his own cup before replying. "And that is wrong?"

"Not in it's purest sense, no," she said, blushing and, for a moment, dodging his gaze. "But some problems can—and should—only be solved by the person who has them." When she looked at Duncan again, she saw that he had arched one dark brow, and he was watching her intently over the rim of his cup.

"And what, by your lights, is this problem I must solve?" he asked.

Phoebe sighed, exasperated. "How should I know?" she countered. "Whatever it is, it makes you play the harpsichord as if you were trying to batter down the gates of heaven itself with a torrent of sound."

"Or of hell," Duncan muttered lightly, refilling her wine cup and his own. "You are right," he allowed after a few moments. And a few thoughtful sips. "It is a private torment, one you can do nothing about. You will only harm yourself by trying."

Phoebe leaned forward slightly on the milking stool, earnest and probably a bit drunk. Instead of guilt, however, she took a defiant and somewhat reckless pleasure in her inebriation, because in point of fact, after all she'd been through lately, it felt good. Time enough for regrets in the morning, when she would have a headache and a queasy stomach and wonder if it was okay to start the first 12-Step group, even though nobody was supposed to do that until 1935. She made a mental note to leave a journal for her descendants, should she be lucky enough to have any, to buy stock in Xerox, IBM, and Microsoft.

She blinked, hiccoughed, and held out her cup.

Duncan shook his head and took the humble chalice from her, setting it aside on the barrel top, where the greasy candle struggled to sustain light. "Thank you," he said, with the merest hint of a smile.

"For what?" Phoebe asked, frowning.

"For caring," he said. "You're safe with me, Phoebe. I'll make you a bed, and we'll set off for safer places as soon as possible."

She peered, squinting into the darkness that pressed close around them. "Lie down in this place? With rats and mice and spiders everywhere? No way, José."

Duncan sighed. "I sleep here myself on occasion," he said in a reasonable tone. "And I have been unmolested by such vermin.'

Phoebe giggled. Either she'd had an even larger share of the wine than she'd thought, or the stuff had been considerably more potent than the brand she usually bought at the supermarket. "You sleep in a cellar? The illustrious Duncan Rourke? *Why*, for heaven's sake?"

"Precisely because I am the illustrious—and more than a little notorious—Duncan Rourke. Now, cease your chatter and take rest. Escaping from Queen's Town might prove quite a challenge, and you'll need all your strength for it."

"I'm afraid," Phoebe confessed.

"That is wise of you," Duncan retorted, holding up the candle so that it spilled its murky glimmer over a cot with a netting of rope for a mattress, one moth-eaten blanket, and a pillow that looked as if it already provided housing for a family of mice. "I think, in you, a little wholesome fear would be an attribute. It might keep you from doing stupid things—though I confess that's a rash hope."

117

"I'm not lying down on that thing," Phoebe said. But she was tired, from the wine and a hard day's work in Mistress Bell's tavern.

"Here," Duncan replied, taking her shoulders in gentle hands. "I'll lie with you. If there's a rat, I'll scare him off."

"Who's going to scare you off?" Phoebe asked, stifling a yawn even as her loins tightened pleasantly at the thought of sharing a bed, narrow or otherwise, with Duncan.

He chuckled. "The Queen's Town detachment of His Majesty's army, if we don't snuff out this candle and you go on talking." The flicker of light died, leaving them in utter blackness, but he lowered her expertly onto the cot, and joined her there, tucking her into the curve of his chest, groin, and thighs.

A fierce arousal overtook Phoebe in those moments of intimacy, but something even more primitive was happening to her heart. Tears filled her eyes, because the emotion was too huge to contain, and she was grateful that her back was to Duncan, and that it was dark.

He found her chin with his hand and turned her face toward him, though, and her traitorous body followed. He kissed her, not eagerly, but as though dragged to her and forced into touching his mouth to hers. A groan—of protest, of loneliness, of need—rumbled up from somewhere deep in his chest, and Phoebe felt the heat and hardness of him against her thigh.

At first, the kiss was a skirmish, but soon it

deepened into something more elemental, and their tongues did battle and then mated. Phoebe was lost, though she sensed that Duncan was still struggling, still trying to hold himself back.

"I promised you would be safe with me," he gasped, when at last the kiss ended.

Phoebe loved Duncan. She realized that fully now, and if she couldn't say so in plain words, she would tell him with her body. She pulled his shirt up, and slid her hands beneath it, to caress the warm, granitelike flesh of his back and his ribs, the downy wall of his chest. He felt sleek and muscular and very dangerous.

He moaned and lowered his head to conquer her mouth, once more, with his. Phoebe gave a little sob, of desperation and pleasure, and thought if he didn't take her completely, and soon, she would surely die.

Duncan, though he plainly desired her as much as she did him, would not be hurried. He stripped her expertly, kissing and caressing each curve and hollow of flesh as he uncovered it, and the reverence in his touch made Phoebe feel like a goddess being worshipped. When he took one waiting nipple between his lips, he simultaneously covered her mouth with his palm, anticipating the long, low cry that trembled against the flesh of his hand.

Phoebe arched her back, whimpering softly now, aware of nothing but the sensations Duncan stirred in her as he stroked and suckled and cherished her. She had not known—had never even imagined, even in her hottest fantasies—that lovemaking could be like this.

When he had nourished himself at both her breasts, and she was soaked with perspiration from the hard, sweet work of wanting him, seeking him, straining instinctively to capture him, Duncan removed his own clothing, and then poised himself over her. She felt his erection at the moist juncture of her thighs and uttered another sob, full of yearning, muffled by his hand.

He kissed her forehead, where tendrils of hair clung to her skin, and whispered to her. "Your body reaches for me," he said. "But what says your mind, Phoebe Turlow? I'll have no woman who does not want taking."

She nodded her head, like someone delirious with fever, and laid her hands to his buttocks, splaying her fingers and urging him to enter her. And she kissed his palm, where it pressed lightly against her lips so that her cries of pleasure would not be heard beyond the walls of the cellar.

Duncan did not torment her further by delaying their joining; he knew she was ripe for him and claimed her in one shattering, explosive stroke.

It was a good thing he'd thought to put his hand over her mouth, for she could not have forestalled the primitive, growling shriek of welcome that seemed to have its beginning in the tips of her toes.

"Oh, God," he murmured, "God." He was moving faster upon her, plunging deeper, and all

120

the while he kissed her cheekbones, her eyelids, her temples, and forehead.

Phoebe tossed beneath him, now arching like a bow tightly drawn, now thrashing, now flinging herself at Duncan, matching him thrust for thrust, her flesh wet and slippery and hot with exertion. Her heart thundered with emotions so ancient that their names had long since been forgotten; she battled for completion, pleaded for it with every wild movement, every muffled groan and whimper, and yet she feared it as a sinner fears judgment. The light, the power, the sheer force of the release Duncan was driving her toward was nuclear in scope, and she truly believed it would consume her.

Suddenly, the end was upon her, upon them both, like some vast, universal cataclysm. Phoebe raised herself high off the rope mattress, her heels braced in the netting, and received Duncan rapturously, and without restraint. He was deep inside her, every muscle of his stallion-like body straining, and she felt his warmth spilling into her womb. She knew, even in her frenzy, what Old Woman had seen in her palm, and why she'd helped Phoebe escape Paradise Island. Even as she buckled helplessly beneath the man who had just conquered her, she knew.

The release went on for some time, catching them both up again when they thought the last flicker of pleasure had already been wrung from them, and the descent was slow and fraught with smaller crises. At last, Duncan collapsed beside

Phoebe, one leg still flung with possessive abandon across her thighs.

Duncan remained in a state of dazed euphoria, and she smiled in the darkness, her fingers woven through Duncan's silky hair. "She knew this would happen, you know."

Duncan shuddered in some belated aftermath, and even that was pleasurable for Phoebe, causing her to give a small, crooning gasp. "Dare I ask whom you're talking about?" he said at length, without raising his head from her breast.

"Old Woman," Phoebe replied, winding a lock around her finger. "She looked at my palm when I told her I wanted to leave Paradise Island, and then she arranged everything." She paused, suddenly worried. "You're not going to punish her, are you? For helping me get away?"

Duncan chuckled and began to nuzzle his way toward a nipple, which immediately turned hard in anticipation of entertaining him. "I wouldn't dare. She'd cast some spell, and all my teeth would fall out, along with my hair and a few other parts I value."

Phoebe felt those same unnamed, overwhelming emotions welling up within her and used both hands to guide Duncan to her breast. She held him there at first, because the wanting was so ferocious, but then she knew he would not leave her, and smoothed his hair gently, and murmured to him while he drew on her.

★ ★ ★

Phoebe's eyes opened wide, the next morning, when she realized that someone was bathing her, quite tenderly, with tepid water. Duncan, of course. She started to speak to him and realized there was a cloth tied around her mouth.

He chuckled, making a deliciously thorough business of washing her most intimate place. "You can take off the gag if you wish, of course," he said, "but I wouldn't advise it. Not with what I'm about to do to you, and me down here where I can't reach your mouth."

Something wicked surged through Phoebe; she was naked, except for the strip of cloth that silenced her, and at Duncan's mercy, and it was glorious.

She watched, fascinated, her blood heating by degrees, as Duncan set aside the basin and parted her legs so wide that one was on one side of the cot and one on the other. With his rough, sea-captain's hands, he stroked the tender flesh on the insides of her thighs, which quivered at each delicious pass of his fingertips.

"All you have to do, if you don't want me to proceed, is shake your head," he said.

Phoebe braced herself on her elbows, but otherwise did not move.

Duncan knelt fully dressed beside the cot and teased her with a devil's grin. Then he bent to her, as though he were thirsty and she were a cool, pure spring. With his fingers, he parted the tangled nest of curls, and she felt his breath on her, and she trembled violently, watching, waiting, swelling for him. And then he touched her with his tongue.

Phoebe whined against the gag, and Duncan began to nibble.

She made a pleading sound and tried to move her hips, but he held them fast and enjoyed her at his leisure, like a rare and exquisite sweet that must be made to last. And last.

Phoebe tilted her head back and groaned, and then Duncan straddled the cot, at the end, and clasping Phoebe's ankle, forced her knees to bend, so that she was totally vulnerable to him. Not one, during this time, did he raised his mouth from her.

The pleasure was keen beyond bearing, akin to pain in its intensity, but woven of a million glittering strands of ecstasy. Phoebe used what movement was permitted her to rock against his tugging lips, his tongue, which tamed and disciplined her even as it spurred her to greater and greater passion.

He knew when she was about to climax and withdrew, murmuring soothing words against her flesh, calming her, making her wait. Only when she was lying back, breathing in deep gasps and shuddering with need, did he take her into his mouth again and suck until she was pitching against him like a mare trying to throw off a rider. When he had exhausted her, made her sing every note of a private rhapsody behind the band of cloth, he raised his head from her thighs and reached up to remove the gag with a gentle tug.

"Wow," Phoebe raised her head to say and then fell backward in complete collapse.

Duncan rose, beaming as if he'd just plucked a thistle from the paw of a lioness, and maybe he had. Phoebe had sublimated her sexual needs for a long time, sine there had been no viable way to fulfill them, and she'd obviously built up a backlog.

"I suppose you expect me to get up and dress," she murmured. Those simple feats sounded physically impossible, given the fact that her bones and muscles had melted like wax.

"Since your hair, unlike Lady Godiva's, will not suffice to shield your virtues, yes. Furthermore, I should think a naked woman riding through the streets of Queen's Town would draw a certain amount of attention—an inconvenient state of affairs in present circumstances, of course." Duncan gathered her dress, torn petticoat, camisole, and drawers, and tossed them to her.

Phoebe raised herself, with considerable languor, and began making hit-and-miss attempts to don her clothes. Duncan, the very soul of chivalry, finally came to her assistance. He was crouching by the cot again, this time to lace her shoes, when she voiced a growing concern.

"Won't we be taking a tremendous risk, trying to leave town in broad daylight?"

"Oh, yes," Duncan said affably, rising and offering his hand to her as though to lead her onto the dance floor for a minuet. "Leaving is a risk, staying is a risk. I've weighed one against the other, you see, and decided it's better to put the place behind us."

Phoebe took his hand and used it as leverage to raise herself shakily to her feet. "I don't suppose I get any say in this? As an interested party who might well be killed in the attempt, I mean?"

Duncan's grin warmed his eyes and made Phoebe's limp, sated senses begin to pulse again, just vaguely. "None at all. I had hoped to exhaust you into silence and docility, but I see I wasn't entirely successful."

She blushed, remembering. "Spare me the false humility," she said. "If you'd been any more successful, I'd be in orbit by now, and the air's mighty thin up there."

He frowned. "What the devil are you talking about?"

"There's no time to explain now," she told him with some impatience, spotting his saddlebags and beginning, without asking permission, to forage for food. "If you must go around kidnapping people," she said, glowering at the piece of jerky she finally unearthed, "you might at least provide decent refreshments."

Duncan only shook his head, but there was a twinkle in his eyes that said he would have laughed outright if he hadn't been afraid of bringing half the King's army down on their heads. "I'll remember that in future." He turned and raised the dusty lid of a trunk, pulling out a scarlet coat with epaulets and gleaming brass buttons, a pair of buff-colored breeches, a simple shirt, and a pair of Hessian boots. For Phoebe, he produced a long velvet cape, hooded and trimmed with gold and silver embroidery.

She looked up at the low, beamed ceiling. Only then had it occurred to her to ask what now seemed an obvious question. "Exactly where are we?"

Duncan had begun to strip off his own clothes and put on the uniform of a British officer, taking no thought, apparently, for the constraints of modesty. His grin was broad, boyish, completely void of the pain and pathos that sometimes caused him to pound the keys of his harpsichord like a demon gone mad. "That's the genius of it, Phoebe, my dear. We're underneath the island headquarters of His Majesty's army."

Phoebe closed her eyes, swaying slightly with the shock, and the torrent of rage hurtling along in its wake. *"Are you crazy?"* she hissed.

"Opinion is divided on that," Duncan said, sitting down on the edge of the cot to pull on one slightly scuffed black boot. "Fate favors the daring—that's my theory. And besides, there's no better place to hide than in plain sight, is there?"

Phoebe's voice was a hissing whisper. "Do you mean to tell me that while we were—while I was carrying on that way, a bunch of British officers were upstairs chatting and having tea?"

Duncan's smile was lavish, blinding. "They do

like their tea," he agreed. "We did, too, before they put so murderous a tax on the stuff. Why do you think I covered your mouth?"

Her knees gave out, and she dropped onto the milk stool, clasping the velvet cloak as though it were the only thing keeping her from drowning. "Oh, my God. I don't believe it."

"I thought I'd convinced you," Duncan said. "Hurry up, now. So far our luck has been good, but fortune is a fickle mistress, and we've got some distance to cover before we dare rest."

"I think I'm going to throw up," Phoebe said.

"If that means what I think it does," Duncan replied, pulling her to her feet and bundling her into the cloak, "it will have to wait until later. Keep the hood over your head at all times, because if anybody gets a glimpse of that hair, we're as good as hanged. Should someone speak to you, just nod and keep your eyes lowered, as if you were timid—which, as we both know, you are not. Any questions?"

"Yes," Phoebe answered miserably. "Why do I get myself into these things?"

Duncan only smiled, for he was busy buttoning his spiffy coat, which made him look like an usher at an old-time theater, or the lead singer of a sixties rock band. He reached for a tricorne hat, and it sat at a rakish angle on his head, casting a shadow over his face. His hair was tied with a black ribbon.

"Couldn't I just wait here until the war is over?" she asked.

Duncan took her hand and drew her toward the steps. "I'll go first. Don't come out until you hear me whistling a tune. Walk rapidly, with your head down, straight to the smithy's. He'll lend us a pair of horses."

"The smithy's?"

"The place where you poured whisky over Billington's poor bleeding back," Duncan said, and then he was mounting the steps, pushing the doors open, stepping out into the bright morning sunshine.

Phoebe waited for shouts, or musket fire, her eyes squeezed shut, but all she heard were the ordinary sounds of a coastal town going about its business—and the clear, whistled strains of "Hail, Britannia."

Guessing that she shouldn't have expected "Yankee Doodle," Phoebe drew a deep breath, gathered the folds of her voluminous cloak, as well as the tattered shreds of her courage, and mounted the cellar steps.

Duncan, she saw in a sidelong glance, was walking on the other side of the street, pausing to exchange jovial greetings with storekeepers and children, foot soldiers and matrons with their maids and marketing baskets. All of them pretended to know him, and looked after him with expressions of good-natured confusion when he'd passed them by.

Phoebe took no such chances. She hastened along the narrow wooden sidewalk to the smithy's and felt a chill of remembered horror before slipping inside. Except for the previous one, she hadn't slept through the night since she'd seen the deep, gruesome lash marks marring Mr. Billington's back.

A moment passed before her eyes adjusted to the dim interior, and when they did, she thought her heart would stop beating. Major Lawrence was standing not six feet away, with the smithy, and he was looking straight at her.

She kept her eyes down and prayed Duncan would tarry a while in the streets. He might fool common soldiers and townspeople with his disguise, but the major would certainly know him for a stranger.

"Well," drawled Lawrence, causing Phoebe's skin to crawl, "what have we here?"

The smithy came quickly to her side and took her arm. "It's my sister, Florence," he said. "You'll forgive her shyness, I hope . . ." He lowered his voice to a confidential whisper. "She's just over the smallpox, you see, and lucky that she survived. It's marked up her skin a little, though, and I'm afraid she's been left a mute, into the bargain. We can't tell if she hears anything we say to her. What the lass needs is a good husband, to look after her and give her a home."

Phoebe felt Lawrence's recoil, graceful though it was, and was torn between elation and a bone-deep desire to claw his eyes out. She tucked herself deeper into the copious folds of the cloak and tried to look meek. Duncan, to her eternal gratitude and relief, did not bungle into the smithy's and ask for a horse.

Lawrence slapped the blacksmith on the shoulder and spoke in the too-loud, too-pleasant tones of a man who wants to escape before he's asked to come for supper and meet the family. "Really must carry on," he blustered. "There's a war to wage, you know. Can't rest on our laurels, down here in the islands, just because we're apart from the fighting, now, can we?"

"No," said the blacksmith, standing close to Phoebe. "Best not do that. They're a tricky lot, these rebels."

Lawrence laughed politely and fled.

"Keep your mouth shut and your head down and listen," said the blacksmith, the moment the officer was gone. "Duncan is waiting in back, with the horses. If anyone speaks to you, pray be silent, reflecting upon the fact that you are a mute. Should you be stopped, he'll say he's escorting you to my brother's house at the cove. Now, be gone, before you bring me the same kind of trouble you got for that wretch Billington."

"Thank you," Phoebe said in a whisper, without raising her eyes. She did not know the smithy's name, nor did she get a glimpse of his face. A diplomat he was not, but she would always remember his courage.

"Be gone," he repeated.

Phoebe found Duncan waiting behind the stables and bit her lower lip to keep from blurting out that she was terrified, that she didn't think she could pull this off, that she was going to be sick all over his boots and that damnable cloak he'd rigged her up in.

He must have felt her trembling when he closed his hands on her waist and lifted her easily onto the horse's back, where she sat side-saddle, as a modest lady would. "Everything will be all right," he said in an undertone. "I promise."

Phoebe did not point out that he had no way of knowing that—since she was supposed to be a mute. That didn't stop her from giving him a subtle kick in the shoulder with the toe of one dainty shoe.

He chuckled, under his breath, and handed her the reins. Then he mounted his own horse and rode off, leading the way down the middle of one street and then the other, touching the brim of his tricorne whenever they met a cart or a wagon or another rider. When they encountered a British officer, flanked by seven mounted soldiers armed with muskets and wearing swords, Phoebe's heart squeezed into her throat and cut off her breath. Duncan rendered a crisp salute, which was returned by the other men, and rode calmly on, making sure Phoebe's mare stayed just a stride behind his borrowed gelding.

By some miracle, they got out of Queen's Town proper without being challenged, and several men with fresh horses were waiting just beyond the first bend in the road. Duncan was off the gelding and out of his British uniform in a matter of seconds, quickly pulling on the breeches and shirt that had been brought for him.

"See that the horses get back to the smithy after the sun sets," he said, and one of the men nodded and rode over to collect the dangling reins of the gelding.

Phoebe did not move or speak, but simply sat there, clinging to the pommel of her saddle, fighting off memories spawned by Duncan's blithe shedding of his clothes.

"What about the lady, here?" asked another man, and something familiar in his voice made Phoebe turn her head to look closely at him.

It was Billington, the man who'd been whipped for defending her against Major Lawrence in the tavern that first day. She felt like a character in one of Shakespeare's plays, doomed to be haunted forever by the ghost of someone she'd brought to an untimely end.

"She stays with me," Duncan said. "She's mute, you know, and ashamed of her complexion. Cobb, the smithy, thinks we ought to find her a husband."

Billington crossed himself and mouthed a prayer that probably included the words "saints preserve us," but there was a smile in his eyes as he drew nearer Phoebe's horse and looked up into her face. "Don't look so surprised, lass," he said. "I told you I was a traitor. Told you Duncan Rourke would come for you, too, didn't I?"

"You're better now?" Phoebe asked in a soft

voice. They were the first words she'd uttered since she'd thanked the smithy for his help.

The small but sturdy man rotated his shoulders and made a grimace. "Still a bit sore, I must confess. But I'll get over it."

Duncan had mounted another horse. Drawing up alongside Phoebe, he curved an arm around her waist and lifted her on in front of him, so that she was squeezed between the saddle horn and something equally solid. "If you don't get yourself out of here, one of the good major's patrols will come along, and you'll find your belly pressed to the post all over again," he said to Billington.

"Always a word of inspiration and encouragement for the lesser folk," Billington retorted, grinning and tossing Duncan a mocking salute. "Whatever would we do without you, Rourke?"

"Probably live long," Duncan replied, and then he spurred the horse, and he and Phoebe were galloping off the main road and into the trees. She clung to the saddle horn with both hands and uttered a cry of protest when the horse took a low stone fence in a graceful leap.

Duncan did not slow down, let alone apologize. They rode deeper and deeper into the dense island foliage, and Phoebe was sweating under her clothes and the velvet cape, which was now something the worse for wear. Finally, after more than an hour of hard riding, the beach came into view, so white against the sparkling aquamarine sea that it dazzled the eyes. Phoebe had been expecting a ship—although Duncan hadn't said so, she was sure he meant to take her back to Paradise Island and leave her in Old Woman's keeping—but the only vessel in sight was a canoe resting on the sand.

"We're not going all the way back in *that?*" she asked, as Duncan eased her gently to the ground before dismounting himself.

Duncan shrugged and pulled the bridle off over the horse's head. "She's seaworthy," he said. "It was she, after all, who brought you here."

"Now I really am going to be sick," Phoebe said. And she was.

7

Duncan paddled the canoe expertly along the shoreline, while Phoebe huddled in the bottom, gazing over the side. The water was clear, and exotic yellow and black fish darted beneath the surface, sometimes mingling with blue ones that looked as though they'd swallowed strips of neon. Once in a while a jellyfish would waft by, like a dancer in pale chiffon, its vital organs clearly visible through its transparent skin.

Phoebe identified with that vulnerable creature, for whenever she risked a glance at Duncan, she caught him studying her, as if he could watch her heart beating, see her lungs filling with air and then deflating. As if he could look upon that deep and secret place inside her, still thrumming in response to his lovemaking, even though hours had passed.

"How is Alex?" she asked, mildly ashamed because she hadn't thought to ask until now.

Duncan watched the tip of one paddle rise from the water, shedding sparkling droplets of water, and then plunge in again, never slackening his smooth, even pace. "His body is mending," he said without looking at her. "Alex is there, physically, but it's as if his spirit has already gone on. He might have dug a grave and crawled into it, for all the interest he shows in anything or anyone around him."

Phoebe started to trail her hand in the water, remembered a graphic scene from a shark movie, and wrenched it back. She'd rolled the elegant cloak, now dusty and snagged, into a cushion, and it was all that kept her bottom from forming a wedge between the tapering sides of the canoe. "Alex needs time," she said gently. "He's grieving for what he's lost—for his leg and for the man he'll never be again, and for all the things he won't be able to do anymore—but that's perfectly natural. You can't expect him to shrug and say, 'Oh, well, I've still got one good leg, haven't I, so why make a fuss about the other?' He's sorting through his feelings, Duncan, and that's a lengthy, complicated process."

At last Duncan met her gaze, and she saw a

terrible sorrow in his eyes, but something else, too. The beginning of hope, perhaps.

"How is that you can be so wise, Mistress Phoebe, and still get yourself into such difficulties?"

She lowered her head, to hide the glow of pleasure his words had caused. Her self-esteem had taken a beating, because of the divorce and the job she'd lost in the twentieth century, and the suffering she'd brought to Mr. Billington in that one. Duncan's compliment, back-handed though it was, had restored some of Phoebe's faith in herself.

"It's just that I believe in taking risks," she answered, after some thought, because she wanted to hold onto her new reputation for being astute. "And when you do that, you make a lot of mistakes. Still, I wouldn't want to live any other way." She paused and smiled broadly, confident, at least, of her philosophy. "A certain amount of caution is appropriate, of course, but that can so easily turn to cowardice."

Duncan said nothing. He just smiled in that slanted way that made Phoebe's heart pound and kept paddling, his eyes, scanning the horizon and then the shore, one after the other.

Some of Phoebe's delight faded. "But then, things happen that make you wish you'd stayed in bed and never troubled yourself to attempt anything."

"What things?" Duncan asked.

"I'll never get over what happened to Mr. Billington," she confessed.

"As you said, that wasn't your fault. Besides, he'd do it all over again, would Jessup, and so would you, so why torment yourself with the whys and wherefores of the matter?"

Phoebe considered. "You're right. There's no point in stewing over it. Still, if you could have seen his back—"

"I did," Duncan interrupted, his tone quiet, clipped, unemotional. "There can be no denying that the work of the lash is ugly to look upon. Feeling it, of course, is even worse."

She stared at him. "Are you telling me that you've been whipped yourself?"

"I'm not telling you anything," Duncan responded. "Except that I wish you'd rest your tongue for half an hour. I have some thinking to do."

How brief, Phoebe thought, is glory. Five minutes before, she'd been wise. Now she felt like a child who'd been misbehaving in church.

She turned her attention back to the fish.

Presently, a dolphin flashed beneath the boat and surfaced on the starboard side, nodding and chattering, its smooth gray flesh gleaming in the sunshine.

Phoebe laughed, delighted, and the animal seemed to know it had pleased her and it began to caper and cavort, for all the world as if it were showing off. When she applauded, the creature redoubled its efforts, and once it swam within touching distance. Its flesh felt hard and smooth under Phoebe's palm, like the outer rind of a watermelon.

The dolphin dove, sounded with breathtaking grace, and then vanished.

Duncan didn't speak, but when Phoebe glanced at him, she saw that he was smiling. There was no need for him to explain his love of the sea and all its creatures; suddenly, it shone in his eyes like sunlight reflected off the water.

He must have noticed the changes in the weather long before Phoebe did. By the time clouds had gathered, marring the aquamarine sky with smudges of glowering black, and the waves supporting the canoe began to play rough, the sleek craft was already gliding swiftly toward the nearest beach.

Phoebe didn't ask whether they were putting in on the same island, south of Queen's Town, or another. She simply clasped the sides of the boat with both hands and watched Duncan's face, which was grim with concentration.

The first warm, pattering drops of tropical rain drenched them and made pockmarks on the unsettled water, plastering their hair flat against their heads and drenching their clothes in a matter of moments. The canoe was filling up by the time it rammed onto the sand, and Duncan shouted at Phoebe to get out and take cover.

She leaped out and ran scrambling up the beach, to watch from under a fragrant, dripping tree while he dragged the boat out of the angry surf, over the sand, and into the shelter of Phoebe's tree. The rain made a deafening roar, thundering upon the sea, the land, and every broad leaf in that island jungle.

Duncan pulled Phoebe farther into the foliage, and she noticed for the first time that he was carrying her cloak, still rolled into a bundle and, miraculously, quite dry.

"Wrap this around you!" he shouted, to be heard over the rising storm.

Phoebe complied without comment. The foliage was thick in the small grotto they found, and the trees made a canopy over their heads, keeping out most of the rain.

Duncan found some dried twigs and leaves and drew his tinderbox from the pocket of his sodden breeches. After a few tries, he had a small fire going and fed it with what bits of wood he could find.

Phoebe, who hadn't realized that her teeth were chattering until she saw the first flames, drew close to the blaze.

"I'm going to find some fresh water," Duncan told her in a raised voice, and she saw that he carried a canteen on a strap over his shoulder and a cap-and-ball pistol in his belt. She hadn't noticed any such gear in the boat, which only meant, she concluded, that she ought to pay closer attention. "I'll be back as soon as I can."

She nodded and, when he was gone, stood up and peeled off her wet clothes and wrapped herself in her trusty cloak. The fire was hungry, and she fed it old, crumbling pieces of driftwood, carried inland by some earlier storm, no doubt, and the flames crackled with happy greed.

Duncan had been gone an hour, at the very least, before she started to get worried. Suppose he'd fallen into a pit and broken a leg? Or been captured by cannibals? She was just about to put her wet clothes back on and go looking for him when he appeared, looking pleased with himself.

He'd found an ancient tin bucket somewhere, and there were two large crabs scrabbling around inside it.

Phoebe wrinkled her nose. She'd grown up in Seattle, so she liked seafood, but she was generally opposed to eating things that tried to climb out of the cooking pot. "Didn't you see any fruit or berries?"

Duncan rolled his eyes. "There is no pleasing a woman. If you want to graze like a deer, then suit yourself. I have other intentions."

He left the crabs in Phoebe's care—they blundered and crawled over one another inside a shallow pit surrounded by stones—and she considered setting them free. In the end, however, she decided it was a risk she didn't care to take.

Duncan returned, made sure his captives hadn't escaped, and set the pail, now filled with water, in the edge of the fire. That done, he untied the tail of his shirt and allowed half a quart of gooey red berries to splatter into Phoebe's lap.

She looked at them for a few moments, then

glumly popped one into her mouth. "Thanks," she said.

He sat down on the sand near the fire, started to pull his wet shirt off over his head, and then stopped.

Phoebe was about to remark that he needn't be shy, since she'd already seen him naked, but the truth was, she hadn't. Their first intimate encounter had taken place in total darkness, and Duncan had been wearing all his clothes in the second. "What are you hiding?" she asked, as the crabs rattled against each other like bones in their pitiful prison. "A tattoo that says 'Mom,' or 'Born to Lose'?"

Duncan stared at her, so genuinely mystified that Phoebe laughed.

"I'm sorry," she said. "I'm still adjusting to life in this dimension." She sighed, looking at his sodden clothes. "All the same, if you sit around in those clammy duds, you're going to catch a world-class cold."

He looked exasperated. "What?"

"You'll be sick," Phoebe translated patiently.

"I've been sick before," he said, peering into the bucket of steaming water and then getting up to find more driftwood to add to the fire. Phoebe hoped the crabs would be reincarnated, poor things, as something inedible.

"Will it hurt them?" she asked. "When you drop them in the water?"

"Who?" Duncan inquired.

"The crabs," Phoebe answered, flushed. Fine

thing if *she* was the one coming down with something, after lecturing Duncan the way she had.

He sighed. "No," he said. "They are very primitive creatures."

"Suppose some giant came along, and plucked us right out of the sand, and dropped us into boiling water. While we might appear primitive to him, we would certainly feel pain."

"Very well," Duncan retorted, annoyed, "let's just give up eating anything besides berries and roots, shall we?" Phoebe was just opening her mouth to deliver a discourse on twentieth-century vegetarianism when he cut her off. "Ah," he went on, with an expression of crazed revelation, "but then, for all we know, plants have feelings, too. Leaving us with no choice but to starve."

"I give up," Phoebe said.

"It's about time," Duncan replied.

The water in the bucket came to a tentative, somewhat grudging boil eventually, and he dropped the crabs into it, first one and then the other. To Phoebe's enormous relief, they both gave up the ghost without delay, and made no pathetic, futile efforts to heave themselves out of the pot.

Duncan's teeth were chattering by the time he fished his dinner out of the bubbling, frothy water with a stick. Phoebe flinched as he popped off a claw and cracked it between two small stones, but the aroma of the succulent crabmeat made her stomach rumble.

He had spread some large, smooth leaves on the ground, and these served as a platter. Shivering, his lips turning a faint shade of blue, he ate.

Phoebe munched her berries and wished she'd never brought up the whole vegetarian question in the first place. She loved both chicken and fish, and enjoyed the occasional filet mignon— or had, when she'd lived in the modern world. It was just the idea of dropping living things into a boiling kettle that had upset her, but she couldn't very well ask for some of the crabmeat after making such a fuss.

Following an interval of triumphant silence, Duncan cracked several claws, placed them on a leaf, and offered them to Phoebe. "Here," he said. "Swallow this, if you can force it past that lump of pride in your throat."

Phoebe accepted the food and ate swiftly and with very little grace. The meal was delicious.

"I still think you should take off your shirt," she said when they'd been sitting in a peaceful silence for a while, listening to the rain. "I won't look, if that's what's bothering you."

Duncan's color, by then, was approaching lavender. Glaring at Phoebe, he untied the laces and wrenched the shirt off over his head. His chest was worthy of Michelangelo's "David," though thickly furred with dark hair, and she couldn't imagine why he'd want to hide. When she took the garment, however, and walked over to hang it with her own things, she saw his back.

Fine white scars marked his flesh from his neck to the base of his spine, and Phoebe marveled that she hadn't felt them the night before, when she'd touched and stroked him in passion. But of course her senses had been occupied elsewhere.

He sat rigid in the firelight and the misty gloom of the storm, allowing her to look at him. Enduring it.

"What happened?" she asked in even tones, moving back to her place by the fire and kneeling in the sand, her hands resting on on the velvet of the cloak where it covered her thighs.

"I was whipped," he said, gazing defiantly into her eyes.

Gall rushed into the back of Phoebe's throat at the thought, but she swallowed hard and would not look away from him because she knew he was trying to stare her down. "God, Duncan, even I could guess that. What I was really asking is, why? Who did such a thing to you?"

He tossed the last of the crab shells into the fire and watched the flames lick them. Phoebe had won the staring match, but she felt no triumph.

"Tell me," she urged quietly. "There is no harpsichord here, no instrument to absorb your fury and turn it into music."

"Isn't this codependent behavior?" he asked.

Damn his memory, Phoebe thought. "No," she said. "I can't change what happened, and I can't make up for it, either. But I can listen, and you might feel a little better for telling the tale."

Duncan was silent for so long that Phoebe thought he had chosen to keep his own counsel, but finally, still staring into the fire, he began to talk.

"I was fifteen," he said. "I lived outside Charles Town, with my family—my father raises cotton on a plantation there. It was a good life, though I was expected to work from the time I could lift a hoe. There were books, and a few paintings, and we had tutors. My mother played the harp and the pianoforte, and she gave me lessons . . .

"But I've gotten off course. I was big for my age, and randy in the bargain. During one of Father's frequent trips to town, on which I accompanied him, I made the acquaintance of a woman—a girl, really—named Francesca Sheffield. She had just been shipped over from England—she'd been married by proxy, and her husband, a British captain, was my father's age. Francesca was beautiful, and miserably home-sick, and the captain was impatient with her.

"We became friends, she and I, because we liked the same music and the same books, and, eventually, we were lovers."

Phoebe waited silently, taking note that Duncan had named his ship for this woman, envisioning the tale as he told it—the handsome young planter, the pretty Francesca, exiled from the only world she knew to what must have seemed a wilderness, at the mercy of a man who could not understand her . . .

"When Sheffield found out—Charles Town is a small place, and there are few secrets—I was accused of . . . forcing my attentions on Francesca, and I was promptly arrested. My father went to the captain with the figurative olive branch in his hand—he knew the truth of the matter, and though he had been furious with me from the moment he found out about my involvement with the lovely Mistress Sheffield, he couldn't stand by and see me charged with such a crime."

He fell silent, stirring the fire with a stick, and Phoebe noticed, to her everlasting surprise, that it was getting dark.

"Didn't Francesca defend you?" she asked after a long time.

"Oh, yes. And Sheffield beat her with his riding crop, according to Bessie, who was their cook at the time, and locked her in her room to contemplate the wages of sin. I was dragged before a magistrate—an intimate friend of the captain's, as luck would have it—and no amount of pleading or reasoning on my father's part—or hers—could alter the course of events. I was bound to a pole outside the town—specially erected for the purpose—and whipped. When I passed out from the pain, Sheffield ordered a dousing with cold water and delivered more lashes. He would probably have killed me if my desperate sire, my brother, and some of their friends hadn't interceded."

Phoebe waited a few moments before speaking,

dealing with another spate of nausea. The whole scene glowed vividly in her mind, even though it had happened when the man before her was still a boy. Then she asked, "Why didn't they put a stop to it sooner?"

"Sheffield was a captain in His Majesty's army," Duncan said. "As such, he had the authority of the magistrate behind him, with a handful of soldiers to make sure the sentence was carried out. My father and brother and the others could have been hanged for what they did—riding into the center of the fray with muskets and swords and demanding that I be set free—but they took that chance."

Tears burned in Phoebe's eyes and ached in her throat. "What happened then?"

"Lucas, my elder brother, cut me loose—I was half-conscious and something less than clean, as you can imagine—and I was hoisted onto my father's horse. He held me against his chest, and we went home." Duncan's voice was far away. "I recall that he wept."

"And your mother?"

"She was hysterical—here was her baby boy, streaked with blood from his head to his feet. But she was soon in charge of her emotions, and of every living soul within a ten-mile radius of the plantation as well. I recovered, in time, and poor Francesca was sent back to England, in genteel disgrace. The captain, as I understand it, has been promoted to major and fights courageously for King and country."

The storm, instead of slackening off, was picking up speed, bending the treetops high above their heads, howling in the twilight like a multitude of ghosts seeking the shelter of their graves.

"You went on living there—in Charles Town—after what he'd done to you?"

"Until my political opinions set father against son and brother against brother, yes. It was my alliance with the Continental Army that made me a prodigal, not the incident with Captain Sheffield."

To call that an "incident" was an understatement of unsettling magnitude. "You mean your father and brother are Tories?" Phoebe asked, unable to hide her surprise.

"To the marrow of their bones," Duncan said without rancor. "My mother had a chapel built, my sister tells me, when I took my share of the inheritance our grandmother left for Lucas, Phillippa, and me, and went off to fit out a ship. She prayed every day—probably still does—that I would see the error of my ways and give up treason and piracy to raise cotton. Or at least help put down this awful rebellion."

"Oh, Duncan," Phoebe murmured, overwhelmed by what such a separation must have meant, to him and to his family. "Do they hate you, Lucas and your father?"

"No," he said, in a strange voice, his face hidden now, in shadow. "It might be better for them if they did, though. Loyal as they are—and

I don't blame them, for there are good and sincere men on both sides of this war, as well as bastards—my activities must make them suspect to the British. I regret nothing, except the pain they've endured on my account."

There was nothing more to say, not then. Phoebe moved close to Duncan and took him inside the soft expanse of her cloak, and they lay together by the fire through the long night, but they did not make love.

By morning, the squall had passed, and the seas were placid again, turquoise under a cloudless sky. Duncan and Phoebe breakfasted on berries and coconut, plucked their still-slightly-damp clothes from the bushes, and got dressed. Then Phoebe climbed stoically back into the canoe, sitting on her cloak again, and Duncan pushed the little craft off the beach and into the tide.

At midafternoon, Duncan spotted a ship in the distance—it was nothing but a speck to Phoebe, who wouldn't have noticed it at all if he hadn't pointed it out—and they went ashore again, into a sheltered cove. Here, flowers grew in riotous colors and gaudy abundance, and Phoebe made a fragrant pink and white wreath of orchidlike blossoms to wear in her hair.

Duncan was distracted, watching the ship, lest it draw nearer to the island.

"Is this when we start shouting, 'The British are coming, the British are coming'?" Phoebe asked. She was scared stupid, but flippancy helped a little, made the whole thing seem more like a game and less like a life-and-death situation.

"No," he said, without a shade of humor in his voice, without even glancing her way. "We'll keep our mouths shut and hope to high heaven they haven't seen us."

Phoebe peered at the thing bobbing on the horizon. "I don't see how they could," she said.

"Through the spyglass?" he suggested bitingly.

"Oh," said Phoebe. Then, after a pause, "Who are they, anyway, if they're not English?"

"That's a pirate ship," Duncan said. He'd already hidden the canoe, and they were watching the water from a copse of spooky trees dangling moss from their branches, but he still looked worried. "Given the way my luck's been running lately, I'd say it's Mornault's, and they were probably watching us before we even knew they were there."

Phoebe swallowed. Her experience with such things was limited to watching one road-show production of *The Pirates of Penzance*, a ride at Disneyland, and a couple of romance novels. She hoped to maintain the status quo.

"Well, at least this time you can't blame me," she said with tremulous cheer.

"I wouldn't be here if it weren't for you," Duncan answered archly.

Phoebe dropped the whole subject and waited, biting her lower lip and squinting at the distant ship. She couldn't tell whether it was moving

151

away or coming closer, and she wasn't about to ask Duncan.

At long last, the ship vanished into a dazzling veil of sunshine.

"It's gone," Phoebe said straightening her wreath, which had dropped down over one eye. "Now we can stop worrying."

"Thank you," Duncan replied, "but I think I'll continue for a while. He might be taking her around to the other side of the island, hoping to surprise us from behind."

"Even your luck couldn't be that bad," Phoebe said. She was tired, she needed a bath, she had a headache, and aspirin wouldn't be discovered for at least a hundred years. She was in no condition to deal with pirates.

"Don't lay any wagers," said Duncan, taking her arm and pulling her deeper into the foliage, where things chattered and chirped and fluttered on all sides and overhead.

Phoebe scrambled to keep up, holding onto her flower garland with her free hand. "What could this guy possibly have against you that would make him go to all that trouble?" she asked with breathless reason.

"I might have stolen his cargo once or twice," Duncan answered, without slowing down. "And there was that time off the Ivory Coast, when I burned his ship down to the waterline."

"Oh, shit," Phoebe said with conviction.

"Exactly," Duncan replied.

He left her beside a spring, in the center of the

island, with instructions to wait there and be quiet until he returned. He offered no explanation for this desertion except to say he wanted to look around.

Everything should have been all right.

Everything *would* have been, if Phoebe hadn't screamed.

And she only did that because of the monkey, which dropped down out of a tree to land screeching in her lap.

The British didn't come, and neither did the pirates, because they were still too far away. But a crowd of natives slipped out of the jungle—a dozen of them, tattooed and scarred, wearing loincloths and carrying spears. They stared at Phoebe, who had just shooed the monkey away, pointing at her clothes, which must have seemed odd to them, and her crown of flowers.

Phoebe's heart pounded. She was thinking of the crabs she and Duncan had for dinner the night before, and of cannibals and giant bubbling cauldrons and divine retribution. If God's eye was on the sparrow, she thought hysterically, perhaps. He kept track of crustaceans, too.

"Duncan," she sang, in a puny tone he could not possibly have heard. It was all she had breath for. "Oh, *Dunc*-an!"

One of the natives dropped to his knees, supporting his spear with strong brown fingers. Another followed his lead, and then another, until they were all kneeling.

They began to chant. *"Doon-can, Doon-can . . ."*

"Oh, my God," Phoebe whispered, covering her mouth.

They rose, as one, with a certain primitive grace, still chanting, and encircled her. A scream surged into Phoebe's throat and died there, too feeble to get past her lips. Then, like actors in a bad movie—if only this *was* a movie, bad or otherwise—they lifted Phoebe onto their shoulders like a football coach who has just led an underdog team to victory.

"Duncan!" she screamed.

"Doon-can, Doon-can," sang her escorts, bearing her through the jungle and never missing a step.

They took her to a circle of huts in the middle of a clearing and set her on a large rock, which she hoped was not a sacrificial altar. The men had obviously decided she was some kind of goddess, but the women, who wore little more than their male counterparts, were plainly less charmed. They walked around and around the stone, poking at Phoebe with their fingers and sneering. The masculine contingent took umbrage at such disrespect, and a heated altercation ensued, raising dust and making birds squawk in the trees.

Phoebe tried to sneak away during the argument, which involved much shouting and making of gestures, but she was spotted and tenderly returned to her throne in the heart of the war zone.

The women finally subsided, in sullen defeat,

and the men circled Phoebe until she was dizzy enough to fall off the rock in a faint. No doubt they were pondering how best to worship such a strange deity. They touched her short hair, and peered into her eyes, and might even have examined her breasts if she hadn't folded her arms and summoned up a makeshift incantation.

It was only a line from an old Beatles song—the first thing that came to her mind—but she said it with authority, and it must have sounded dire, for her little flock drew back a little way and henceforth kept their hands to themselves.

Phoebe held them at a distance with a glare, which was more and more difficult to sustain as the day wore on. She had to go to the bathroom, and it didn't look like Duncan was going to rescue her, and who knew what these people did to their goddesses—burned them at the stake? Dropped them into live volcanoes? Previous deities, if there had been any, were conspicuously absent, and historically, the field had always had a high mortality rate.

At sunset, the natives built up the fire and tried to feed Phoebe what looked and smelled like the digestive tract of a good-sized animal, and she fended them off by reciting every word of Elton John's last album in a stern voice. There was no telling how long that trick would work, however. Sooner or later, the plot was bound to thicken.

It was sooner, as it happened. There was a great rustling of foliage, and Phoebe's heart soared. Duncan had come, at last, to save her. She would polish his boots for a year for this and make a real effort to stop talking in twentieth-century lingo just to irritate him . . .

There was a great hubbub and snatching up of spears within the village, and Phoebe held her breath. Duncan was only one man, after all, and clever as he was, he couldn't hope to prevail against so many people with that antique pistol of his.

Then a man stepped out of the trees, and Phoebe almost screamed a warning, but a grim realization stopped her. This was not Duncan; this was an ugly, long-haired pirate, with a complexion like cornmeal and part of his nose missing. He wore high boots and a striped shirt and one gold earring, and Phoebe would have appreciated how well he suited the part if she hadn't been so busy sliding to the ground in a swoon.

She awakened all too soon, to find the man talking to the natives in their own tongue. He was surrounded by other pirates now, all of whom had bad teeth, if they had any at all, and were surely disappointments to their mothers. There was an exchange of money—Phoebe wondered, in her light-headed state, what a good goddess was going for these days—and then she was carried off through the jungle.

She considered struggling, decided it would be futile if not outright stupid, and tried to think of an escape plan. Nothing came to mind, but the effort kept her from panicking, at least until she'd been taken on board a stinking ship and tossed into the hold like so much ballast.

By then, Phoebe was sure Duncan hadn't rescued her because he was already dead, or being held in some other part of the ship.

No. She brought her frantic, runaway thoughts under shaky control. The fact was, she didn't *know* where Duncan was, or what had happened to him. Something almost certainly had, and it was unlikely that that something was good. Only one thing was absolutely clear: If she was going to be any help to him, she'd have to help herself first.

8

Phoebe sat in the darkness, feeling like Jonah in the belly of the whale, but without the happy prospect of being barfed up on some distant shore in three days, safe and sound. She huddled, almost in a fetal position, with her knees drawn up under her chin and her arms tightly clasped around her shins, taking slow, shallow breaths, like a creature lapsing into hibernation. She concentrated on the measured *thud-thud-thud* of her heartbeat, to keep herself from thinking of what would happen when Mornault's inevitable summons came. A scrabbling sound at the door interrupted her meditation, and she raised her forehead from her knees, mutely terrified, her skin clammy with sweat. There was a creaking of hinges, followed by a muttered imprecation. The portal was flooded with light, and then blocked again by the figure of a giant.

"For God's sake," hissed a familiar voice, "don't scream."

Duncan.

Phoebe could hardly believe it; indeed, she thought she must be hallucinating. All the same, she scrambled awkwardly to her feet and staggered toward him, tripping over crates and coiled rope, and an involuntary mewling sound flowed tremulously from her throat.

Duncan took her into his arms and held her fast for a few moments, and she knew then that he was real and could have died of the relief. Overhead, Mornault's men were making a great deal of noise.

"How did you get here?" Phoebe whispered, holding on to the front of Duncan's shirt with both hands and allowing herself to be weak. She could always deny it later.

"Never mind that," Duncan said. "We have to get out of here."

Phoebe had been in such a deep state of shock that she didn't realize his clothes were wet, that he smelled of kelp and brine, until that moment. "You didn't *swim*?"

"I did, and so will you," Duncan replied, already leading her out of the hold and into the narrow passageway beyond.

"But how . . .?"

"There is a game of dice going on in the galley," Duncan told her in an impatient whisper as he pulled her up some steps. "I believe you are the prize, and if you don't tame your tongue and make haste, they'll have the both of us."

Phoebe quelled her other questions and followed Duncan across the darkened, empty deck. There was a crescent moon out, offering precious little light, and when her rescuer started over the side, she balked, but only for a second. They'd been lucky so far, but casino night might end at any time, which meant they would have a crew of sore losers to deal with, as well as an eager winner, primed to celebrate.

She followed Duncan over the rail, only to find him poised to slide down the anchor rope and herself left with no choice but to do likewise. It was a long drop to the water, and even if she managed to avoid doing a belly flop, there would certainly be an audible splash.

Closing her eyes and holding on to the rope with both hands and both legs like a fireman descending a pole, Phoebe lowered herself down and down, into the waiting sea. Duncan was there already, of course, and he put an arm around her waist, because she was already foundering a bit, and spoke into her ear.

"You'll have to leave the gown," he whispered. "It's too heavy."

Water lapped against the creaking side of the ship, warm as the contents of a bathtub, but alive beneath their feet with all sorts of terrifying creatures. Phoebe was not inclined to argue—her thoughts were focused on escaping pirates and other monsters of the deep—and she shed the tattered dress quickly.

Duncan laid a finger to her lips when she would have spoken.

"Silence," he told her, in a voice so soft it was hardly more than a breath and yet so urgent that she could not have ignored it. "They will miss you soon, and an alarm will be sounded. We have a long way to swim." He caught her hand and placed her fingers around his belt. "Sound carries a long way on the water. Do not try to hurry, and no matter what happens, do not scream or even speak. Just hold on to me.

She nodded, and Duncan moved away from the ship's side, through its broad, mobile shadow, and she gripped his belt and carried her own weight as much as she could. They had not gone far when Duncan's prediction came true—someone had counted noses and come up one goddess short.

There was hue and cry aboard the sleek vessel, and lanterns glowed along the rails as disgruntled sailors rushed to peer into the gloom. Bursting with fear, Phoebe bit her lower lip and swam doggedly beside Duncan. The salt water stung her rope-burned palms like fire.

The sails had been lowered, since the craft rode at anchor, and she and Duncan were surely swimming into shallow waters, but there are other ways of giving chase. Phoebe heard ropes whirring over pulleys and the splashing *smack* of a skiff striking the surface.

Blind panic threatened, but Phoebe clung to Duncan and kept moving.

The light of a lantern spilled over the water, in the end, and found them, and the skiff gained steadily. There were three men aboard, the disfigured Mornault, the lamp-bearer, and an oarsman.

Duncan stopped, treading water, and pushed Phoebe behind him. "Keep going," he said.

She didn't.

Mornault laughed, looking especially ludicrous in the thin, wavering light, with his glittering earring and one nostril open to his sinus passages. "So," he crowed, "it is you, my friend. I should have known! Who but Duncan Rourke would have the gall to climb an anchor line like a monkey and steal away my ladylove?"

Phoebe waited, her chemise moving around her like the tentacles of some sea creature, her heart pounding in her throat. Duncan reached back and pried her fear-numbed fingers from his belt.

"Go!" he commanded again in a hoarse whisper, and then he disappeared beneath the surface.

Mornault and his friends were too worried about what Duncan might be doing to bother with Phoebe; the pirate captain swore, peering over the side, the oarsman fretted in antique

161

French, and the old lamplighter stood up, rocking the boat.

Phoebe backstroked a little distance and waited. Whatever happened, she wasn't going to leave Duncan. He would be furious with her, if they survived, but that didn't matter. Besides, she was only a mediocre swimmer—had never gotten beyond the "turtles" class at summer camp—and her chances of making it to shore on her own were practically nil.

There was a strange sound, from under the skiff, followed by much shouting. Duncan reappeared at Phoebe's side, sleek as a dolphin, put an arm around her, and propelled them both through the water. The rowboat began to sink, while Mornault stood up in it, waving his fist and screaming comments about Duncan's heritage. The oarsman and the guy with the lantern just screamed, period.

Duncan sounded only slightly breathless as he dragged a now-wilting Phoebe along with him. "I know you're dying to ask," he said, "so I'll spare you the effort. The point of my dagger caused a small leak in the bottom of the captain's dinghy. An accident, of course."

Of course, Phoebe agreed silently. She heard violent splashing in the distance and more yelling. She closed her eyes, aching with weariness, and briny water rushed into her face, filling her nose and mouth. She choked and coughed, and Duncan kept going.

"Pay attention," he said. "This is an ocean. It has waves."

Phoebe called him a name even Mornault had not thought to use, and he responded with what might have been a chuckle.

After that, she lapsed into a state much like the one she'd been in while crouched in the hold of the pirate ship. She functioned; she moved her legs and her free arm, drew breath and expelled it, endured her burning hands and the pain of forcing her body to its limit and beyond. An eternity passed, it seemed, and then they reached shallow water at last, and Duncan half dragged, half carried her onto dry land.

She gave a convulsive sob of relief and plunged her fingers deep into the sand, holding on as if the sea might find her and try to pull her back into its embrace. Duncan loosened her hold, gently, and brought her to her feet.

"No," she said. She was so spent that she could not say more, nor take another step.

"Just a little farther," Duncan urged. He was barely able to stand himself, but he lifted her into his arms all the same. He carried her a long way, or so it seemed to Phoebe, who was in a half-stupor by then, seemingly incapable of sustaining the same thought for more than a few moments.

Finally, Duncan laid her down on something— it felt like a grass mat—she felt her chemise being pulled away and replaced with a dry blanket. It was bliss, not to have to swim, or walk, or even be carried any farther, and Phoebe gave herself up to a profound, deathlike sleep.

She awakened once or twice and knew she was inside a hut of some kind and that Duncan was nearby, but she drew no other conclusions. She simply sank back into the quiet blackness, like a stone settling to the bottom of a pond, and dreamed no dreams that she could remember.

When she finally meandered to the surface of consciousness, Duncan was there, holding a wooden bowl and spoon. She blinked and became aware of her aching muscles and the stinging rawness of her palms.

"How long have I been asleep?" she asked, stretching cautiously and then raising herself on one elbow.

Duncan held the spoon close to her mouth, and she tasted the steaming, savory broth. "Probably sixteen or seventeen hours," he replied, giving her more soup. "We're the guests of Monna Ungalla—she claims to be a distant relative of Old Woman's."

Phoebe took another spoonful of broth and then collapsed onto the mat with a groan. Her soreness went deeper than the marrow of her bones, into some inner infinity. "Good. We can ask her Old Woman's true name."

Duncan made her sit up again and gave her the bowl and spoon. "I tried that. She said we might say it aloud, if we knew it, and make big magic."

Realizing that she was hungry, Phoebe

discarded the spoon and drank the soup from the lip of the bowl, with no concern for etiquette. After all, Emily Post and Miss Manners wouldn't be born for a long, long time.

"You know what I think?" she asked, when she was finished with the broth. "I think they've all forgotten what they called her in the first place—maybe she's even forgotten herself—and this whole 'big magic' thing is just a way to save face."

"Monna's right about one thing," Duncan conceded, still on one knee next to the mat. His arms were folded, and he was wearing the same breeches and shirt he'd had on when they left Queen's Town. "If I knew the name, I'd say it, just to see what would happen."

Phoebe grinned. "Yeah," she said, relishing the prospect. "So would I."

Presently, Monna herself appeared—she was a large woman, and the robes Phoebe wore and was practically lost in must have been hers. She touched Phoebe's forehead in a motherly way, frowned, and shook her head.

"What?" Phoebe demanded, alarmed. Duncan was sitting on another mat by that time, juggling a small, sleek knife one-handed.

"Too soon. You stay. Rest longer."

Duncan did not look away from the knife, and with good reason. The blade glittered as he sent it flying, end over end, caught it smoothly by the handle, and repeated the whole unnerving process. "If Mornault finds us before I'm ready," he observed, "we might rest forever."

Phoebe shuddered, remembering the danger, the stark, numbing fear, and the vast, star-dappled sea, like black velvet under the night sky, seeming to go on forever and ever. She caught Monna's eye and said, "What's Old Woman's real name?"

Monna laughed. "You find that out on your own," she said.

"Damn," Phoebe muttered.

"I don't think that's it," said Duncan.

They sailed that night, in a fishing boat, with two of Monna's many sons for escorts. Phoebe sat huddled in the rough, muumuu-style robes the native woman had given her and thought private thoughts. Duncan stood in the prow, like Washington crossing the Delaware, keeping watch, and the boys, both teenagers, worked the tides and currents with impressive skill.

It was nearly dawn when Phoebe was jolted out of a doze by a hand on her shoulder.

She opened her eyes and stared at the handsome, rumpled man bending over her, in his salt-stiffened, costume-party clothes, and a few moments passed before she recalled where she was. Then she remembered coming to Paradise Island, stepping out of an elevator . . .

"It's just a short walk to the house from here," Duncan said, and his smile, incredibly white, contrasted nicely with his suntanned skin. "Can you manage it?"

Phoebe gave him a look of mock rebuke and rose awkwardly to her feet. "Can I manage it?" she echoed. "Didn't I climb down an anchor line? Didn't I swim a hundred miles through shark-infested waters?"

Duncan put out a hand to steady her, his grin on high-beam. "It was more like five miles," he said. "I did most of the swimming, and sharks are harmless, unless they're hungry." He paid Monna's sons with a silver coin, stepped out of the boat into shallow water, and reached up for Phoebe. He carried her ashore, set her on her feet, and looked down at her with a serious expression. "You were very brave."

The compliment pleased Phoebe, and she might have been blushing a little when she smiled up at him and said, "So were you."

They set out for Duncan's grand house together, bantering as they made their way through the foliage, following a well-beaten path.

There was great joy when they returned—Duncan's crewmen came from their quarters to shake his hand and slap him on the back, and the housemaids surrounded Phoebe, chattering like birds. Old Woman fussed and fretted and led her to the kitchen, saying she looked half-starved.

Simone did not greet Phoebe, or even look at her. She was standing at the rear of the crowd that had come to welcome Duncan, with her soul luminous and sorrowful in her eyes.

Phoebe felt sorry for her and, at the same time, fiercely possessive of Duncan.

"I knew he would find you and bring you back," Old Woman said when they were alone in the large cookhouse, with Phoebe seated at one of the long trestle tables, a cup of tea and a plate of coarse, sugary biscuits in front of her.

"Of course you did," Phoebe retorted. "That's why you let me leave in the first place."

Old Woman laughed and added a bowl of fruit to the feast. Her gentle eyes were watchful and bright with affection. "You look different."

Phoebe ignored that. They were both aware of what had changed, but it was a very personal matter, after all, and Phoebe did not wish to discuss the details. "What did you see in my palm that day?"

"You know," Old Woman said.

"Besides babies," Phoebe urged.

Old Woman sighed, as though some glorious vision glimmered before her. "A good place, far from here, with laughing and much music."

Phoebe resisted an urge to bend down and beat her forehead against the table. Even when Old Woman answered a question, she didn't really *answer* it, she simply deepened the mystery.

Peeling a banana, grown no doubt on that very island, Phoebe presented another inquiry all the same. "What would happen if I said your name? And don't say 'big magic.' I want the truth."

Old Woman merely looked at her with a wry expression.

"Okay, don't tell me your name. All I want to know is this—if I discover it on my own, will the magic work?"

"Yes," Old Woman said. "Finish your food. You want a bath and a bed."

Phoebe sighed, her eyes narrowed as she mused. "Daphne," she speculated. "Evelyn. Almira . . ."

There were no thunderbolts.

Phoebe took the promised bath, in a large copper tub reserved for the purpose and stored in a room behind the kitchen. Old Woman brought her a gown and wrapper—more belongings of that poor, nameless, shipwrecked lady whose wardrobe had washed up on the beach without her.

"It would be a native name," Phoebe ruminated, scrubbing. "Of course . . ."

Old Woman poured a pitcherful of warm water over her head.

Alex stood on the veranda, late that afternoon, facing the sea and leaning on a cane. His leg had never taken an infection, God be thanked, but it was withering, like a blighted branch on an otherwise healthy tree. Duncan paused, indulging, yet again, in the futile wish that the British musket ball had struck him instead of Alex.

His friend turned, and his mouth shaped itself

into a too-careful, highly polished smile, but his eyes were hollow. "You've found her, then. The prodigal wench with strange tales to tell."

"Yes," Duncan said, leaning against the porch rail, a few feet from Alex. "She earned Jessup Billington a beating before I could get to her, but otherwise the damage was minimal."

"I don't suppose she meant it to happen."

"No," Duncan admitted, recalling the look in Phoebe's eyes when she spoke of tending Billington on the floor of the smithy's back room. She had nightmares about it, too, ones that made her thrash and cry out, though he doubted that she remembered them on wakening. "It's just that if there's trouble anywhere within a day's ride of where she is, Phoebe will find it, hoist up her skirts, and wade in."

Alex chuckled, but the sound, like his eyes, was empty. "You ought to marry the minx," he said. "Such a match would produce the kind of sturdy, adventurous children our new country will need." There was a certain sorrow in his manner, despite his attempts to seem cheerful, and Duncan suspected it was rooted in Alex's oft-mentioned desire to father a pack of rowdy patriots himself.

"There's nothing to stop you from marrying," he told Alex quietly. "It was your knee that took a musket ball, my friend, not your man-parts."

Alex's face contorted for a moment, and his struggle to regain his composure was painful to watch. "We've discussed this before," he said, when the inner battle was over and he had won—or lost. "I won't have some woman take me for a husband out of pity, apologizing for me, making excuses, saying, 'it happened in the war, you know.'"

"She wouldn't say any of those things about you, this imaginary wife of yours. You say them about yourself, you damnable fool. Don't you see that? We can't govern what happens to us, to any significant degree, but *by God* we can choose the attitude we take toward it!"

"All very inspiring," said Alex bitterly. "Perhaps you should have been a cleric, instead of a pirate and a mercenary. But that wouldn't do for you, would it, Duncan? Because you're a whole man, with two good legs!"

"Christ, Alex—why are you doing this to yourself, to me, to everybody who cares about you? We're all cripples, one way or another—that's part of being human. Your affliction shows on the outside, that's all—but it's in your heart that the poison lies, and in your mind. You feel exceeding sorry for yourself, don't you?" He saw the fury rising in Alex's eyes, and Duncan exulted in it because it meant there was still somebody inside that once-perfect body. "Well, damn it, why don't you just get drunk, like any other man would do in your circumstances? Why don't you lay your head down on your arms and weep for what's gone and let some comely wench give you comfort? God in heaven, Alex, don't you see that this is a chance to be better, to be more than you

171

ever could have before? Yes, something like this can break a man. But only if he elects to be broken."

There were tears standing in Alex's eyes. "Leave me alone," he said. "If you have an ounce of pity in your black, bloody soul, *leave me alone!*"

"I will not," Duncan vowed. "I will follow you to the grave if that's what I must do. I will plague you even in death, my friend, but I will never . . . *by God I will never* let you rob the world of the gifts only you can give! Never!"

Alex began to weep and then to sob. "Jesus God, Duncan, you don't know how it is . . ."

Duncan gripped Alex's shoulders, to lend him strength, to share the very substance of his soul if that was what it took. "No," he said. "I don't know, and I wouldn't presume to say I did. But you can't give up and die, Alex. You talk about our new country—well, it must have people like you to survive. For the sake of your countrymen, if for no other reason, you've got to get past this. We need you in this fight, and beyond it, too, when the victory is won."

Alex shuddered with grief. "I can't do it. I'm not strong enough."

"You can," Duncan argued, still holding his friend. "Don't turn your back on us, Alex. We've come so far, we rebels, and fought so many bloody battles. We're hungry and footsore and, heaven help us, all we want is our liberty, the freedom to choose our own fate! Have you forgotten the dream so easily? Will you abandon us now, when we need you the most?"

"You promised," Alex wept. "You swore you would help me die, if I decided not to live!"

"And I meant what I said," Duncan replied softly. He embraced his friend. "But I never promised not to make a case for living. We will go to Queen's Town, Alex. You can drink and wench and expel your demons. And then we shall go back to the business of winning this war."

Alex smiled; his face was still wet with tears, and though it was fleeting, it had been a genuine smile. "How can you go a-wenching, when it's plain you love Phoebe Turlow?"

There are some things one does not try to deny, not to one's closest friend, anyway. "Alas," Duncan admitted, "I am smitten and want no other but her. I have retained sufficient wit, however, to make a *show* of sowing wild oats, and I can still drink, thank God."

"Very well," Alex said gravely. "I shall accept this challenge, if only to prove to you, once and for all, that you are defending a eunuch. But heed me and heed me well, Duncan—I have not released you from your promise to aid me if my final choice is death."

Duncan felt a chill of foreboding at Alex's words, but he was, in many ways, at his best in a crisis, and he spoke in easy tones. "You've been such a horse's ass of late that I may decide to spare you the trouble of choosing and shoot you myself."

"Then perhaps I shall endeavor to make myself even more obnoxious," Alex replied with weary humor and stumped past Duncan, on the crutch he'd whittled for himself, to take refuge in the house.

Duncan swore, watching him go, and thus did not hear Phoebe approach from the other side of the veranda. She simply appeared next to him, rested and fresh, her funny hair newly washed and sticking out in places. She wore a frock fashioned of some smooth fabric, and the dusty rose color suited her well, lending a healthy glow to her clear skin and casting a soft reflection upward into her eyes. He caught his breath, for the love he bore this woman, an emotion only recently discovered, went deeper than the very roots of his soul. All that he had told Alex about her was truer than the purest truth, and so were the things he hadn't yet dared admit, even to himself.

"Phoebe," he said stupidly.

She smiled, that was all, and he felt himself overtaken by her, possessed, pirated, and plundered, like a ship commandeered by the crew of swifter, better craft. Dazed, he decided that the situation was much more serious than he had guessed, for this was not a passing fancy, like the many liaisons littering his past. No, this was an eternal thing.

"Is something wrong?" she asked, a frown creasing her forehead. "You look pale."

"I have just come face-to-face with my own future," Duncan said. "Or the lack of one, which

174

is probably more likely, given my line of work. I need you, Phoebe. Will you be my mistress—share my bed and my table?"

"No," she answered, without hesitation. There was nothing coy in her expression or her bearing.

He was taken aback, for he was not accustomed to refusals. Furthermore, her responses to his lovemaking had not been those of a reluctant woman. She was, he suspected, as insatiably lusty as he himself, and would want, even crave, the release he could give her.

"Why not?" he managed, after a moment or two of stricken pause.

She smiled, but her splendid blue eyes were solemn. "Because I deserve better. I won't live with the knowledge that I can be discarded when someone younger and prettier comes along."

He tried to protest, but Phoebe did not give him a chance.

"Oh, I know better than anybody that a wedding band is no guarantee of lasting devotion," she went on. "Still, it's much harder to get a divorce in your time than it was—will be—in mine. Marriage is not taken lightly."

Duncan saw then that there would be no reasoning with her. She was as obdurate as any of those rabble-rousers up in Boston, though in a sweeter and gentler way, of course. He did not even attempt to explain that marrying him would make her an enemy of the Crown, every bit as guilty of treason and piracy, in the King's view, as her husband. Nor did he remind her how easily she could become a widow within weeks, days, even hours of her wedding.

"You will deny me your bed unless I take you to wife," he said slowly. "That is blackmail, Phoebe."

"No," she responded, and he caught the scent of lemon on her skin and remembered how brave she had been, swimming away from Jacques Mornault's ship, how she'd felt, warm and supple and eager, thrashing beneath him, meeting him as an equal on that plane and on every other. "You've taught me to want you, Duncan, and I will suffer as much or more than you for my decision. But I have learned to value myself, and I will not be used."

Duncan considered the lectures he had given Alex, concerning the taking of wives and the fathering of children. And he did love Phoebe, though he could not yet tell her so. He must find the proper words first, or perhaps convey his message in the language of music. "Very well," he said. "If you want a wedding, you shall have it. This very day."

Phoebe looked surprised. "Don't we need a license or something?"

"Papers can be drawn up and witnessed, if you want them," Duncan allowed. "I am the captain of a ship, you will recall, and I have the authority, even in wartime, to perform a marriage ceremony."

"Aren't you supposed to be the groom?" she asked.

He laughed, drawing her close and planting a light kiss on her forehead. His heart ached at the contact, however innocent, and there came a painful grinding in his loins. "Yes, and when the service is ended, Phoebe, you shall be my wife in deed and in truth. Alex can serve as my proxy—it might do him good to pretend he's a bridegroom, with all the delights of the wedding night before him."

Phoebe's color was high. "You're sure this is legal?"

He kissed her, this time lingeringly, on the mouth, and then bent to touch his lips briefly to the swell of flesh above her bodice. She shivered in his arms, and he resisted the temptation to seduce her, to lead her quietly to his bed and tease her until her cries of rapture made the tiles rattle on the roof. "Yes," he replied at last. "The marriage will be binding, in heaven and on earth, and you'll have all the papers and rings and baubles you want to prove it. I'll write my family in Charles Town, and if anything happens to me, you shall have a home with them."

She stiffened against him. "Nothing is going to 'happen' to you," she insisted. "I haven't come all this way and been through all this trouble, just to lose you. Besides, I don't think your family would appreciate my politics very much."

Duncan touched a finger to the tip of her nose. "Phoebe, Phoebe," he scolded gruffly, "we must be realistic. There is a war being fought, and I have other enemies besides the British. I could be killed at any time. And I must have the assurance you'll be safe, with my father and brother looking after you. They won't agree with your rebel ways, it's true, but they'll love you, you may be sure of that."

Tears glistened in her dense eyelashes. This woman, who could face scoundrels and sharks and natives with spears with such aplomb, wept at the mere suggestion of Duncan's death, and her display of emotion touched him more than he dared allow her to see. "Okay, okay," she said, in that strange bastardized English Duncan had yet to master. "Let's just handle this one moment at a time, shall we? Tomorrow will take care of itself, and so will all the days after it."

Duncan cupped his hand on her chin and raised her face for his kiss.

"Think carefully, Phoebe," he said when it was over. "This is a dangerous thing you are doing, aligning yourself with the likes of me. The penalty for treason is still death."

"I know," she said quietly. "The penalty for *living* is death, Duncan. It's what you do that really matters, not what you wish or think or fear will happen."

He smoothed her odd hair. "So be it," he said. "We will be married before nightfall, and dance while there is music. Go now, and make yourself ready for me, while I tell Alex he's about to be a bridegroom."

9

Phoebe went back inside the house in a daze, trailing her hand along the ornate bannister as she climbed the stairs. The whole situation seemed more like an impossible dream than ever before, now that Duncan had proposed. Although she wanted to be his wife, she was afraid—no, terrified—of waking up to find herself in the old life, where the man she loved was no more than words on the tattered, discolored pages of an obscure history book. She might pop back into the twentieth century at any time, like that guy in the TV reruns who was always making "leaps," with no warning and no chance to say goodbye.

She entered her room, sat down on the chair in front of the vanity table, and stared at her image in the mirror. She could face the British if she had to, and even the pirate Mornault, but leaving Duncan would be an anguish beyond bearing. Especially if he was her husband.

Phoebe sat there in confused silence, one part of her quaking with fear, another bursting to celebrate, for quite a long time. Her trance was broken when someone knocked at the door, and she turned on the vanity seat, expecting Old Woman, or perhaps Duncan, come to say he'd changed his mind about the wedding.

"Yes?" she called, her voice a little shaky.

It was Alex who entered, leaving the door ajar, for the sake of propriety she supposed, and moving with painful slowness into the center of the room.

"You'll pardon the intrusion, I hope," he said, his eyes kindly and sad as he pondered her. "I've come to make certain this marriage is truly what you want and that you're not being forced into it."

"You don't think much of your friend Duncan," Phoebe commented. "When I first came here, you believed he'd been keeping me prisoner in the cellars."

Alex sighed, and Phoebe saw fine beads of sweat glistening on his forehead. He had expanded considerable effort to see her. "On the contrary," he replied, "I know Duncan Rourke to be the finest of men. The fact remains, though, that when he gets an idea into his head, he's likely to assume any sensible person would agree with it. Even if they're kicking and screaming in protest. As for the cellar incident, well, he once locked me in one, as a jest, forgot I was there, and went off on a hunt."

Phoebe smiled. "I suppose he thought you'd keep," she said, gesturing toward the window seat. "Sit down, Alex."

He made his difficult way to the bay window, with its fluttering gauze curtains, and sat. After pulling a handkerchief from an inside pocket of his spotless azure blue waistcoat, he dried his face and neck and sighed. "We grew up together, Duncan and I," he said after a few moments of agitated rest. "I am not as close to my own brother as I am to him."

Phoebe's smile had fallen away. "You must have been there, then, when the British captain took the whip to him."

Alex flinched visibly and went so pale that Phoebe jumped to her feet and fetched him a cup of water from the carafe beside her nap-rumpled bed. "He told you about that, did he?"

"Yes," she said. "Including the *affaire de coeur* with Mrs. Sheffield."

"I was away at school at the time," Alex said, between sips of water. His color, such as it was, was beginning to return. "My father rode with Mr. Rourke, and with Lucas, when they freed Duncan by force. It was very nearly too late, even then."

"He said it took a long time to recover."

"It was a year before he was right," Alex told her, his eyes haunted, fixed on some distant scene. "Duncan got the pneumonia, the beating had weakened him that much, and he nearly died from that."

Phoebe was silent, hoping that Alex's thoughts were following the same track her own had taken. If Duncan had survived a savage beating, and the illness that followed, then Alex should be able to find a way through his present troubles.

"He never really got over it, you know," Alex

reflected. "It's why he plays that splendid, dreadful music of his."

Phoebe nodded. "Do you hope to persuade me not to marry Duncan?" she asked. It had crossed her mind that Alex could think her unsuitable for the match—after all, she had appeared out of nowhere, blathering about elevators and other things that were still unknown in the eighteenth century. Too, her short hair must seem bizarre to him, since the women of his time usually didn't cut their tresses between the cradle and the grave.

Alex shook his head and made at least an attempt at smiling. "No, mistress. He loves you, though he'll not say so until he's good and ready, so you must be patient with him. Now I know, at least, that my closest friend will be happy, provided he's fortunate enough to survive this rebellion of ours."

"What about you, Alex?" Phoebe asked. "Do you mean to survive, too?"

He rose tremulously to his feet, with the help of his crutch, and it took all Phoebe's forbearance to keep from rushing to his aid. "We shall see," he said. "In the meantime, there is to be a wedding, and I am to play at being a bridegroom." He paused and assessed her fondly. "He's a lucky fellow indeed, our Duncan. Have patience with him, Phoebe—he's good to the core of his soul, but sometimes he thinks he ought to seem otherwise. I know him better, perhaps, than any man alive, and I can tell you he'll be a faithful husband, because honor is second nature to him. Should you betray him, however, Duncan will be the very personification of fury, and though he would not deny you, you'd never again know his trust."

Phoebe's heart swelled at Alex's tribute to her future husband, but it ached, too, because he so plainly believed he could never experience happiness and passion of his own. "You are a splendid man," she said and meant it. "Someday soon, there will be another wedding—yours—and we'll all be joyous."

"Yes," Alex replied, in that same distracted, beleaguered voice he'd used before. "Or perhaps a funeral, at which I shall expect you to weep."

Phoebe swallowed tears, knowing that sometimes people who are drowning in despair simply cannot be reached, no matter what. "And what would you expect of Duncan, in such a circumstance?"

"Music, of course. Thunderous, discordant stuff, fit to bring every dead sailor up from his watery grave, with his hands pressed to his ears." He had reached the doorway, by the same laborious effort he'd exhibited all along, and he turned on the threshold to meet Phoebe's gaze. "Do you think I don't know how highly my friend regards me, Phoebe, and what it will do to him if I die? Well, mark you this: I understand full well, and the grief of it, added to my other burden, is nigh unto unbearable." With that, Alex was gone.

Phoebe was still sitting there, staring at the

space he'd left in the doorway, when Old Woman came in, carrying a dress trimmed in ecru lace draped over one arm. Her face seemed polished with merriment, glowing like fine, dark wood, and she would not countenance sorrow in the bride.

"Good thing we got you a bath and a rest," Old Woman chattered, laying the gown on the bed and smoothing it with her broad, competent hands. "Won't be no sleep for you this night, miss, and you'll smell sweet for your man."

Phoebe sighed. "Have you ever looked at Alex's palm?" she asked. "What did you see there?"

"Calluses," said Old Woman. "You don't worry about him. He got his own charts to follow."

Phoebe stood and went to examine the dress. Alex's visit had put her in a reflective mood, but she was to marry within the next few hours, taking a man she loved for her husband, and she knew better than anyone what joys the night would bring. "Did this belong to that poor woman, too?" she asked, smoothing the creamy satin of the gown. "The one who was shipwrecked?"

"No," Old Woman replied. "I made it with these black hands, before Mr. Duncan found you wandering in the cellar. This dress, it never belong to nobody but you."

"More magic," Phoebe said with a smile.

"It be magic that brought you here," Old Woman said. "I give you another gift, too, on this happy day. I tell you my name, but you do not say it, you hear? Not 'til the time comes!"

Phoebe was caught up in the spell. After all, if she could travel through time, then certainly Old Woman's true name could make magic. "Can I tell Duncan?"

"No," Old Woman said adamantly, scowling a fierce scowl. "You got to promise me you won't. Not until after."

"After what?"

"You never mind that. You'll *know* when it's right."

Phoebe sighed, but her curiosity wouldn't let her miss this chance. "All right, I promise," she said.

Old Woman whispered the name in her ear. It was an English word, after all, embodying everything good.

"If my firstborn is a daughter, I will call her by that name," Phoebe said, touched to the heart, and smiling through tears.

"Your firstborn will be a man-child," Old Woman replied briskly. "And he be called John Alexander, for his grandfather and Mr. Alex."

Phoebe didn't take the trouble to argue. She knew Old Woman's true name, and she was going to marry Duncan, and for the time being, that was enough. Besides, she'd already made up her mind to let Duncan name his first son.

"Help me put on this beautiful dress," she said instead, and Old Woman's eyes glowed with pride and satisfaction as she obliged.

The gown was a perfect fit, delicate and simple, its skirts making a whispery rustle when Phoebe moved. If she could have gone to any Seattle bridal boutique and chosen a wedding dress for herself, she would have hoped to find something like this. "It's so beautiful," she breathed, turning from side to side before the vanity mirror.

"Yes," Old Woman agreed. She caught both Phoebe's hands in her own and looked deeply into her eyes. "There still be much to give you trouble, mistress. You must be stronger than strong."

Phoebe felt a chill of fear. "What do you mean?"

"You have a babe inside you, even now. A boy-child, like I said. No matter what happen, to you or your man, you look after that little one. He has important business in this world, John Alexander Rourke."

Phoebe sank onto the vanity bench and knew she'd gone pale as parchment.

"Not to think of trouble now," Old Woman scolded. "Think of Mr. Duncan, and the wedding, and the night ahead, which will bring you both much pleasure."

Phoebe was reminded of her own words, spoken to Duncan that very afternoon on the veranda, about taking life as it came. Old Woman was telling her to live for the moment, to make every precious second worthwhile. How simple, that philosophy, and how difficult to follow!

She took her friend's hand and squeezed it, and there was nothing more to say.

The wedding was to be held on the beach, with the sky for a church, the sunset for stained-glass windows, and a group of servants and misfit mercenaries for witnesses.

Phoebe could not have been happier.

When she stood beside Alex, facing her future husband—who held a Bible in his hands, along with a bouquet of purple orchids that he handed to her—she gave no thought to pirates, wars, and time warps. She wanted to tell Duncan about the child she knew was growing within her, the boy Old Woman had already christened John Alexander Rourke, but she would wait for just the right moment.

It was odd, hearing Duncan say the holy words, and ask for vows in return, and to have Alex return them, as if Phoebe were marrying him. At one point, she panicked, thinking Duncan might have tricked her, and Alex, too, into wedding themselves to each other. But then she realized that Duncan called Alex by his, Duncan's, name, and she was reassured.

The vows were made, and when Duncan had pronounced himself and Phoebe to be man and wife, it was the clergyman who kissed the bride, and not the groom-by-proxy.

A noisy, energetic celebration followed. Bonfires were built along the beach, and sailors produced harmonicas and fiddles and small accordions. Phoebe danced with her new husband in the sand, and for her, that night, nothing and no one else existed.

There was much wine—which Phoebe did not touch—and the music was joyous, compelling her into dance after dance, until she was winded and gasping. It was while she was resting, and Duncan was whirling round and round one of the bonfires with Old Woman, that she noticed Simone walking away, toward the cone of moonlight shimmering on the waters.

Phoebe followed, frowning, and caught up to the girl at the edge of the surf, grasping her arm.

"What are you doing?" she demanded.

Simone looked her up and down with cold, empty eyes. "I want to swim," she said. And she let her saronglike robe fall to the sand, revealing her perfect body. "You mistress of Paradise Island now. You can send me away."

Phoebe shook her head. "This is your home."

"And yours," said Simone, turning and wading gracefully into the water. "Mr. Duncan is my man, too. When you get big with the babe that's in you, he'll come to me."

Phoebe clung to what Alex had said: Duncan would be faithful to her, and to the vows they'd made. Except that Alex had been the one to make them, albeit in Duncan's name. "Let go of him, Simone," Phoebe answered, wading a little way into the foamy tide herself. The water felt good. "There's another man for you, and you'll meet him in time. Duncan is mine, and I won't share him."

"You might not have a choice," Simone said. She was treading water, just a few yards offshore, and her grace and ease in the sea reminded Phoebe that this was Simone's world, not her own. Phoebe had come to Paradise Island, and to Duncan, by accident, but Simone had been born, like a mermaid, to sand and salt water and tropical nights. To underestimate the native woman's appeal to a man like Duncan would be a grave mistake.

"I do," Phoebe insisted. "I love Duncan, and I meant what I said before—I will not share him."

Simone was floating on her back now, her firm breasts and flat belly glistening like polished teakwood in the moonlight. "He is mine, as well as yours," she said.

Phoebe was shaken by the other woman's placid confidence. Perhaps Duncan had never broken off with Simone in the first place. In this time and this place, men took mistresses as a matter of course. Even men who considered themselves happily married.

"No," Phoebe said and turned away.

She met Duncan, come to search for her, at the top of the beach.

He took both her hands in his. "What is it?"

"Simone," she said. There was no point in avoiding the subject. "Have you been making love to her, Duncan? Since I came to the island, I mean?" She could not see his eyes, for the darkness, but that was all right. She listened for his answer with her heart.

"Not since you came to the island," he said.

"But before?"

"Yes."

Phoebe nodded. "You have a past," she said softly, "and so do I. But what matters to me now, Duncan, is the future. And if you are unfaithful to me, I promise you, nothing the British or Mornault could do would compare with my vengeance. Do we understand each other?"

Duncan pulled her against his chest. "Yes," he said. "But I will not betray you, Phoebe. You can trust in that, if nothing else."

She looked up, into the face of her husband. "Nor I you," she said softly. "I love you so much, Duncan."

He did not speak, but kissed her and then led her toward the house, via an indirect path that skirted the wedding celebration by a wide margin. For Phoebe, for the time being, it was enough that Duncan had made her his wife. He would declare himself, just as Alex had said, when he was ready.

The interior of the great house was laced with shadows and colored lights from the improvised paper lanterns outside, where the celebration continued. Clasping her hand, Duncan led Phoebe up the stairs, along the passageway, and into his room—which was now hers, too.

"That must have been the most unconventional wedding on record," Phoebe said, suddenly as nervous as a virgin, even though Duncan had already initiated her, quite thoroughly, into connubial bliss. And before that, of course, there had been Jeffrey. Poor, arrogant Jeffrey, who hadn't a clue about what it meant to stir a woman to true passion, to drive her beyond the boundaries of her own soul and then draw her back again, utterly satisfied, and soothe her to sleep.

Duncan did not light a lamp, and scant moonlight flowed through the towering windows, with their view of the sea. "Yes," he agreed. "But it was only the preliminary."

Phoebe shivered, with anticipation and, yes, a touch of fear.

Her husband clasped her shoulders in gentle hands. "What is it?"

She was grateful for the dimness of the room; it allowed her to hold onto some shred of dignity. "It's only that—well, when you make love to me, the pleasure is so great . . ."

Duncan's thumbs made circles on her shoulders, comforting ones that struck sparks, nonetheless, in the furthest reaches of her womanhood. "You do not want me to give you pleasure?" he asked, disbelieving.

Phoebe rested her head against his chest, trembling, laughing a little, and very close to tears. "Of course I do. It's just that—well—I lose control."

"That is as it should be," Duncan said, turning her, deftly unfastening the buttons of the wedding dress Old Woman had made before even meeting her. The gown that fit perfectly. "I, too, am lost,

191

and quite helpless, when you take me inside you and render my seed from me." He smoothed away the dress, and the chemise beneath it, and stood still, as if stricken by her beauty.

"Take off your clothes, Duncan," she commanded gently. "I want to see you as clearly as you see me."

He obeyed, kicking off his boots first, then hauling his shirt over his head and tossing it aside, and finally removing his breeches. He was hard and erect, like the mast of his ship, and the sight of him filled Phoebe with wanton longings and with daring.

"My God," she whispered. "You are so beautiful, like a statue carved to celebrate some sensuous deity."

Duncan lowered himself gracefully to one knee. "It is you," he said in a hoarse voice, "who was made to be worshipped, pleasured, and adored." He stroked her thighs, causing them to quiver almost imperceptibly beneath his fingertips and palms, and finally parted the silken delta for conquering. "I will have you well, Phoebe Rourke, and this time I shall not muffle your cries. I want the whole island—the world—to know that you are mine, and that I please you in our bedchamber."

She tilted her head back and gave an exultant sob when he kissed the pulsing nubbin he'd bared and then took slow, greedy suckle. A shudder moved through her warm, compliant body, and she knew she would have melted to the floor, like so much wax, if Duncan hadn't grasped her buttocks and pressed her even closer to his mouth.

Phoebe cried his name and clasped her hands behind his head, urging him on. Her breasts seemed to swell with her mounting pleasure, and she knew the wedding guests might hear and know the master was taking his bride, and she didn't care. She didn't care about anything except satisfying Duncan, and being satisfied.

She rocked against him, crying out like a she-cat in the jungle, joined to her mate, and Duncan gave her the wall for a brace and put her trembling, boneless legs over his shoulders. He consumed her with ruthless hunger, and when she begged and promised and flung herself fitfully upon his tongue and his lips, sobbing, he merely teased her. There was no attempt, as he had said, to quiet her.

While the wedding guests celebrated on the beach, with their bonfires and fiddles and jugs of potent island wine, the marriage of Duncan and Phoebe was duly consummated, to the satisfaction of both parties.

The message arrived the following morning, via the usual complicated network of sailors, tavern keepers, and native couriers. Duncan was already up and dressed when it reached him, drinking coffee on the terrace outside the room where Phoebe, now his wife, still slept. She'd held nothing back the night before, but given him everything and more, and received him as if he'd been a missing part of herself.

Old Woman appeared in the open doorway to the terrace, and from her secretive, self-satisfied smile, anyone would think she'd engineered not only the new marriage, but the entire universe as well. Without a word, she handed him the battered, much-creased vellum envelope and left.

Duncan recognized his sister, Phillippa's, personal stationery, even though her name did not appear anywhere on the outside. His own name was coded, as always; the letter had been sent first to the Apollo Tavern in Boston, where a friend watched for such missives and forwarded them by whatever means came to hand.

He hesitated, half afraid to read the lines his sister had written. Duncan was close to Phillippa, as he was to Lucas, their brother, despite several profound philosophical differences, but it was an arduous thing to send a letter, especially in time of war. Such an undertaking precluded trifles.

"What is it?" Phoebe asked from behind him, laying her hands on his shoulders. It was the second time she had taken him by surprise that way, and he was troubled because he hadn't heard her approaching.

Duncan used his knife to slit the envelope open and pulled out the folded pages. "A message from my sister," he said, and even Phillippa's affectionate salutation did not settle his fears. He'd been right to worry, he discovered as he scanned the neat, flourishing script, for the news was not good.

Phoebe sat down across from him at the small metal table, her hair bright in the sunlight. She was wearing one of his shirts, and there was a warm, apricot glow to her skin. She waited, in silence, until Duncan was ready to speak.

"I must go to Charles Town," he said at last. "My father has been ill."

She reached out to touch his hand, soothingly, with the tips of her fingers. "But Charleston is occupied by the British," she reminded him carefully. He'd told her himself, on the way back from Queen's Town, how General Clinton had taken the city in May.

"Yes," Duncan answered. "I'm sorry to leave you so soon, my love."

"No problem. You're *not* leaving me," replied Mrs. Rourke, with all the authority of her position as mistress of the house. "I'm going with you."

He had risen from his chair, set on making preparations and departing immediately, but her words stopped him cold. "No," he said. "Absolutely not."

"Don't force me to stow away, Duncan," she warned, rising and walking over to stand toe-to-toe with him. "Or catch a ride on the first passing ship. I will do whatever is necessary, but I will not be left behind."

Duncan gave a long sigh and shoved a hand into his hair, which was still loose from the night.

"What makes you so bloody stubborn?" he demanded angrily.

Phoebe raised one shoulder in an impudent shrug. "I don't know. It comes naturally to me. What makes *you* so bloody stubborn?"

"Kindly do not swear," he said in a taut voice, turning from her and leaving the terrace for the bedchamber. "It is not becoming."

"That was swearing?" she countered, following him and dressing while he threw shirts and breeches and other necessities into a trunk. "You should have told me before. I might have said the wrong thing at a tea party."

Duncan clenched his jaw, then relaxed it by force of will. "Damnation, Phoebe, I don't need this kind of vexation from you. My father may already be dead."

"I know," Phoebe answered with gentle implacability. "On the other hand, he could be thriving by now—how long ago was that letter written? If he's gone—and I doubt that very much, since he's your father and must therefore be quite as intractable as you are—you'll need me to comfort you. If he's well, he'll want to meet his daughter-in-law."

Duncan stood stiffly for a while, like a mule about to be driven down a road knee-deep in mud, and then relented. Phoebe would try to follow him if he left her on the island and probably get herself killed or kidnapped in the process. At least, if she was with him, he could protect her.

196

"Will I never win another argument?"

She drew close to him and slipped her arms round his waist. Her hair smelled of sunlight, and there was a faint, musky perfume on her skin, the scent of their lovemaking. "Not while you're married to me," she answered.

Even then, Duncan knew her words were prophetic.

They sailed with a full crew in the early afternoon, and both the tides and the wind were with them. It was Phoebe, out to explore the ship, who found Simone huddled behind a crate in the hold, looking scared and defiant.

Her possessions filled the small bundle beside her.

"What are you doing here?" Phoebe asked, placing her hands on her hips and keeping her voice down.

"I'm leaving. That ought to make you glad. 'Course, if you tell Duncan, he'll send me back."

Phoebe sighed and sat down on another crate. The light in the hold was dim, and the place made her uncomfortable anyway, reminding her, as it did, of her brief adventure aboard Mornault's ship. "It doesn't make me glad," she said. "The island is your home. You were born there, weren't you?"

"No matter," Simone replied tonelessly, glaring at Phoebe with an obdurate gleam in her eyes. "I'll find a new place."

"I thought you were determined to stay and seduce my husband," Phoebe said. "Just last night, you told me . . ."

"You wish me to try?"

"Of course not. But if Duncan is the sort of man to take a mistress, he'll do so, whether you're on Paradise Island or in Timbuktu. These are difficult times, Simone, and dangerous ones. You would be better off staying put."

"I imagine you would be, too. But you didn't."

Phoebe laughed softly and shook her head. "You've got me there."

"You planning to tell Duncan I'm aboard?"

Phoebe considered. "No," she said at length. "You're a grown woman, and if you want to leave, that's your business. Where will you go?"

Simone rested her head against the ship's side, closed her eyes, and sighed. "To the big island. I can get work there."

"Try the Crown and Lily Tavern," Phoebe suggested. "Ask for Mistress Bell. And whatever you do, don't tell her I sent you. My brief career as a serving wench wasn't exactly a stunning success."

In spite of everything, and obviously against her will, Simone smiled. "So I've been told."

"I'll bring you water and food," Phoebe said, standing up. "And I'll keep your secret, as well. But I want one question answered in return."

"What?" Simone asked. Her eyes were still

closed, and she'd been humming very softly during the brief lapses in their conversation.

"What made you change your mind about staying?"

"The change I see in Duncan," Simone said. "I tried not to recognize it at first, but it was there, right from the beginning. You give him something more than pleasure. You touch a part of him that other women just can't reach."

Phoebe didn't reply, but left Simone with her bundle and her dignity and took herself up onto the main deck, to watch the island recede into the glittering horizon.

Duncan was busy, as were all his men, and Phoebe made a point of staying out of the way, trying to go unnoticed, as if she, too, were a stowaway.

When the midday meal was served, below deck in the galley, Phoebe collected her share of food on a large wooden trencher, plus a little extra, telling the cook she preferred to eat in the captain's cabin. She did go to the small chamber she would be sharing with Duncan during the voyage—the berth looked hardly wide enough for the two of them—in case someone was watching. She ate, then packed cheese, bread, dried meat, and a banana into a leather bag, along with a jar of water, and slipped down to the hold.

Simone accepted the food with dignity and offered grudging thanks.

Phoebe returned to the upper deck and the cabin, where she took off her dress, lay down on the berth in her chemise, and went to sleep. When she awakened, Duncan was beside her, his hair unbound, wearing only his breeches and an insufferable grin.

"It was good of you to wake, Mistress Rourke," he said. "I have business with you, as it happens." With his right hand, he caressed her thigh, from knee to hip, displacing the wispy slip in the process.

Phoebe gave a shivery croon and stretched contentedly. "What sort of business?" she asked, as he bared her breasts and prepared them for pleasure with light, brushing motions of his fingertips.

"The most intimate kind," he replied and put his tongue to her nipple.

Phoebe arched her back and groaned. "You— know how much noise I make," she managed to sputter, her fingers already deep in his hair, holding him close to her. "What will your men say?"

Duncan raised his head just long enough to answer. "That I'm a lucky bastard," he replied.

10

"Now," Duncan said, when he and Phoebe lay spent with lovemaking on the berth in his cabin, their arms and legs still entangled. "Tell me who you are hiding in the hold."

Phoebe drew breath to deny the accusation, then stopped herself. She could not begin this new and wonderful marriage by lying to her husband—to do so would weaken the whole foundation of their relationship, and that was most precious to her. "I promised I wouldn't tell," she said miserably. "Not that it'll matter. When you go down there to look for yourself, she's going to think I betrayed her."

" 'She,' " Duncan mused, tracing the line of Phoebe's jaw with the tip of his index finger, caressing her lips, which were still pleasantly sensitive from his kisses. "It cannot be Old Woman, for she would not trouble herself to hide. Indeed, she would probably demand this cabin and take over my duties and those of the cook and navigator as well. So our traveler must be Simone."

Phoebe sighed, with sincerity. "Just when she was beginning to like me," she lamented.

Duncan's expression was thoughtful. "Simone is not a slave or a prisoner," he told his worried wife in his own good time. "If she wishes to leave the island and make her way in the world, she is free to do so, like anyone else in my household. Except for you, of course." He chuckled and tasted her mouth as though he were sampling a vintage wine. "You, I cannot spare."

Phoebe fretted, her body already reawakening, blossoming again, under Duncan's skillful attentions. There were things she wanted to ask him, important things, but her thoughts were unfocused, as though she'd had too much to drink. "Ummm . . . that feels *very* good. But if you make me cry out like last time, I'll be too embarrassed to set foot outside this cabin . . ."

"That would be fine with me," Duncan said throatily, showing neither haste nor mercy as he proceeded to bring her, once again, to a fever pitch of arousal. "At least you can't get into trouble here."

"That's—oh, God, Duncan—that's what you think . . ."

He had her again soon after the fragments of her sentence fell away into insensible moans, and with meticulous thoroughness, kneeling between her thighs and grasping her hips to raise her to him, and pull her hard into each thrust. She bucked against him, making a sound that was at once a series of sobs and a single unbroken groan. When Duncan came, at last, she had long since been satisfied, and fallen still in exhaustion and utter contentment.

She watched his marvelous face as he surrendered to pleasure, and she was filled with joy, for this was the one time he could not hide his emotions from her.

"If we keep this up," she said, stroking Duncan's head after he'd collapsed beside her, his cheek resting upon her breast, "we'll have more children than I really want to give birth to, without anesthetic and Lamaze classes."

"Speak English," Duncan said, his voice muffled by her flesh.

Phoebe laughed. "I'm trying, darling. I truly am." She was solemn again, remembering Simone. "What are we going to do about our stowaway?"

Duncan sighed. "What *can* we do?" he grumbled.

"I could go down there and tell her that you saw me taking her food—that is how you knew, isn't it?—and guessed that she was on board."

"She won't believe you."

Phoebe's frustration was mounting. "No. And Simone is fiercely proud, Duncan—I think she would rather ride out this whole trip in the hold than have you know her heart is broken."

Duncan raised his head and looked into Phoebe's eyes. "Kindly do not romanticize the situation," he said. "Simone is young and very beautiful. She is free. In time, she'll get over her infatuation and wonder what she ever saw in me."

She slipped her fingers into his soft, glistening hair, loving the way it felt. Loving him. "Nope," she said. "You were her first love, I think. There will always be a small bruise, somewhere in her heart, that will ache whenever she remembers you."

He uttered an exaggerated groan of misery and despair. "I see I can depend upon you, not only to prevail in every disagreement, but spare me absolutely nothing."

Phoebe lifted her head just far enough to kiss his chin, which was already stubbly even though he had shaved that morning, before they boarded the ship. "As an eighteenth-century wife, it is my duty to keep you on the straight-and-narrow path, and I'll use a staff with a hook on the end if I must. Now, about Simone . . ."

Duncan groaned again. More loudly than before.

"I'll continue to take her food and water, until we get to Queen's Town and she can make good on her escape," Phoebe decreed, undaunted. "You can turn a blind eye to her in the meantime and make sure she isn't discovered before we make port."

"We're not going to Queen's Town," Duncan said, with pained logic. "The place is festering with British soldiers, in case you've forgotten, any one of whom would like to hang me from a sturdy branch and use my carcass for bayonet practice."

"Well, we can't take her to the States—the colonies, I mean," Phoebe protested, her face warm because, incredibly, she *had* forgotten that Queen's Town wasn't a port Duncan could sail

204

into with flags flying and trumpets sounding. But then, neither was Charles Town, and he certainly meant to go there.

Something else tugged at the edge of her mind, a vague but urgent concern, but it eluded her in her intoxicated state.

She lowered her voice to a whisper. "Simone is black."

"Yes," Duncan replied dryly, "I had ascertained that much."

Phoebe slugged him in the shoulder, though just hard enough to indicate irritation. "Duncan, you cannot take that woman—that *girl*—to a place where she might well be made into a slave!"

"No," he said. "But it was her choice to make this journey, not mine. I will not risk the lives of my wife and my crew—"

She laid a finger to his lips. "You needn't do that," she pointed out reasonably. "Just send Simone ashore in a skiff, when we're close enough to Queen's Town. She will make her own way after that."

Duncan had that intractable look on his face again. "That will destroy the illusion that I didn't know she was traveling in the hold, won't it? God in heaven, Phoebe, this is all so complicated, so *female*. It would be far simpler to simply tell the chit that I've found her out, and that she needn't hide in the hold like a bilge rat, living on scraps. We could put her off the ship tomorrow night—I have friends who would see her to the big island."

Phoebe waited patiently for him to finish.

"That's a good idea," she allowed. "The second part, I mean, about letting your friends take Simone to Queen's Town. But until tomorrow night, husband, you must leave her be. When the time comes for her to go ashore, tell me, and I will handle it."

"How?"

"I don't know, but I have twenty-four hours to figure it out."

Duncan muttered a curse and flung himself off the berth to wash and put his clothes back on. He still had a ship to captain, after all, and could not while away the daylight hours in his cabin, making love to his wife. *More's the pity*, Phoebe thought. He really was a spectacular creature, in body as well as mind, with his well-defined muscles, tanned skin, and longish, somewhat shaggy hair—even the whip marks on his back didn't detract from the physical wonder that was Duncan Rourke.

Pirate. Patriot.

Father-to-be.

Phoebe smiled, cherishing her secret. She would not tell Duncan about their child until she was sure she was pregnant. And since her periods had never been regular, it might take a while to be certain.

When Duncan had made himself presentable again, bent over the berth to kiss Phoebe's forehead, and left the cabin, she got up, took a sponge bath of her own, and donned another of the ship-wrecked woman's dresses.

"He knows," Simone accused, the moment Phoebe stepped into the hold at suppertime, carrying a plate of hot food, a fork, and a ewer filled with fresh coffee, the latter being a luxury only smugglers and pirates possessed. "You went and told Duncan about me."

Phoebe put the plate and ewer down carefully on top of a crate and laid the fork in perfect alignment with the other things, as though setting the table for a fancy dinner party. "I didn't tell him," she declared in a thin but earnest tone of voice. "Not exactly."

" 'Not exactly'?" Simone echoed pointedly, but she took up the fork and began to eat.

"You must be dying to take a walk," Phoebe said. "And how do you go to the bathroom? Is there a chamber pot?"

Simone refused to answer; she just glared at her unwilling jailor, chewing.

The confession erupted from Phoebe. "All right, yes, Duncan knows you're here. He asked me who I was hiding in the hold, and I said I couldn't tell because I'd promised." Simone's glare intensified, the whites of her beautiful eyes glittering in the dimness. "Well, I couldn't lie to him!" cried the captain's bride. "I happen to love the man, and love and lies don't mix."

Simone was silent for so long that Phoebe was turning to leave when she finally spoke. "I can't face him," she said. "Nor the crew."

"You don't have to," Phoebe replied gently. "Tomorrow night, Duncan will send you ashore in a skiff. He says someone will escort you safely to Queen's Town from there.''

Simone's eyes glistened with tears, but Phoebe knew better than to show pity. Here was a woman every bit as proud as Phoebe herself, and she understood what it was to hurt the way Simone was hurting, and want to hold fast to your dignity because you believed, at the moment, that you had nothing else left.

Phoebe went to the doorway and paused there, without looking back at the woman who might have been her friend, if circumstances had been different. At last, it had come to the surface of her mind, the question she needed to ask. "Will you betray Duncan, and all of us, to the British, when you reach Queen's Town?''

Duncan must have thought of that possibility, but had not troubled himself to mention it. Simone, out of spite or for some other less obvious reason, could guide the enemy to Paradise Island.

"There is something you forget, Mistress Rourke,'' Simone said, with bitter sorrow and with weariness, but now no rancor. "I love your husband as much as you do, maybe more, because I've known him longer. I've seen the scars Duncan bears and heard him cry out in the night because his dreams had carried him back to that whipping post and to that pain. I couldn't bear to draw another breath if I was the cause of that happening again, but there's a difference this time. Before, they just whipped him, those redcoats. Now, they'd hang him, too."

Phoebe felt her stomach roil, and bile scalded the back of her throat. She couldn't speak.

Simone went ruthlessly on. "You remember, mistress, what I said, and you be careful. Otherwise, you might find yourself watching your man pay the price for something you said or did."

Phoebe closed the door to the hold and fled back to the captain's cabin. She had, of course, known about Duncan's involvement with Simone from the beginning. All the same, Simone had struck her mark, referring to the scars on Duncan's back and the nightmares that must have haunted him for half his life, and perhaps tormented him still. She was not jealous, exactly, but sorely wounded by the knowledge that Simone, and probably many other women, had been so close to him.

It wasn't reasonable, she knew that, but knowing did nothing to change the way she felt.

An even heavier burden was the knowledge that she herself might so easily be the cause of his downfall, his suffering, and his death.

Phoebe stayed in the cabin until Duncan appeared, wanting to know why she'd missed dinner. She was surprised, and just a little flattered, that he'd noticed, considering all he had to do on deck. She told him she had a headache, which was perfectly true, though she made it sound much worse than it was, and he soaked a cloth in tepid water and laid it on her forehead before leaving the room again.

Guilt compounded her other agonies.

Presently, Duncan returned with a bowl of stew and some bread and sat on the edge of the berth, kicking off his boots, while she stared at her food, and then at him, and did not take a bite.

"It would appear," he ventured, "that the interview with Simone did not go well."

Phoebe wanted to cry, or throw up, or both. In the end, she just sat there, holding the stew bowl and feeling wretched. "It hurts," she said.

"What does?" Duncan asked tenderly, turning to look directly into her face.

"Knowing someone else touched you, slept beside you, felt the same things I feel when you made love to them."

"Ah," Duncan said. "Yes."

"It's unreasonable," Phoebe declared, "and I'm sorry."

He smiled, took the spoon, and prodded her mouth with it until she accepted a taste of stew. "Unreasonable, yes—and also human," he agreed. "Do you imagine, Phoebe, that I never think of the man you were married to before me, and wonder if he made you laugh, and cry out in pleasure, and if you caused him no end of trouble, as you do me?"

Phoebe uttered a little sobbing chuckle, her mouth still full. After chewing and swallowing and refusing a second spoonful, she said, "Don't loose any sleep over Jeffrey, my love—he isn't—

wasn't—*won't be*, ever, even remotely comparable to you." At Duncan's arched eyebrow, she rushed to explain further. "Jeffrey is still a boy, playing games, at thirty-five. You have been a man since your teens. And he'll never be more than a child, really, because he's complacent and hasn't even guessed that he should be anything more than he is."

Duncan stretched out on the berth beside Phoebe, having taken off his boots but still fully clad otherwise, and cupped his hands behind his head. "The way you talk baffles me sorely," he said quietly. "I've never heard anything like it." He reached over, took the spoon from the bowl of stew, which she was still holding, and nudged her hand with his until she took the utensil. "Tell me about that other world of yours, Phoebe— while you're having your dinner."

The emphasis on the part about continuing to eat was subtle, but Phoebe could tell he intended to press the matter if she didn't cooperate. She wasn't hungry, but there was the baby to think about, and a body needed fuel to function, like any engine, so she began to nibble stoically at the food.

Between bites, Phoebe related the story of her life. She told Duncan about her childhood, and about Jeffrey, and how she'd truly believed she loved him, only to find out very recently that she'd merely been infatuated. Also, because her mother and stepfather had been killed in an accident during her last year of high school, and her half brother, Eliott, had paid almost no attention to her, she'd wanted to start a family of her own and belong to someone. She described Murphy, that ungrateful dog, and how it had felt, being out of work in a culture where a large part of a person's value is determined by what that person does for a living, and how much money they earn.

Duncan frowned. "It will come to that, then? Such superficiality, after all we're suffering here in the hope of laying the foundations of a great civilization?" He sounded disappointed, and it was little wonder, given the very real sacrifices he and other men and women were making every day, in their desperate struggle for liberty.

Phoebe didn't have the heart to tell him about income tax and the national debt, AIDS and the rising crime rate, or the ongoing tensions in the Middle East. She could see no reason to burden Duncan with things he had no need to know; he was playing his part, in his time, and that was more than enough.

Maybe it was true, what Shakespeare had written, she concluded—perhaps all the world truly was a stage, and men and women merely players, with roles assigned before they ever stepped out of the wings.

"Yes," she admitted. "But it's a great country, Duncan. There isn't another like it on the face of the earth."

"Tell me something you like about this nation," he said with touching eagerness. "Something simple."

She smiled. "Well, there's the Fourth of July—we call it Independence Day. People celebrate the signing of the Declaration of Independence by cooking outdoors—hot dogs, corn on the cob, steaks and hamburgers,that sort of thing, and at night, there are always fireworks—beautiful explosions of colored light."

Duncan's eyes twinkled. Phoebe didn't know if he believed what she was saying or was merely humoring her, and at the moment, she didn't care. He was *listening*. "You eat dogs?" he asked. He sounded amused, but at the same time, Phoebe could see that he was worried.

She explained the term.

"Ah," he said. "Sounds dreadful. For all of it, Ben Franklin and that lot would like knowing the people take the trouble to remember after so long. It was hard-won, that consensus in Philadelphia."

"Oh, they remember, all right," she assured him, touching his hand. "When I left, we'd been celebrating every year for well over two centuries. And a lot of other Americans have died to preserve what you and Mr. Franklin and all the others began." Phoebe could almost hear a fife and drum, but she didn't care if she sounded sentimental; she was a patriot at heart and always had been. "There are problems ahead, Duncan—big ones. And the country is far from perfect. But it's by striving toward the ideals the nation holds that progress is made."

"Yes," Duncan agreed. "Truly, men shall tread upon the moon?"

"Only the beginning," Phoebe said. But she was frowning, thinking again of Simone and all the harm she might do, despite her angry assertion that she loved Duncan too well to sell him to the British. Judas had loved Christ, too, at one time.

"What troubles you?" Duncan asked, for he had learned to read her expressions rather more easily than she would have liked.

"Simone vowed she wouldn't tell the British how to find Paradise Island—and you. But I'm still afraid. That old saying about hell having no fury like a woman scorned should not be taken lightly."

Duncan smiled. "No," he agreed. "A man ignores that element of the female nature at his peril. Still, we cannot hold the islanders as hostages lest they betray us. There are others who could do so as well, of course—a seaman with a grudge, for example. We've had two or three men jump ship in the past months. Or one of the native lads, with ambitions to see the broader world, and the need for gold to carry out his plans . . ."

"If you're trying to reassure me," Phoebe advised, "it isn't working."

"Reality is almost never reassuring," Duncan countered. "But it is what it is, nonetheless, and only the imprudent allow themselves to forget that. "Now," he said, rising from the bed to remove his clothes and extinguish the lamp, "we must have our sleep, Mistress Rourke. The new day will make many demands."

It was sound advice, but more than an hour passed before either of them closed their eyes.

In the morning, Phoebe awakened to find that Duncan had already left the cabin, as usual. She washed, as best as she could—Kathie Lee Gifford wouldn't be singing and dancing on *this* ship— and donned a gown from the trunk Old Woman had packed for her. Dressed and groomed, she took herself to the galley, there to consume a hasty breakfast of porridge and wonderful, thick slices of bacon.

There was no need to be secretive, and yet Simone remained stubbornly in the hold. She accepted the food that Phoebe brought and ate it with a hunger she could not hide. Phoebe sat on the same crate as before and watched her in silence, until she'd finished.

"Have you been for a walk on deck, at least?" Phoebe asked when Simone had devoured the last crumb.

"Of course I have," Simone answered testily, but with a note of grudging appreciation in her voice. "I go out when it's late, and there are fewer men on watch. They pretend not to see me."

"You pay a high price for your pride," Phoebe pointed out. "You might have had the first mate's berth, and all the fresh air and exercise and food and water you could want. Instead, you insist on sitting here in this dark hole, like Joseph at the bottom of the well. And the worst part is, you're

215

proving nothing, punishing yourself this way, except that hurt feelings have made you foolish."

Simone lowered her head for a moment, and Phoebe felt a pang, for she had never sought to wound the girl. Beyond wanting to scratch her eyes out on a few occasions, of course, for lusting after Duncan with such stubborn devotion, and that had only been a figurative desire.

"At least," Simone said softly, "I am foolish where he cannot see me and laugh at my foolishness. Or worse, feel pity for me."

"He," of course, was Duncan. "The captain"—out of simple kindness, Phoebe did not say, "my husband"—"does not pity you, Simone. Nor does he find the situation amusing. Won't you come up on deck with me and stand in the sunlight? It's glorious today, and there's a fresh breeze, too."

But Simone did not rise from her seat between the boxes, her bundle of possessions resting on her lap. "No," she said. "Please—just go and leave me be."

Phoebe left, feeling depressed. If you want to make a situation worse, she thought, just send me as an emissary. With the very best of intentions, I'll botch things up so badly that a team of diplomats couldn't mend the damage.

"Perhaps I should talk to her," Duncan said. He was waiting on the deck, arms folded, when Phoebe emerged from below. "From your expression, I might conclude that you made little or no progress with the recalcitrant Simone."

"Progress?" Phoebe echoed forlornly. "Thanks to me, she'll probably hurl herself overboard at the first sign of circling sharks. Still, the very worst thing you could do, Duncan, would be to go down there and confront her now. Let Simone meet you another time, when she's stronger and in charge of her life again."

"Have you noticed," Duncan asked, after a nod of capitulation, "that you are starting to speak our language?"

Phoebe sighed. "All this formality tends to rub off on a person. I'll have to practice modern idioms in my spare time, just to keep my memory fresh."

He laughed and took her arm. "Come," he said. "I want to show you how the ship is managed. You may need to know someday."

Phoebe wanted to understand the complexities of controlling such a craft, it was true, but her reasons were rooted in curiosity, and a deep, insatiable desire to learn all about everything. She did not want to "need to know," however; that would mean that something had happened to Duncan.

"You are quite forward-thinking—in some ways—for a man of the eighteenth century," she said.

"The men of the twentieth are more so?"

Phoebe considered. "Well, no," she admitted at long last. "Some of them *want* to be, I think. They're just learning to be sensitive—watching *Donahue*, beating on drums, and getting in touch with their feelings about their fathers, things like that."

Duncan followed as he escorted Phoebe forward, toward the wheel-house, where the lessons would begin. "Beating on drums?"

"It's a way to validate the primitive side of their psyches."

"I take back everything I said before. You are not starting to speak our language, and I am not learning yours."

Phoebe laughed. "Perhaps, over the next forty or fifty years, I'll be able to explain it all properly. What this new nation of yours has come to after two hundred and twenty years."

"I'm not sure I wish to know," Duncan said, only half in jest. He could not have guessed, though Phoebe had had inklings, when on the edge of sleep or waking, that he was fated to find out firsthand. Whether he wanted to or not.

Shortly after sunset, which was a glorious spill of crimson, gold, apricot, and pink light over a turquoise sea, a skiff was rigged and lowered over the side of the ship. Simone descended to it, via a rope ladder, with a minimum of fuss from the crew and no apparent notice at all from the captain. Two able seamen awaited her and pushed off when she was safely aboard.

She had, Phoebe knew, a pouch of gold coins in her possession, and a paper stating that she was a free woman, and not a slave. The document had been signed, not by Duncan, of course, but by Phoebe, and witnessed by the first mate and the ship's surgeon.

Phoebe waved from the rail, and she thought Simone saw the farewell gesture, but she did not respond. Silently, Phoebe wished her rival Godspeed, and prayed she would never tell, on purpose or unwittingly, that she had worked in the household, and taken pleasure in the bed, of one Duncan Rourke. Rebel, pirate, and enemy of the Crown, marked for severe punishment—he would make a splendid example—and ultimately marked for death.

Phoebe prayed silently, her hands folded, her heart humble. Please. Let Simone forgive Duncan for not loving her. Let her keep her peace and go on to have a happy life.

There was no knowing then, of course, whether that prayer would be answered, and though she had tried, mostly, to be kind, and always to be honest and fair in all her dealings, Phoebe was not a particularly religious person. She did not pretend piety, for if there was a God, He would surely recognize such a deception, being omnipresent and omnipotent. But if that Deity of deities cared at all for the affairs of the men and women on one paltry but beautiful blue-green world, a speck in a vast configuration of stars and asteroids, comets and meteorites, moons and planets, Phoebe would be most grateful for any help.

Meanwhile, Simone and the two crewmen were skimming over the water in a fleet little skiff, and presently the thickening shadows swallowed them, and Phoebe turned from the rail.

She returned, alone, to the cabin belowdecks, where a lamp was burning, lit by Peter Beedle, one of Duncan's most trusted men, who was there still, arranging the contents of a tray on the small, fold-down slab of carved wood that served as both a desk and a dining table. He favored Phoebe with a deferential, rather shy nod and murmured, "Mistress Rourke."

"Hello," Phoebe replied. She felt the ship bobbing on the water, a sensation she'd gotten used to long since, deeming herself a born sailor. Then she realized the vessel was not at anchor, but under way, and wheeling to the starboard side, if her senses were correct. She frowned, puzzled. The men with the skiff could not have deposited Simone on shore and arranged for her escort to Queen's Town so quickly. "Are we leaving those men behind?" she muttered, musing aloud rather than expecting Beedle to answer her.

He did, being a polite and knowledgeable sort. "Yes, mistress," he said. "There's hard sailing ahead of us this night, for we've spotted a ship nearby, with no colors flying to tell us who she be. Not that that would be proof," he added as a wry afterthought, thinking, no doubt, as Phoebe was, of the collection of flags carried by the *Francesca* herself, allowing Duncan to pass the ship off as Dutch or French or Spanish or British, as he might choose.

Phoebe was troubled and had not touched the wine or food, but only sat staring at it, when Duncan came in five minutes later. Beedle, of course, had already returned to his post, whatever and wherever that was.

"Mr. Beedle has clean hands," she said, when Duncan entered. "Thank you for that."

Duncan chuckled; there was a chart rolled under his arm, and he laid it on a shelf, secured by the bolted-down clock in front of it, before crossing the room to wash at the basin. "You surprise me, Mistress Rourke. I expected a harangue because we had sailed off without two members of our crew—along with a very sturdy skiff, I might add, that was much prized by the captain."

"Beedle told me we were being pursued," she said, as her husband came at last to the narrow table and sat down next to her. The lamplight made shadows on his aristocratic face, sharpening the angles and deepening the hollows, and she thought of a mountain range at sunset, as seen from an airplane window.

Duncan smiled, filling Phoebe's plate first and setting it authoritatively before her, then attending to his own. "Pursued? Was that the word he used, or merely your interpretation?"

Phoebe hesitated. "My interpretation," she admitted, when she could sustain the silence no longer."

"Ah," said Duncan and ate two small, roasted potatoes, with impeccable manners, before going on. "We believe the other vessel is a British supply ship," he said. "Given that she flies no colors, it is safe enough to assume that she's carrying a cargo her officers wish to keep secret. She is also a vessel of war, however, and surely takes us for either pirates or patriots—rebels to her—and is therefore sworn to sink us to the bottom at the first opportunity."

Phoebe, who had been swallowing a green bean, choked in the process. When she'd recovered, which Duncan waited with patient vigilance for her to do, she gasped, "You expect them to attack us?"

Duncan drained a cup of wine, and Phoebe wished sorely that she dared indulge, too, but she had fetal alcohol syndrome to consider, and she was taking no chances with their child's health. The child she already thought of as John Alexander Rourke, thanks to Old Woman.

"They'll try," he said at long last. "We are, at present, leading them into an ambush—one of the many small, sheltered coves these islands offer. If they follow, we will, of course, be certain of their intentions. You shall be put ashore, naturally, before the fighting begins."

Phoebe did not particularly want to be present for the battle, but neither did she feel inclined to leave Duncan, even—especially—in those circumstances. "You must know what I think of that idea without my bothering to tell you."

He picked up a chicken leg and pondered it, never glancing in Phoebe's direction. "That you refuse to leave my side," he said, sounding almost bored. "I must confess, it's a trait I admire. However, in this case, my beautiful and lusty bride, you shall not be given a choice."

11

Phoebe considered carefully before responding to Duncan's edict. He was indeed being arbitrary, decreeing that she would have no say in her own immediate destiny, insisting that she was to be removed from the ship before any encounter with the unmarked vessel tagging after them. On the other hand, his intentions were unquestionably good; he was trying to protect her. If his methods were slightly highhanded, well, he could not be blamed overmuch. After all, he was a man of his times.

"Everyone has choices," she countered moderately, her hands folded in her lap.

Duncan had abandoned his supper and was busy plundering a battered but ornately carved oaken chest, ferreting out various woolly-looking garments and tossing them into a pile on the floor. "Yes," he agreed, almost as an aside, "and here are yours: You may leave the ship with dignity, comporting yourself like a lady, or you may leave it kicking and screaming. In either case, you shall be put ashore."

Phoebe sighed. She must control her impulses, all of which favored open rebellion. A rash action on her part could seal Duncan's fate, and that was a prospect she couldn't live with.

"Stand up," he commanded, crossing the small cabin with an unwieldy garment in his hands.

"Listen to me," Phoebe said, just a shade of impatience creeping into her tone. All the same, she stood.

Duncan held the top to a set of woolen underwear against her, frowning as he measured its fit with his gaze. "What?"

"I'll be safer if I stay with you," she told him, her voice trembling slightly—with conviction, though, and not trepidation. "Think about it, Duncan. I could be eaten by sharks before I ever reached the shore. Or drowned. And let's just suppose I was lucky enough to reach dry land. I might be captured by natives, or another band of pirates. At least if I'm with you, you'll be able to keep me safe."

He lowered the undershirt, and his frown gave way to an expression of beleaguered exasperation. "I suppose you're right," he conceded at long last. In a breath, his conciliatory manner was gone. "You'll keep yourself belowdecks the whole while, Mistress Duncan," he warned, "or I swear you'll never make another voyage aboard this ship."

Phoebe smiled tentatively and took the

scratchy shirt from his hand. "It would have been a poor disguise anyway," she said.

"It wasn't meant for deception," Duncan countered impatiently, just as an urgent bell began to sound somewhere up on deck. He was already moving toward the door as he finished speaking. "But for warmth. People do perish from the chill, you know, even in these southerly islands."

Phoebe nodded, still standing beside the table. "Take care," she whispered.

He opened the door with a kind of hasty grace. "Stay here," he said. A moment later, the heavy wooden panel had closed between them, and she heard a key grate in the lock.

A wild, totally instinctive desire rose within Phoebe, urging her to fling herself against the door, screaming like a cat crammed into a fishing creel, and then subsided again. In the next instant, something struck the side of the ship with such violent impact that she had to grasp the back of a chair to keep from falling. Simultaneously, a terrible sound, a monstrous, grinding screech of wood-against-wood, filled the passages of Phoebe's ears and threatened to explode there.

That sound was followed by even more disturbing ones—the metallic clash of swords, the thunder of cannonballs, the shouts of angry men, and the screams of wounded ones.

Phoebe was terrified and, for long moments, paralyzed in the bargain. But as the din on deck increased to deafening proportions, she forced herself to consider the very real possibility that Duncan and his men would lose the battle. If that happened, she must be prepared to defend herself.

Her first thought was a cowardly one: that if Duncan was dead, she didn't want to live anyway. Then she remembered the child nestled inside her, and she knew she could not give up.

A quick search of the room yielded two pearl-handled cap-and-ball pistols, but whether or not they were loaded was anybody's guess. Phoebe laid them on the bed and studied them doubtfully. A firearm in the hands of an untrained person, she knew, was worse than no weapon at all. The pistols could blow up in her face, or simply click ineffectually when the invaders burst through the door. Furthermore, she would have only a single shot with each one, since reloading was beyond her. She had to make those musket balls count.

Biting her lower lip, Phoebe picked up one of the guns and grasped it in both hands. It was cumbersome and unbelievably heavy, and just holding the thing made every inch of her skin tickle with sweat. Her wrists trembled, and her knees felt like jelly, and she had yet to face a single pirate.

So much for courage.

She put the pistol down with a shaking hand, dragged a chair into position facing the door, and reclaimed both weapons. Then she sat, waiting, her heart hammering at such a rate that it made her dizzy.

Above decks, the fighting and shouting and shooting went on and on. There were lulls, but the din always started up again. She could not guess how much time passed, whether hours or only moments. Terror held her in a suspended state, a dimension of its own.

Half-moons of perspiration formed under her arms, and she had to dry her palms on her skirts more than once. The cold terror in the pit of her stomach finally dissolved, and exhaustion nearly overwhelmed her. She felt as if she'd been drugged, and her eyelids seemed weighted. And so she kept her vigil, pistols lying dense in her lap, one damp palm resting lightly on each handle. When at last, in the midst of an oasis of quiet, someone tried the door, Phoebe started violently. One of the guns crashed to the floor, and she braced herself for an explosion, but there was none. Nor was there time to retrieve the lost pistol. She raised herself to her feet, the remaining one aimed and wavering in both hands, and held her breath.

A stranger filled the chasm. "Put that thing down before you hurt yourself," he said.

A tiny muscle on the inside of Phoebe's trigger finger twitched, sending a chill down her spine. "Where is my husband?" she demanded.

"I presume that would be Duncan," replied the man, stepping into the dust-flecked light streaming through a porthole high overhead.

There was something familiar in his manner and his build, though Phoebe was certain she'd never seen him before. In his scuffed boots, dove gray breeches, linen shirt, and tailored waistcoat, he looked more like a gentleman farmer than a pirate, and nothing at all like a British sailor.

Phoebe swallowed the hard lump that rose in her throat. "Don't come any closer," she warned.

The intruder remained where he was, just over the threshold, but he was clearly not intimidated. No, he was attempting to mollify her, and Phoebe would have been furious if every organ in her body hadn't already turned to water.

He grinned, and another stab of familiarity shot through Phoebe, nearly painful in its intensity. She guessed his identity a fraction of a moment before he told her who he was.

"Lucas Rourke," he said, extending one gentlemanly hand. "Duncan's elder brother."

Phoebe retreated a step, the weapon trained on Rourke's midsection. "You're a Tory," she said.

"I regard myself as a patriot," he replied in a smooth, reasonable voice. He shrugged. "It's a matter of definition."

"Where is Duncan? Did you kill him?"

"Kill my own brother, misguided though I think he is?" Lucas Rourke rolled his eyes, which, unlike Duncan's, were brown. Their shape and expression were remarkably similar all the same. "I admit I've been tempted on occasion, but I wouldn't actually follow through. Our mother would be furious."

Phoebe glanced uncertainly over his shoulder, for the door still stood open behind him, hoping for some sign of her husband. All she saw were more strangers, broad-shouldered men like Lucas.

"Tell me where Duncan is, or I'll shoot you," she said. "I swear it."

Lucas smiled reassuringly. Like his brother, he had a set of dazzling teeth. "No need of that, Mistress Rourke," he said. "Duncan is fine, except for a few bruises." He looked back at the men crowding the narrow passageway outside. "Bring him in. Gently."

A small scuffle ensued, and then Duncan, speechless with rage, hands bound behind him, was shoved into the chamber.

Lucas looked at him with a sort of disapproving affection and clucked his tongue. "Brave to a fault," he muttered. "It would behoove you, Brother, to learn prudence. Even cowardice has its place."

Phoebe lowered the pistol, staring at Duncan, wanting to rush forward to set him free, knowing the effort would be useless and perhaps even fatal. "Shall I shoot him?" she asked her husband.

Duncan shocked her with a low, hoarse burst of laughter. "God, what a wonder you are. No, love—you mustn't deprive me of the aspirations that sustain me."

She glanced uncertainly at Lucas, who stood

with his arms folded, unruffled and unperturbed. He surely hadn't taken part in the messy conquest of the *Francesca*—no doubt he was strictly management. "But . . .?"

"My brother will do you no harm, Phoebe," Duncan said gently. "For all that he's a bungler and an idiot, with a head like the top of a newel post and all the political sophistication of the scarecrow in our mother's garden, I've never known him to rob, rape, or pillage."

Lucas crossed the small cabin and took the pistol from Phoebe's hands. She was light-headed with confusion and fear.

"Sit down," Lucas said, taking her arm and squiring her to the bed. When she was settled nervously on its edge, his gaze skirting his furious brother, he spoke to his henchmen. "Leave us."

One lingered. "Shall we set a course for Charles Town, sir?"

"You know the plan," Lucas replied wearily, with a small sigh.

Phoebe's heart had risen to her throat, where it thrummed softly, like a moth imprisoned in a walnut shell. Duncan faced his brother, his stance every bit as arrogant as if he were still free and in control.

"What happened?" Phoebe asked, when neither man spoke. Her eyes were on Lucas. "Was it *your* ship that overtook us?"

"Not exactly," Lucas answered, with a certain reluctance. He had closed and latched the cabin door, and now he leaned against it. Duncan was glaring at him, and he met his brother's gaze squarely, solemnly, while he made his reply. "We came upon the battle—which you were losing, may I say—and interceded. The offenders were routed."

A muscle leaped in Duncan's jawline, and he strained at his bonds. He must have known it was hopeless—even Phoebe could see that—but he couldn't help the attempt, being who he was. "All right," he said, in a tone wicked for its chamois softness. "You saved me, Lucas. You saved us all. Now if you will be so kind as to untie my hands, get back on your own ship, and leave me to my business . . ."

"Sorry," Lucas said with a note of what sounded like genuine regret. "I have orders from our esteemed father to bring you to Charles Town, forthwith."

"We were on our way there anyway," Phoebe pointed out, brightening.

The look Duncan hurled in her direction caused her to slump slightly.

"Is that true, Duncan?" Lucas asked, moving to stand close to his brother. Closer, in fact, than Phoebe would have done, considering Duncan's current state of mind. "Were you going home?"

Duncan stared at him in stubborn silence for a long time, but finally, in low, grating words that Phoebe had to strain to hear, he replied. "Not in the way you mean. Phillippa wrote that Father had been unwell. I meant to look in on him, like a dutiful son, and leave again."

Phoebe thought she saw Lucas's broad shoulders sag slightly, but she couldn't read him because his face was turned from view. "I dare say he'll be glad to see you," he said. "It would have been better, of course, if you'd come of your own accord."

"I tried," Duncan growled. A vein in his forehead was pulsing, an indication that the new stillness in his manner was not to be trusted. "How is Father?"

"He's old," Lucas said forthrightly. "And he's fragile. The war is hard on him, and having you turn traitor is worse still."

"Beware of words such as 'traitor,'" Duncan warned softly. "They're as deadly as an overheated cannon."

Lucas sighed and turned away from Duncan to plunder a cabinet. He found liquor and a glass and poured a drink, which he offered to Phoebe.

She could certainly have used it, but she shook her head, mindful of the baby. Her brother-in-law favored her with a cordial nod and a slight bow and turned again toward Duncan, raising the whiskey to his lips as he regarded his brother.

"I suppose there's nothing for it but to let you go," he said, as though it were the last thing in the world he wanted to do. He uttered yet another lengthy sigh. "Great Apollo, it will be like letting a copperhead out of a tobacco pouch."

"True," Duncan said. His whisper had a bite to it, like the sound of a whip drawn back swiftly.

Phoebe, somewhat recovered by then, rose to

232

her feet in the interest of peace and went to stand between the two men.

"The solution is simple," she said. "Lucas, you will take your crew and leave the *Francesca* immediately. Once you've gone, I'll set Duncan free. That way, no one will get hurt."

Lucas chuckled, though he was looking at Duncan and not her. "That's a fine idea," he said. "Would that I could trust my brother to proceed to Charles Town as planned, but I can't. Therefore—"

"But we are going there," Phoebe said quickly. She turned, gazing up into Duncan's eyes. "We are, aren't we?"

"Of course," Duncan drawled, returning his brother's stare. "How else will I have my revenge?"

Now it was Phoebe who sighed. "Can't we forget that? Your father has been sick, Duncan. Lucas was only trying to make sure you visited him. And as for you, Lucas Rourke—your methods of persuasion leave something to be desired."

"I am properly chagrined," Lucas said, the splayed fingers of one well-shaped but calloused hand spread fanlike over his heart. "I'm sure you will concede, however, that something more than common persuasion is required when dealing with the likes of my brother."

Phoebe put her hands on her hips and assessed Duncan ruefully. "There's no possible way I can deny that," she admitted.

"Stand back," Lucas told her in a cordial tone, taking a small knife with a jet handle from a sheath inside his coat. "I'm about to open the tobacco sack."

Duncan stood ominously still while his brother severed the rawhide ties that bound his wrists together. Phoebe watched with wide eyes, her breath stopping up her lungs, as an almost imperceptible ripple moved through Duncan's powerful frame, reminding her of a panther stretching outside the door of its cage.

He rubbed one wrist and then the other, but the cabin fairly vibrated with the undercurrent of his anger.

"Get off my ship," he told his brother, just when Phoebe could bear the suspense no longer. "I will come to Charles Town in my own good time, and not as your prisoner."

Lucas narrowed his eyes and rubbed his square chin with one hand. "Try to see this from my point of view," he said. "And Father's. If we detain you in our custody until after the rebellion has been put down, you won't be shot during one of your infernal raids or hanged by the King's men. Our aim, quite simply, is to save your life."

Duncan ran a forearm across his mouth. "Yes. I would live to a great age, no doubt, hating the pair of you with every breath I drew."

Phoebe saw the logic behind Lucas's and their father's plan, even though she knew it would never work. Cautiously, she laid a hand on Duncan's arm. "You're both wrong," she said quietly, turning her gaze to Lucas's face. "The one thing Duncan treasures most is his freedom. You might just as well cut his throat, right here and now, as lock him up somewhere."

Lucas's nod was so slight as to be almost imperceptible. "Yes," he said gruffly, "I suppose that's true." He looked into Duncan's blue eyes, which were still blazing with suppressed outrage. "Do I have your word that you'll come home and speak to Father straightaway?"

"Yes," Duncan said evenly. "My wife will be my bond."

Phoebe frowned. "What?"

Duncan took her elbow and gave her a subtle push toward his brother. "I needn't tell you how many perils lie between here and the Carolina coast," he told Lucas. "Phoebe will be safer with you."

She opened her mouth to protest, only to have Duncan press an index finger against her lips.

"No arguments," he said. "Please."

Phoebe muttered a swearword. She wanted to stay with Duncan, wanted that more than anything, but she knew he was right. Lucas's ship was obviously well armed, and that alone would deter most pirates. The British navy wouldn't bother him because he was known for his loyalty to the Crown.

"What about you?"

Duncan smiled, smoothing her hair with a light gesture of one hand. "I'll be along, Phoebe," he promised. "Just as soon as I've recovered my dignity."

Tears burned behind Phoebe's eyes, but she refused to let them fall. The awareness that she might never see Duncan again was bitterly poignant; she felt it in every tuck and corner of her heart. She laid one hand on his chest. "I love you," she whispered.

He bent his head, touched her mouth with his. Then, straightening again, he gave her a long, searching look. "Be careful," he said. With that, he was gone, and the separation, for Phoebe, was a wrenching one.

She left Duncan's ship for Lucas's a few minutes later, with her trunkful of secondhand belongings, and stood at the rail, staring back at the *Francesca*, trying her best to be brave, as the *Charles Town Princess* sailed on a tide crimson with sunset. The *Francesca* followed them slowly out of the cove.

Phoebe remained where she was until darkness fell. They were on the open sea by that time, and Lucas pried her gently from her post and squired her into a brightly lit dining room. Luscious smells made the air savory, and Phoebe's stomach rumbled.

Servants bustled about as Lucas seated his sister-in-law at the largest table and then took the chair across from hers.

"I won't pretend I approve of how you've handled things up to now," Phoebe said straight out.

Lucas smiled, shook out a linen napkin, and spread it in his lap. "If you're referring to Duncan's wounded pride, I would advise you not to fret. My brother is the most resilient man I have ever known and is at this moment, I assure, laying plans to repay me for my transgression."

A black man in pristine white clothes brought a platter of roasted meat to the table, followed by a bowl of mashed potatoes, green beans boiled with bacon and onion, and a carafe of wine.

Phoebe was glad her principles did not require her to forego the meal; the events of the afternoon and evening had taken a toll on her system, and she was starving. She helped herself to vegetables, a heap of potatoes, and a thin slice of meat. She was well aware, all along, that she should have waited for her "host" to serve her. Etiquette, the eighteenth-century variety or otherwise, was beyond her.

"This had better not be a trick," she warned, after swallowing a mouthful of mashed potatoes.

Apparently reflecting on her remark, Lucas filled his wineglass and signaled the waiter, who hovered a few yards away. Only moments passed before the steward appeared with water for Phoebe.

"Thank you," she said, and the man inclined his head slightly in acknowledgment before walking away. When he was gone, she leaned forward and spoke in a lowered voice. "Is that poor man a slave?"

"I don't know," Lucas replied. "He came with the vessel."

"This isn't your ship?"

"Of course not." He began cutting a slice of roasted meat into small, precise pieces. "I'm a planter. Duncan is the only seagoing man in our family. And the Rourkes do not keep slaves."

"How did you know where to find him? Duncan, I mean?"

"I didn't," Lucas answered in his own good time. He was obviously one of those people who like to have everything on their plate arranged just so before they start eating. Phoebe was already half finished and thinking about seconds. "It was a happy accident—for all of us, as it happens—although I knew, of course, that Duncan frequents this part of the Caribbean Sea."

Phoebe laid down her fork, her appetite forgotten. "Someone told you."

Lucas gave her a rueful look. "No one needed to do that," he said. "My brother is the object of a dozen warrants. The British want to hang him."

The reminder made Phoebe's stomach churn. "How can you possibly take their side against Duncan," she asked, "when you know what the English did to him before?"

He pushed his plate away. "He told you about that, did he?"

Phoebe nodded.

"It's true that Sheffield's actions were unconscionable," Lucas admitted, and the pallor beneath his tan told Phoebe he was remembering the day Duncan had been whipped in vivid, bloody detail. "On the other hand, Duncan knew better, even at fifteen, than to"—he paused to clear his throat, and a faint blush pulsed on his cheekbones—"than to be—er—intimate with another man's wife. Few things wound more deeply than that."

"He was fifteen years old," Phoebe insisted. "He might have been grounded, or sent to bed without his supper. But *whipped?* An animal shouldn't be treated that way, let alone a human being!"

Lucas had gotten snagged further back. "'- Grounded'? What the deuce does that mean? It sounds absolutely brutal."

Phoebe had almost forgotten, by that point, that she was a time traveler, and had lived a very different life in another world. "Never mind," she said.

"No, please—I'm curious. Tell me."

She bit her lower lip. A thorough explanation would involve things she didn't really want to go into—she'd have to tell him about airplanes, and how the term "grounded" meant they couldn't fly, for one reason or another. Even if she managed to steer Lucas past the concept of flying machines, he still might not see the correlation between keeping planes on the ground and making a kid stay home as punishment.

"It's a colloquialism," she said lamely, because

she knew Lucas would insist on some definition. "Meaning Duncan couldn't go out for a few weeks or so."

Lucas frowned. "That would hardly have served as chastisement," he replied. "He'd have slept and read, indulged his penchant for music, and bedeviled the servants the whole while."

"You think he deserved to be whipped?"

Lucas paled again. "Of course not!"

"Then what?"

"I think," Lucas said briskly, setting his napkin on the table, "that Duncan should have stayed away from Francesca Sheffield in the first place."

It was an impasse, a Mexican standoff. Phoebe sighed and looked forlornly at her food. It had tasted so good, but now she felt as though someone had wadded a beach towel and stuffed it down her throat.

"What happened to your hair?" Lucas asked, after a long and awkward silence.

Phoebe considered several replies, excluding the truth, of course, and decided on a convoluted version of the O. Henry yarn. "My dear old mother was dying. I sold my gossamer tresses to pay for her medicine."

Lucas stared at her for a moment, obviously confounded, and then rose from his chair. "Come, Mistress Rourke," he said. "You are obviously exhausted. I'll see you safely to your cabin."

Phoebe balked. Duncan had said she'd be safe

with Lucas, but he might not know his brother as well as he thought he did.

Lucas smiled, linked her arm with his, and patted the back of her hand. "I am a gentleman," he said. "Even if I weren't, I could not forget for a moment that you are my brother's wife."

She felt a blush warm her face. Lucas was telling the truth; she knew that, though she couldn't have explained the instinct in concrete terms.

He escorted her to her cabin, which was comfortable and private, equipped with a washstand, towels, and a soft berth with crisp linen sheets, and waited properly on the threshold while she surveyed her quarters.

"Get your rest, Phoebe," he said. "And don't worry overmuch about Duncan's coming to Charles Town. He's remarkably good at evading the British."

"Yes," Phoebe replied evenly. "As long as he's not betrayed by someone he trusts, I'm sure he'll be quite safe."

Lucas colored slightly. "Do you think I'm leading Duncan to his doom, the way a Judas goat leads sheep to the slaughter?"

"Are you?"

"No." Although Lucas spoke the word softly, it was as if he'd shouted. "No," he said again, more moderately, straightening his waistcoat. "Despite our political differences, my dear, I love my brother. I would sooner forfeit my own life than see him perish." He paused and inclined

241

his head, somewhat stiffly, by way of a farewell bow. "Good night," he said and closed the door.

Phoebe went over and threw the heavy brass bolt before turning away. After undressing, using the chamberpot, and finally giving herself a splash-bath at the basin, she donned a nightgown, blew out the oil lamp on the wall, and crawled into bed. Her concern for Duncan ached in her stomach and throat and behind her eyes, like some kind of psychological plague. Despite Lucas's assurances that her husband would be safe in Charles Town, the fact remained that the city had fallen to the British General Clinton in May. The place was crawling with redcoats, any one of whom would be thrilled to claim the bounty for collaring the notorious Duncan Rourke.

For the hundredth time, Phoebe wished she'd read all of that worn-out copy of Duncan's biography, instead of just skimming. If she had, she would have known whether or not he would be captured in Charles Town—and how long he was destined to live. Among other things.

She shivered although the tropical night was balmy. It was better going into the Charles Town situation blind; to know the exact date and means of Duncan's death would be unbearable.

Tears threatened again, but Phoebe pressed her fingertips under her eyes until the urge passed. Maybe she was doing all this worrying for nothing, she thought, with an inelegant sniffle.

He'd palmed her off on his family; maybe he had no intention of going to Charles Town . . .

She shook her head, unable to deceive herself. Duncan hadn't changed his mind about seeing his father; she'd seen the look in his eyes earlier, aboard the *Francesca*, when Lucas had said the man was old and fragile. No, whatever the cost, her husband was bound, as surely as she was, for his family's plantation on the Charles River.

Duncan stood at the rail of the *Francesca*, watching his brother's hired ship sunder the spill of moonlight quavering on the dark waters. His wrists still burned a little, and he was aware of a hundred bruises in as many parts of his anatomy, but the worst injury had been to his pride. Being a pragmatic man, however, he had already dealt with his feelings about nearly losing his ship to a band of pirates and then being rescued by Lucas.

For now, Phoebe was safe, that was the important thing. The only thing.

He smiled. She was bound to liven things up, once she reached the family plantation.

Duncan rested his elbow on the rail and rubbed his chin. He doubted he would ever forget how Phoebe had looked, standing in the center of his cabin with that ancient pistol in her hands, holding her ground to the last. It was God's own blessing that she hadn't known how to load the damned things; she probably would have shot off one of her feet and sunk the *Francesca* in the bargain.

243

He frowned. Perhaps it was time to give the ship a new name.

In the next moment, Duncan brought himself up short. None of his men had been killed in that day's skirmish, but several were wounded, and he had no business standing about on deck thinking fanciful thoughts. He was asking his crew to sail into the mouth of the yawning jaws of the lion by taking them to Charles Town, and that was a matter for sober reflection. His fingers itching for the strings of a fiddle or a lute, the keys of a pianoforte or a harpsichord, Duncan turned from the sight of the retreating *Charles Town Princess* and set his mind on work.

The next morning, Phoebe used the last of the water in the pitcher on her washstand to make herself presentable, put on fresh clothes from her trunk, and hurried out of the cabin, eager for the sight of the *Francesca*. The ship was a magnificent, stirring sight, and there was always the chance that she might catch a glimpse of Duncan.

But there was no sign of the other ship. The *Charles Town Princess* was alone.

Lucas must have been watching for her, because he appeared almost immediately, and the look of amused compassion on his face told her he had a pretty good idea what she was thinking. And feeling.

"The sea has different routes," he said, "just like the land. You'll see Duncan when we make port, I promise."

"What makes you so sure?" Phoebe asked in a small voice, still staring at the empty horizon. She felt a little queasy, and she was reconsidering last night's theory that Duncan might have hit the road, now that he'd discharged his "responsibilities" to the woman he'd so rashly married.

"It's quite simple," Lucas replied. "He can't live without you."

12

They were a full eight days at sea, during which time Phoebe failed to catch so much as a glimpse of the *Francesca*, though she spent hours pacing the decks. Despite Lucas's constant reassurances, she was desperately worried about Duncan.

Charles Town Harbor was splashed with sunlight and crowded with British warships on the morning of their arrival. There were also American clippers, obviously confiscated, with their sails folded and redcoats patrolling at their rails. The city itself, to Phoebe's twentieth-century eyes, looked like a theme park, except for various real-life touches, like sweating slaves carrying barrels and cobbled streets dotted with horse dung.

The *Charles Town Princess* tied up to a long jetty, and a contingent of British officials came out to greet the ship as her passengers began to disembark.

Phoebe's blood froze at the sight of them. Lucas might be on their side, politically at least, but they were bound to ask questions. They could not help noticing her short hair—she wished she'd thought to cover it, using a curtain or even a lace tablecloth for a mantle—and if they connected her with Duncan, she would be arrested.

"Be silent and keep your eyes lowered," Lucas rasped, though he was smiling broadly at the approaching Brits. "I'll handle this."

Phoebe stared at the warped boards of the jetty, her heart thudding in her ears. She didn't need to remind herself that these were people who wanted to hang her husband; the thought was branded on her mind.

"Hello, Rourke," one of the men said, in a blustery voice. Through her lashes, Phoebe saw a heavyset fellow with snow white hair, bright blue eyes, and a ruddy complexion. He looked like someone's grandfather and probably was.

"Major Stone," Lucas replied smoothly. "To what do I owe the honor of a personal welcome?"

Stone's chuckle turned into a cough, and several moments had passed before he was ready to frame an answer. "Damn tobacco," he said. "Got to give it up."

Lucas said nothing, and Phoebe remained silent as commanded, though she couldn't help shifting nervously from one foot to the other.

Major Stone coughed again, then went on in a booming, jovial voice Phoebe suspected was quite typical of him. "Can't be too careful," he said. "Thought you might have seen that brother of yours in your travels."

Phoebe's heart stopped, then started again with a painful lurch. Here, however unexpected, was the moment of truth. For all his pretty promises, Lucas was a loyal subject of His Majesty, King George III, and he might well betray both Phoebe and Duncan.

"Duncan is lost to us, I'm afraid," Lucas said sadly. "Would that it were not so, but, alas, he has strayed from the fold, never to return."

Phoebe let out her breath. Lucas had kept his word, but there was still a very real possibility that he'd arouse suspicion with his bad acting.

"And who might the young lady be?" Major Stone asked with cordial curiosity.

Phoebe very nearly looked up and met his gaze, which might have been disastrous, given the fact that her emotions were usually plainly visible in her eyes.

"Her name is Phoebe," Lucas explained, taking a rather rough hold on his sister-in-law's upper arm. "She's a serving wench—a mute, as it happens." He ruffled her hair indulgently, as if she were a pet, and Phoebe seethed. "Suffered a head wound once, and they had to shave her like a monk."

"Looks to be a sturdy creature," Major Stone

commented, as though discussing a prize heifer. "Where did you say you picked her up?"

"I got the chit from another planter, down the coast a way. He owed me for four suckling pigs and a dray horse."

Phoebe felt her face turning crimson.

"A good bargain," thundered Major Stone. There was a short, resonant pause. "You'll send word, won't you, Rourke, if you hear from your brother?"

"Of course," Lucas said. "But don't stay up nights waiting. Duncan is too crafty by half to show his face around Charles Town."

Major Stone made a *harrumph* sound, then signaled his men to precede him back along the wharf to the shore. He hesitated, and Phoebe felt his eyes on her, and although she knew the man wasn't evil, she felt a chill of fear all the same. That was the trouble with wars: there were good people on both sides, doing what they saw as their duty, believing what they had been born and raised to believe.

"Mind you keep the wench close by whilst in Charles Town," the British officer said. "My men are randy, and while they'll leave the ladies alone or feel the bite of the lash, they see these poor wretches as fair game."

Phoebe's heart was now pounding so hard that she thought surely both Lucas and the major could hear it. Her opinion of the lash as punishment notwithstanding, she was keenly annoyed that only "ladies" were protected; bondswomen, slaves, and prostitutes were on their own.

Lucas's grip tightened, as though he sensed Phoebe's rising ire. "Don't worry, Basil," he said, in the soothing tones of an old friend. "I look after what belongs to me and mine."

Phoebe, again peering through her lashes, saw Major Stone hesitate and then turn and follow his men down the jetty.

"He suspects something," she murmured. Lucas was hustling her along in the major's wake. He retained his hold on her arm, though there was a subtle difference; before, his hold had been protective. Now, he was restraining her, probably fearing that she would do something stupid.

"One can suspect a great many things," Lucas remarked, "and never come up with the required proof. Now hold your tongue—you're supposed to be mute, remember?"

They reached the foot of the jetty, a crowded, noisy place, full of strong smells. Phoebe double-stepped to keep pace with her brother-in-law's long strides, and took in the scene in sidelong glances. For all the dangers, it was a fascinating experience walking through revolutionary Charles Town, and she was pierced by a sudden, poignant wish that Professor Benning could see the place. He was probably the one person she knew in the twentieth century who would have given any credence at all to her account of this amazing odyssey.

A fine black carriage waited on the low, cluttered shore, among wagons and carts and pack mules. A man in footman's livery climbed down from the high box to tip his three-cornered hat in greeting. He was dark-skinned, with a ready smile and an abundance of bristly white hair, and Phoebe liked him immediately.

"Hello, Enoch," Lucas said.

Enoch inclined his head slightly. "Suh," he responded. He opened the carriage door and produced a set of wooden steps from inside, placing them carefully on the ground and testing them with a motion of one hand before gesturing for Lucas to enter.

Much to Phoebe's surprise, Lucas mounted the stairs, climbed into the vehicle, his sizable frame causing it to rock on its springs as he settled himself, and left her standing outside.

Biting her lower lip to keep from muttering, and thus giving away the fact that she wasn't a mute bondswoman collected as payment for pigs and a plow horse, Phoebe followed under her own power. Enoch hovered but did not offer his assistance.

Perched on the hard, narrow seat across from Lucas, Phoebe folded her arms and waited until the carriage was in motion before speaking. "That was very rude," she remarked stiffly.

"You are supposed to be a bound servant," Lucas reminded her, tugging at the fancy cuffs of his expensive shirt. "Basil Stone is a shrewd fellow, as you've clearly deduced for yourself, and he might well have been watching to see if I treated you as such."

Phoebe's irritation subsided a little. "We're certainly not out of the proverbial woods," she said. "Every man on the *Charles Town Princess* knows you didn't get me from another planter. They saw me board from the *Francesca*—"

Lucas stopped her with a wave of one hand. "Most of them have been with our family, in one capacity or another, since before Duncan was born. They're not going to hand him over to the hangman any more than I am."

"You have an unwarranted confidence in human nature," Phoebe observed.

"And you are a cynic," Lucas answered, not unkindly. He assessed her hand-me-down clothes with a pensive expression. "I'm afraid you suit the role of a serving wench only too well. No need to worry, though—Mother and Phillippa will see that you're properly turned out."

The carriage rolled and shifted over the cobblestones, and Phoebe was developing a case of motion sickness. It seemed ironic, given the fact that she'd never had any such trouble on the ocean. "If I'm to be presented to the world as a bond servant, whyever should I be 'properly turned out'?"

Lucas sighed. "You will simply have to live two lives—one in Charles Town, and one in the country. Our plantation is a considerable distance from the city, after all, and Major Stone is hardly a regular guest in our home."

251

Phoebe groaned as a wave of nausea swept over her, leaving her trembling and clammy when it passed.

Lucas reached across and took her hand, his aristocratic face a study in concern. "Are you all right?" he demanded.

She sighed, rested her head against the back of the seat, and closed her eyes. "We bondswomen are a hardy lot," she said. "Just throw me a crust of bread once in a while and let me sleep on the hearth on cold nights, and I'll probably live to be, oh, thirty-five."

For a moment, Lucas was silent. Then he realized she was joking and chuckled.

The plantation was indeed a long way outside Charles Town. After an hour's travel, they left the carriage behind and boarded a boat to travel miles down the Charles River. It was probably well after midnight when Lucas awakened Phoebe, who was curled into an awkward heap on a plank bench, to tell her they had reached their destination at last.

There was another carriage waiting at the pier.

Twenty minutes later, sleepy, cramped, and hopelessly rumpled, Phoebe disembarked from the second coach. It was dark, but the Rourke house was visible in the bright moonlight, a palatial structure with pillars and enormous arched windows trimmed in fine stonework. Two women in cloaks hurried out the front door and down the walk, both carrying lanterns.

"Where is he?" the younger one demanded of Lucas. "Where is Duncan?"

She was beautiful, dark-haired like her brothers, but her eyes were charcoal gray and trimmed in thick lashes.

"Hush, Phillippa," the older woman interceded. "Duncan could hardly come to us so openly, with half the British army looking for him."

Lucas cleared his throat. "Mother, Phillippa— may I introduce Phoebe? She is Duncan's wife."

Phillippa laid one hand to her chest, which was hidden beneath the voluminous folds of the cloak. "*Wife?*" she echoed in plain disbelief.

Phoebe was all set to dislike Duncan's sister and braced for the inevitable question about her hair, when a dazzling smile suddenly lighted Phillippa's features.

"But that's wonderful," she cried. "Perhaps he'll settle down now and behave himself."

Mrs. Rourke, Duncan's mother, with her translucent skin and Grecian-goddess features, was as delicate as a madonna. She smiled sweetly and took Phoebe's arm, linking it with hers. "Come, Phoebe—you must be exhausted. And hungry. We'll get you settled into your room for a good rest."

Phillippa hurried after them as Mrs. Rourke ushered Phoebe toward the front door. Lucas remained behind, probably to help Enoch put the team and carriage away.

"But I have a thousand questions to ask!"

protested the girl. Phoebe figured she was around eighteen.

"You may save them," said Mrs. Rourke, gently but firmly, "for the morning."

The task was evidently beyond Phillippa's powers. "Where is Duncan?" she chimed, following them through the darkened house and up one side of a beautiful double stairway. "Is he all right? Did you wear a lace wedding dress? What happened to your hair?"

Mrs. Rourke sighed. "Good heavens, Phillippa, sometimes you are a trial. Go and wake Marva, please. Ask her to bring some of that pheasant we had for supper."

"No, please," Phoebe protested quickly. "Don't disturb anyone. I'll be fine until morning."

"Nonsense," said Mrs. Rourke. "You are dreadfully pale."

With obvious reluctance, Phillippa turned and went back down the stairs, in search of the unfortunate Marva. Phoebe, meanwhile, allowed herself to be squired into a large chamber, its furniture reduced to bulky shapes in the darkness.

Mrs. Rourke set her lantern on a table and proceeded to light several candles from its flame. Phoebe looked with gratitude upon a large feather bed, longing to lose herself in its softness and slumber like Sleeping Beauty, until Duncan came and awakened her with a kiss.

"You poor dear," Mrs. Rourke said. "I vow,

you are nigh unto swooning, even now. Come here, and I'll help you out of that dress."

The lady was obviously of gentle breeding. She had been roused from her bed in the middle of the night, confronted with a strange, short-haired woman in a shipwreck victim's hand-me-downs, and promptly informed that she'd just inherited a daughter-in-law. She was remarkably unruffled, considering all that.

"You are very kind," Phoebe said, almost croaking the words.

Mrs. Rourke took a nightgown from a massive chest and held it out to Phoebe. "You are a member of our family," she replied, gently and at length. She helped Phoebe out of her dress and into the nightie, as though she were a weary child. "I'll bring water and a basin from my room," she said and went out.

After Phoebe had washed, and eaten the pheasant and buttered bread Phillippa brought to her, she settled back against a mountain of feather pillows and sighed, wearily content. She closed her eyes and did not open them again until late the next afternoon.

Phillippa was perched in the windowseat, sketching. She wore a gray dress, and her gleaming black hair was wound into a heavy chignon. "I thought you were going to sleep forever," she announced. "Are you hungry?"

Phoebe's first priority was the chamberpot, though of course she couldn't be quite so blunt as to say so. "I—"

"Or maybe you'd like to have your bath first? Mother's found some lovely clothes for you to wear, until we can send for our dressmaker. Shall I go and ask Marva and Easter-Sue to fill the tub?"

A bath sounded heavenly, and the errand would buy Phoebe the privacy she needed to attend to an urgent and basic need. "That would be wonderful," she said. "The bath, I mean."

When Phillippa returned some twenty minutes later, she was accompanied by her mother. Mrs. Rourke was even more beautiful in the light of day, and she fairly exuded serenity. Phoebe wondered how that was possible, when there was a war on and one of her sons was, for all intents and purposes, a wanted man.

"Have you rested well?" Mrs. Rourke asked, and her smile seemed genuine, as well as gracious. She had yet to really pursue the subject of Duncan's whereabouts, though she'd had ample opportunity the night before, and Phoebe wondered if the woman was a model of restraint or simply disinterested. Of course, she had probably spoken with Lucas.

"Yes," Phoebe responded, sitting up in bed. "I feel like a new woman."

Phillippa was staring at her hair and frowning. Her expression was curious, rather than hostile, and Phoebe took pity on her. She formulated what she hoped was a credible story, and she was ready to try it out.

"I was in a nunnery for several months," she

256

confided, warming to the outrageous tale even as it spun like gossamer from her tongue. "I wanted to be a nun, but, well, in the end I found out I didn't have the calling."

Phillippa's eyes were the size of portholes. "Duncan *married a nun*?" she gasped. Then she smiled, and it was blinding, luminous with delight. "Great Zeus and Apollo, that's superb!"

"Hush!" Mrs. Rourke said, more sharply than she had the night before. "How many times have I told you that a lady does not swear?"

Phillippa ducked her head, but her eyes were glowing with mischief. "Sorry, Mother," she murmured, while Phoebe began to wish she'd thought up a less spectacular lie; this one was bound to get her into trouble.

Phoebe made a mental note never to say "Great Zeus and Apollo," not that there'd ever been much danger of it, and spoke demurely. "I wasn't actually a nun. I hadn't taken my vows, you see."

"There is no need to explain," Mrs. Rourke pointed out, as a black woman, probably Marva, entered with a tray. Behind her clattered two maids, lugging a huge copper bathtub.

Marva, who was thin and wiry and had an air of innate dignity, set the food tray gently in Phoebe's lap. "Poor little thing," she said, with a cluck of her tongue. Then she turned, shaking her gray head, and scooted out of the room. Mrs. Rourke and Phillippa left, too, after seeing that the bathtub had been positioned correctly on the hearth.

While one last maid puttered with the fire, Phoebe consumed a planter's breakfast of sausage, hotcakes dripping syrup, eggs, and fried potatoes—fat grams be damned. She was hungry, and she needed her strength.

When she'd finished eating, the tray was whisked away, and people began arriving with buckets of steaming water, which were poured into the waiting tub. Phoebe was naked and stepping into her bath practically the instant the door closed on the last servant.

It was bliss. Phoebe sank to her chin, feeling decadent. A nice hot soak could make up for a multitude of small adversities, she thought, smiling. Between this and the meal she'd just consumed, she'd be her old self in no time.

For nearly an hour, by the mantel clock, Phoebe luxuriated. Then, because the water had grown chilly, she scrubbed herself, from head to foot, with a cloth and the sweet-smelling soap that had been left for her by one of the maids. She was out of the tub and bundled in a towel as big and soft as a blanket, when a soft tap sounded at the door.

"Phoebe?" a familiar female voice called. "It's me, Phillippa."

"Come in," Phoebe called, with a rueful half-smile. It was question time.

Phillippa entered, carrying an armful of fluffy, eyelet-trimmed garments. "I've brought you drawers, a camisole, and petticoats. Mother's had a cornflower gown brushed and aired, and Marva will bring it up in a few minutes. It will compliment your blue eyes."

Phoebe accepted the linen undergarments gratefully and stepped behind an ornately carved and painted screen to put them on. A part of her was waiting for Duncan to arrive, listening for his footstep in the hallway outside the door of her room.

"I'm so glad you've come to Troy," Phillippa said.

"Troy?" Phoebe purposely spoke in a bright, happy voice, although she was beginning to be afraid. Perhaps the British had captured her husband, perhaps he had already been hanged for a criminal.

"It's the name of our plantation," Phillippa said happily. "I'm not surprised that Duncan didn't tell you. He thinks it's silly, and so does Lucas."

Phoebe came out from behind the screen, smiling. "What do you think?"

Phillippa looked mildly surprised by the question. "That it's wonderfully poetic," she confessed. She was seated on a hassock, near the dying fire, her fingers interlaced. "My grandmother, Jenny Polander Rourke, chose the title when she came here to marry my grandfather, some sixty years ago. She loved the Greek classics."

"Troy" seemed an odd choice for a young

bride, given the fact that the fabled city had eventually fallen. Had that been Jenny Rourke's vision for her husband's plantation, that it would be invaded by enemies, razed to the ground, and remembered only in legend? Phoebe considered what she knew of the nation's future, and a brief uneasiness fell over her heart like the shadow of a dark angel. Even if the great house survived the remainder of the Revolution—there were four years of fighting left, if she remembered her history correctly—the Civil War was still ahead.

That was nearly a hundred years away, Phoebe reminded herself. The hormonal upheaval caused by her pregnancy, coupled with her worries about Duncan's safety, caused her to be macabre. What she needed was some fresh air and sunshine.

"Phoebe?"

Only at Phillippa's troubled prompting did Phoebe realize she'd left her end of the conversation hanging in midair while she ruminated about hormones, Duncan, and the fate of Troy. "I'm sorry," she said with a laugh. "I've been under a lot of strain lately, and I tend to be easily distracted."

Phillippa's smile was as spectacular as those of her brothers. "I should think so," she agreed. "One minute you were a nun, the next you were my brother's wife. That would be enough to distract anybody."

"Yes," Phoebe agreed with a soft smile. There was another knock at the door, and Mrs. Rourke entered, carrying the promised blue dress over one elegant arm.

"I do hope you have not been prattling," the older woman told her daughter affectionately. "Phoebe has been through enough these past weeks, I'm sure, without enduring one of your interrogations. Here—let us see if the gown suits."

Phillippa sulked a little, chin in hand, while her mother helped Phoebe into the blue dress, which fitted almost perfectly.

"It's so dull around here," the girl protested. "This wretched war has changed everything. And as soon as someone comes along that I might talk to, I'm accused of prying."

Mrs. Rourke's eyes were soft with laughter as she looked at Phoebe. "I'm afraid our Phillippa is incorrigibly inquisitive."

"I don't mind," Phoebe said, and it was true. She had to tell some lies—after all, she couldn't very well say that she'd come back in time from another century—but it was only natural for Phillippa to be curious.

As soon as Phoebe's gown had been buttoned and her unruly crop of hair had been tamed just a little with a damp brush, Phillippa fairly dragged her out of the bedroom and down the stairs. The house, seen only dimly the night before, proved to be a spacious, uncluttered place, with good paintings on the walls and Carrara marble fireplaces in several rooms. Phoebe spotted several statues, very probably Greek, that would have made a modern museum curator drool.

"I want you to meet Father," Phillippa explained, as they left the house through a set of French doors leading into a garden.

Phoebe's first sight of John Rourke, the man for whom her son would be named, if Old Woman's prophesy was correct, caused a bittersweet tug in her heart. A smaller, gray-haired composite of Duncan and Lucas, he was seated on a bench, absorbed in a leatherbound volume of *Richard III*. Instantly, Phoebe recognized his strength, but his weakness—failing health—was visible, too. At the sound of Phillippa and Phoebe's approach, he raised his eyes from the book, smiled, and stood.

"So this is Phoebe," he said in a gentle, cultivated voice.

An image of John Rourke collecting his youngest son from a British whipping post and carrying him home flashed in Phoebe's mind. She felt the color drain from her face and curtsied in a belated effort to hide it.

"Welcome to Troy," he told her, stepping forward to kiss her lightly on the cheek when she stood straight again. He held both her hands as he assessed her with warm, mirthful eyes. "For all that his politics will surely get us all hanged one day, I must confess that my second son has impeccable taste in women."

Phoebe was charmed, and some of her self-consciousness seeped away. Okay, so she had hair like a candidate for brain surgery. In time, it would grow, and she would feel less like a misfit. "Thank you," she said.

"Phoebe used to be a nun," Phillippa announced, bringing another rush of color to Phoebe's face.

A sort of skeptical humor danced in Mr. Rourke's blue eyes, along with some deep sorrow, bravely borne. "Very interesting," he said. "Tell me, my dear—when will Duncan come to collect you?"

Phillippa took a seat on another bench, listening with interest. Phoebe sat beside her, at a gesture from her father-in-law, and he returned to his bench.

"I don't know," Phoebe answered belatedly. Suddenly, she wanted to cry, though she did not indulge the desire. "It's a terrible risk, Duncan's coming here."

"Yes," Mr. Rourke replied quietly. "Duncan thrives on such escapades. I don't mind admitting that I wish he'd been blessed with a modicum of common cowardice. Just enough, mind you, to keep him from taking foolish chances."

Mrs. Rourke joined them in the garden just then and deftly steered the conversation in another direction. "Lucas has returned to Charles Town on business," she said. "I've asked him to bring our dressmaker back with him, if she's free to travel. You were quite right earlier, Phillippa." She paused to touch her daughter's shoulder. "Life here at Troy has become tedious.

A ball would be just the thing to raise our spirits, as well as those of our neighbors.''

Phoebe's smile faltered on her mouth, but she kept it from slipping away. Duncan was bound to arrive soon, and a house full of guests would present a very real danger to him.

"Do you think that's wise, Margaret?" Mr. Rourke asked. "Many of our friends are members of the King's army. We can hardly exclude them from the festivities."

"Of course we can't," Margaret agreed. "What better way to allay suspicion, though, than to invite all our friends for a celebration? Ours is a sizable holding, Mr. Rourke. There are countless places to hide."

Phoebe didn't volunteer an opinion; she was too confused.

Phillippa had no such problem. "It's a grand idea," she said cheerfully, beaming at her mother. "May I have a new gown? A lavender one, with lace trim?"

"We are at war," Mr. Rourke reminded his daughter, his tone carrying a gentle rebuke. His kindly gaze shifted smoothly to his wife's exquisite, ageless face. "It would behoove you to remember that as well, my dear."

"I haven't forgotten," Margaret said, undaunted, sitting down on the bench beside her husband and opening an ivory fan with a slight, graceful flick of one wrist. "We shall have simple gowns made," she added, no doubt for Phillippa's benefit. "Do give the idea serious consideration, Mr. Rourke. We could have dancing, and surely we can spare one or two hogs for roasting?"

Mr. Rourke—Phoebe thought it was romantic that Margaret addressed her husband in that formal way—sighed heavily. "We might as well cook that old boar before either the King's army or Mr. Washington's appropriates him for rations."

As easily as that, it was decided. There was to be a party at Troy. Not just an afternoon affair, either—this gathering would last for days, with guests traveling long distances to attend.

Phoebe and Phillippa were appointed to draft the invitations that very evening, and neither objected. Phillippa was delighted at the prospect of a festivity, and Phoebe was simply grateful to have something to occupy her mind. If left to her own devices, she would have fretted herself into a dither, worrying that Duncan wouldn't show up and, at the same time, that he would.

There was no sign of him that night.

Lucas returned in the morning, bringing a weary dressmaker and a number of bolts of fabric with him, and was immediately dispatched to Charles Town again, with a manservant, to deliver invitations. John Rourke himself carried the others to neighboring plantations, while Phoebe, Phillippa, and Margaret busied themselves planning decorations and menus.

The dressmaker, who spoke French even though she appeared to understand English very well, concerned Phoebe and took her measurements. Soon, a flurry of sewing was going on in the rear parlor. Mrs. Rourke and Phillippa were fitted as well, and there was an air of excitement throughout the great house.

As busy as she was, Phoebe was still waiting for Duncan. After three days had gone by, she was so anxious that she walked to the end of the Rourke driveway, a distance of some two miles, hoping to meet her husband along the way. Instead, she encountered her father-in-law, driving a buggy pulled by a gray horse.

He drew the vehicle to a stop beside her, and the compassion she saw in his face was nearly her undoing. Instead of speaking, John Rourke simply patted the seat beside him.

Phoebe hesitated a moment, then climbed aboard, her eyes burning with tears she refused to shed. She stared straight ahead, her hands clasped tightly in her lap. "I don't suppose it's safe to stray so far from the main house at this hour," she said.

Her father-in-law brought the reins down on the horse's back, and the buggy lurched forward. "Not in these times," he agreed quietly. "Are you unhappy here, Phoebe?"

She turned to look at him, forgetting her earlier desire to hide her emotions. "No," she said quickly. "You've all been wonderful, as though you were my family . . ."

" 'As though'? But we *are* your family, my dear."

Phoebe wanted that to be true. She'd been so lonely, for so long, and belonging was a new experience for her. Still, she couldn't afford to forget that she was a rebel, and these good people were loyalists. For all their kindness toward her, and her affection for them, the Rourkes were technically her enemies. And she was theirs.

"How can you say that, when you know I'm not a Tory?"

Rourke smiled in the gathering darkness, holding the reins loosely in his calloused hands. The horse plainly knew its way home. "You are wedded, before God and man, to my son. As Duncan's wife, you are as much my child as he is."

Phoebe could no longer hold back her tears, though she wiped them away hastily with the backs of her hands. "Duncan is a fortunate man, to be born into such a family," she said with a sniffle.

Her father-in-law patted her arm. "He is indeed a lucky rascal," he replied, with a warm smile. "Just look at his wife."

13

The preparations for the grand celebration went on, and still there was no word from Duncan.

The days were long and sultry, and Phoebe

did her best to keep busy, hiding an agony of suspense behind a ready smile and a flurry of frenetic activity. At night, she lay sleepless in her vast feather bed, obsessing, imagining all the ghastly fates that might have befallen the man she loved.

Lecturing herself on the pitfalls of codependency did no good at all. Where Duncan Rourke was concerned, it seemed, she had reached roughly the same evolutionary level as the jellyfish.

Guests began arriving ten days after the invitations had been dispersed, rattling up the long driveway in carriages and wagons and carts, mounted on horses and mules, even on foot. The mansion seemed to swell with people, and Phoebe kept a low profile, unsure how to present herself. John and Margaret Rourke seemed proud, even eager, to introduce her as their daughter-in-law, and Phillippa regaled everyone who would listen with the nun yarn Phoebe had made up to explain her haircut.

When Major Basil Stone arrived in a fancy coach, on the afternoon of the ball, Phoebe was watching from a window in the upstairs hallway and nearly suffered a heart attack. Lucas had told that august and dangerously British personage that she was a mute bond servant.

She stepped back with a gasp, the fingers of one hand spread over her thumping heart, those of the other crushing the fabric of the curtain.

Strong hands gripped her shoulders and, for

one moment of joyous terror, she thought Duncan had come to Troy at last. But she knew her husband's touch—it was imprinted on her nerve endings for all time—and no more than an instant had passed before a mingling of disappointment and relief swamped her.

It was Lucas who turned her to face him.

"There are shadows under your eyes," he said gently. He was attentive and affectionate with Phoebe, was Lucas Rourke, but in a brotherly fashion. "The strain of being my brother's bride shows plainly, I'm afraid."

Phoebe sighed and turned her head slightly, briefly, as if to glance at Major Stone through the window glass again. A tremor of dread went through her, closely followed by a flash flood of pure irritation. "Your friend is here," she said, ignoring his comment about her appearance. "The one who met us when we arrived in Charles Town. I believe you told him I was a mute bond servant."

Lucas moved past her to lift the curtain and look out. To her annoyance, he chuckled. "Ah, yes," he said. "It's Basil. Oh, what a tangled web I've woven."

Phoebe took a moment to contain her temper. It would do no good to panic. "Of course, Major Stone will hear a different story from your parents, won't he? How do you intend to explain my coming up in the world so quickly? Not to mention the spectacular way I've managed to overcome my affliction?"

He turned to look at her over one broad shoulder. There was no fear in his eyes, only amusement and a sort of tender concern. "I'll simply tell him I lied," he said, as though the answer should have been perfectly obvious.

"But he could arrest us both . . ."

Lucas smiled. "And spoil my mother's lovely party? Believe me, Phoebe, Basil has better manners than that."

"You are impossible," Phoebe hissed. The strain of waiting and worrying, compounded by sleepless nights and days of running hither and yon, trying to stay one step ahead of her fears, had stretched her self-control to a thin thread. "We are talking about your brother's life here, in case you've forgotten. That man down there, alighting from his fancy carriage, would like nothing better than to put a noose around Duncan's neck!"

Lucas touched her face with light, cool fingertips. "There are a great many people who want to hang your husband," he said reasonably. "Major Stone will find himself standing in line for the privilege. Still, he who would execute my brother must first capture him, and the task is far beyond lesser men, requiring an equal. For good or ill, Duncan has few of those."

Phoebe was only mildly reassured. "He has his weaknesses, like everyone else," she argued in a hushed voice, remembering that the rooms of Troy were crammed with guests of all political persuasions.

Lucas arched an eyebrow. "Such as?"

"Such as this place," Phoebe whispered. "Such as you, and Phillippa, and your mother and father—"

"And you," Lucas supplied thoughtfully. "Yes, I see. A clever enemy might use you—or any one of us, come to that—as bait for a classic trap."

"Exactly."

"Then we shall have to take great care not to put ourselves in such a position," he said.

"Talking to you is like chatting with the Cheshire cat!" Phoebe sputtered, in a fresh burst of frustration.

"The what?" Lucas inquired, frowning.

"Never mind," Phoebe said. "It hasn't been created yet." She moved around Lucas to return to the window, but Major Stone had already been admitted to the house,and the coach was being taken away by grooms. "I'll just have to keep to myself until everyone is gone," she muttered, speaking to herself rather than to her brother-in-law. In her anxiety, she had all but forgotten he was there.

He reminded her quickly enough. "Mother and Phillippa will never permit that," he said. "You, Phoebe Rourke, are cause for celebration."

She did not ask him to explain his comment; nothing he'd said so far made sense, and there was no cause to expect any change.

Phoebe went to her room, locked the door

behind her, and proceeded to pace. Her presence in that house could only serve to endanger Duncan, provided he hadn't already been captured. Perhaps the best thing to do, the *only* thing to do, was to leave Troy before she could be used to hurt a man she would have died to protect.

The question was, where was she to go? She knew nothing about the terrain surrounding the plantation, and even if she managed to avoid British patrols, she might still fall into the hands of brigands or hostile Indians. Yes, the twentieth century was every bit as dangerous, but the singular perils of the eighteenth were unfamiliar ones, and that put her at a distinct disadvantage.

For all her fretting and stewing, for all her pacing, her standing up and her lying down, Phoebe was no closer to coming up with a viable plan at sunset than she had been when she first crossed the threshold of that room. She heard music in the garden and was drawn against her will out onto the terrace, where she stood looking down on a fairyland scene.

Chinese lanterns glowed in the branches of the trees, shedding jewel-like light on women in gowns of glimmering silk and satin. A thick spray of stars crowded the sky, bright as fireworks, and soft laughter mingled with the chime of costly crystal glasses and the low strains of fiddles and mandolins and dulcimers. The notes of a harpsichord curled out through the French doors below like smoke, seeking the tunes played by the other instruments and drawing them into an invisible, magical dance.

Phoebe closed her eyes, remembering the thundering, tempestuous music of another harpsichord, so different from the tinkling and merry strains of the one she was hearing now. Remembering the man who had played with such skill, such fire, that he had virtually become the instrument, shaping the sounds inside himself, spilling them through his fingertips like a wizard directing an orchestra of the elements.

The weight of a man's hands, coming to rest on her waist, caused her to start and draw in her breath.

His voice moved softly past her ear, a hoarse whisper underlaid with laughter and mischief, passion and promise. "Come inside, Mistress Rourke, and greet your husband like a proper wife."

Phoebe felt a sweet, violent tug somewhere deep inside, and a sort of ecstatic apprehension raced through her veins like electricity, raising goose bumps on her skin and turning her nipples hard as buttons under the bodice of her ball gown. She said nothing—could not have spoken if she'd had to—as Duncan eased her backward, over the terrace threshold, into the lonely chamber where she had alternately mourned and cursed him for so many nights.

The room was in shadow; she saw Duncan's outline, watched as the shape slowly solidified into a flesh-and-blood man. He was dressed in a farmer's clothes, a muslin shirt, dark brown breeches of some rough-spun cloth, scuffed boots. He was rumpled and smudged and slightly gaunt, and Phoebe was so glad to see him that she drew back one hand and slapped him hard across the face.

He grasped her hand, after the fact, caressing the fragile underside of her wrist where, beneath the translucent flesh, a tangle of blue veins still pulsed with the visceral news that he was back. His teeth flashed white and perfect in the sultry gloom of that room, so private and yet echoing with voices and music from the party below in the garden.

"You've missed me," he said.

Phoebe might have slapped him again, if he hadn't still been holding her. She shuddered violently as he raised her wrist and brushed his lips across that warm and pulsing place in a feather-light kiss.

"Damn you, Duncan," she managed at last, her voice no more than an anguished whisper, "where have you been? And why did you come here now, of all times? And how did you get into this room, when I locked the door myself?"

"So many questions," he scolded, nibbling the fragile flesh he had just kissed, sending shards of fire ripping through Phoebe's system. "All of them will wait until I've had my way with you, Mistress Rourke."

Phoebe tried to swallow the soft, murmured whimper that rose in her throat as he lifted her into his arms, but the effort came too late. She was one big melting ache as he carried her to the bed and laid her down. He removed her left dancing slipper and kissed her instep, and she felt herself opening for him, a void yearning to be filled.

Duncan towered over her, plainly aware of her response to him, enjoying the power he wielded. With a pass of one hand, he caught a curved index finger in her neckline and tugged, causing her bare breasts to spring free of their confinement, full and warm and weighted with the need to nourish him. He chafed each nipple with the callused side of his thumb, preparing them for conquering.

Phoebe arched her back and uttered a small, strangled gasp. She had had enough, even then, of the preliminaries; if Duncan had raised her skirts and petticoats, opened his breeches and taken her with no further delay, she knew she would have climaxed with the first stroke. She knew better than to think he would appease her so quickly, however, and the knowledge filled her with sweet despair.

He chuckled, as if he knew her thoughts, knew she was damning him to hell even as she longed to take him deep inside her, and moved away from the bed. He crossed the room, closed the terrace doors, and pulled the heavy draperies into place.

Now, even the thin, wavering light of stars and Chinese lanterns was shut out, and Duncan was back before Phoebe's eyes had adjusted. He moved unerringly in the darkness, turning her onto her stomach to unfasten the buttons of her gown, turning her back to pull it down and away.

Her camisole followed, then her voluminous, ruffled petticoats, then her drawers. He took her stockings last, separately and with excruciating slowness, rolling each one down and down, over her thighs, her knees, her calves and ankles. Finally, she lay naked in the thick gloom, still unable to see Duncan, utterly vulnerable to the skilled motions of his hands.

She bit her lower lip as he sat on the feather bed beside her, weighing her breasts in his hands, toying with the nipples, finding her waist and her hips, cupping her buttocks and raising her, trembling, off the mattress. His name escaped her in a whispery rush.

His laugh was low and smoky, curling along her clamoring senses like mist from a genie's lamp. "I've missed you, too," he said.

Phoebe was utterly helpless, her resonant body an instrument in the hands of a virtuoso, but the feeling was one of freedom, of splendid abandon. With this man, she could explore the furthest reaches of pleasure, knowing all the while that she was safe, and that he would lead her slowly, tenderly back to herself when they'd both been thoroughly satisfied. "Please," was the only word she could remember.

He withdrew just long enough to take off his clothes—she knew what he was doing not by sight, for she was still in darkness, but by sound and the drafts his motions produced in the heavy air. The party noises were muffled and faint, but the music was a presence, entwined about them, part of their lovemaking.

At last, Duncan stretched out beside her on the feather-stuffed ticking, his bare flesh smooth under her palms and fingertips, except for the V of tangled hair on his chest. Phoebe followed it to its apex with her hand, found his member and closed her fingers around it. The gesture was not a caress, but a conquest, a claiming.

Duncan uttered a low and probably involuntary groan, and when she stroked the tip with her thumb, he gave a senseless exclamation, groped for her shoulders, and thrust her beneath him. Poised over her, he found her mouth with his and kissed her with a depth and thoroughness that left her dizzy with need.

She said it again, the only word she remembered, the plaintive expression of her need, her yearning, her loneliness.

"Please . . ."

Still, Duncan would not appease Phoebe. He kissed her again, as hungrily, as powerfully as before. Then he traced the edge of her jaw with his lips, the pulsing muscles along the length of her neck, the curve of her shoulder, the slight swelling above her breasts. When at last he found a nipple, ravished it with his tongue, and then took it greedily into his mouth, a new level of arousal struck Phoebe like a careening boxcar turned broadside. He showed no quarter as he plundered her, but his fingers were gentle on her lips, muffling her cries of wanting and welcome.

Presently, he moved down her body, nibbling, trailing his warm, moist lips between her ribs, over her belly and abdomen, into the delta of curls that sheltered her femininity. When he parted the silken curtain and took her boldly to suckle, she exploded, instantaneously, powerfully, completely, her hips rising high off the bed, her buttocks cushioned in his strong hands, his fingers squeezing them as though they were fruits, ripe with sweet juices. He stayed with her, through all the wild twists and pitches of her release, relentless, gentle, fierce.

Phoebe's climax was so shattering that she could not have imagined what lay beyond it. She expected to lie beneath Duncan, replete and sated, while he mounted her, and took his pleasure. She would stroke his back and shoulders, buttocks and thighs with her hands, speaking soft nonsense words, comforting and cajoling, urging him on, floating in the peace he had given her.

It wasn't like that.

He entered her like a conqueror, with a hard, deep thrust that reawakened all her desires at once and brought them surging to the surface like lava in a live volcano.

She gave a low, guttural cry, one he made no effort to silence, and rose to meet his second thrust, her hunger as ferocious and urgent as his. At her response, he withdrew, but only long

278

enough to turn her over and raise her onto her hands and knees; theirs was the primitive, exhaustive joining of a stallion and his mare, woven of nature and need.

Duncan cupped Phoebe's breasts, squeezing and stroking them, plucking at the nipples as he rode her, and she flung herself back upon him, taking him deep and deeper still. She was ruthless, finally rendering his seed from him, along with a strangled shout of satisfaction, and moistening the flesh of his rod and his belly with nectar of her own. He bucked against her as aftershocks rocked both their bodies, then fell upon her, trembling with exhaustion, her nipples pressing hard into his palms.

They were a long time recovering, and when Duncan finally raised his head, he began kissing the small, jutting bones of Phoebe's spine. He slid one hand downward, from her breast to her belly and then to the tender and innately feminine place at the juncture of her thighs. She whimpered into her pillow as he began to tease her with a slow, rolling motion of one finger.

"I don't believe this," she muttered, amazed to discover that she was responding. Again.

He tasted her shoulder blade while continuing to play with her. "Allow me to convince you," he said.

"Are you aware that this house is crawling with redcoats and Tories?" Phoebe demanded furiously, sometime later, when her muscles were solid again and she could trust her legs to support her. She had lighted a lamp and stood at a safe distance from Duncan, out of his reach.

Duncan remained in bed, lying on his back, his hands cupped behind his head. He was the classic picture of male indolence, contented and damnably certain that he'd given satisfaction. "I noticed them when I came in," he said. Either he didn't understand the gravity of the situation, or recklessness had become such a habit that he'd forgotten how to exercise any sort of caution. "We should be perfectly safe, unless someone happened to hear you howling like a she-wolf when we were making love."

Color flooded Phoebe's cheeks. "Okay," she hissed, "so I made a little noise. If you were a gentleman, you wouldn't mention such things."

"If I were a gentleman," Duncan countered, with a grin, "you wouldn't have been carrying on like that in the first place."

Phoebe had already donned her camisole and drawers; now she stepped into her petticoats and wrenched the waistband into place. A glimpse of herself in the bureau mirror revealed an incriminating glow to her skin and a sparkle in her eyes, and both had their beginnings in something other than her current exasperation. "How did you get in here?" she asked, attempting to keep her voice down. Now that her mind was relatively clear again, she was afraid. "I *know* I locked the door."

Duncan's grin broadened. If he was worried about Major Stone or any of the other Englishmen on the premises, he gave no indication of it. "Locked doors are nothing to me, Phoebe," he teased. "Not when you're on the other side, eagerly awaiting the attentions of your husband."

She snatched up a pillow from the settee near the fireplace and flung it at him, albeit half-heartedly. "Don't flatter yourself, Mr. Rourke. As it happens, I wasn't thinking about you at all. I was considering my chances of escaping Troy without being scalped by Indians or captured by redcoats!"

He frowned, then sat up and reached for his breeches, which were draped around one of the bedposts. "You aren't happy here?"

Phoebe averted her eyes. Her pride kept her from admitting that she wouldn't be happy anywhere without him. "Everyone in your family has been wonderful to me," she said softly. "But I was afraid."

"Of what?" Duncan was out of bed, pulling on his breeches, fastening the buttons. She hesitated so long that he came to stand facing her, took her chin in his hand, and made her look at him. "Tell me what you were afraid of, Phoebe."

She blinked, because she wanted to cry and she wasn't about to show that kind of weakness. "I was scared you would be stupid enough to come here," she answered at last. "And I was right."

His smile was unhurried and more than a little cocky. "Don't pretend you weren't glad to see me," he said. "You obviously were."

Phoebe twisted free of his grasp. Outside, the music played on, and the laughter ebbed and flowed, but it was only a matter of time before Duncan's presence would be discovered. When that happened, nothing would save him from a British noose, not her love, not the influence of his father and elder brother. She was outraged by the scope of the risk he was taking. "There are men at this party who want to hang you!"

He uttered a philosophical sigh. "And a few women as well, no doubt," he allowed. "Dear Phoebe—will you please cease your fretting? I've avoided the scaffold since before the war began, and I shall continue to do so. Besides, you knew I was on my way to Troy."

Phoebe heard footsteps in the hall and voices. Her heart skidded past a couple of beats and then resumed a pace only slightly faster than normal. "Your timing is rotten," she whispered. "You might have come before the party, or after it—any time but now."

He had drawn near again, and he kissed her forehead lightly. "I want to see my father," he said. "Once I've satisfied myself that he is well, I will leave again."

Something in his manner, in the tone of his voice, worried Phoebe even more deeply than his badly timed return to the family plantation. "Taking me with you, of course."

Duncan hesitated. "Phoebe . . ."

She folded her arms. "Don't bother making a speech about how I'll be safer here at Troy," she warned, "because it isn't true. Once some of these Tories and lobsterbacks figure out that I'm not a nun or a mute servant after all . . .' "

Laughter lighted his eyes and made one side of his mouth kick upward. " 'A nun or a mute servant'? What in the devil are you talking about?"

Again, Phoebe felt heat surge into her face. "It's partly my fault," she confessed, in a rush. "I told Phillippa I was in a convent—you know, to explain my hair. It was the only thing I could think of at the time. But Lucas was the one who told Major Stone I was a bond servant with no voice." She sighed. "It was a handy story at the time, given the fact that the major met the *Charles Town Princess* with an escort of armed soldiers and seemed more than a little suspicious about me. Now it's a problem, though, because he's here, at this party, and your mother and father have been telling everyone that I'm your wife."

"I can see the dilemma," Duncan said, though he didn't seem very concerned.

"Can you?" Phoebe demanded, getting angry again. How could such an intelligent man be so obtuse? "I'll be questioned, at the very least, and perhaps even arrested . . ."

He curved a finger under her chin, which was trembling a little, even though she held it at a defiant angle. "No," he said. "The British shall not have you, for questioning or for any other purpose. You belong to the Revolution, and to me."

Phoebe's heart lightened, though there was a certain poignant sorrow in the knowledge that she would be leaving Troy soon, leaving the family she had come to think of as her own. "How will you manage to see your father with so many people around?"

With that same finger, Duncan traced her lips, which were still swollen from his kisses. He smiled fleetingly at some memory, though whether it was a recent one or not she could not guess. "You will be my messenger," he said. "Find Father, if you will, and tell him the Prodigal has returned, hungry for the fatted calf."

Phoebe opened her mouth to protest, then closed it again, knowing it would be a waste of time. "All right," she agreed doubtfully and at length, straightening her hair, which was growing out and therefore hopeless, and the skirts of her ball gown, which were rumpled. "If I'm not back in fifteen minutes, assume I've been slapped into cuffs, taken downtown, and booked."

Duncan looked puzzled, which pleased Phoebe, though of course it was small consolation for the risk he was forcing her to take.

She turned the key in the lock, opened the door, and looked down the hall in both directions. Two young girls hurried by, giggling, the crisp satin skirts of their party dresses rustling pleasantly, paying Phoebe no notice whatsoever.

Pulling the door closed behind her, Phoebe set out for the stairway, head held high, strides purposeful, looking neither to right nor left. The

lower part of the house was thick with guests—
couples were dancing in the parlor-turned-ball-
room on the first floor and strolling in the garden.
While searching for John Rourke, Phoebe took
equal care to avoid Phillippa, Margaret, and
Lucas; any one of them would guess, with one
look at her eyes, that Duncan was in the house.

Eventually, Phoebe found Marva, bearing a
tray of fruit tarts through the crowd, and inquired
about her father-in-law. Marva nodded toward
the closed doors of Mr. Rourke's study.

"He be there, mistress," the woman said with
weary kindness. "You knock and tell master that
Marva says he'd better have some supper."

Phoebe thanked the servant and turned to
make her way toward John Rourke's private
domain. She had tapped at one of the towering
doors, been invited in, and stepped over the
threshold before she thought to wonder if he was
alone. By that time, of course, it was too late.

Major Basil Stone stood by the cold fireplace,
one crimson-sleeved arm resting against the
marble mantelpiece, a snifter of brandy in his
other hand. His pale blue gaze fastened on
Phoebe the moment she entered the room, and
it was plain that he remembered their meeting
on the jetty the day she had arrived in Charles
Town.

"Well," he said thoughtfully.

John, who had been seated behind his desk,
rose from his chair with a broad, fatherly smile on
his face. There was no forestalling the inevitable.

"Here you are, my dear—I was wondering what became of you. Major, may I present my daughter-in-law, Phoebe? Phoebe, this is Major Basil Stone."

Phoebe stood as boneless as a scarecrow in the center of that graciously masculine room, fingers so tightly interlocked that the knuckles ached, heart wedged into her sinuses and pounding there.

"Your daughter-in-law," mused the major. "He's a sly one, your Lucas. Didn't mention he'd taken a bride when I met him in Charles Town just about a fortnight ago. In fact, he introduced this lovely young lady as a servant."

Phoebe tried to smile, but she knew her expression was brittle and her eyes were probably a bit glassy. For the moment there was no need to pretend she was mute, as Lucas had claimed. She couldn't have uttered a word to save herself from pitching headlong into perdition itself.

John Rourke laughed. "I guess Lucas must have thought you'd make a pest of yourself," he said to Stone, who was obviously a trusted friend. "My eldest son has yet to take a wife, though God knows his mother and I wish he would settle down and start a family. Phoebe is wedded to Duncan."

The ensuing silence was thunderous. Phoebe's heart seemed to swell until it filled the room, causing the very walls and floorboards to throb in time with its too-rapid beat. Perspiration tickled her upper lip and the space between her shoulder blades, and still she just stood there, with a foolish smile teetering on her mouth.

"Phoebe is wedded to Duncan," Stone repeated, after considerable time had passed. His gaze was speculative, boring deep, seeing far too much.

She cast a desperate glance in her father-in-law's direction and saw in an instant that he knew Duncan was in the house at that very moment. Perhaps he had intended to betray his younger son all along, out of some misguided sense of political loyalty . . .

John Rourke gave a deep sigh and reached out to her, and despite her doubts, Phoebe went to him. He patted her hand and gave her a look full of sorrowful affection. "I fear my son is no sort of gentleman. He married Phoebe on an impulse and then abandoned her to our care."

"Do you know where your husband is?" Major Stone demanded of Phoebe, crossing the room to stand only a few feet from her.

Phoebe did not dare even to think of the room just upstairs, where Duncan waited, where he had made such thorough love to her only a little while before. She was afraid the major would see the truth in her face. "No," she murmured, gazing steadfastly at the old man's nose in order to avoid looking into his eyes. Tension welled up inside her, along with a generous splash of hormones, and she burst into tears. "And I don't care if I never hear his name again, sir, for he's a rogue and a rascal, and he never had any intention of being a proper husband to me!"

"There, there," said John Rourke solicitously, still patting her hand. "Duncan is not worthy of your tears, my dear." He met the major's eyes squarely. "Believe me, Basil, when Duncan is found at last, I shall want a word with him myself."

"You realize," Stone said, after taking a sip of his brandy, "that it is a crime against the Crown to harbor a wanted man? Even when that fugitive is one's own flesh and blood?"

"There are many different transgressions under heaven, Basil," Mr. Rourke replied. "A man is called upon, on occasion, to weigh one against another and attempt to choose the lesser of the two."

Phoebe held her breath, watching the major out of the corner of her eye. Stone was no fool; at any moment, he would surely summon his men and order them to search Troy from the wine cellars to the rafters.

"If that outlaw is here," Basil replied, "I will find him."

Rourke merely gestured with one hand, issuing a silent invitation. Had it not been for his tight grasp on Phoebe's arm, she might have done something rash, like bolting from the room, shouting for Duncan to run for his life. As it was, just keeping herself from fainting or throwing up on the Persian carpet required all her concentration.

Stone set his brandy snifter on the mantel, his face as chilled and hard as the marble from which the fireplace had been sculpted, and left the room without another word. There was no need for talk now.

Phoebe whirled on her father-in-law, her eyes burning with furious tears. "How could you?" she whispered, wrenching free and retreating a step. "How could you betray your own son?"

"Dear God!" Mr. Rourke expelled the exclamation on a bitter sigh. His eyes were hollow with despair, and he looked much older than he was and tired to the very marrow of his soul. "He *is* here, beneath this roof. If Duncan isn't hanged for a traitor, he shall surely be hanged for a fool."

14

Lucas's prediction that Major Stone would never be so ill-mannered as to spoil a party proved to be grossly inaccurate. Phoebe and Mr. Rourke left the study just in time to hear the old soldier making a startling announcement to the assemblage of soldiers and farmers, Tories and closet-patriots.

Stone, the man of the hour, stood on the stairs, in order to be seen and heard.

"By the authority of His Majesty, King George the Third of England," he announced, "I hereby place John and Lucas Rourke under house arrest." As a horrified murmur rose from the crowd, Stone raised his voice. His eyes were cold, his cheeks ruddy with conviction, a life led mainly outdoors, and a high-cholesterol diet. "Seize them immediately."

Lucas, who had been in the center of the ballroom, guiding a pretty young woman through the minuet, reacted with a shouted exclamation, abandoning his partner to push his way through the gathering. In true Rourke fashion, he was not attempting to escape, but advancing on Stone, who was trouble personified, as if he, Lucas, were invincible. His expression was mildly murderous.

Beside Phoebe, John Rourke stood quite still, showing no sign of temper, nor any sign that he planned to resist arrest. He had expected something like this, Phoebe thought, quelling her own repeated surges of hysteria one by one.

A flicker of shadowy movement on the first landing of the great staircase, not ten feet from where Stone stood, compounded her fears a hundredfold.

Duncan.

Please, she pleaded silently, uselessly, *don't do anything stupid.*

"Take him," Major Stone commanded, when Lucas had shouldered his way through to stand practically at his feet. Apparently it was a family trait, heading straight into the teeth of a crisis when any fool would have known to turn and run.

Reluctantly, men in crimson coats and buff breeches separated themselves from the other guests, worried and pallid, intent on the daunting task of subduing Lucas Rourke. Duncan's elder brother struggled violently and, in the end, was stilled not by the efforts of the six grappling soldiers who had surrounded him, but by the quiet authority of his father's voice.

"That will be quite enough, Lucas," John Rourke said simply, as his own hands were wrenched behind him and bound. He held his head high, and his voice was as level as his gaze. He might have been resigned to his fate, Phoebe reflected, but he was no more intimidated than his son. He was, however, much wiser.

Flushed, clearly acting against his own better judgment, Lucas stopped resisting.

Appearing from out of nowhere, Phillippa launched herself at the unfortunate young lieutenant who had taken her father captive. The boy-soldier, pimply and probably homesick, was caught off guard, and raised one arm as if to shove her roughly aside. At this, the elder Mr. Rourke spoke again. His voice was as calm as it had been moments before when he'd reprimanded Lucas.

"Lay a hand on my daughter, sir," he said, "and I shall kill you for it."

The lieutenant took heed and lowered his arm to his side, while Phoebe drew Phillippa in a frantic embrace and pulled her back out of the way.

Margaret appeared, slightly pale but otherwise self-possessed and full of dignity.

"What is the meaning of this, Basil?" she demanded coolly. "Ours is a Loyalist household, we are subjects of the King. How dare you treat us in such a fashion?"

A shadow of shame moved briefly in Stone's shrewd eyes, then vanished. "I apologize for the necessity, Mistress Rourke. However, these are desperate times, and regrettably, harsh measures are sometimes required." He paused and turned to glance behind him, up the darkened stairs, effectively stopping Phoebe's heart, and then went on in a determined voice. "Men who would shelter an enemy of the King cannot be counted among His Majesty's friends. John and Lucas Rourke shall be remanded to headquarters in Charles Town, there to be tried as traitors."

"You have no proof!" Lucas spat, appalled and furious. He was still bound at the wrists, like his father. "Perhaps they're right, these rebels, when they accuse the King and his government of tyranny. Only a despot detains honest citizens without just cause!"

The guests, who had been stunned to silence until then, began to murmur among themselves. Phoebe held Phillippa, who was sobbing silently; she did not dare to look toward the top of the stairs again for fear of revealing what she had guessed—that Duncan was there, just beyond the reach of the lamplight, listening, watching. Planning God only knew what.

"Silence!" shouted the major. "There is no tyranny here. It is Rourke who has broken the law, not me, nor my men."

"*British* law," some intrepid soul scoffed from within the knot of dumbfounded partygoers. "Not our own!"

There was a flurry of agreement, incendiary, traitorous. The Tories were heard, as well. What an eclectic party group, Phoebe reflected— Trojans and Greeks.

Again, John Rourke spoke, the voice of reason in a room thrumming with violence barely restrained. Margaret stood straight-spined and square-shouldered at his side, her hand resting lightly in the curve of his arm. They might have been going in to dinner, for all the alarm either of them showed, instead of facing possible tragedy.

"Shhh," Phoebe said to Phillippa. The room was an emotional tinderbox, ready to erupt into chaos at any moment. John and Margaret Rourke understood that, Phoebe could see, though she had her doubts about Lucas, and Phillippa was on the point of giving way to hysteria.

With considerable ceremony, Stone left his dais on the stairs and crossed to face his host and hostess. "I *am* sorry," he said.

"I know," John replied hoarsely.

At that, the Rourke men were taken from the room.

"Mama," Phillippa moaned, trembling, her face wet with tears.

Margaret's command came quickly and

brooked no argument. "Collect yourself, Phillippa," she said. "Your father and brothers, you and Phoebe and I, we must all be strong and share what courage we can muster among ourselves."

With that, she swept away, following John and Lucas and their armed guard toward the back of the house. Phillippa straightened her back and dashed at her cheeks with the back of one hand. "Duncan is right," she whispered, and Phoebe released her, though she remained close by. "This is oppression!"

Another convert to the rebel cause, Phoebe thought, but she took no joy in the fact. Nothing in her high school and college careers had prepared her for the fact that real people had staked everything, their lives, their fortunes, and their personal freedom, such as it was, on one of the greatest gambles in the history of the western world. The players on both sides of this drama were not the flat, lifeless figures in paintings, the fancy handwriting in eighteenth-century diaries, actors in a miniseries, or the subjects of outdated biographies—they were real. They were innocent, idealistic children like Phillippa, skinny boys with bad complexions and a yearning for home, whether that was London or Boston, Brighton or Yorktown. They were good and honorable men, like John Rourke and like Major Basil Stone. They were courageous, beautiful women, like Margaret, like the women who surely waited and worried and made the age-old sacrifices on both sides of the fray.

Phoebe stood, stricken, watching as Major Stone conferred briefly with several of his men. When the conversation had ended, he came to her, as she had expected him to do.

"When next you see your husband," he began, not unkindly, not even disrespectfully, but with a sort of obdurate reason that turned Phoebe's blood to splinters of ice, "I trust you will tell Mr. Rourke that the lives of his father and brother are now in his hands."

"I imagine he knows that," Phoebe said. She, like Phillippa, had drawn strength from Margaret's brief parting speech.

"I imagine he does," Stone agreed.

Phillippa had recovered her composure, though her eyes were still puffy and red-rimmed and the skirts of her gown were rumpled where she had grasped and crushed them in her fists. "Perhaps," she said to the major, "you should take Mother and Phoebe and me as hostages, too. Surely chivalry cannot matter to you, not if you would betray men who have long been your friends."

Phoebe said nothing, made no attempt to stop her sister-in-law's diatribe.

Major Stone glared at them both for a long moment, then moved through the scattered remnants of the crowd and disappeared.

Phoebe waited until she was certain no one was watching, then made her way slowly, casually, up the main staircase, Phillippa following. There was no sign of Duncan, but something of his essence lingered in the weighted summer air, and she knew he had been a witness to the arrest of his father and brother. She was thankful he had not attempted to intervene.

Not yet, at least.

Phoebe hurried along the upper hallway, holding her hem off the floor to keep from tripping over the rustling skirts of her ball gown, with Phillippa still close behind. She opened the door to her room and burst in, expecting to find her husband there, pacing, perhaps, while he laid plans to implement a rescue.

The chamber was empty, though the curtains had been thrust aside and the terrace doors gaped open, admitting mosquitoes, the rise and fall of human voices, and the night sounds from the stables and the dark, dense woods beyond the garden and the lawn.

Phillippa cast a glance at the rumpled bed, which was clearly visible by the light of a lamp lit earlier, when Phoebe and Duncan had finished with their lovemaking, but she asked no questions.

"Is there another way out of this room?" Phoebe asked, keeping her voice down and hoping the state of the bedclothes didn't tell too clear a tale. "Besides climbing the outside wall like Dracula, I mean?"

"Dracula?"

"I'll explain another time," Phoebe replied,

exasperated with herself. She was going to have to stop mixing up her centuries if she wanted to live happily in this one. Not that she was likely to achieve that modest dream, given the war and the fact that she was married to one of America's Most Wanted. "Sometimes these houses had—have—secret passages. How about this one?"

Phillippa went to the terrace and looked out before closing the doors carefully against the night and turning to face Phoebe. She hesitated, and Phoebe realized, with a slight pang, that the girl was making a final, down-to-brass-tacks decision—to trust or not to trust.

She waited in silence. If she had not proven her loyalty to the family by now, there was, in her opinion, no hope of ever doing so.

"Yes," Phillippa said at long last. "Come here, and I'll show you." Behind one of the floral tapestries flanking the fireplace on either side was an almost seamless panel. With a push of her hand, Phillippa opened it, revealing the cramped passage inside. Rather than a full-sized hallway, this was a rabbit warren, one of many entrances, Phoebe later learned, to a maze covering most of the house. Anyone larger than a child of five or six would be forced to crawl through it on hands and knees.

Phillippa knelt and peered inside. "I suppose he's long gone," she mused.

"Duncan?" The name left Phoebe's lips aboard a mocking tone. "He doesn't have the sense to run away. He'll get himself horse-whipped, and finally hanged, trying to save your father and Lucas from the evils of a British stockade."

Rising, Phillippa closed the Alice-in-Wonderland door, and the tapestry fell into place, as it was intended to do, with no help from anyone. "Now that I've had time to think about it," she said, using a damask towel from Phoebe's washstand to wipe her hands, "I understand that Major Stone means Father and Lucas no real harm. He is using them as bait, that's all."

"To trap Duncan," Phoebe agreed ruefully. Perhaps some of Phillippa's fears had been erased, but Phoebe herself was still terrified. Trap or no trap, her husband would try to spring the prisoners. For him, the knowledge of their captivity would be unbearable, reason enough, in and of itself, to attempt their release. "Phillippa, if you have any idea where your brother would hide, you must tell me. It's important that I speak with him."

"Why?" Phillippa asked, walking resolutely over to the bed and making it up, as she had probably seen the servants do many times. "You won't be able to change his mind, you know."

Phoebe feared her sister-in-law was right. "No," she said sorrowfully. "I don't suppose I will." She sat down on the edge of the bed she had shared so happily with Duncan such a short while before, and Phillippa took a seat beside her, frowning.

"I want to go away with you and Duncan,"

Phillippa finally proclaimed. "I've decided to join my lot with the rebels and do what I can to help throw off this miserable king."

Phoebe smiled sadly. "You have a great deal of confidence in your brother's ability to escape," she observed. "What makes you so certain he won't be caught, tried, and hanged?"

"He's far too clever," Phillippa said.

Phoebe was skeptical, but for the sake of her sanity she chose to believe that Duncan would prevail, as the colonies themselves would prevail, shaping themselves into the beginnings of a great if often troubled nation. "I'm not sure Duncan will agree to take you away from Troy," she warned quietly, after a long and thoughtful silence. "He might not be willing to subject you to that kind of danger, Phillippa. After all, you are his only sister."

"And you are his only wife," Phillippa pointed out, "but he'll take you with him when he leaves."

Phoebe could only sigh and wait.

And wait.

Duncan's father and brother were being held, predictably, in a cramped, musty corner of the cellar, a tiny room with a dirt floor and a drapery of cobwebs overhead. They were provided with a single tallow candle for light; it smoked and wavered and sputtered in the fetid gloom of their dungeon.

He watched them for a while, to make certain they had been left alone to meditate on the gravity of their situation. Duncan could have told Stone, that pompous old maid of a soldier, that no amount of time or reflection would induce them to betray him. He was not a criminal in their eyes, but merely a misguided mischiefmaker who would come to see reason, once the rebellion had been put down and matters had been properly explained to him.

Duncan smiled for his own benefit, raised the loose metal grating hidden amongst the dust and spider-spinnings of the ceiling, and let himself down through the narrow opening.

Lucas leaned forward, as if to rise, and simultaneously opened his mouth to speak. John, who sat beside his elder son on the cold floor, stayed both impulses by grasping Lucas's arm.

Duncan dropped to his haunches, took up the candle, and held it in such a way that its dim light fell over his father's worn, kindly features. He saw anger in the set of John Rourke's face, as well as exhaustion and an unsettling degree of sorrow. It was true, then, what Phillippa had written in her letter to Duncan so many weeks before: their sire was tired and ill. Perhaps even inclined to die.

"My men wait in the woods," Duncan said, taking care to keep his voice low. There were guards outside; he had seen them moving sluggishly through the heavy night air, their coats discarded, their shirts wet with sweat, their palms slick, no doubt, on the stocks of their muskets. "There is room for you, aboard the *Francesca*."

Lucas spoke at last, in a spitting whisper. "You are mad, coming here!"

Duncan did not explain that he'd come to see their father; Lucas knew that, had known it since their last encounter, in a distant cove. "The simplest things surprise you, Brother," he said. "I have no time to cajole or convince. Will you leave with me, or allow yourselves to be hanged for depriving the good major of an opportunity to earn yet another medal?"

John took the tallow from Duncan's hand and set it aside. "You must know," he said, "that I cannot leave your mother or Phillippa. Or Troy itself, for that matter."

Duncan felt a tightening in his throat. He, too, loved the land, and hoped to live upon it again one day, as a free man, but there was no time to elaborate. "Mother and Phillippa are not in danger of being executed for treason," he pointed out. "You are, and so is Lucas."

"No," John said firmly.

A vision of his father swinging from a length of rope on a scaffold flashed before Duncan's eyes; he had seen other men die that way, for lesser crimes, and had come near to such an end himself, on several occasions. "God in heaven, Father, does your life mean nothing at all? And you." He turned a blazing stare on Lucas. "You are a young man, with many fruitful years left to you. Will you never marry, never sire a child— never live unfettered, knowing that you won that liberty for yourself?"

A pained expression contorted Lucas's face for a moment, but he brought himself swiftly under control. "Major Stone will see his error and set us free," he said, though the words lacked a certain conviction.

Duncan started to protest, but his father cut him off by taking his wrist in a grasp still strong enough to be mildly painful. "Tell me, Duncan," he said, "what would you do in my place? If this were your land—and it will be someday, in part, by the grace of God—if it meant abandoning your wife and your young daughter, abandoning all the workers who depend on you for every bite of food that goes into their mouths, every scrap of cloth that covers their backs, *what would you do*?"

Duncan was silent, defeated now, half-strangled by the frustration he felt, the rage, and the empathy.

"Speak," John pressed sternly. "I will not allow you to leave my question unanswered. What would you do in my place?"

Duncan lowered his eyes. "I would stay," he admitted.

"Yes," his father agreed and laid a hand to Duncan's shoulder. "Take your wife, if you must, and put Troy behind you, now. Do not return until this bloody rebellion has ended."

A sound rose in Duncan's throat and was aborted before it could find utterance. He had seen a phantom in his father's eyes, the spirit that

302

would live on after John Rourke was dead. And death, he knew, would not be long in coming.

"Be gone," John insisted, with a note of sad amusement in his voice. "I am that weary of looking at you, Duncan Rourke." Having so spoken, the patriarch stood, raising Duncan with him, and embraced his son. "God be with you," he said.

Duncan did not turn from his father's farewell, but returned it, as near to weeping as he could afford to be. Before him was the man who had loved him unequivocally, despite their difference, who had taught him to read, to hunt and shoot, to anticipate the weather by the signs the earth offered, the man who had cut him free of a British whipping post and carried him home, delirious and soaked in blood, on his own horse. John had taught him to be strong and stubborn, had shown him that he must learn to govern himself before he could lead others with any success.

Lucas rose, too, and shook Duncan's hand. "I'll look for you to come back home," he said, "when this fighting's over."

Duncan nodded, not trusting himself to speak. After a last long look at John Rourke, he drew a cask out of the corner, climbed onto it, and hoisted himself through the hole in the ceiling. For some time afterward, he lay in the cramped, filthy space above the wine cellar, listening, thinking, remembering. Imprinting his father's image on his mind for all time.

Eventually, he allowed himself to weep. His

sobs, though silent, were deep, wrenching ones, rooted in some part of him he had never acknowledged before. When at last the worst of his grief had passed, he moved back through the bowels and walls of the great house, traveling routes he had learned in childhood.

When he reached the chamber where Phoebe waited—it had been his room, once—he pushed the tapestry aside and found his wife lying on the bed, fully clothed and sound asleep. Her arms were thrown wide of her slender body, and she was snoring ever so slightly. She had exchanged her ball gown for a divided skirt made for riding astride, a pair of boots, and a long-sleeved shirt that might have been his at one time.

Duncan stood over Phoebe for a time, watching her sleep, coping in silence with a storm of poignant emotions, fully aware of other sounds— a light step in the hallway, guests in the rooms on either side of this one, settling in for the night, talking, making love. He never considered leaving Phoebe at Troy; with the events of that night, the plantation had, for all intents and purposes, fallen to the enemy. He bent and kissed her lips like the prince in a tale he'd heard once, long ago, beside the fire on a winter's night, and she opened her eyes.

Duncan did not speak; he merely gave her his hand. She was on her feet in a moment, and he led her out onto the terrace. The party had ended, the Chinese lanterns were extinguished, and the garden appeared empty. He whistled and heard the corresponding signal return to him on a balmy breeze.

They descended from the terrace by means of a rope, Duncan going first, Phoebe following. She did not hesitate or utter a sound as they fled across the darkened lawn and into the night.

Men waited deep in the woods, patient, silent, well versed in such tactics, with horses and muskets. Duncan mounted a gelding, bent to extend a hand to Phoebe, and swung her up behind him. They rode hard, a score of men, Duncan and Phoebe, and a small, cloaked figure he did not notice until nearly sunrise, when the sea was near enough to smell.

Phillippa flung back the hood of her cape and beamed at her grim, exhausted brother. "I've decided," she announced, "to participate in the Revolution."

A glance back at Phoebe revealed that she'd known Phillippa was present all along. Perhaps she had even helped arrange the deception, and his men had participated, too. Duncan swept them up, one and all, in a single, scathing glare, warning them without words that they would suffer for their foolhardy audacity.

Finally, he spat a curse, but secretly he was pleased that one member of his family, at least, had seen the light. "Mind you don't get underfoot," he told his sister, "or make a liability of yourself."

Phillippa laughed, though he could see that she had been weeping during their long flight from

Troy. Perhaps she knew, as he did, that their father was sick unto dying, that she might never see her home again. "I will do my best to behave," she promised.

The *Francesca* awaited them on turquoise waters frosted with white foam, but it was nightfall before they dared to board her and set sail for friendlier waters. Phoebe had seen the anguish in her husband's face and guessed at its cause, but she did not offer him comfort until they were alone in their cabin, long after midnight.

Phillippa was sleeping soundly, just across the passageway; Phoebe knew that because she had looked in on her sister-in-law only minutes before Duncan came belowdecks and let himself into their tiny chamber.

Phoebe had given herself a sponge bath and donned one of Duncan's shirts in place of a nightgown. She was certainly no expert on masculine emotions, but she knew how to console one particular man.

Gently, she removed his shirt, which was stiff with dust and sweat, and began to wash his upper torso with tepid water from the basin on the washstand.

Duncan submitted in silence, tilting his magnificent head back, closing his eyes. The muscles in his jawline, for all of that, were rock-hard, ridged, the muscles of an ancient warrior, caught forever in marble.

"Thank you," she said.

He did not open his eyes. "For what?" he asked, his voice low and somehow broken, though he was trying hard not to let her see that he was suffering.

"For not leaving me behind," she replied. "Now . . ." Phoebe paused, sighed deeply. "If only you would talk to me."

He met her gaze at last, and she saw utter despair in his eyes, along with the conviction that he had failed. "There is nothing to say."

"Isn't there? You were forced to leave your family—most of it, anyway—in the hands of the British. You have no way of knowing what will happen to them. I'd say that was something to talk about."

Duncan pushed her hand away, when she would have continued to sponge his chest and belly with light, tantalizing strokes. "What do you want me to tell you?" he rasped. "That I'm a coward?"

Phoebe dunked the sponge, squeezed it languidly, and moved around him to begin washing his back. It was a beautiful, well-muscled expanse of sun-browned flesh, even with the whip marks crisscrossing and rooted deep. "You, a coward? Good Lord, Duncan, sometimes I actually wish you *were* a little less daring—that way, you might live longer."

Something moved in him, some emotion he quickly suppressed. Phoebe's heart ached.

"My reasons are selfish, of course," Phoebe prattled on, continuing the sensuous bath. "I love you very much. I want to be a wife for a good long time—so mind you don't make me a widow."

He sighed, gazing straight ahead, pondering some scene Phoebe couldn't see. She unbuttoned his breeches, freed him, and went on wielding the sponge. Duncan gasped before he could stop himself, and he had no control whatsoever over the response of his body. His member rose against his belly like the mast of a ship. Despite his state of mind, he was more than ready for further attention.

It was the only way Phoebe knew of to get past the barriers he'd erected and meld her soul with his. In that fusion, Duncan might know a few minutes of peace, and Phoebe wanted to give him that gift, however fleeting.

She put the basin and sponge aside and stroked him. She told him to kick off his boots, and he obeyed her. When she had removed his breeches, he was utterly vulnerable to her, and so completely, perfectly masculine that he took her breath away.

The lamp guttered out just as she knelt, to worship and to conquer.

Duncan groaned and plunged his fingers into Phoebe's hair. She imagined those hands, moving with graceful fury over the keyboard of a harpsichord or the strings of a mandolin, as she enjoyed him. For once, for that night if never again, Duncan was the instrument, and she was the musician.

She played him with tender, relentless skill,

made him spend himself, led him to their bed, and extracted still more music—melodies, thunderous rhapsodies, crescendos. He gave himself up to her completely, and she loved him all the more for having the strength to submit. Duncan had trusted her with far more than his body; while she made love to him, at least, he entrusted her with his soul as well.

"Tell me about Troy," she whispered, when they lay entwined on the bed, emptied, for that night at least, of all their passions. "Tell me about your father and your beautiful mother, about Lucas and Phillippa."

Duncan was silent for a long while, and when Phoebe reached up to caress him, she felt tears on his face. It was time, she knew then, to reveal her secret.

"Okay, then," she said, "*I'll* tell *you* something. I'm going to have a child."

He drew her on top of him in a single motion, the effects of his repeated releases evidently forgotten. She saw his face in the moonlight flooding in through the high porthole and knew that he could see her clearly, too. She felt his gaze probing the deepest, most private parts of her being, and the sensation was not entirely pleasant.

"What did you say?"

"I believe you understood me the first time, Mr. Rourke," Phoebe whispered. She was less sure of his reaction than she had been a moment before, a little frightened now that he would not want her, would not accept the baby they had made together. "You will be a father—sometime in March, probably."

"My God," he breathed, and Phoebe wished he would show some emotion other than mere surprise—joy or sorrow, fury or regret. *Something.*

"Old Woman says our baby will be a boy. She's already named him John Alexander Rourke—for your father, of course. And Alex."

For an excruciatingly long moment, he simply stared into her eyes. Then, just when she had almost lost hope, he pulled her very close, as if expecting someone to try to tear her from his arms. "Trust Old Woman," he said, close to Phoebe's ear, "to know all about my child before I do. Good Lord, Phoebe—why didn't you tell me?"

"Things kept coming up," she teased.

He laughed, and the sound was better than music, better than good news. "A child," he repeated. But as he held Phoebe against his side, some of the joy seemed to seep out of him. "What kind of man will our son grow up to be," he asked, "with an outlaw for a father?"

"He won't have 'an outlaw for a father,' Duncan," Phoebe pointed out, snuggling close and holding on tight. "He'll have a hero—a man who helped give him a free country to grow up in."

Duncan plunged the fingers of his right hand into her hair, much as he had earlier, in passion, though this time the reason was different. Slowly, halting every few moments in order to regain control, he told her that his father and brother had refused to be rescued, that they had preferred to take their chances with the hangman, that he'd seen a ghost in John Rourke's eyes and knew that he would soon perish.

Phoebe listened—she had led Duncan to this point, after all, through the sponge bath, the easy words, the lovemaking, and the tenderness that had followed. Now, she would simply hear him and hold him in her arms while he told her things that were both important and trivial. While he talked, she took his right hand and laid it on her bare belly, to remind him of the tiny life growing beneath his palm.

15

The closeness Duncan and Phoebe enjoyed that night was not destined to last. Before the sun rose, Duncan was out of bed, washing and dressing silently in the slowly fading darkness of the last hour before dawn. Phoebe, sensing his reticence, knowing his mind almost as well as her own, pretended to be asleep.

When he was gone, without kissing her forehead or murmuring a farewell as he had always done, she cried. Duncan had opened his soul to her the night before, but now he had retreated into his private regrets again, and Phoebe knew he was suffering the agonies of the damned, as surely as if he'd been hurled into some medieval hell. His father and brother were captives of a government he opposed, and the home he dreamed of returning to one day was in the hands of his enemies. His despair was overwhelming, and, strong as he was, Phoebe could not be certain he would recover. Human beings had limits, even the special ones, like Duncan.

She waited, drifting in and out of a fitful sleep fraught with nightmares, until the sun filled the cabin with golden light. Then she got up, washed, pulled fresh clothes from the trunk at the foot of the bed, and dressed. She paused at Phillippa's door, but there was no answer, and when Phoebe gained the busy deck, she found her sister-in-law standing at the bow, gazing out at the sea as if spellbound.

Phoebe stepped up to the rail beside her. "Good morning," she said.

Phillippa turned that brilliant Rourke smile on her, dispelling all Phoebe's worries that the girl might be regretting leaving home. She did not seem to have Duncan's grave doubts about the futures of John and Lucas, and of Troy itself, but then Phillippa was very young. In her sheltered experience, no doubt, everything had always worked out in the end—dragons slain, castles conquered, princesses rescued from the clutches of the evil magician.

"I thought you would sleep all day long,"

Phillippa scolded. "Heaven knows, I have no one to talk to—the men are all busy, and Duncan is in one of his moods."

"He's worried about your father and brother," Phoebe said without rancor.

Phillippa's smile faded, and she nodded slowly. "Yes," she said. "As am I." Her countenance brightened again, but the effort was visible. What brave, sturdy people they were, these Rourkes. "Father and Lucas will be set free," she said determinedly. "After all, they've done nothing wrong, and that incident at the party was all a ruse on Major Stone's part, an attempt to force Duncan to surrender. By now, the major must know he's failed, and I should imagine he's quite ashamed of himself in the bargain."

Phoebe's assessment of the situation was, like Duncan's, considerably less optimistic than Phillippa's. Basil Stone was not a monster; his fondness for the Rourke family, with the exception of Duncan, of course, had been plain to see. But he was first and foremost a soldier of the King, and he had done his duty as he saw it. Duncan's escape from Troy would probably make matters worse for those left behind, not better.

"I hope you're right," Phoebe said. She felt sick, despondent, and weak and wanted to return to the captain's cabin, climb into bed, and curl up in a fetal position, but she denied herself that questionable luxury. For the sake of her child, for her own good and Duncan's, she would keep putting one foot in front of the other, go on moving and hoping and believing. Eventually, things would get better.

Please God.

Phoebe and Phillippa went below to the galley, where they ate a modest breakfast and talked. Phoebe told her sister-in-law about Paradise Island, spoke of Old Woman and the wonderful, sprawling house overlooking the sea, and even mentioned the child she would bear Duncan in the early spring.

That afternoon, a gathering storm darkened the sky and turned calm blue waters to churning charcoal. Phillippa went green as clover, but she remained on deck, doing what she could to help as the sailors scrambled to secure the ship. In the long days that followed, Phoebe felt a new respect for Phillippa. The girl was naive, but she was as innately courageous as any other member of her family, and her intellect was formidable.

At last, they reached Paradise Island and dropped anchor in the natural harbor well down the shore from the house. Phoebe recalled, with no small sorrow, that a cluster of condominiums would be built here, late in the twentieth century, replacing the dense tropical foliage that grew on the hillsides, driving away the colorful, raucous birds rising now like a living rainbow against the sky. The coral reef would be destroyed, to make swimming and boating easier, forcing the gaudy neon fish to go elsewhere.

Phoebe wished she could hold back the future

and keep Paradise Island a secret from the outside world forever.

Duncan was silent as he rowed his sister and wife ashore, leaving the crew to attend to the *Francesca*. Phoebe simply watched him, pondering the mysteries of marriage. Each night, when they were alone at last, and the cabin was immersed in darkness, Duncan had turned to Phoebe, had given and taken comfort in her embrace, and their love-making had been as explosive as ever before.

Except that there was no true intimacy, no fusion of souls. Although he was obviously in pain, he took care not to share his emotions with Phoebe, not to let down his guard again and show her the inner passages of his heart.

She was desolate, but she also felt the angry sting of betrayal. Duncan had trusted her the first night, but then, for some reason she had not been able to discern, he had closed her out.

If Phillippa noticed the strain between her brother and her sister-in-law, and she must have, for she was a bright girl, she gave no sign of it. She chattered incessantly, and when they were near the shore, took off her slippers and stepped over the side to wade happily onto the beach.

Phoebe couldn't help smiling at Phillippa's happiness, despite her own bruised feelings. Duncan, on the other hand, sent the rowboat skimming onto the dry white sand, jumped out, and went into the surf after his sister, grabbing her hand and practically dragging her ashore.

"Don't ever do that again," he growled, towering over the girl, his hands resting on his hips. "There are sharks in these waters, and venomous eels!"

Phoebe climbed carefully out of the boat, grateful for the feel of solid earth beneath her feet and at the same time furious with her husband. "Duncan . . ." she began, in protest.

But Phillippa needed no defending, as it happened; she took care of herself in true Rourke fashion. She raised both her small hands and thrust them, palms first, at Duncan's chest, nearly knocking him off his feet with the unexpectedness of the blow. "I will not be dragged about and shouted at!" she yelled. "Furthermore, I cannot see how a shark or a water snake could possibly be worse company than you are!"

Phoebe applauded and earned herself a furious glance from her husband.

"You stay out of this," he snapped. Then he turned back to Phillippa, prepared to shake a finger at her and go on with his lecture.

Phillippa was having none of that; she simply walked away, holding her skirts high, moving on swift, bare feet over the hot, sugar-fine sand. "Are you going to let him treat you like that?" she demanded, looking back at Phoebe and squinting against the dazzling tropical sun.

"Like what?" Duncan demanded, before Phoebe had a chance to respond one way or the other. "Pray, bestow upon me the benefit of your

316

worldly wisdom, little sister, and tell me how I am mistreating my wife!"

Phoebe stepped between them, hoping to put an end t to the argument before it could escalate into something that would scare away all the wildlife. "Duncan," she said calmly, "you are making a fool of yourself. Phillippa, you are the sister I have wished for all my life, but you *will* not interfere in my marriage. Do you both understand, or must I knock your heads together?"

There was a short silence, full of dire portent, but then Duncan scowled and stormed off up the beach, and Phillippa subsided, her shoulders slumping a little, her eyes downcast. After one apologetic glance at Phoebe, she fetched her slippers from the bottom of the rowboat and pulled them on, hopping comically from one sandy foot to the other as she did so.

"I'm sorry, Phoebe," she said, somewhat breathlessly, as they watched Duncan disappear into the foliage. "I was only trying to help."

Phoebe linked her arm through Phillippa's and smiled. "I know," she said gently. "Duncan is going through something that will one day be referred to as a dark night of the soul," she went on, ushering Phillippa up the path that would eventually bring them to the great house. "He'll get over it, I'm sure, being a resilient type. In the meantime, we must simply leave him to work things through on his own."

Phillippa looked very young and very vulnerable, with her wet skirts, sunburned nose, and teary eyes. "That's going to be hard," she said.

"Yes," Phoebe agreed with a sigh. "I know."

With that, the two women proceeded to the house, where they were met by a gleeful Old Woman, who embraced them both and led them inside to be fed, provided with baths and fresh clothes, and generally fussed over.

"You seem delighted that Phillippa is here," Phoebe remarked to Old Woman hours after their return, when she was in the master bedchamber, newly awakened from a long and much-needed nap. Old Woman had brought cold lemonade, made from springwater and lemons and sugar raised on the island, along with a tray of small sandwiches and pretty cookies. "I suppose you foresaw our arrival in your crystal ball?"

Old Woman took Phoebe's teasing in her usual good-natured way. "This is a good place for Miss Phillippa," she said. "She is needed here."

Phoebe sighed. She was sitting in a chair near the terrace doors, looking out at the sea as she nibbled and sipped the refreshments Old Woman had prepared for her. "You've noticed Duncan's black mood, I expect," she said. She always put on a front when he was around, never letting him see how much his attitude troubled her, but with her friend she could relax a little.

Old Woman was unfolding and shaking out the contents of Phoebe's trunk, which had been brought from the *Francesca* while she was sleeping. "There's a feeling in the air," she admitted, "like before the sea and the wind get angry. Trouble's coming."

Phoebe took a sip of her lemonade. She had no appetite and wouldn't have touched the food if it hadn't been for the baby. "Yes," she agreed. "Trouble is definitely coming. How is Alex doing, by the way?"

Old Woman examined a gown, frowned, and tossed it to one side. "He's feeling sorry for himself mostly," she sniffed. "What that boy needs is a good thrashing."

Phoebe was shocked. "You can't be serious," she said. She'd never have dreamed Old Woman, with her gentle tones and mystical ways, was an advocate of violence. "You think someone should strike Alex?"

"He's got to be straightened out, that one. He wants a talking-to." Old Woman stopped her sorting for a moment and stood very still, gazing out the window at the water, wearing its sequined mantle of sunlight. "Might go either way, Mr. Alex."

Phoebe shuddered in the aftermath of a quick, icy chill. "What do you mean?" she asked, setting her glass on the small table beside her chair and rising quickly to cross the room and stand facing the other woman. "Did you foresee something?" she demanded in an anxious whisper. "Something about Alex, I mean?"

Old Woman was slow in meeting Phoebe's eyes. When she did, there was compassion in her face, and sorrow. "There's a chance he'll come around," she said. "There's always hope of that, long as a body can draw breath. But he's in deep waters, Mr. Alex is, and he's got to a place where even Mr. Duncan can't reach him."

"Isn't there something we can do?" Phoebe pleaded.

Old Woman smiled sadly and patted Phoebe's cheek. "You might ask that God of yours to send an angel," she said. "That's what Mr. Alex needs now. An angel with a stubborn mind and a hot temper."

Phoebe was reminded of Phillippa, who certainly had a stubborn mind, as well as a hot temper. It was the angel part that came into question.

Phillippa found Alex Maxwell on one of the downstairs terraces, a crutch leaning against the wall near his chair, one foot propped on a wicker hassock. He didn't see her at first, which gave her a few moments to admire him, to remember the long-ago days when he had come often to Troy. Alex and her brothers had been great friends, and Phillippa, a child then, had adored Alex and dreamed of marrying him someday. She'd thought he was the handsomest man she'd ever seen, and now, as her heart turned itself inside out, she realized that she still cared for him. In a new and very troubling way.

She almost lost her courage—she, Phillippa Rourke, the most inveterate tomboy in the colony of South Carolina, the despair of a score of

English and French governesses—but in the end she forced herself to step over the threshold and speak.

"Alex?" she said, pretending she hadn't instantly recognized him. Pretending her soul hadn't twisted itself into a painful knot at the first glimpse.

He turned, and she saw shadows under his eyes, an unnerving gauntness in his face. But if he knew her, he did not reveal the fact.

"It's Phillippa," she said gently, noticing his maimed leg, really noticing, for the first time. "Don't you remember?"

A tattered vestige of the old smile spread across the familiar mouth. She knew those lips from a thousand girlish daydreams. Alex started to rise, grappling for his crutch, then gave up the effort, as if a new and somehow deeper awareness of his disability had just struck him. "Phillippa," he said, and she saw something broken in his eyes and grieved. "I wouldn't have recognized you."

Phillippa ventured out onto the terrace and took a chair near his without waiting for an invitation. Far from feeling confident, she wanted to bolt, to go somewhere and sob because Alex—beautiful, comical, dashing Alex—had been destroyed. Clearly, the injuries to his body were nothing at all compared with those to his soul. "Am I so different?" she asked. "That you wouldn't know me, I mean?"

Alex stared deeply into her eyes for a long moment, alert for pity, ready to brace himself against it. Then he looked away. "You were an imp," he reflected, "with grubby hands and skinned knees and pigtails. Yes, Phillippa, you've changed—from a freckled little monkey to a very beautiful woman."

Something surged into Phillippa's heart; for a second, she thought it would actually burst. She put a hand to her chest and took several deep breaths to steady herself. "You've changed, too," she said when she could speak.

Alex avoided her gaze, but she saw him stiffen and knew her words, meant in the kindest way, had pierced him like a spear. "Yes," he said at length. "I'm different, too. Tell me, how does my family fare? And yours?"

Phillippa wanted to weep and at the same time to dance along the stone railings of the terrace. She had half expected to see Alex when she reached Paradise Island; where Duncan was, Alex could usually be found as well. What she had *not* anticipated was this agonizing renewal of old feelings, this awakening of dreams she'd carefully tucked away, long ago, with her dolls and storybooks. She felt a sudden, swift anger because no one had warned her that loving a man could hurt the way it did.

She schooled herself to answer in dignified tones, void of emotion. "My father and Lucas have been arrested by the British," she said. "I imagine my mother is attempting to secure their release, through official channels, of course."

Alex gave her his full attention. Evidently, he

322

had not yet seen Duncan, else he would have heard the tale from him. "And Duncan left them?"

"He had to," Phillippa pointed out. "They wouldn't be saved. Father and Lucas believe that British rule is best for the colonies, that all the current problems can be worked out. Which brings me to your family. They are well—I saw your mother and father at our party."

Alex was silent for a long time, gazing through Phillippa, as though she were transparent. That, she found, was even worse than before, when he'd refused to look at her at all and fixed his attention on the sea.

"Duncan must be in a state," he murmured at last.

"He's utterly impossible," Phillippa agreed. Phoebe had warned her not to interfere, which meant she had to keep her opinions to herself, or at least make the effort to do so when her brother and sister-in-law were around. Surely, though, she could confide in Alex, her secret prince, who had saved her from so many dragons and witches and hairy trolls in her musings.

"He will be more so as time passes," Alex predicted. There was a certain gruff affection in his tone; part of his anger, Phillippa suddenly realized, stemmed from his inability to fight at Duncan's side, to help his friend through a difficult time. "What of the lovely Phoebe, then? Is she safe and well?"

Phillippa had that much good news to offer,

at least. She smiled. "Phoebe is going to be a mother," she confided, blushing. It was unseemly to speak of such things in mixed company, according to her long line of vanquished governesses, but this was Alex. She could say anything to him. "I think she's very happy about it."

Another pause, full of meanings Phillippa could not quite grasp. "And Duncan?" He spoke gruffly, almost abruptly. "How is he taking this momentous news?"

Phillippa hesitated. "I think he's afraid to be too pleased," she said. "Besides, he has a lot on his mind."

Alex merely nodded, and Phillippa was not to know if the conversation would ever have gone further, because Duncan spoiled everything, in that way elder brothers have. All he had to do was appear in the terrace doorway, looming there like a stormcloud sculpted to the shape of a man.

"Go and eat your supper, Phillippa," he said.

For Phoebe's sake, Phillippa held her tongue and marched into the house. She consoled herself with the theory that she wasn't really obeying her officious brother's command, she was having supper because she was hungry, and for no other earthly reason. Duncan had his share of gall, she reflected furiously, calling the *King* a tyrant.

Alex looked thinner, weaker, a man of sorrows caving in upon himself. Duncan's discouragement deepened immeasurably at the sight of his friend, and he had been harsh with Phillippa because of it. He promised himself that he would find her later and apologize.

"I hear you are to be a father," Alex said, without looking at Duncan. At Phillippa's departure, he had taken a glass from the table next to his chair and filled it from a decanter. "Rum," he explained unnecessarily. "The scourge of all pirates."

"I'll take some of that," Duncan replied, and Alex accommodated him by pouring a second glassful and extending it to his friend.

"Are we celebrating," Alex inquired, after taking a deep draft, "or commiserating?"

"Time will tell," Duncan said. He raised his glass, even though Alex wasn't looking, and tossed the rum back in a single swallow. His eyes watered and his throat burned and he wondered, briefly, when he'd turned into an old maid who couldn't handle a simple shot of good contraband liquor. "How have you been feeling, my friend? As if I didn't know."

"I'm rotting, from the soul out, like a piece of fruit fallen from the branch," Alex answered. The lack of emotion in his voice indicated that he believed the grim analogy.

Duncan refilled his glass and went to stand at the marble railing, looking out at the sea. Usually, the sight renewed him, lent him strength, but that night it was merely a meaningless mass of water, just something that was there. "Perhaps it might help the situation," he said presently, "if you would rise off your self-pitying ass and make yourself useful in some way."

"Harsh words," Alex commented tonelessly.

Duncan would have preferred for his friend to fling his glass at him, to bellow insults or throw a punch, as he would have done in the old days. Of course none of those things happened, because all the fight had gone out of Alex Maxwell. He had died, Alex had, the day a British musket ball had shattered his knee; what Duncan saw, what they all saw, was merely his corpse. Moving by reflex, carried about by the memories of his nerves, like a beheaded chicken dashing around the chopping block.

"Christ, Alex," Duncan muttered, "you picked a hell of a time to give up."

"I know," Alex said. The shame in his voice struck Duncan between the shoulder blades like a mace. "I'm in pieces." Duncan heard the clink of glass against glass as Alex took another dose of rum. "Can't seem to gather myself back into the old shape."

Duncan finished his drink. He would have another, he supposed, and another after that. But alone, in the privacy of his study, with nothing but the harpsichord for company. He'd have preferred to go to Phoebe, to tell her he didn't know what to do, to weep in her arms and spend himself in her exquisitely receptive body, but like Alex, he was ashamed. He'd allowed her to see his weaknesses once before—what blessed solace that had been—but he couldn't afford to do it again. For all their gentle philosophies, women wanted strength in a man, not fragility. If he showed that side of himself to Phoebe again, she might stop loving him, and if that happened, he would be utterly lost.

What a hypocrite he was, Duncan reflected bitterly. He could not admit to Phoebe that he loved her, even now, and yet he feared the loss of her affection for him above all things. The whip, the hangman's noose, the judgment all men must one day face, none of that frightened him overmuch. But one small woman held his heart, his very being, in her hands, and had the power to crush him like a clod of dry dirt.

"We are a sorry pair, you and I," he said to Alex. "Perhaps the world would be better if we simply crawled into our graves and pulled the sod over our heads like a blanket."

"The idea appeals to me," Alex replied, his words somewhat slurred now, as he got down to serious drinking. "You, on the other hand"—he paused to belch ignobly—"have a child on the way. Nothing for it, old friend—you'll have to grow up now, and stop dashing about, playing at being a pirate."

"What about you, Alex?" Duncan asked, turning around, setting his empty glass on the chair-side table with a resounding crash. "When will you pull your thumb out of your mouth and comport yourself like a man?"

Alex offered no reply.

★ ★ ★

327

Phoebe lay awake and alone in the master bed-chamber, long after full darkness had fallen and a deep silence had settled over the house. When the music shattered that uneasy peace, she did not know whether to be relieved or heartbroken. She listened to her husband play his furious, terrible music, and concluded that she was a little of both. Duncan had found an outlet for his grief, and it was a comfort to know that, but she despaired, too, because he had not come to her.

She was awake, many hours later, when Duncan entered their room. Although he had left the harpsichord some time before, it was plain that he'd been attempting to drown his demons in alcohol.

He stripped and stretched out beside her on the bed, but did not reach for her. Although Phoebe would have refused him—making love to a drunk was not on her list of wifely duties—she was still aggrieved that he didn't even try to touch her.

She supposed that made her as crazy as he was.

Sunny and uneventful days passed, rapidly turning to sunny and uneventful weeks, and Phoebe began to gain weight and to throw up promptly at eight o'clock every morning. If she'd ever had any doubts that she was pregnant, those misgivings were gone with her waistline. Duncan was as uncommunicative as ever, gone all day and hammering at the harpsichord half the night, like Zeus flinging thunderbolts from his fingertips. Sometimes, he tried to drink himself into

328

unconsciousness, and succeeded admirably, but on other occasions, he came sober to Phoebe's bed and asked her to take him inside her, and she did not refuse him. Their lovemaking was as tempestuous, as fiercely satisfying, from a physical standpoint at least, as it had ever been. Emotionally, however, Phoebe felt abandoned, untouched, and most especially, unloved.

Alex grew worse with every passing day, despite regular visits from both Phoebe and Phillippa. Phoebe could not reach him, and neither could Duncan, but Phillippa often succeeded in making the patient so angry that he flung things and shouted injunctions to "leave him the bloody hell alone." These outbursts only seemed to encourage Phillippa to torment him further.

Then some of Duncan's men, spies he had left behind in South Carolina, arrived on Paradise Island, and they brought Margaret Rourke with them.

She was the picture of dignity and grace as she approached the front entrance of Duncan's house. Margaret's younger son awaited her on the veranda—Phoebe and Phillippa were watching from a ground-floor window—as she made her way up the curving walk and then the glistening white marble steps to face Duncan.

Duncan made no move to embrace her—as far as Phoebe could tell, from her admittedly awkward vantage point—he didn't even smile. She knew, and hoped Margaret did as well, that it was shame that kept him from greeting her properly, and not a lack of affection.

"What news do you bring?" he asked. Phillippa and Phoebe strained to catch the words.

Margaret stood straight and tall. Despite the sultry island heat, she was wearing a hooded cloak over her traveling clothes. "I have borne my journey well," she said, when he failed to inquire. "But I am weary, and in need of hospitality."

Duncan descended the steps very slowly, and something in the set of his broad shoulders made Phoebe's heart ache. She and Phillippa dashed for the front door, which stood open, lest they miss whatever might come next.

When they reached their destination, however, Duncan had drawn Margaret into a brief embrace and was just releasing her.

"You shouldn't have come here," he said, as he turned to lead her into the house. He scowled to find his wife and sister filling the doorway, eavesdropping without compunction. "The seas are dangerous these days."

Phoebe hovered, grasping the door frame, while Phillippa rushed to hurl herself into her mother's arms.

"Mama," the woman-child cried. "It's terrible! Alex is here, and he's been shot, and he won't let himself get well . . ."

Margaret held her daughter, there on the veranda of Duncan's grand house, her gaze moving from Phoebe's face to Duncan's in silent question. Duncan started to speak, then expelled an exasperated breath and went inside, favoring Phoebe with a scathing glance as he passed. Margaret came next and paused to kiss her daughter-in-law lightly on the cheek, her arm linked with Phillippa's.

"My dear, strong Phoebe," Margaret said. "You're as much a Rourke as any of us, and suffering for it, I'll wager."

Phoebe smiled sadly and cast one brief, sorrowful glance after her departing husband. Then she focused her full attention on their weary guest, who had traveled far and braved many perils to be with them. "Come inside and rest," she said. "Phillippa, do go and ask Old Woman to please prepare a room and something to eat."

"Knowing her," Phillippa sniffled, regaining her composure now that she'd given vent to her frustration over Alex, "she's already done all that and more." But she hurried off to do Phoebe's bidding, after squeezing Margaret's hand once in parting.

Phoebe escorted her mother-in-law into Duncan's study, usually the coolest room in the house. He was there, as she had thought he would be, leaning against the edge of his desk, arms folded, expression unreadable, waiting.

He nodded formally to his mother and wife as they took seats, Phoebe settling on the leather settee after Margaret had dropped gracefully into a wing-backed chair. It was, Phoebe supposed, an acknowledgment of sorts, but she was left with a bereft feeling, as though Duncan had grasped

331

her shoulders and set her out of his path. Both literally and figuratively.

He invited Margaret to speak with a gesture some would have considered insolent, probably without being able to say why.

Margaret flinched slightly, as if he'd struck her, then raised her chin and folded her aristocratic hands, long-fingered and graceful ones, disposed, like Duncan's, toward the making of music, in her lap. "Troy has been confiscated by the Crown," she said, and the faintly defiant note in her voice was the only indication of her anger, which must have been profound. "Your father and Lucas are being transported to London, there to be tried and no doubt cast into prison. I have attempted to secure justice through the magistrates, and I have failed. Therefore, I mean to go to England and seek audience with the King himself. Is that direct enough for you, Duncan?"

He was reeling inwardly, though there was no outward sign of it. Phoebe was aware of his true reaction only because she knew him so well, and she suspected that Margaret did, too.

"My God," Duncan rasped at long last. "You expect to reason with that pox-ridden madman? As for Father and Lucas, they'll rot in Newgate or some other filthy hole before they get a fair trial from that lot!"

"I do not think your father will survive long enough to be imprisoned," Margaret said quietly. Phillippa had just entered with a tray, which she promptly dropped, sending glassware and silver crashing to the floor. She uttered a strangled scream and then started to swoon, though Duncan caught her and lifted her into his arms before she reached the floor.

Phoebe was off the settee in an instant. "Put her here," she said.

Margaret rose from her chair and went to stand over her daughter, laying a gentle hand on Phillippa's forehead. "Ask yourself, child," she commanded softly, "how your father would want you to behave in this crisis. And then act accordingly, for his sake as well as your own."

Phillippa opened her eyes, which were brimming with tears. "Oh, Mama, I cannot bear it— I cannot."

"You must," Margaret said. She spoke with unshakable firmness, but there was no cruelty in her manner or her tone. She loved her daughter, as she obviously loved her husband and sons, and she was determined to see things through, whatever fate might hold. In the meantime, she would maintain her composure, and she expected each member of her family to do the same.

"What ship carries them to England?" Duncan asked, the sharpness of his voice puncturing the moment.

Margaret turned and met his gaze stalwartly. "They are aboard the *Northumberland*," she said. "You must not try to intercept this vessel, Duncan. I came here to ask your help in reaching the King, not to inspire a fool's errand."

333

Duncan did not reply. He simply strode out of the room, and minutes later, the clamorous peals of a brass bell shattered the serenity of the island. It was the signal for his crew to man the *Francesca* and fit her out to sail.

16

The *Northumberland* proved easy to track, but then, her captain had intended it so. What the British had not anticipated, or so Duncan hoped, was finding a disabled Dutch trading ship in their sea-lane, listing to starboard and taking on water. Everything—the *Francesca*, his own life, the lives of his crew—depended on the success of this deception, flimsy as it was. To board the *Northumberland*, they must lure her alongside. If her officers guessed that a trap yawned before them, they would simply turn their cannon on the already foundering ship and finish her with a few rounds of grapeshot.

Duncan kept out of sight, lest he be recognized, as the captain of the English ship raised a horn to his mouth to address them. Beedle had gotten himself up in a cap and a fancy coat with shiny brass buttons, and now he stepped up to the rail and answered the *Northumberland*'s hail with his own. Beedle was a master mimic and he had presented himself as a Dutchman before, when the situation called for it.

"We beg your aid, good sir," Beedle shouted cheerfully through his horn. Below, men were ready to patch the *Francesca*'s side with tar swabs, but this would not be done, by Duncan's own order, until the other ship had been boarded. "We seem to be taking on water, and we've a full crew aboard, all of them much too young to die."

Duncan watched the British captain, a man he did not recognize, and felt alarm clench coldly in the pit of his stomach. The fellow was suspicious, as well he might be, but in this case, failure was not an option. Duncan could endure losing the *Francesca*, if it came to that, but his crew was another matter, and the lives of his father and brother were even more precious to him. To make matters worse, he suspected—though he'd searched the ship from stem to stern and found no sign of her—that Phoebe was aboard somewhere.

Christ, he thought, closing his eyes for a fraction of a moment. His wife, his child. His father and brother, and his crew. His ship.

Whatever it cost, this gambit must succeed.

"Show your crew!" demanded the *Northumberland*'s sea master.

The men stepped up to the rail, grasping it to maintain their balance as the *Francesca* bent her masts and rigging toward the water, creaking mightily under the strain. It was then, of all times, that Phoebe showed herself, dragging herself up the slippery incline of the deck to join the startled crew at the rail.

She waved a handkerchief. "Help!" she cried, with a convincing note of hysteria in her voice. "We'll all drown if you don't save us!"

Nobody was going to be able to help that woman, Duncan vowed to himself, as fresh fear surged, bile-bitter, into the back of his throat, when he got his hands on her. In the meantime, he could only hope that chivalry, a trait the British loved to ascribe to themselves, would prevail, and the *Northumberland* would sail within rappeling distance.

"Hold fast!" the English captain boomed, true to form. "Assistance is on its way!"

Duncan drew his sword as the awkward prison ship lumbered toward them. When the *Francesca* tipped again, with a great, grinding moan of timbers that reverberated along his spine, he saw Phoebe lose her tentative grasp on the rail. She slid backward, arms wheeling, and Duncan caught her with his free arm and held her against his chest.

"You," he said past her ear, "are in more trouble than you have ever dreamed."

"So," she replied, only a little breathless, "are you."

"Find something to hold onto," Duncan commanded, "and stay put until the fighting is over."

"Yes, dear," Phoebe promised very sweetly, turning to look up at him and bat her eyelashes.

"You must know that I wouldn't dream of disobeying you."

The *Northumberland* was alongside; he could not stay and throttle her. Instead, he embraced her briefly and bolted into the fray.

The battle was long and it was bloody, and the British, as always, gave as good as they got. Blue sparks filled the air as Duncan's sword clashed with that of an English captain, and all around, his men fought with the tireless, savage intensity that had enabled the fighting force to survive more than four years of warfare. At one point, when Duncan glanced around him, looking for Phoebe, a new opponent descended upon him and cut a deep slash into his right shoulder.

The pain would come later, if he was fortunate enough to live to feel it, Duncan knew. For the moment, all he could see was smoke and blood and the flash of sunlight on swords. He heard the shouts of his own men and the crew of the *Northumberland*, the terrible scream of timber from the *Francesca* as she succumbed.

Phoebe. Had she stayed aboard the doomed ship, or was she on this one, getting in the way of swordplay?

Duncan fought his way across the deck, wielding his sword and casting glances to left and right when he could afford to, searching desperately for any sign of his wife. He did not catch so much as a glimpse of her, and he was terrified to consider the possibilities, but he did not yet despair. Phoebe would do what she must to survive, for the sake of their child and for herself. That was the sort of woman she was.

Behind him, he felt the *Francesca* go into a death roll, as if she were a part of him, an extension of his own body. Soaked in sweat, choking on the acrid smoke of cannon and muskets and burning cargo, Duncan did the only thing he could—he continued to fight.

The *Northumberland* was a transport ship, rather than a war vessel, and when the tide of battle turned at last, it favored the rebel forces. Once the trained soldiers had been defeated, those put on board to lie in wait for Duncan and his raiders, only the crew was left to offer resistance. They were sailors, not men of war, and they had been reduced to swinging barrel staves and mop handles in the effort to protect themselves. One by one, then by twos and threes, they saw reason and surrendered.

Duncan lowered his sword in time to turn and see the *Francesca* tumbling beneath the water's surface like a whale turning up its belly. He stopped Beedle as he passed and caught at the man's tattered sleeve with a bloodied hand.

"Where is my wife?" he asked, his voice hoarse.

"Below," Beedle said, casting a glance toward the corpse of Duncan's ship. "She's safe, man—gone to find your father and brother and see if they need looking after. Here, let's have a look at the shoulder, if we can find it for the blood . . ."

Duncan shrugged away when his friend would

have taken hold of him. "Later," he replied, though Beedle could not have heard, for Duncan had already turned by the time the word left his mouth, making his way toward the companionway leading belowdecks.

He encountered several of his men as he went; each one tried to waylay him and was shaken off. He found the hold, where the prisoners were kept, and stood on the threshold, appalled by the stink of the place, temporarily blinded by the gloom.

Phoebe's form, slightly plump now that their child was growing inside her, was the first one he recognized. He could see that she was whole, with no blood on her, and the relief that rode the wake of this realization made him sway in the doorway. He grated out her name.

She turned and looked back at him, her face a smudged, pale oval in the darkness. "Over here, Duncan," she said. "Come quickly."

He stepped over prone bodies, neither knowing nor caring if they were alive or dead, and reached her side. She was kneeling on the filthy, straw-littered boards of the lower deck, holding a man in her arms. Duncan dropped to one knee when he recognized his father. He was dimly aware of Lucas, grubby and gaunt, close by.

John Rourke smiled up at him. One hand was splayed over his sunken chest, as if to keep his heart beating by an act of will. "If I were a well man," John said, "I swear I would get up off this floor and thrash you for a fool. Don't you know a bloody trap when you see one? They might have had you, Duncan. God in heaven, they might have had you."

Tears burned in Duncan's eyes, and, for once, he made no effort to hide them. It would have been futile. "Are you going to lie there and die, old man," he challenged gruffly, "after all I've been through to save you from a British prison?"

Phoebe had withdrawn a little way, so Duncan could be closer to his father. Lucas, he saw, through a sheen of tears, was slumped across from him, clasping the older man's free hand against his own forehead. His broad shoulders moved with his weeping, though there was no sound from him.

"It is my time to die," John replied slowly, and with obvious difficulty. "I reckon I'd have done so anyway, right about now. The circumstances probably don't matter much, in the scheme of things."

"Stay with us," Duncan rasped. He felt Phoebe's hand on his back, providing a counterpoint to the pain awakening in his wound, and was amazed at the comfort that came from such a simple caress. "There are doctors . . ."

His father gave a long, shuddering sigh—there was a faint echo of amusement in the sound—and then shook his head. "I am too weary," he said. "This I cannot grant you, Duncan. But there are things I will ask, of both you and Lucas."

"Anything," Lucas said. It was the first time he'd spoken.

"Remember, when this war is ended—no

matter who prevails—that you are brothers. I enjoin you to look after your mother and sister, of course, but also to forget your differences when the fighting ceases and set yourselves to the task of raising Troy from the ashes. It must be held for the Rourkes who will come after us."

Across their father's fragile, dying body, Duncan and Lucas looked at each other. There was no need to speak; they had always been close, and although they had argued many times, and even come to blows on occasion as brothers will, they loved each other. There had never been any question of that.

"Phoebe?" John looked about, blindly, for his daughter-in-law.

"I'm here," she said gently, drawing near again, so that he could see her.

He smiled, and she smoothed his hair with a light, soot-smudged hand. "You'll comfort Margaret, won't you?" he asked. "And Phillippa? And this great brute of a son of mine?"

"Yes," she promised. She looked tenderly at Duncan and then told her father-in-law in a soft voice, "There will be a child in March. We're going to call him John Alexander Rourke."

John's gray face took on a translucent quality; he seemed to welcome death, to see things Phoebe and Lucas and Duncan could not. "John Alexander Rourke," he repeated, making the name a benediction on his own life.

With that, John Rourke closed his eyes, sighed once more, and perished.

Lucas doubled over with a soundless cry, laying his forehead to his father's chest, and Duncan, half-blinded by his own grief, rested a hand on his brother's heaving back, lending the only comfort he could give. He did not know how long they sat like that—ten minutes? an hour?—before Beedle and other members of Duncan's crew came and led Lucas away.

Only then did Duncan realize that the other prisoners, probably all dissidents on their way to England for trial, had been ushered out.

Phoebe laid cool, dirty hands on either side of Duncan's face. "Come with me," she commanded softly. "You can do nothing more here, and you're wounded. I'm going to keep my promise to John and look after you."

Duncan supposed he was in a mild state of shock. He rose awkwardly to his feet—the wound in his shoulder was throbbing in time with his heartbeat now, and the pain was like the touch of a smoldering branding iron. And yet, in the face of his father's death, it was no more than an annoyance.

She took him to a room filled with long tables; the mess, no doubt. There were men everywhere, moaning and bleeding, being tended by freed prisoners and, in some cases, by those who had wounded them in the first place. Lucas was there, looking grim but whole, and he helped Phoebe press Duncan onto one of the improvised cots.

The pain grew keen and sharp, clawing at him

342

like talons, like claws attempting to wrench his muscles out through his skin. And his father, the man he'd thought would live forever, was dead.

Lucas peeled away shreds of Duncan's bloody shirt, while Phoebe peered at the wound.

"It looks pretty bad," she said.

Duncan uttered a strangled laugh. "An astute observation, Mistress Rourke," he said. "I want whiskey. Now."

"Too bad," Phoebe said. "What we had went down with the *Francesca,* and as near as we can tell, the captain and crew of the *Northumberland* are simply not drinking men."

"What are we going to do?" asked Lucas. He looked like a dead man himself, as soiled and befuddled as if he'd just dug his way up out of the grave to inquire what all the wailing was about.

"Clean the wound as best we can, and then stitch it closed."

"You know how to do that?"

"I saw it in a movie once," Phoebe said, with alarming confidence.

Lucas opened his mouth, only to be stopped by the back of Duncan's hand coming to rest against his belly.

"Don't bother asking what a 'movie' is," Duncan told his brother. "You won't understand the answer."

"Shut up," said Phoebe. "I need to concentrate."

Duncan passed out then, and it was probably just as well.

Phoebe joined Beedle on the deck of the *Northumberland.* It was sunset, and half a dozen lifeboats bobbed on moving patches of pink and apricot waters, dappled with bits of crimson and gold. The captain, the crew, and the tattered remains of the redcoat contingent were aboard, with water and food to last them until they were found or reached shore on their own. Understandably, the prisoners who had been incarcerated below, with John and Lucas, had chosen to remain on board.

Among them were a surgeon and two barbers, who had done an admirable job of mending the wounded, Duncan included. The suturing had proved to be too much for Phoebe after all, and she'd been grateful to hand over her needle and thread to the doctor.

"The captain all but turned the *Francesca* onto her masts, searching for you," Beedle said with some amusement in his tone. His spiffy coat was somewhat the worse for wear, now that the fighting was over, and the brass buttons were either missing or dulled with blood. "Where were you hiding, Mistress Rourke?"

Phoebe might have smiled, if John hadn't been dead and Duncan severely injured, body and soul. She thought of the book she'd read about Duncan's life, lying open somewhere, far off in the twentieth century, and remembered that it had mentioned his sword wound. "I was in the hold, crouched inside a coil of rope. I believe there were two or three bilge rats in there with me."

Beedle waved to the crewmen of the *Northumberland*, and one sporting fellow waved back. "Duncan will have my hide for saying it, but I don't care," he said, without looking at her. "I'm glad you were close at hand today, Mistress Rourke. Your husband had need of you, though only God knows whether he'll ever admit it or not."

"Thank you," Phoebe replied. "I expect, when Mr. Rourke recovers, he'll lecture me until I'm ready to cover my ears with both hands and jump overboard. He was not, to put it plainly, pleased to find me on board the *Francesca*, today of all days." She paused, truly aware, for the first time since the action had begun, of her own weariness. "Now, I must go and sit with my husband," she said.

"He'd prefer it, I think, if you'd lie down," Beedle said kindly. "I'll find you a place to rest and come for you straightaway if the captain needs you."

She thought, as she did every day, every hour, every minute, of their child. "Yes," she said. "I'll rest. Thank you again, Mr. Beedle."

The plain man blushed and offered his arm.

Phillippa and Margaret, Old Woman and all the servants were waiting on the beach with muskets and whatever other weapons they'd been able to find, as the *Northumberland* sailed ponderously into port. When the vessel was near enough that they could recognize Phoebe and Lucas and Beedle at the rail, they lowered their guns and simply waited.

Phoebe came ashore in the one remaining lifeboat, escorted by Lucas and the elderly surgeon, Dr. Evan Mars, who had been on his way to England to stand trial on charges of treason. He had been in the pay of General Washington himself, until his capture.

Slumped between Phoebe and the doctor, rummy with fever, was Duncan.

Margaret Rourke did not wait for the rowboat to reach the shore; she waded out to meet it. "Where is John?" she asked, her gaze moving from her firstborn son to her second, and lingering on the latter even as she addressed the former. "Tell me, Lucas."

"Father is dead," Lucas said quietly. Phoebe's heart went out to him, and to Margaret, whose face showed that she had known the truth before she had asked. "It was his heart."

Margaret gripped the side of the boat, standing waist-deep in the surf, her dress floating gauzily around her. She stared at Duncan for a long time, then turned her gaze on Phoebe. "Will he recover?"

"I don't know," Phoebe replied in all honesty, wishing again, as they all made their way toward the house, Lucas and the surgeon all but carrying

Duncan between them, that she'd read the end of that damnable biography before she left the twentieth century.

Duncan was taken to the master bedroom, where Phoebe and Old Woman stripped him down and bathed his scalding flesh in cool water. He was in a waking stupor and wholly uncooperative during the process, writhing and twisting about, singing snatches of bawdy songs, calling out orders to a phantom crew.

"Let me get Simone to help," Old Woman said, watching Phoebe. "You look near to collapsing yourself."

"Simone is back?" Phoebe asked, surprised and somehow troubled by the news. "When did this happen?"

"She showed up two nights ago. Said she came down from Queen's Town. Now, you don't bother Old Woman with no more questions. You just go and put your feet up."

Phoebe didn't want to be too far from Duncan, but she *had* been under a considerable strain lately, and she was tired. Too, the news of Simone's return had upset her, in some vague, indefinable way. She laid protective hands over her stomach. "Something is wrong," she mused.

"A whole lot is wrong," Old Woman amplified. Then she covered Duncan tenderly with a linen sheet and crossed to the doorway. "Mr. Alex, he ready to put a gun to his head. Miss Phillippa, she so torn up about her papa being gone, I don't

347

know how we'll put her back together. Mr. Lucas and Mistress Margaret, well, they just broken-hearted. It's a sad place, this house."

"Yes," Phoebe agreed, but she was still thinking about Simone and wondering why she had returned to Paradise Island.

The next day, Duncan's fever was down, and his fits of delirium gave way to a profound, healing sleep. The day after that, John Rourke was buried on a hilltop overlooking the sea, with a clergyman, one of the prisoners from the *Northumberland*, to perform the ceremony. Like Dr. Mars, Lucas, and the others, the Reverend Franks had been a prisoner. Franks was accused of preaching sedition and readily confessed his guilt.

Phoebe attended the funeral, and so did Duncan, although he could barely stand. The *Northumberland* was taken out onto the open sea, though still within plain view of the mourners on the island, there to be set ablaze with torches. She made a fitting tribute, Phoebe thought as she stood watching the ship burn, for John Rourke, the gentle Viking. Those who had sailed the craft on her brief and final voyage were returning to shore in small boats.

Alex was the first to turn away and hobbled slowly down the hill on his crutch, brushing off the help Beedle attempted to lend with a motion of his hand. Phoebe glanced up at Duncan's face, just then, and saw that he was not looking at the magnificent fire, or pondering his father's fresh grave. He was watching Alex.

"Will you join us?" Duncan asked of Lucas, later that night, when he and Beedle and several other members of the crew had gathered in his study. Alex was notably absent.

Lucas sighed. His face was shadowed with grief, but he was sturdy of mind and bone and spirit, and he was mending in spite of himself. "Join you?" he echoed. "But you have no ship, Brother. Of course, you might have refitted the *Northumberland* for your own use, if you hadn't been so eager to provide a spectacle for us all."

Duncan took a sip from the snifter of brandy he'd poured for himself, taking care to avoid Phoebe's gaze. He was completely aware of her, nonetheless, standing near the fireplace, watching him with her arms folded and that devious little mind of hers spinning like the blades of a windmill. "That cumbersome old tub? It would be easier to maneuver a whale's carcass. Besides, the British would have known her at a glance for one of their own." He took another swallow of brandy, making sure Phoebe knew he'd enjoyed it. "It's true that we're in want of a ship, and we'll have one."

"How?" Lucas asked with pointed reason, raising both eyebrows. Duncan had forgotten how irritating his elder brother could be when he got bogged down in details.

"Well, hell," Duncan said, exasperated, "we'll

steal one. Did you think I was going to row into the harbor at Charles Town and put in an order for a fleet clipper, specially designed for piracy and high treason?"

Lucas got to his feet. "I won't be a party to thievery."

Duncan uttered a long-suffering sigh. "Sit down," he replied. "And leave the moralizing to our good and subversive friend, the Reverend Franks." He paused to give that man a nod of polite acknowledgment. "What is your decision, Lucas?"

The elder Rourke son shoved the fingers of one hand through his dark hair. "Good God, Duncan, we buried our father not six hours past, and you're talking of stealing ships!"

"I will do my mourning privately," Duncan said, in a moderate voice that contained, never-theless, a warning. "The war, I fear, will go right on as if nothing had happened. I intend to fight until we fall or they do. Now, Lucas—on which side shall you stand?"

Lucas hesitated. For a beat too long.

Duncan leaned forward in his chair, setting the brandy aside with a thump. "Can it be?" he breathed. "Can you really be so thick, Lucas, as to hold to your Tory beliefs after they took your land, threw you aboard a prison ship without a trial, and killed your father?"

Lucas was breathing deeply, rapidly. He'd gone pale, and his flesh glistened with sweat, but Duncan knew his brother well—despite the outward signs of it, Lucas was not afraid. He was angry. "Those things were unfair," he bit out, meeting Duncan's gaze squarely. "But they are to be expected, when one member of the family is a wanted man, seeking to overthrow a just government!"

"A *just government?*" Duncan rasped. "You think it is *just* to arrest an old man for the sins of his son? God, Lucas, if you truly believe that sanctimonious rot, then I fear for us all."

"Damn you," Lucas cried, on his feet again. "Who shall I blame for the death of my father—the King, for wanting to enforce his laws? Or you, Duncan, for breaking them with such dedication?"

A charged silence settled over the room, smothering all but the smallest sounds.

In the end, it was Margaret Rourke who spoke next, from the doorway of the study.

"You will both hold your tongues," she said. She was slender and fragile in her widow's weeds, her flawless skin white with grief and the strain of bearing it with dignity. "Duncan, you claim to love liberty, but adventure is your true mistress, and you would risk anything for it, including the freedom you profess to cherish. You might indeed have become a pirate if you hadn't had a cause to take up. And you, Lucas, have said a thing many men would be loath to forgive, even in a beloved brother."

Lucas's broad shoulders slumped a little, as though his mother had struck him. Duncan was doing his share of squirming as well, but inwardly, and he hid it well.

"Do you think," Duncan persisted evenly, his gaze fixed, scalding, on his brother, "that Father died because of me?"

"I don't know," Lucas answered. Then, without looking at anyone else, including Duncan, he strode out of the room.

There was no more talk of stealing ships that night.

Phillippa was huddled on the end of a stone bench, in an isolated corner of the garden, weeping softly. Alex watched, from a little distance, wanting to console her, not knowing how. Loathing himself for his helplessness.

She must have heard something or sensed his presence, for even though he kept to the shadows, she raised her head, sniffled, and said his name.

He came toward her, his gait graceless and slow, as always, because of the crutch and the small, slippery stones and broken shells that made up the garden walk. The effort to remain upright, and not humiliate himself by collapsing at her feet, raised perspiration on his upper lip.

"Sit with me for a little while?" It was a plea, not a command. She patted the bench.

Alex made no move toward her. "Your father was a good man," he said. It was the best he could manage, under the circumstances. The world was a black place to him, treacherous and unjust, fraught with ugliness and pain. In point of fact, he envied John Rourke for escaping it.

Phillippa sniffled, her face aglow with moonlight. Even with her eyes red-rimmed and her nose swollen from crying, she was painfully pretty, a lily blooming in a landscape of waste and rubble. "Yes," she said softly. "Like you."

Alex flinched inwardly, as if she'd pierced him with a lance. "No," he argued brokenly. "John was nothing like me. What will you do now, Phillippa?"

"Do?" She widened her gray eyes, and he saw that the thick, dark lashes surrounding them were spiky with tears. "I'll cry a great deal, I should think, for some time. I'll always miss Father, and I expect it will hurt when I think of him, at least for a while. But of course I shall go on. That, after all, is what he would want."

Several awkward moments passed before Alex was able to speak. Here was a mere girl, delicate and fragile, and yet she had more courage than he'd ever possessed, even in his best days. He felt a bittersweet yearning whenever he saw Phillippa, or merely thought of her, but in point of fact he wasn't fit to speak her name.

He stood in the darkness, his hand trembling where he grasped that cursed crutch. He had fallen in love with Phillippa, during some unguarded moment after her arrival on Paradise Island, and he knew that she cared for him as well. The idea of taking Phillippa to wife, of lying with her every night, consumed him, filled him with an unholy desire.

But he was a cripple. To wed such a woman would be a travesty on his part; she deserved a man who could protect her, provide for her, teach her pleasure . . .

"Alex?" Phillippa said gently. "I love you."

He turned his back on her, turned his back on all hope of finding his way again. And he told himself it was for her sake.

She caught up to him before he'd gained the French doors leading in from that part of the garden and slipped her arms around his waist from behind. In another woman, the act would have been brazen, but it was not so with Phillippa. The gesture was one of sweet innocence, even though the reaction it stirred in him was downright contemptible.

"Why are you afraid?" she asked, resting her cheek against his spine and holding him fast. "I know that you love me."

He did not have the heart, or the willpower, to break out of her embrace. He felt consoled, truly and deeply, for the first time since that musket ball had shattered his knee. His withered soul drank of her kindness and was soothed, temporarily at least. "Yes," he admitted at length, his voice broken and gruff. "Yes, Phillippa, I love you. Too much to doom you to a lifetime of sorrow and pity."

She moved, standing in front of him now, but still holding him fast in her arms. If he had ever

354

doubted his ability to respond to a woman, and of course he had, he could no longer do so. The evidence of his desire was embarrassingly prominent.

"Sorrow and pity?" Phillippa echoed. "All the sorrow is yours, Alex Maxwell, and so is the pity. You're the only one around here who feels sorry for you—the rest of us just want to shake you until your teeth rattle."

He let the crutch clatter to the ground and gripped both her shoulders, hard. "Listen to me," he seethed, too angry now, too frustrated, to think of propriety or of a young girl's sensibilities. "I am a freak. If we married, and I took you to my bed—" Alex realized what he was saying and abruptly stopped speaking.

There was an unsettling twinkle in Phillippa's eyes. "Do you think I don't know what men and women do together?" she asked. "I grew up on a plantation, Alex. We raised horses and cattle, sheep and pigs."

Perhaps she wasn't embarrassed, but Alex was. "Stop," he pleaded.

She laughed, and the sound was moist, because she'd been crying earlier. What a contradictory creature she was, delightful and infuriating at one and the same time. "Of course you'll have to marry me first," she announced. "If you don't, my brothers will kill you."

Alex tilted his head back and searched the starry sky, a smile tugging at one corner of his mouth. This, he thought, was a form of suicide he had not yet considered.

17

Phoebe waited until everyone but Duncan had left the study. He did not meet her eyes, or rise from his chair, when she came to stand beside him. She laid a hand on his shoulder, where the sling was tied, and he flinched at her touch, although she had been careful to avoid his wound.

"Lucas didn't mean what he said," she told him. "About John dying because of you."

Duncan was a long time in answering. "Yes," he said finally. "He did."

Phoebe knelt next to him, pressed one hand to his face, made him turn his head and look at her. "You know it isn't true—don't you? John was sick long before . . ."

He sighed, brushed her cheek with the knuckles of his right hand. "I don't know anything," he told her, "except that my father wouldn't have wanted me to believe I'd done him harm. Lucas is hurting, and he has no pretty wife to bind his wounds." Here he paused and offered up a slight, sad smile as he raised Phoebe to her feet and then drew her down onto his lap. "Considering that my brother never had much tact in the first place,

356

I guess it's not surprising that he would say what he did."

Phoebe took a deep breath and let it out slowly before speaking. "You don't really plan to steal a ship?" she ventured. She would have to find a way to go along if Duncan went pirating again, but she hoped it wouldn't be necessary. She enjoyed an adventure as much as the next person, but she'd had enough swashbuckling to last her. "Couldn't we just stay here and mind our own business for a while?"

Duncan chuckled, but his eyes betrayed the depth of his suffering. "Phoebe, Phoebe," he scolded. "Harrying the British *is* my business. If I stay here and wait for them to find me, it will spoil the fun—theirs as well as mine."

Frustration surged within Phoebe, and she controlled it. She'd learned a lot about self-restraint, she reflected, since meeting this man. "Couldn't you just lie low for a month or two? The British are bound to be in a bad mood, after what you did to the *Northumberland*, and by now they surely know who did it."

" 'Lie low,' " he mused, seeming to savor the phrase. "Another interesting term." He moved one thumb over Phoebe's lower lip, as if preparing her for his kiss, and she felt a spilling warmth, somewhere deep inside, followed by a singular ache in a much more specific place. Where this man was concerned, she was an absolute harlot.

She shivered. Duncan hadn't touched her in

an intimate way, and yet there could be no denying that the lovemaking process had already begun; mysterious, elemental things were happening inside her—passages widening, needs awakening, tiny muscles contracting. And contracting further, like the spring in an old-fashioned clock.

"You deliberately misunderstood," she said in a somewhat tremulous voice. Phoebe wanted to make love to Duncan and to have him make love to her, but not in the study, with so many people around. "To 'lie low' just means not drawing attention to yourself."

"Hmmm," Duncan replied, pretending to ponder her words. At the same time, he dipped a finger beneath her neckline and found a nipple with which to amuse himself. "I am sorely in need of a wife's loving attention," he said. "Will you pleasure me, Phoebe?"

She gasped as he bared the breast he had been teasing. "Yes," she managed. "But not here—for heaven's sake, Duncan—*not here.*"

He laughed, low in his throat, and set her, wobbling, on her feet. "But here is where I want you," he said reasonably. "Here and, certainly, now."

Phoebe grabbed the back of the chair, since she was feeling a bit weak-kneed. "No," she said, watching as he crossed the room. He closed the terrace doors first, and then went to shut and lock the ones opening onto the hallway.

"No?" he echoed. He returned to her and

kissed her, at the same time tugging down the front of her bodice to free the eager swell of her breasts.

"Duncan," she whimpered, in lame and admittedly ineffectual protest, when he released her mouth. He was holding one of her breasts, preparing the nipple with the pad of his thumb, just as he had made her lower lip ready for his kiss minutes before.

He bent his head and took suckle, at the same time raising her skirts and untying the ribbons that held her drawers up. It occurred to Phoebe that her husband was remarkably agile, for someone with only one good hand.

Phoebe swayed in his embrace, her head flung back, completely lost.

"Do you still want to refuse me?" Duncan inquired, with damnable confidence, when at last he had apparently satisfied himself at both her nipples.

She sighed dreamily, bemused. "Refuse?" The exact definition of the word eluded her.

He kissed her again, making everything worse—or better—and she was vaguely aware that her drawers were down around her ankles. Furthermore, there was a breeze coming from somewhere. "Step out of those pantaloons, Mistress Rourke," Duncan instructed gently. "Or you might trip over them."

Phoebe obeyed and would have tripped anyway, if Duncan hadn't steadied her. He brought her to the chair where he had held her on his lap before and did the same again, only with a difference.

Early the next morning, when Duncan was already locked away with his men, no doubt laying plans to rip off half the British navy, Phoebe went in search of Simone. Phoebe herself was subdued, grieving for John Rourke and, because the echoes of last night's pleasures were still thrumming in her nerve endings, inclined to be charitable.

Simone was alone in the washroom, bent over a tub full of soapy water.

Phoebe stood in the doorway and waited until Simone acknowledged her presence with a grudging, desultory nod.

"He's got you breeding," Simone commented, without undue malice. She was scrubbing a linen shirt and went on with her work.

"You found your way back rather quickly," Phoebe replied, since Simone's remark did not require an answer. Since she'd become the mistress of Duncan's house, she hadn't been near the laundry room. She had to admit, she hadn't missed the place. "I guess everyone else has been too distracted to ask, but I'd like to know how you got here."

Simone shrugged, keeping her eyes averted. Gone was the bristling defiance of old; something vital had gone out of the girl, and Phoebe took no satisfaction whatsoever in the knowledge. "I was born in these islands," Simone said. "I can find my way betwixt them."

Phoebe left the doorway, where she had been framed in an aureole of sunshine, and came to stand on the other side of Simone's washtub.- "What happened when you got to Queen's Town?" she asked, reaching out and stilling the servant's strong brown hand with her own.

Misery flickered in Simone's lovely dark eyes as she looked, at last, into Phoebe's. "I found out that I should have stayed here," she said. "There was no honest work for me—they wanted me for a whore or a slave."

"I'm sorry," Phoebe said, and she meant it.

A tear followed a crooked path down Simone's cheek. "Don't waste your pity on me," she warned fiercely. "I don't want it." She lowered her gaze to Phoebe's still-flat stomach, and there was something like contempt in her face. "Soon, Duncan will be wanting a mistress. He'll come back to me."

The words stung Phoebe, as they were intended to do, even though they hadn't come as any sort of surprise. She straightened her shoulders and raised her chin. "I'm not going to argue with you, Simone, so you can stop trying to make me angry." Then, since there was nothing more to say, she turned and went back to the main house.

Seeing Simone had done nothing to ease her apprehensions, but it wasn't the prospect of Duncan's infidelity that Phoebe found so disconcerting—he was a man who appreciated the bounties of nature, and she suspected that the further her pregnancy advanced, the more intrigued he would be. No, it was something else that was bothering her, some nameless nuance, insubstantial as smoke, subtle as a viper slithering through deep grass.

An hour after dawn the following morning, when Phoebe lay curled against Duncan's side, recovering from another bout of lovemaking, there was a sudden, deafening boom, causing the whole house to shake.

Duncan spat a curse and flung himself out of bed, tearing off his sling and hurling it to one side before hauling on his clothes.

"What just happened here?" Phoebe asked in a thin voice. She was more inclined to huddle, with the covers pulled up to her chin.

"We're under attack," Duncan replied, with a sharpness that gave Phoebe to believe he considered her question a stupid one. There was another crash, followed by the sound of their terrace crumbling. "Son of a bitch!" he bellowed, going to the window. "They've gotten to the ridge, the blighters, and turned our own cannon on us!"

Phoebe hopped out of bed and yanked on a wrapper. They'd already knocked out the terrace, whoever "they" were, and being a sensible woman, she wasn't about to stay around until the outside wall went, too. All of the sudden she knew, as she dashed for the door, what it was in Simone's manner that had bothered her so much.

Guilt.

"What do you want me to do?" Phoebe asked, as Duncan hustled her through the doorway and then gripped both her upper arms and wrenched her onto her toes in a highly successful effort to get her attention.

"Find my mother and Phillippa. Old Woman will hide you. That's all I have time to say, except this: If you disobey me now and bring harm to yourself or our child, I will never forgive you."

The words gave Phoebe a chill; she knew he meant them.

"Be careful," she said.

Duncan didn't answer; he planted a hasty kiss on her forehead and vanished.

Phillippa and Margaret had been roused, with the rest of the household, by the cannon fire, and the assault continued unabated as they all raced downstairs in their nightclothes, carrying whatever other garments they'd been able to snatch up before fleeing. Old Woman was waiting in the entryway, looking serene and serious, ready to usher them into the cellars, along with the female servants.

There was no sign, Phoebe noticed, of Simone.

"Is it the British, come to hang Duncan?" Phillippa asked when they were all huddled in a dank room, with a single candle for light, clad in their mismatched, hodgepodge clothes.

"It is the pirate," Old Woman said. "Jacques Mornault."

Phoebe, seated on a crate, drew up her knees and wrapped her arms around them. Her gown was of rough, colorless cloth, lent to her by one of the maids. "He got past the watch," she mused aloud, "and took over the cannon on the ridge above the house."

"Yes," Old Woman answered, reflected candlelight flickering in her eyes as she looked at Phoebe. Simone's name wavered between them like a specter, but neither of them mentioned it.

"Are we going to die?" one of the younger servants asked, lip trembling.

"No, child," Margaret Rourke said confidently. She moved to sit beside the girl and put a motherly arm around her. "There's no reason to think matters will come to that."

Phoebe was not concerned with her own safety, just yet, but she was only too aware that Duncan was in mortal danger. All the worse, she thought miserably, that the damn fool didn't have the sense to be afraid and take precautions to protect himself.

"Where do you suppose Alex is?" Phillippa asked, in a small voice. "I didn't see him."

Phoebe and Margaret exchanged glances, but neither of them spoke.

Another round of cannon fire shook the house, and Phoebe bit back a terrified sob. Was this how it was going to end? she wondered. Had she traveled through time and fallen in love with

364

Duncan Rourke only to end up dead, at the bottom of a pile of rubble?

Phillippa stood up and began to pace.

Phoebe rested her chin on her knees and waited, in a daze, and time became irrelevant. Above their heads and outside, the battle raged on, endless, earsplitting, and for all the hoopla, oddly monotonous. Some of the servants actually went to sleep, and Old Woman murmured low, wordless chants, prayers to some ancient island goddess. Margaret seemed lost in a private reverie; perhaps, despite her brave assurances that they were not about to die, she expected to join John in some better, brighter world.

The candle burned out, and Old Woman replaced it with another.

As the new light spread, stronger and brighter, Phoebe looked around for Phillippa—and found no sign of her.

Phillippa groped her way up the cellar steps, which were littered with fragments of the walls and ceiling. The light was dim, and the air was so filled with smoke and dust that she could barely breathe. She heard men talking, somewhere in the distance, but the shooting had stopped, at least temporarily.

At the top of the stairs, she waited, and listened.

The voices were far away and dearly familiar. She heard Lucas, and Duncan, and thanked God, with tears blurring her vision, that they were still alive and whole enough to argue with each other. No doubt Alex was with them, safe and sound.

Phillippa would not return to the cellar until she knew for sure.

She made her way through the wreckage of Duncan's beautiful house, stepping over books and fallen statues and shattered pieces of furniture. She did not call out, lest she attract her brothers' attention and be sent, or more likely dragged, back to the assigned hiding place. She must see Alex for herself, and then she would return to the cellars of her own accord.

Another volley struck as she was crossing the main palor, with a violence so swift and stunning that Phillippa was hurled to the floor as forcefully as if someone had grabbed her arm and thrust her down. She lay still for a few moments, the breath knocked out of her, collecting herself and coping with the brutal surprise of what had happened. She must have cried out at some point—the soreness in her throat indicated that—but she had no memory of making the smallest sound.

Phillippa raised herself to a sitting position just as another round shook the house on its sturdy foundations. Part of the ceiling came down, and she screamed in fear, curled on the floor, her arms covering her head.

She heard a stumping sound and raised her head just in time to see Alex coming toward her, moving quickly on his crutch, carrying a pistol in his hand. He was dirty, and his clothes were

366

torn and sweat-stained, but he was standing under his own power, and there were no visible wounds.

It was all Phillippa had wanted to know. She smiled and got to her feet, albeit awkwardly, dusting her hands together.

Alex scowled at her, flushed beneath the layers of soot and marble dust. "Go back to the cellars," he ordered furiously. "Now!"

Phillippa started a little and laid one hand to her breast. "You dare to shout at me?" she asked, though of course the question was superfluous, since he was *already* shouting.

"*Yes!*" Alex bellowed, drawing a step nearer. "And I'll do more than that if I catch you up here again!"

Something moved in the pit of Phillippa's stomach, and it was not, she was chagrined to realize, an entirely unpleasant sensation. Before he could clarify the obvious—that he was threatening her—another devastating round of cannon fire struck the nearest wall. A huge chandelier, probably Austrian, swayed over their heads, then came loose from its moorings with an ominous cracking sound. Alex abandoned both crutch and pistol to leap upon Phillippa like a panther, sending them both sprawling.

The chandelier came to a musical landing only inches from their feet.

"I'd better stay with you," Phillippa said, making her eyes big and biting the inside of her lip to keep from smiling. "I don't think I'd be quite safe anywhere else."

Alex looked at her with something very like disgust, but she forgave him because she knew he didn't mean it. He wanted to marry her, and when the war was over, take her home to his family's plantation, which was conveniently near Troy, where she would bear his children, see that he ate properly, and advise him in important matters.

"Count yourself fortunate, Miss Rourke," he said coldly, hauling himself painfully to his feet, "that I am completely occupied with the task of keeping you alive. Had I so much as five minutes to spare, I would paddle you within an inch of your life!"

Phillippa fluttered her eyelashes at him. "But you don't have time," she reminded him, bold in the knowledge that she was safe. From that ignoble fate, anyway.

"Come with me," he rasped, clasping her hand. Both his crutch and pistol were under the mountain of shattered glass that had once been a magnificent work of art as well as an instrument of light. After one rueful glance, during which he must have concluded, as Phillippa did, that there would be no recovering either item without a great deal of effort, he pulled her after him across the ruined parlor. His steps, though slow and measured, were not those of a man with any permanent need for a crutch.

He located a closet, one used to store linens

for the dining room, and thrust Phillippa inside it. "I will be back for you," he told her grimly. "If I were you, however, I would not look forward to the encounter."

With those unromantic words, he slammed the door in Phillippa's face, and before her eyes had adjusted to the dark so that she could see and grasp the handle, he'd wedged her in, probably by bracing a chair under the latch.

Phillippa flung herself against the heavy panel and shrieked in fury, but it did her no good. She was stuck, maybe for eternity, maybe until the pirates found her and did unspeakable things to her. And if perchance they spared her, Alex would probably murder her himself.

"I want to marry your sister," Alex told Duncan and Lucas furiously, when he rejoined them in what remained of the garden. They had a line of small cannon, guns Duncan kept for emergencies, and had been giving Mornault a steady dose of grapeshot for the past hour. Their faces were black with gunpowder, like Alex's own, and their clothes hung in shreds. The rest of the crew had taken up different posts all around the outside perimeters of the yard.

"Fine with me," Lucas said generously, "if you give your word not to beat her."

"From the look of him," Duncan remarked to his brother, "I'd say our Alex isn't quite prepared to make that promise. You've seen Phillippa?"

"I've locked her in the linen closet," Alex

369

explained. It was an odd conversation, and he supposed he might see some humor in it one day, provided any of them lived long enough to put matters into their proper perspective. "I had to do *something* to keep her out of trouble."

Duncan and Lucas looked at each other, and Alex thought he saw a smile pass between them.

"The poor, naive bastard actually thinks that's possible," Duncan said, marveling. His grin was a slash of white in his filthy face.

Lucas laughed at Alex's look of consternation and gestured toward his brother. "Heed the wisdom of a married man," he advised.

"I still want to marry her," Alex insisted.

Duncan arched one brow, his arms folded. He'd discarded his sling, and blood was beginning to seep through the filthy fabric of his shirt, but he didn't seem to be in pain. "We've yet to hear your promise not to beat her," he pointed out. There was a vague twinkle in his eyes, for despite the seriousness of their situation, Duncan reveled in matching wits with the likes of Jacques Mornault.

Alex sighed. He had always been an honest man, and he saw no point in changing at this late date. "When this is over," he said evenly, "I plan to go back to that closet, free Phillippa, take her across my knee, and raise blisters on her backside. Are you satisfied?"

Duncan and Lucas exchanged another look.

"Sure," said Lucas.

"If you are," agreed Duncan with a shrug.

There was no moon that night, and Duncan thanked the gods for that. If there had been, he and his men would not have been able to come up behind Mornault and his crew and put an end to the siege.

It was too easy, after all the waiting and enduring. For one primitive, telling moment, as he stood clasping the hair of Mornault's head, his dagger resting against the pirate's throat, Duncan wished things had been different. Perhaps his mother was right, he thought, lowering the knife, as the fierce desire to sever his enemy's jugular seeped out of him. Perhaps it was not the love of liberty that drove him, but a passion for just such encounters as this one.

He wrenched Mornault to his feet and sheathed the knife.

The pirate faced him, grinning, his halved nose all the more grotesque for being in shadow. "It will be the death of you," Mornault said. "This honorable nature of yours."

Duncan suspected his old enemy might be right, though of course he did not say so. "Who led you to these cannons?" he demanded.

"The wench," Mornault said. He was as crazy as Duncan himself, was the pirate, for he was laughing now. "You know what they say, old friend, about a woman scorned. Give me a knife, and I will give you what you want—a fight to the death."

The prospect raised Duncan's blood in a way that troubled him. He still wanted, God help him, to cut Mornault's liver out. He was accomplished at self-denial, however, and revealed none of what he felt. Instead, Duncan folded his arms and frowned.

He could blame the attack of Paradise Island on a woman scorned, Mornault had said. Duncan had no memory of scorning anyone; at least, he hadn't done so recently. In fact, before Phoebe had come into his life, he'd had a run of bad luck where females were concerned and gotten himself thrown out of some pretty impressive places.

Then Simone entered the circle of light from the lanterns Mornault had so thoughtfully provided, her eyes downcast, her shoulders slumped, and suddenly Duncan understood.

It was as if he'd been kicked in the stomach.

"You," he breathed.

Simone raised her face to Duncan; he saw her tears but hardened his heart. Phoebe might have perished during the day-long siege and taken their unborn child with her. The rest of his family had been in danger of the same fate, and his house, as far as he could tell, was little more than a ruin, creaking on its foundations.

"Do you know what you've done?" he asked.

Lucas put a restraining hand on his arm. "Duncan . . ."

Duncan shook off his brother's grasp. He was

weak with anger and the loss of blood. "Damn you," he told the girl, who was trembling now. There was no fear in her, he knew; only spite and anger and pride. Her eyes—he'd once thought them beautiful—glittered in the night like those of some wild, stalking creature deprived of its prey.

She spat at his feet.

He turned from her, back to Mornault, who was still spoiling for a fight, even though his hands had been bound by then, as had those of his men.

The pirate laughed. "Are you a coward after all, Rourke?"

Duncan's hand rested for a moment on the hilt of his dagger. It was a sore temptation to cut the other man's bonds and tear into him with his bare hands, but there was no time for such an indulgence.

"It would seem," Duncan said, ignoring the challenge and looking the other man up and down coolly, "that I've found myself a ship after all. Pity it was so bloody easy, though."

There was a stockade of sorts, well back from the main house and hidden from general view. Duncan gave orders for Mornault and his men to be taken there. Then he turned his back on his captives and started down the darkened hillside.

"What will you do with them?" Lucas demanded, keeping pace. Duncan supposed he was concerned about the girl and the pirates. "After this, I mean?"

"I haven't decided," Duncan answered with

wry, quiet fury, gritting his teeth because his wounded shoulder was beginning to feel as though someone had filled it with molten lead. "Maybe I'll burn them all at the stake. Or feed them to the sharks, one digit at a time."

"Damn it all to hell, Duncan," Lucas barked, "I'm serious. You can't turn Mornault over to the British, though God knows they probably want him as badly as they want you, because he'll tell them where to find you. And you can't simply release these bastards—they'll only come back for you later, with more guns and another ship. As for burning them at the stake or feeding them to the sharks—well, I can only assume you were making a jest."

"Assume what you like," Duncan replied, supporting his weak arm with his other hand and hoping Lucas wouldn't notice and put up more of a fuss than he already had. In the meanwhile, he was enjoying himself; he'd forgotten how diverting it was to bait his brother. "What do you think Mornault and his band of merry men would have done to me, had Fortune favored their efforts over ours?"

Lucas made a sputtering sound, which meant he didn't have a response at the ready.

Duncan stumbled, caught himself. For now, he only wanted Phoebe, washing his wound, prattling in her strange English, perhaps allowing him a sip or two of whiskey for the pains he'd taken in saving her from the proverbial fate worse than death.

"Are you all right?" Lucas demanded. Sometimes, he could be quite observant, and unfortunately, this appeared to be one of those instances.

Duncan quickened his pace, hoping to reach Phoebe, and what remained of his house, before he passed out. "Splendid," he answered. "Today was an interesting exercise, wasn't it? Perhaps we should keep Mornault just long enough to really piss him off, then send him on his way with our thanks. We could always invite him back another day, to stir things up again." He went down as far as one knee, and Lucas hauled him back up again. Duncan couldn't see clearly, and his stomach, fortuitously empty, was doing slow rolls, like a drowned seal drifting in an ocean current.

"You are talking nonsense," Lucas said. He touched Duncan's forehead with the back of his hand, for mixed in with his other relatively innocuous faults was a tendency to be something of a mother hen. "Great Zeus and Apollo, I could fry an egg on your forehead!"

"I would advise you not to try," Duncan replied. And then he laughed at the sheer insanity of the exchange.

The house was before them, luminous in the gloom, like some Grecian temple. Duncan supposed the damage could be repaired, but the task would take months, if not years, and craftsmen were in short supply, given his occupation and the stringencies of war. He might have wept, if he hadn't known Phoebe was waiting for him somewhere.

Lucas left him after they passed through the garden doorway, ordering him to sit down and wait while he, Lucas, sought out the physician Mars. Duncan ignored his brother's command and proceeded to the cellar, making his way carefully down the stairs, which were littered with rubble. Just the effort of keeping himself upright brought out a cold sweat, soaking his ruined clothes and making his hands slippery.

"Phoebe!" he shouted into the darkness, and for one truly unbearable moment, he thought she wasn't going to answer, that Mornault had managed to kill her after all.

Then she appeared at the foot of the stairs, holding a lantern aloft. Seeing him, she shoved the light into someone else's hands and hurried to his side, tucking herself under his arm.

"Idiot," she fussed. "What are you thinking of, wandering about like this, when you can barely stand . . ."

"Are you hurt?" he asked, allowing himself to lean on her just a little.

She led him the rest of the way downstairs, since the trip back up would be too difficult for both of them. "No," she answered. "Have you seen Phillippa? I wanted to go looking for her, but Old Woman wouldn't let me . . ."

"Phillippa is probably bent over Alex's knee at this very moment, getting her backside blistered," Duncan replied. "I think it will do them both good."

"Don't get any ideas, Mr. Rourke," Phoebe warned briskly, leading him along the passageway where he'd found her wandering that first night of their acquaintance. It all seemed so recent and, conversely, so very long ago. "If you ever try to do such a thing, I'll shoot you."

He laughed again. "Another of your poetic promises," he said. "Where the devil are you taking me?"

"Back to the room where we women have been hiding all day," she answered. "We'll try for the first floor later, when you're a bit stronger."

Duncan staggered a little. His head was as light as if he'd guzzled a kegful of rum all by himself, and just as he thought he would collapse, the gloomy passage was filled with a blinding dazzle.

It was as if the doorway to heaven itself had opened before them.

"Oh, My God," Phoebe whispered. "It's the elevator!"

"What?" While Duncan was still trying to make sense of what must be an illusion, a product of his fever and his wound, Phoebe pulled him deeper into the glare. "Where . . .?" His knees buckled and he folded, knocking his head against the wall in spite of the small, strong hands that attempted to steer him safely to the floor. "Phoebe . . ."

"I'm here," she said gently.

The pain was all-consuming, like a voracious

fire. Duncan said her name again, as a prayer, and then slipped into the enfolding darkness.

Phoebe knelt beside Duncan on the elevator floor, holding him close. He was unconscious and bleeding and covered with dirt, and she hadn't the first idea how she was going to explain him to the hotel staff, the police, and/or anyone else in the twentieth century. Her decision had been instinctive; he needed medical help, of the modern variety.

The elevator stopped, and the doors glided open, revealing the lobby she remembered. Phoebe felt a dizzying sense of relief. On some level, she'd been afraid of finding herself in some other period of history, rather than her own, but she heard familiar sounds. Somewhere, a telephone was ringing, and the theme music of a popular sitcom blared from the speakers of an unseen television set.

Phoebe dragged Duncan out of the elevator and looked around.

The desk clerk appeared, a blond Adonis, wearing the obligatory T-shirt and a pair of khaki shorts. He snapped his chewing gum as he came toward Phoebe and her prone husband. "Hey, who's that, and what happened to him?"

Phoebe was not inclined to explain, with Duncan lying on the floor, losing blood and burning up with fever. "Never mind who he is," she said. "Is there a hospital on this island?"

"Sure," said Adonis. His real name, according

to the plastic tag on his T-shirt, was Rodney. "I'll call an ambulance."

"Thank you," Phoebe replied. One of the maids appeared with a blanket, and out of the corner of her eye, she saw the woman with the light-up hat and varicose veins—the one who'd been on the same charter flight to Paradise Island as Phoebe had.

"Now I see why you missed the party tonight," the woman said. "What happened to your date? He looks like he fell down a flight of stairs."

Phoebe frowned up at her, distracted and a little impatient. "Tonight?"

"Yeah, you know. It's part of the deal—we come here and look at the condos, and we get a party."

Realization struck Phoebe with the impact of a city bus. She'd been in 1780 long enough to fall in love, marry, get pregnant, and have more adventures than any sensible woman would ever wish for, but here, in 1995, the clock must have virtually stood still.

"What time is it?" Phoebe asked, staying close to Duncan, who was beginning to stir. He was going to get a shock when he came around, and she wanted to be close by, so she could lend moral support. A few pointers on adjusting to the twentieth century probably wouldn't hurt either.

The woman consulted her watch. "Ten after nine," she said. She studied Duncan, eyes narrowed in speculation, then raised her gaze to Phoebe's face. "You play rough, honey. I wouldn't have figured you for the type, which just goes to show that life is full of surprises."

"Isn't it?" Phoebe agreed, looking down at Duncan, who was still cradled in her arms. Then she kissed his forehead and simply waited.

18

The island hospital was a small, unhurried place. The staff wore loose cotton shirts in bright prints, sandals or sneakers, and white slacks or shorts. The elderly woman at the admittance desk was unruffled when Phoebe acknowledged there was no health insurance and, for the moment, no money to pay the bill. (A fact that raised the possibility that they weren't in the real world at all, but on another planet or at least in a different dimension.) Duncan was examined, bathed, and put into bed, with an IV dripping glucose and various antibiotics into his veins.

He was disoriented and confused, and considering the circumstances, Phoebe thought that was preferable to full alertness. If he'd been aware of what was really happening to him, needles and blood tests and the application of antiseptics aside, he might have had to be restrained.

When she was sure he was comfortable, Phoebe called information and got the number of her bank in Seattle. The number, fortunately, was toll-free, and there were operators on duty twenty-four hours per day.

She explained that she'd lost her ATM card—leaving out the fact that it had been missing, technically, for well over two hundred years—and gave them the information required to verify her identity. The new card, she was assured, would be on its way to Paradise Island the next day, via an express service. She was to have the same personal identification number.

A slender black woman, wearing the hospital's tropical, freestyle uniform, appeared in the doorway just as Phoebe was hanging up the telephone receiver. She bore a striking resemblance to Simone, but without the hostility and angst.

"Mrs. Rourke? Maybe you'd best go back to the hotel and get yourself some rest. We'll take good care of your husband while you're gone."

"I can't leave him," Phoebe said.

"He isn't critically ill—you do understand that?"

Phoebe nodded—the antibiotics and a few days of enforced leisure were just what Duncan needed. God only knew, however, what would go through that eighteenth-century mind, sharp as it was, when he found himself in a future he couldn't possibly have imagined, with tubes running into his flesh and strange machines blinking and bleeping all around him.

"Yes," Phoebe answered belatedly. The nurse's name tag read "Sharon." "I just want to be here when he comes around, that's all."

Sharon's smile was gentle and reassuring. "Okay, no problem. How about if we send somebody over to the hotel for some of your things, though? If you had a shower and something to eat, you might feel lots better, don't you think?"

Phoebe was grateful for Sharon's kindness. Although she wasn't about to leave Duncan, she was dirty and tired and still wearing the dress she'd borrowed—that morning or two hundred years ago, she didn't know which—from a servant. And while her appetite was virtually nonexistent, she hadn't forgotten her unborn child. To protect her son—or daughter, if Old Woman had guessed wrong—she would eat and try to sleep.

The staff set up a cot in Duncan's room, and Phoebe left him long enough to take a shower. A makeshift supper, consisting of a wilted BLT, a glass of milk, and a bowl of cream of tomato soup, awaited her on a tray. She ate, clad in a hospital robe, and went to sleep well after midnight.

Her husband's voice awakened her bright and early the next morning, and even though Duncan spoke calmly, Phoebe sat bolt upright on her cot, braced for an explosion of questions.

"What is this place?" he asked, in an understandably incredulous tone.

Phoebe nearly tripped over her suitcase, which someone had apparently brought over from the hotel during the night, reaching his bedside. She took his hand, the one with no IV needle taped to it, and gave him a wavering, watery smile. "Just don't get excited," she said. "I can explain everything. Sort of."

"I am not excited," Duncan ground out. There were other indications, besides his clenched teeth, that his self-control was slipping.

"We've left your century," Phoebe said, "and now we're in mine. The year is 1995, and you are in a hospital . . ." When his eyes widened in growing horror, and he started to sit up, Phoebe pressed him gently back onto his pillows. "It's all right, darling. Hospitals aren't like they were in your time. They've given you medicine, and by tomorrow or the next day, you'll be your old self again."

Duncan was still agitated, that was obvious, but he did a good job of keeping his composure. He looked around, taking in the television set affixed to the wall, the phone, the transparent bag of liquid suspended above the bed, the machines that had monitored his vital signs during the night.

"Is the whole world like this?" he whispered, clearly dreading the answer.

Phoebe smiled, touched to the heart, and kissed him. "No, of course not. As soon as you're ready to leave the hospital, we'll travel to the mainland and I'll show you something utterly, completely American."

"What?"

"I'm keeping it for a surprise," Phoebe said,

383

as a nurse entered with breakfast trays for both of them.

Duncan stared at the staffer's short skirt and tank top. "Great Zeus and Apollo," he muttered, when they were alone again. "That was indecent!"

Phoebe dipped his spoon into something that might have been either pudding or cereal and stuck it into his mouth. "You ain't seen nothin' yet," she teased.

After they'd eaten, she turned the TV on, and Duncan's education in modern American life began—with a syndicated episode of *Lifestyles of the Rich and Famous.* He was amazed by the moving figures, the colors, and disembodied voices of television, but Phoebe hardly glanced at the screen. Watching Duncan's reactions was more entertaining than any program could ever have been.

Phoebe spent most of that day preparing Duncan for what was ahead, using dog-eared magazines from the waiting room to show him how men and women dressed, what houses looked like, and what kinds of foods people ate. Automobiles and airplanes, pictured in the advertisements, fascinated him, and after lunch he drifted off to sleep. Phoebe's diagnosis was a case of information overload.

She sat in a chair near his bed, too keyed up to nap, wondering when the police would come and ask her how Duncan came to be on Paradise Island, out of his head with fever, wearing clothes that were a little too authentic, even for a costume party, and sporting a neatly stitched sword wound on one shoulder. It was a good thing the law didn't show up, because no viable story presented itself.

The next day was eventful; Phoebe's new ATM card came, and Duncan was released from the hospital. Even wearing white chinos and a flowered shirt, loaned to him by one of the orderlies, there was something of the pirate about him.

They returned to the hotel in a taxi, and Duncan found the reality of an automobile somewhat more disconcerting than a four-color picture in a magazine. When he saw his beautiful house, reduced by time and neglect to a shabby, second-rate inn, his mood went into retrograde.

There was a cash machine in the lobby, and Phoebe made the first foray into her savings account. Duncan watched with a thoughtful frown, but said nothing. "This will give us a start," she said, "but there's still the hospital bill to pay."

"We have debts?" Duncan asked. He'd probably never owed anyone a cent in his life, unless you counted the cost of all the weapons and supplies he'd filched from the British government during the Revolution.

"Come on," Phoebe said gently, taking his hand. "We'll talk about it in the piano bar, over a piña colada and a glass of ice tea."

The bar had once been Duncan's study, and he plainly disapproved of the changes. While he stood glowering at the jukebox, as though it were some mesmerizing tool of the devil, Phoebe ordered drinks at the bar and carried them to a secluded table. The piña colada met with his approval, unlike most of the things he'd seen since leaving the hospital.

"Tell me about our debts," he insisted, after consuming his drink.

"We have to pay the hospital for taking care of you," Phoebe said. "Don't worry about it, okay?"

"What of this currency that you took out of the wall?"

Phoebe smiled at the quaint, if apt, description. "Not enough," she said. "The twentieth century is frightfully expensive." They were going to need airline tickets to Orlando, too, since the charter had already gone back to the States for another batch of prospective condo buyers. Then there was food, and the hotel bill . . .

"I have gold," Duncan said.

Phoebe sighed. "No, you don't," she said. "Trust me, I checked your pockets after they'd stripped you down at the hospital. And even though this place may look like home, it isn't. Two hundred and fifteen years have passed, for all intents and purposes, since the day Mornault practically blasted us off the planet with your cannon."

The expression on her husband's face indicated that it hadn't been a good time to mention his old enemy and the damage that had been done to the house. He leaned toward her and spoke in a low, impatient voice. "I have gold," he repeated, measuring the words out slowly, as if he thought Phoebe might have trouble comprehending them. "Shall I prove it?"

"Please do," Phoebe said, with a sigh. "My savings account won't keep us going for long."

Duncan glanced suspiciously at the bartender. "Later," he replied.

They spent the hottest part of the day in their room—Phoebe was sure Duncan wouldn't enjoy a tour of the condominiums or a look at what modern business acumen had done to the cove where the *Francesca* had once bobbed at anchor—alternately napping and watching television. Her husband, the pirate, was withdrawn and grim, and although Phoebe would have welcomed his lovemaking, he made no attempt to touch her. And even though she ached, if only to be held, Phoebe kept her hands to herself.

After dark, and a room-service meal that Duncan pronounced unpalatable and would have hurled into the hallway, cart and all, if Phoebe hadn't stopped him, they went downstairs. The hotel, not exactly a mecca for tourists, was all but deserted, and it was easy to find the cellar steps and sneak down them.

Phoebe felt a pang of loneliness for the eighteenth century as Duncan pulled her along behind him. What must Margaret and Lucas and Alex and Phillippa be thinking? The servants, if any had still been close enough to witness the strange disappearance of the master and mistress, would have seen the wall open onto a cubicle of light, and then close again, leaving no trace.

The modern cellar was well lit, and Duncan had no trouble finding what he was looking for—a small storage closet of some type, with a brick floor and rotting rafters. He knelt, pulling the butter knife he'd swiped from the room-service cart out of his belt, and began prying an ordinary-looking stone out of the wall. When it finally gave way, he reached into the chasm and drew out a small metal box.

"We'll open this in our room," he told her, tucking the dusty little chest under his flowered shirt with a pirate's deftness. "If the new tenants get wind of it, they'll probably use it to wreak still more havoc on my house."

Phoebe let the possessive pronoun pass unchallenged. Duncan was an intelligent man, and he knew the mansion no longer belonged to him. He had probably already figured out, too, that he was a ghost of sorts; technically, he didn't exist because there was a grave somewhere with his name on it. For that matter, Phoebe hadn't legally lived in 1780, either, because she hadn't been born until 1969.

It was all so damn confusing.

"You're the boss," she agreed wearily. It wasn't entirely true, of course; in Phoebe's mind, she and Duncan were equals, but, after all he'd been through, she figured she could forego semantics for a little while.

When, behind the locked door of Room 73, he opened the box, wielding the same butter knife he'd used to dislodge the stone in the cellar wall, Phoebe drew in a sharp breath. The thing was brimming with thick gold coins, their glow undimmed by the passage of time.

"Duncan," Phoebe whispered, "that's a small fortune!"

He smiled. "A wise man," he replied, "is prepared for the unexpected."

Phoebe lifted a gold piece from the box and held it up for a closer look. The coin was large and heavy and stamped with the image of a lion. The average collector would probably pay far more than face value for specimens like these, she reasoned, but there was no sense in being greedy. "We'll have to be discreet," she said. "There aren't a lot of these floating around, and there'll be questions if we try to pass them at McDonald's or the supermarket."

A glance at Duncan's puzzled face reminded Phoebe that they hadn't gotten to American Consumerism 101.

"Leave everything to me," she said.

Duncan rolled his eyes.

The next day, Phoebe and Duncan left the island on a small propeller-driven aircraft. Fortunately, passports would not be required, since Paradise Island was an American possession, rather like Puerto Rico, and money was no longer a problem.

Soon, they landed at an airfield outside Orlando.

Duncan had not said a word since takeoff, and he was white as a Bing Crosby Christmas. When the plane touched down and bounced along the runway, engines roaring in reverse thrust, he gave Phoebe a look that would have curdled yogurt. Translation: *Don't ever ask me to do this again.*

She began to wonder how he would react to her surprise. Scratch Space Mountain and Star Tours, she thought with some regret.

They checked into a room, then caught a cab to a shopping mall, and Phoebe used her ATM card again, this time to replace the cash she'd spent on their airline tickets. Later, she would find a pawnshop in a bad neighborhood and hock one of Duncan's gold coins, just to get a feel for their value. In the meantime, the pirate in her life needed a change of clothes—she still had the rumpled contents of the suitcase she'd brought from Seattle—so she outfitted him in jeans, athletic shoes, and a blue cotton shirt.

"Ummm," she said, admiring him.

Duncan, overwhelmed all over again by the mall and the crowds of scantily dressed shoppers, was starting to turn testy. Phoebe took his hand and dragged him out onto the concourse and into the food court, where she purchased double-bacon cheeseburgers, french fries, and milk shakes.

"This is a distinct improvement," Duncan

390

said, brightening, "over that swill we had at the hospital."

Phoebe smiled. "Don't get too used to it. Good as this stuff tastes, a steady diet of it would *put* you in the hospital."

Duncan had finished his fries and started in on Phoebe's. There was color in his face again, and an evil glint in his eyes. "Do you presume, woman," he said, pretending to ferocity, "to dictate what I will and will not eat?"

"Of course," Phoebe answered blithely. "I'm your wife."

He sighed. "I suppose that means you won't buy me another of these"—he turned to consult the sign over the counter at the fast-food franchise—"Belly-busters?"

"That's exactly what it means," Phoebe said. "Do you want to die of clogged arteries before you turn two hundred and fifty?"

Duncan laughed. "I shall be two hundred and forty-five on my next birthday," he said, and a woman pushing a stroller between the tables of the food court paused to stare.

That afternoon, they visited one of Orlando's major tourist attractions.

"We did not revere mice in quite the same way, in my time," Duncan confided behind his hand, as a giant and very cheerful rodent skipped by on two legs. "Nasty little creatures, for the most part."

Phoebe elbowed him gently, mindful of his sword wound and general debilitation. "You speak sacrilege," she warned, with a smile in her eyes. "Come with me, Captain Rourke—there is something I want to show you."

Duncan seemed shaken when they came out of the ride—Phoebe's personal favorite—featuring pirates, skeletons, heaps of treasure, and a convincing battle between ship and shore. "You might have warned me," he said, a muscle flexing once in his jaw, "that there would be gunplay!"

Phoebe laughed. "I told you it would be realistic," she said. "How do you feel about ghosts?"

He didn't reply.

Later that night in their hotel room, when they were both immersed to their necks in the Jacuzzi, Phoebe asked, "Well, Mr. Rourke? What do you think of modern America?"

Duncan pondered his answer, taking his wineglass from the tiled edge of the tub and sipping from it. "That," he countered dryly, at considerable length, "was modern America?"

Phoebe splashed him for being so pompous. Still, she had to concede he had a point. "One facet of it, yes," she admitted, when his wine had been swamped with bathwater and his hair drenched. She went to him, slipped her arms around his lean, bare waist, and laid her head against his good shoulder. "Tell me what you thought," she urged. She really wanted to know.

Duncan hesitated, then allowed his hands to rest on the small of her back. "The pirates were amusing," he said, and the sorrowful mischief in his eyes was unsettlingly reminiscent of his father, "though I confess I almost threw you to the floor of the boat once or twice, to save you from stray musket balls. The haunted house, however, was nearly my undoing."

She stood on her tiptoes to kiss him. "But you don't like it here."

He paused again. Then he smoothed her hair and said, with touching reluctance, "No, Phoebe. I don't belong."

Phoebe bit her lower lip as tears threatened. "It's my fault," she said. "I gave you the impression that the whole place is one big amusement park, and that's not true. The country you and your friends fought to establish is so much more, Duncan—"

He quieted her with a brief, light kiss. "I know," he assured her hoarsely, pulling her close to him. "We're together, Phoebe. That's the important thing."

She sniffled. "Yes," she agreed. "But you know what? For all its trials and hardships, I think I like your world better, too. It was more graceful, somehow, and everything seemed more substantial. More real."

Duncan curved a finger under her chin and lifted. "But it will be better for you here," he said. "Better for our baby."

Phoebe nodded. They'd watched a PBS special on pregnancy and childbirth earlier in the evening, and Duncan had been captivated. "I'll see a doctor tomorrow," she promised, seeing the concern in his eyes, "just to make sure everything's all right. And then I'll show you another side of America."

"I love you," he said softly. He had told her before when in the throes of passion, but this was different. A milestone, somehow, a decree that what they shared together was permanent. Even eternal.

She stared at him in wonder and joy, because, for all Duncan's tenderness, all his protectiveness and his passion, he had never said those words in quite that way. And she had yearned to hear them, in just that context, the way a desert flower longs for the cool mist of morning.

"And I love you," she replied. "In this world or any other."

Duncan kissed her again, very deeply and very thoroughly, and then brought her out of the water. They dried each other with soft hotel towels and took their time making love.

Phoebe saw an obstetrician the next day and came out of the exam room smiling, with a prescription for prenatal vitamins in her hand. The examination had gone well, and the baby's heartbeat was strong and steady. Duncan was in the waiting room when she emerged, staring in the direction of the sea.

She saw the forlorn expression on his face before he'd had time to replace it with one of those knee-smiling grins of his.

"Come along, Mr. Rourke," Phoebe said tenderly, taking his hand and brushing her lips across his knuckles. "There is something else I want you to see."

A little over an hour later, they were on the freeway, in a rented car, headed for Cape Kennedy.

"It's time we talked about islands and oceans and supernatural elevators," Phoebe announced, keeping her eyes on the road.

Beside her, in the passenger seat, Duncan frowned. "What about the baby? You haven't told me what the doctor said."

"Our child is fine," she assured him, her throat thick with emotion. "It's you I'm worried about."

They had hamburgers, Duncan's favorite food, at a fast-food place near the base. Then Phoebe took her eighteenth-century husband through the space museum, explaining moon shots and other modern wonders as best she could.

On the way back to their motel in Orlando, Phoebe made a few comparisons of her own. There were things she liked about the twentieth century, of course, but she knew she didn't belong there, any more than Duncan did. Quietly, in the most private part of her heart, she said good-bye to the 1990s.

"We're going back," Phoebe proclaimed.

"Back?" Duncan echoed. He'd been deep in thought since they'd left the museum. Little wonder. "How?" he asked in a distracted tone.

"We'll start by flying—okay, we'll take a boat—back to Paradise Island. Then we'll check into the hotel, there to wait and watch and hope to high heaven that the magic elevator takes us back to 1780."

Duncan's smile was rueful—and sad in a way that hurt Phoebe's heart. "That would be a miracle," he said.

"Maybe it would," Phoebe agreed, reaching over the gearshift to squeeze his hand. "But it isn't as if it hasn't already happened twice. Could be that the third time, as they say, is the charm."

He sighed. "Even if it were possible—what about the baby?"

"What about him? He was conceived in the eighteenth century. Maybe he's supposed to be born there."

Duncan seemed unconvinced, but they sold a pile of gold coins to a shop owner that afternoon, and by evening they were aboard a chartered yacht, speeding toward Paradise Island. Standing in the wheelhouse with the skipper, listening to an in-depth lecture on how the instruments worked, Duncan looked truly happy for the first time in days.

The Eden Hotel was as depressing as before, but Phoebe knew in her heart that returning had been the right thing to do. They settled in, Mr. and Mrs. Duncan Rourke, and spent their days reading and exploring and talking, and their evenings making love. Phoebe was perfectly content and could have gone on living in that aimless way forever, but she sensed a restlessness in Duncan, an impatient longing for the world he knew.

Phoebe searched high and low for Professor Benning's book about Duncan's life, without saying anything to her husband, but she turned up exactly nothing. Probably some tourist had found the little volume and taken it home. Calls to the island library and to a book search service on the mainland were fruitless, and Phoebe reluctantly gave up on finding out how her story, and Duncan's, would end.

Perhaps, she reasoned, it was for the best.

Phoebe's pregnancy was starting to show, and the proceeds from the coins were running out, when Duncan developed insomnia. She often awakened in the night, with a start, and found him gone, and she was always terrified by the discovery.

Usually, she found him on one of the terraces, or sitting at the piano in the bar, running his hands tentatively over the keys, as if afraid to unleash the music inside him. On occasion, he walked the beach, and later described the constellations he'd seen in wistful tones, as though the stars he'd looked up at were not the same ones he'd always known.

Although he loved her, and said so often and eloquently, with words as well as with his body, Phoebe began to fear that she was losing Duncan, that he was slowly slipping away from her. She wanted to cling to him, keep him at her side night and day, but she loved him too much and too well to make herself his jailer.

And so Phoebe waited and watched the ever-changing temperament of the sea, and beneath her heart, the baby grew.

Duncan got out of bed slowly, in the depths of that still and sultry night, some three months after their return to the hotel on Paradise Island, taking care not to awaken Phoebe. He'd gotten to know the bartender, an affable black man who called himself Snowball, and sometimes he was still behind the bar when Duncan came downstairs, polishing glasses or wiping tables.

The television set, an apparatus Duncan had come to despise after an initial and very brief period of fascination, was tuned to a twenty-four-hour news channel when he entered the lounge.

"Duncan, old buddy," Snowball greeted him, flashing that broad ivory smile. He called everybody "old buddy," but Duncan didn't mind because the term made him feel welcome. As much as he loved Phoebe—enough, he sometimes thought, to sacrifice his soul for her—he missed the companionship of like-minded males, like Alex and Beedle and his brother, Lucas. When he let himself consider the fact that they were all long dead, these men who had been his friends, the grief was hard to bear.

"Hello," he said, glancing at the clock on the wall behind the bar. Still an hour until closing time, he thought. As usual, the place was empty, except for the two of them.

"Hey, do me a favor, will you?" Snowball asked. "I got half a case of Grand Marnier down in the cellar, in that little room at the bottom of the stairs. You mind gettin' it for me, so I don't get into Dutch for leavin' before my shift's over? Soon as I step out of this place, somebody'll be in here wantin' a maitai, and the night manager will have my ass."

Duncan smiled. He hadn't learned to speak twentieth-century English, in all its varieties—Snowball called it "lingo"—but he could usually understand it. "Sure," he said and set out for the cellar without asking for directions. He'd stored wine in that same small chamber in his time, along with contraband rum.

"Thanks, man," Snowball said.

At the top of the cellar stairs, Duncan flipped the light switch—one of the many modern inventions he had come to appreciate—but nothing happened. He hesitated, waiting for his eyes to adjust to the gloom, and then he saw a strange, faint glow in the passageway, and heard a bell chime.

The elevator. For a moment, his heartbeat quickened, but then he remembered: The contraptions were commonplace in the 1990s. Every building of any size had one, including this seedy hotel.

He went down the steps, opened the door to the storage room, and by the glow of the lingering elevator, found the half case of Grand Marnier Snowball had asked for. Lifting the box, Duncan started back toward the stairs, then stopped, grinning. The elevator was still there, with its doors open, waiting. Why walk?

Duncan stepped into the cubicle, congratulating himself on his understanding of modern devices, pushed the button for the lobby, and watched as the doors slipped shut. The machine glided upward and stopped, and Duncan stepped out, yawning a little. He'd have a drink, talk with Snowball for a while, and then go back upstairs, to lie beside Phoebe and wait for morning. If his wife awakened in a malleable mood, he would make love to her . . .

He had stepped out of the elevator, and heard the doors whisper closed behind him, before he realized what had happened.

The lobby was no longer a lobby. It was an empty, moon-washed room, littered with broken statuary, shining crystal splinters from the fallen chandelier, and bits of molded plaster from the ceiling.

Duncan whirled, the crate of brown bottles still in his arms, and found the elevator gone. The wall was smooth and utterly bare, except for a hook and a dangling wire that had once held a painting in place.

He lowered the liquor to the floor, his heart pounding in his ears, his eyes burning. Then, knowing that he was back in 1780, without Phoebe, he flung himself at the place where the elevator had been and screamed her name.

★ ★ ★

400

Phoebe sat straight up in her bed, wrenched from the depths of a sound sleep as surely as if a fist had grasped her brain and jerked her awake. She was drenched in perspiration, her nightgown clinging to her skin, and the sound of her own name echoed in her ears, like the shriek of a banshee.

"Duncan?" She fumbled for the switch on the bedside lamp, turned it, and the glow verified what she had already known: Her husband wasn't there. "Duncan!"

He was downstairs, she told herself, as the terrible urgency that had awakened her subsided into despair. Or walking on the beach, or reading in the lobby . . .

The assurances didn't help. Phoebe got out of bed, peeled off her cotton nightgown, found one of the sweat suits she'd sent away for instead of maternity clothes, and got dressed, fumbling all the while.

She kept murmuring Duncan's name, over and over again, like a crazy woman repeating a litany, but she didn't care how she sounded, didn't try to stop herself. Her gut told her what her mind wanted to deny: that something awful and profound had happened.

Their room was on the second floor, and Phoebe didn't bother summoning the elevator. She dashed down the stairs, barefooted, hair sticking out all over her head, and raced into the cocktail lounge.

Snowball was there, and he looked up expectantly when Phoebe slid into the room like a deer on ice. "Phoebe?" he said, narrowing his eyes for a moment.

"Where's Duncan?" Phoebe demanded breathlessly. She knew the answer, even then, but she wasn't willing to face it yet, wanted to hear somebody deny what she was thinking.

Snowball rounded the bar, took Phoebe's arm and ushered her to a chair. "I sent him downstairs for something," he said. "He must have got to talkin' to somebody. Here, you sit tight, and I'll get you a nice glass of milk."

Phoebe stood up, then sat down again. She was out of breath, and her knees were trembling so badly that she was afraid she'd fall. She began to cry, softly at first, and then harder, and then in great, hysterical wails.

Snowball patted Phoebe's back and murmured that everything would be all right, and she laid her head down on her folded arms and sobbed.

"You got to stop that," the bartender said. "It ain't good for you. You want me to call a doctor before I go and find that damn fool husband of yours?"

Phoebe raised her head and hiccoughed. "He's gone," she said.

"What you mean, 'he's gone'?" Snowball demanded, but he was beginning to sound worried. "I just saw the man a few minutes ago! Why, he'll probably walk through that door in a second or two. When he does, how you goin' to explain carryin' on like this?"

She pretended to be calm and waited, but Duncan did not return. By dawn, Snowball and the desk clerk and the island police knew what Phoebe had realized at the outset.

Duncan Rourke had vanished like a memory made of smoke.

19

"Where the hell have you been?" Alex demanded, white-faced with annoyance and the residual pain of his knee injury, when he entered the ruins of the study to find Duncan there, pouring a drink. To spare his family and friends as much of the shock as necessary, Duncan had hidden the case of Grand Marnier first, then gone to the bedchamber, there to exchange his twentieth-century garb for breeches, boots, and a loose linen shirt. He'd barely been able to tolerate the place even long enough to change his clothes, knowing that Phoebe was gone, that he might never see her again.

The mere prospect was all but unbearable; the reality, day upon day, night upon night, would be pure torture.

"How long was I away?" Duncan countered grimly, calling upon all his inner resources, marshaling his thoughts into a semblance of order. As much as he wanted to give in to despair, he did not have that luxury. There was a war to win, and people depended upon him.

He took in the restored Alex while he awaited an answer. His friend sported no crutch, figurative or otherwise, though he had a pronounced limp. A pistol stuck into his belt, as of old, and his hair was brushed and tied back in a remarkably tidy fashion. His skin was sun-browned.

The question took Alex visibly aback, as it should have done. "Good Lord," he said finally, "I'd have thought you'd know that. It's been weeks since you vanished into thin air, like some bloody ghost! Lucas and I have been over every inch of the island, searching for any sign of either you or Phoebe. What the *devil* has been going on in this place?"

Duncan felt hollow and raw on the inside, and bruised on the outside. Being dragged down a rocky road behind a horse would surely have hurt less than being parted from his wife this way. And he did not look forward to telling the tale.

He took a fiery sip of brandy and collapsed into the chair behind his desk before replying. "You'd better get yourself a drink, my friend, and take a seat. It is a long and tangled story, full of twists and turns."

Alex stared at Duncan in curious irritation while taking his advice. When he had a cup in his hand and had planted himself on a hassock, he lifted an eyebrow and muttered, "Well, get on with it."

Duncan did not expect to be believed.

Nonetheless, he began with the night of Phoebe's arrival—Alex himself had been present for that event, so there was a chance that he might accept at least some of the account, incredible as it was—and then described more recent experiences. Starting with his own elevator journey to the future.

Doggedly, Duncan related the important things and had to keep clearing his throat when he described the circumstances of his final separation from Phoebe. By that point, he did not care whether Alex believed him or not.

"Great Scot," Alex marveled when it had ended, and Duncan sat, broken, his head resting in one hand and his cup empty. "Mice as big as men? Carriages with no need for horses to draw them? Rocket ships capable of reaching the moon? Why, five minutes in the place would drive a normal man mad, from the sounds of it!"

Duncan sighed and then gave his friend a level look. "So you think me mad?"

"I would think any other man mad, who told such a tale," Alex allowed. "Since I know you to be damnably sane, I can only assume you are telling the truth." His brows drew together in a deep frown as he considered further ramifications of the situation. "If such a thing can happen, we can claim to understand little or nothing of the world and its ways." He paused and gazed earnestly at Duncan for a long time before asking, "How will you carry on, without Phoebe?"

"I don't know," Duncan replied. He yearned

for more brandy, indeed, for enough to render himself insensible, but that was a comfort reserved for other men, who had the leisure for truly exquisite suffering. He scanned the room with an expression of wry accusation, noticing the damaged walls and ceilings. His desk and chair were practically the only things still standing. "What have you and Lucas and the others been doing while I was away?"

Alex's neck turned crimson and he averted his eyes for a moment, indicating to Duncan that his friend had been occupied with some private matter. Phillippa, for instance. It was at once amazing and heartening, the change in Alex, though Duncan was too distracted to really appreciate the true scope of this resurrection.

"I've married your sister, for one thing," Alex said, meeting Duncan's eyes.

Duncan knew his smile was wan, perhaps even grim, but his pleasure in the news was genuine. "Congratulations," he said. "If I'd known the baggage could work so miraculous a transformation as this, I'd have brought her to Paradise long ago."

Alex's flush deepened and then slowly subsided. Apparently, all was well with the bride and groom, even though the outside world stood in shambles around them. It was a thought Duncan did not care to pursue too far.

"We have not been idle," Alex hurried to add. "Lucas and Beedle and the rest of us, I mean. We've—er—appropriated Mornault's ship.

She's a fine craft, and only wanted cleaning up, really. Lucas has seen to getting her fitted out and ready to serve our purposes."

"Mornault and the others?" Duncan asked. "What have you done with them? Especially, the girl, Simone?"

Alex stood, limped over to the desk and refilled his glass. "Mornault and his men are still in the stockade," he said, and a faint hesitation, a note of reluctance, made Duncan brace himself for the rest of the story. "The girl is dead," he finished.

Duncan felt his stomach roll. "Dead?"

"We couldn't put her in with Mornault and that lot, of course," Alex said, and his bleak tone indicated that he was recalling, all too vividly, the details of Simone's death. "She came here, and slept in her old room, and was given her usual tasks to do. She got a length of rope from some-where and hanged herself from one of the rafters in the washroom. It was Phillippa who found her."

Simone—beautiful, troubled Simone, dead at such a young age. The knowledge burned itself into Duncan's being like a spattering of acid. "My God," he said and was silent for a while, absorbing and assimilating this fresh sorrow, making it part of him, like so many others before it. "And my mother?" he asked, at length. "How fares that dear and formidable woman?"

"Mistress Rourke is as well as can be expected," Alex replied, "considering the events of recent weeks. She misses your father, and like the rest of us, she's been very worried about your and Phoebe's disappearance. How are you going to explain this to them?"

Duncan sighed. Telling Alex what had happened was one thing, but describing elevators and what he knew of the mysteries of time to the others was more of a challenge than Duncan felt ready to undertake. "One day," he replied, after some consideration, "I shall, of course, have to tell them the truth. In the meantime, I will simply refuse to say anything. I expect your cooperation in this, Alex."

Alex looked skeptical—which was nothing, of course, in comparison to the way his family and his officers would react to so outlandish a tale. "I don't think they'll accept it," he said. "However, their relief that you have returned, albeit without your lovely wife, will probably occupy them for a time. What do you want to do now?"

"Die," Duncan answered, facing a lifetime without Phoebe. God's blood, but the years ahead looked insufferably dull, as well as lonely beyond his ability to bear. "I don't suppose Fate will be quite so merciful, though."

"Probably not," Alex agreed. "Come—it is time for Lazarus to emerge, trailing his burial clothes, from the tomb. You must show yourself, Duncan, put an end to your share of the distress that's been plaguing this household, and tell the rest of us what to do next."

Duncan nodded, dreading the prospect, and hauled himself out of the chair and onto his feet.

He spread his hands and made an attempt at a grin.

"Behold," he said, "as your unlikely Lazarus steps, bedazzled and blinking, into the light."

Phoebe's hysteria eventually subsided, leaving a waking stupor in its place. A week passed, and then another, and no trace of Duncan was found anywhere on the island. This did not surprise her, of course, since she knew precisely what had happened to him. She stayed on Paradise Island, living in the same room she and Duncan had shared, waiting and thinking and, often, crying. Sometimes, she sat in the cocktail lounge and talked to Snowball, but that didn't change the fact that she was alone again, except for her unborn baby. He wasn't much company yet, of course.

One rainy afternoon, when her money was running low and her mood was even lower, Phoebe stumbled across her copy of Duncan's biography, lying on a metal table on the screened veranda. Her heart hammered when she recognized the familiar cloth cover.

It was as though the volume had assembled itself out of nothing.

Now, here it was, before her. The end of the story, the answers to the questions she had wondered about. Had Duncan lived a long life, or been caught and hanged by the British? Had her visit to the past altered history, and would those changes, if any, be reflected in the musty pages of that slim and tattered book?

Phoebe bit her lower lip, gathering the biography against her bosom for a moment.

The rain made a thick sheet of gray beyond the rusted screens, blotting out the view, hiding the exotic flowers and the lush foliage, driving the bright, raucous birds into silent seclusion. Knowing what had happened to Duncan might bring terrible, unending pain, she reasoned. Suppose he had been captured by the British and been executed, or killed in battle?

Phoebe put the book down, even turned her back, meaning to walk away, but in the end she couldn't.

For better or for worse, she had to find out what became of Duncan.

She slumped into one of the vinyl upholstered patio chairs, picked up Professor Benning's copy of *Duncan Rourke, Pirate or Patriot?*, and opened it to the first page. Immediately, the story gripped her, and she was immersed in it. There were things that made her smile, and, at other times, she had to tilt her head back for a few moments and close her eyes against a fresh and stinging rush of tears.

The author mentioned that Duncan had taken a wife, a mysterious creature thought to have escaped from some prison or asylum, but she had vanished one night, in the aftermath of a battle, and had never been seen or heard from again.

Phoebe ached over those words, sniffled once,

and made herself go on reading. The final chapter was upon her within an hour, for it was a short and very concise book, with few embellishments or poetic graces. Sitting up very straight, her heart in her throat and her stomach in a knot, thinking how odd it was to be in such suspense over things that had happened two centuries before, she hoisted her mental skirts and waded into the truth.

The facts were devastating.

Three weeks after capturing Mornault and his motley crew, after their cannon assault on his home, Duncan had taken the lot of them to a place just south of Queen's Town, all bound and hobbled. He'd used Mornault's own ship, now christened the *Phoebe Anne*, in the process, and turned the group over to friends of his, who would in turn deliver them to British authorities.

The mission had been successful—up to that point. Jacques Mornault and his men were eventually tried before an English magistrate—their crimes alone had taken half a printed page to list—and finally faced a firing squad.

Duncan had sailed back to Paradise Island, only to find a detachment of British soldiers, led by one Captain Lawrence, waiting there for him. He was promptly arrested, along with his crew, and so were Lucas and Alex, but only after Lucas was gravely wounded, trying to save his brother.

Tears streaked down Phoebe's cheeks as the story got worse.

Captain Lawrence, the same man, no doubt,

who had served in Queen's Town and beaten Mr. Billington to a bloody pulp for defending Phoebe in the tavern that day, was determined to make an example of Duncan Rourke. Lawrence had probably heard about the affair with Francesca Sheffield, too, though the writer didn't cover that element of the story, and felt compelled to take an extra pound of flesh on his comrade's behalf.

Duncan had been bound to a tree and savagely whipped, but this time there had been no John Rourke to come to the rescue, to cut him free and carry him home and bind up his wounds. Lucas had been incapacitated in the preceding fracas, Alex and the others bound and made to witness the fate that awaited them on the morrow. No, on this second occasion, Duncan had suffered the full measure of his fate, untempered and undiluted by mercy or justice.

He had been left tied to that tree, throughout the night, that he might have an opportunity, in Lawrence's words, "to contemplate the wages of his sin." By morning, Duncan was dead.

Phoebe closed the book, groped her way through a screen door and out into the tropical downpour, where she was violently ill. She could not have imagined a crueler or more ironic death for Duncan, and she would have gone back through time and suffered the whole ordeal in his place, had that been possible.

Anything—she would have done *anything*, to change history.

412

When her stomach was empty, she stood in the rain, pregnant with the child of a man who had been dead for more than two centuries, heartbroken and sick to the marrow of her bones. She honestly did not know how she would endure the rest of her life with the image of Duncan's execution vivid in her mind; but for the sake of John Alexander Rourke, her son, she must find a way.

It was Snowball who found her standing there in the courtyard, soaked to the skin, face turned to the torrent, hair plastered to her head and dripping. He took her hand and led her inside to the lounge, where he gave her hot coffee to drink and went off in search of towels and a robe.

Phoebe sat on a stool at the bar, her coffee untouched, staring into the long mirror behind Snowball's workspace. Instead of her own pitiful reflection, though, she saw Duncan. He was on his knees before the tree that had served as his whipping post, his hands still tied and extended high over his head, his hair matted with blood and sweat, his face abraded by the rough bark. The flesh of his back was shredded.

She watched Duncan die, powerless to help him or to lend even the simplest comfort. Then she gave an involuntary wail of despair and fainted.

Snowball returned to find her on the floor, struggling to raise herself, and made a soblike sound in his throat. "Phoebe," he said. "Poor little Phoebe."

413

He called an ambulance, over Phoebe's protests, and she was taken to the hospital. Ironically, they put her in the same bed Duncan had occupied during his visit to the twentieth century.

She opened her eyes the next morning to find Sharon, the nurse who resembled Simone, standing beside her bed. "You looking to lose that baby, Mrs. Rourke?" the other woman asked, her voice at once stern and kindly. "Because that's what's going to happen if you don't get yourself calmed down somehow."

Phoebe had already lost her husband, the only man she had ever loved or ever would, and the loss of their child would be the final blow. "Good advice," she admitted. "If only I knew how to act on it. Maybe I need a shrink."

Sharon frowned and drew up a chair. "What happened to that good-looking man of yours?"

Explaining was futile—any attempt would probably get her airlifted to some loony ward on the mainland. "He's gone," she replied. Those two words said everything, and nothing at all. Duncan was more than gone—he'd been a hero, in all senses of the word, and the fates had rewarded him with a horrible death.

The nurse sighed. "Guess it's just you and Baby, then. Lots of women in that predicament these days. Me, for instance."

Phoebe welcomed any distraction from her own miserable situation. Besides, she was genuinely interested. "You're a single parent?"

Sharon smiled. "I've got two boys—Leander and Martin. Things get pretty tough sometimes, but we always seem to make it through." Her expression turned somber in the space of a moment. "Their daddy was killed in the Persian Gulf."

"I'm sorry," Phoebe murmured. She wondered if Sharon's husband had suffered, as Duncan had, or if his death had been quick and merciful. Of course, she wasn't about to ask.

"Yeah," Sharon said with a wistful smile. "I'm sorry, too. My Ben was a good man. But you can only do so much crying and hurting and carrying on, you know? Then you just gotta stop it and get yourself moving again. The sooner you do that, Mrs. Rourke, the better off you and that little baby are going to be."

Phoebe nodded. "I know you're right," she said, as fresh tears burned in her eyes. "And I'm trying."

Sharon rose from her chair, came to Phoebe's bedside, and patted her hand. "You just rest, okay? Just close your eyes and try to think serene thoughts . . ."

It was in that moment that Old Woman's name came back to her, and she recalled the power it was supposed to have. She felt the first tremulous, fragile hope, and began to repeat the word, silently, in the sorest part of her heart.

Phoebe was released the following morning, into the jaws of a raging tropical storm, and Snowball took her back to the hotel in his jeep, the rain thundering so loudly on the vehicle's canvas roof that they didn't try to talk. She was preoccupied anyway—she'd been gaining strength *and* determination steadily since she'd remembered Old Woman's true name.

Once they'd reached their destination, Phoebe went to her room, and Snowball returned to his job. He'd been a good friend, though their association had been short, and she would always be grateful for his kindness.

All day, the storm went on, bending palm trees almost double in the wind, causing the T-shirted staff to fasten all the shutters and close all the doors. The electricity was shut off, just in case, and supplies of canned food and bottled water were taken to the cellars, along with blankets, pillows, and a first aid kit.

Phoebe was agitated; it seemed she'd absorbed the energy of the angry elements. Her mind was racing with plans and possibilities, and with every breath she repeated the secret, one-word litany that had been Old Woman's gift to her.

By nightfall, the storm was at its height, ripping shingles from the roof and rattling the hotel on its foundations. Phoebe, two other guests, and the staff descended to the cellars, carrying lanterns and books and portable radios, talking nervously among themselves.

Phoebe knew, had told herself over and over, that even if she managed to get back to Duncan, she might not reach him in time to keep him from sailing into the hands of the British. She had learned only too well that time did not pass at the same rate in both places—she might get there before Duncan was captured and killed, but she might also find his grave, high on the hillside, beside his father's.

"Don't you want to come and sit with us, dear?" asked Mrs. Zillman, one of the guests, a friendly old woman with blue-rinsed hair. She and her husband, Malcolm, had bought a condo during a previous trip to Paradise Island and were back to take legal possession of the place.

Phoebe stared at the closed doors of the elevator and then lifted her disposable flashlight to the panel above. The numbers indicating the different floors were dark, of course, since the power was off. "I'm too nervous," she answered, and that was certainly true enough. She said Old Woman's name again, in the privacy of her mind.

Mrs. Zillman smiled sympathetically—she'd probably heard the surface details of Phoebe's story from members of the staff—and went back to her husband and the others. An instant after she'd gone, there was a soft chiming sound, and the elevator doors whisked open.

Her heart hammering—after all, it might mean nothing except that the power had been turned on again—Phoebe stepped into the cubicle. Had it not been for her flashlight, she would have been in complete darkness when the doors closed behind her.

"Duncan," she pleaded in a soft, ragged

whisper, "be there. Please, be there, alive and safe and stubborn."

The elevator made a humming sound, though there was no other indication that the thing was powered by electricity, but Phoebe could feel it moving, rising, lifting her. She held her breath when it stopped, and the doors opened.

Duncan's ruined parlor loomed before her, and she lunged into it, without a moment's hesitation, clutching her purse and the flashlight. The doors swept closed behind her, and Phoebe didn't have to look back to know they had vanished entirely.

She was back in Duncan's world.

Phoebe stood in the center of the gracious room, frowning. There was no storm here, and it was daytime instead of night. She started to call Duncan's name, then stopped herself. If the British had already taken over the island, she didn't want to alert them of her presence.

Not that she could qualify as a threat, armed with a flashlight and a purseful of prenatal vitamins and other such perks of life in modern America.

Was Duncan still alive, or had she arrived too late?

She was still standing there, biting her lower lip and wondering how to proceed, when Margaret Rourke appeared. At the sight of her daughter-in-law, Margaret gave a little cry and rushed to take Phoebe into her arms.

Phoebe returned the hug, then drew back to study Margaret's face. The exquisite features were drawn, the eyes shadowed and a little sunken, but the Rourke strength was still very much in evidence. Margaret was dressed in mourning clothes, and Phoebe prayed there was only John to grieve for, and not Duncan, too.

"We thought you'd left us forever," Margaret said.

Phoebe shook her head. She was terrified to ask the question, but could delay it no longer. "Where is Duncan?"

Margaret's expression was blank for a moment, as if she couldn't remember the answer, and Phoebe held her breath.

"Why, he's gone to Queen's Town," Margaret said at last, brightening a little. "They took that wretched pirate and his men there, to be turned over to the authorities. Oh, my dear—Duncan will be overjoyed to find you here!"

Phoebe's relief was like balm to a throbbing wound, but she couldn't afford to indulge in it for long. Duncan was still on a collision course with Captain Lawrence and a shipful of British troops, and if they didn't find a way to warn him, Phoebe would probably be forced to witness her husband's final ordeal. The thought brought gall surging into the back of her throat.

"And the British? Have they arrived yet?"

Margaret shook her head. "We haven't been expecting them," she said.

"Trust me, they're on their way. Are we alone here on Paradise Island—just us women?"

Margaret nodded. "It's only Phillippa and Old

419

Woman and me. The servants have gone to other islands, and all the men are with Duncan."

"Good," Phoebe said, linking her arm with Margaret's. "Here's what we're going to do . . ."

It was the dead of night, and there was no moon, but Duncan pushed Mornault's refitted ship, now called the *Phoebe Anne*, toward Paradise Island. His gut told him there was trouble brewing, and his mother and sister were alone there, with only Old Woman to protect them.

Not that the latter wouldn't make a formidable opponent.

Alex, who had not liked being parted from his new bride, was every bit as impatient to return, and he joined Duncan at the bow.

"The sea's almighty quiet tonight," he said, and though the words painted a calm picture, Duncan heard the uneasiness behind them.

"Yes," he said. "One would almost think these were times of peace, offering no peril to men abroad on the waters."

"It is women at home on the land that I'm thinking of now," Alex replied. "I shouldn't have left Phillippa behind."

Duncan was not unsympathetic. He had wanted to protect Phoebe, too, when she had been with him. Now, he would have given anything he owned to have her at his side again, no matter what the danger to either of them. "What could you have done, Alex?" he reasoned. "Brought your lovely wife aboard and allowed her to rub elbows with the likes of Jacques Mornault? Risked having her captured by the British and taken to England or somewhere else as either a prisoner or a prize?"

Alex shook his head, but his attention was fixed on the dark waters. He narrowed his gaze and frowned. "Do you see a light?"

Duncan peered into the gloom. Sure enough, there was a faint, flickering glow, far off. Not landward, certainly, but well away from the coast of any of the islands, and directly in their path. Without speaking to Alex, he turned and summoned the crew from their quiet pursuits with a shout.

The cannons were prepared for combat, and those few men who had been unarmed strapped on swords or tucked daggers or pistols into their belts. Duncan climbed the rigging himself, trying to make out the origin of the light, but they were still too far away to assess the situation with any real accuracy.

"Maybe we should just go round," Alex suggested. He was a raider at heart, striking suddenly, taking the enemy by surprise when he could, and staying out of their way when he thought they were laying a trap.

"No good," Duncan disagreed, with a shake of his head. "They know we're here. That's why they've shown themselves."

"But it may be an ambush," suggested Lucas, who had come on deck when the alarm sounded and immediately sought out Duncan and Alex.

Despite his Tory tendencies, the man appeared to enjoy the life of a rebel. Perhaps they would yet win him to the cause of liberty.

"A clumsy one, if that's the case," Duncan said.

They drew nearer, skimming almost silently over the obsidian waters, riding the night wind under a starless sky, and the cannons were loaded and tamped and ready for firing. It was a surprise when they came upon two small skiffs, bobbing on the tide. One had been set ablaze like a Viking funeral pyre, and would go under soon, and the other held four cloaked figures with lamps upraised.

"Don't shoot," a female voice shouted over the crackle of the burning boat.

The bottom seemed to fall out of Duncan's stomach. Phoebe? But that was impossible; he'd left her behind, however unwillingly and inadvertently, in that crazy century of hers.

Nonetheless, her name escaped him anyway, a hoarse shout, carrying over the water. "Phoebe?"

"Duncan!" she screamed back, and the sound was full of joy.

Duncan closed his eyes for a moment, in an effort to hold onto his emotions. "Phoebe," he whispered, as Lucas and Alex gave shouts of delight.

When the skiff had drawn alongside, and a rope ladder had been thrown over the *Phoebe Anne*'s sleek side, Duncan was the first to descend. He did not speak to Phoebe, but simply wrenched her into his arms, nearly oversetting the small boat in the process, and buried his face in her neck. He didn't give a damn if she felt his tears on her skin.

She clung to him, and he felt her belly, full of his baby, pressed against him.

While they stood there, holding each other, swaying with the motion of the great sea, Phillippa, Margaret, and even Old Woman ascended the ladder to the deck. The burning rowboat sputtered and went under.

"How—?" Duncan began, capable of speech at long last.

Phoebe touched his lips with her fingers. "No time for that now, darling," she said. "We've got to get away from here, quick, or your story, as told in *Duncan Rourke, Pirate or Patriot?* is going to end on a real downbeat."

He laughed, because he was so full of joy, because life had surprised him and brought her back. He would ask nothing more of it than that, he thought. Phoebe, his baby—they were more than enough.

Phoebe started up the ladder, and Duncan followed.

On the deck of the ship that bore her name, Phoebe told her husband that the British were waiting on Paradise Island, and for once in his life, he did not question her. He nodded, but did not give the expected command to turn the ship in another direction. Instead, they sailed steadily on.

Phoebe was alarmed. "Aren't we going to turn aside?"

"No," Duncan replied, in a damnably calm tone of voice. "Paradise Island is my home. I will not let them have it without a fight."

An image of Duncan tied to a tree flashed into Phoebe's mind, and she thought she would be sick. "Have you gone mad while we were apart?" she whispered, horrified. "I've just told you what the future holds . . ."

Duncan touched her face in a gesture that was at once reverent and defiant. "I love you, Phoebe Rourke, and having you here beside me again is all I would ask of heaven. But don't you see? There is no turning from our destiny—if we do not go out to meet it head on, it will follow us."

Phoebe lowered her head, and Duncan drew her into his embrace.

"I'm afraid," she whispered. "I'm so afraid I only found you to lose you again."

He cupped his hand under her chin and made her look at him. "As long as you are nearby," he said, "I am invincible."

Phoebe simply clung to him, knowing it would do no good to argue.

A few hours later, Phoebe sat with Phillippa and Margaret in the galley, waiting, offering silent, frantic prayers. The gloom was so impenetrable that she could not see her companions, who were on either side of her. The only sound, besides their breathing, was the rhythmic slap of water against the sides of the ship.

The first cannon blast, when it came, reverberated through every timber of the vessel and set Phoebe's very soul a-tremble within her. The three women clasped hands, but no one spoke.

There was another explosion, then another, before the objects of Duncan's attack fired back. The *Phoebe Anne*'s bow shuddered under the impact, and there was shouting above decks.

Phoebe pictured British soldiers boarding the ship, bayonets drawn, and suddenly she could not sit and wait for another moment. She pulled free of Margaret and Phillippa, who tried valiantly to restrain her, and stumbled through the galley to the portal, feeling her way, bruising herself on tables and benches as she went.

Finding the door, she threw back the bolt and flung it open.

A wash of lantern light spilled into the companionway from the upper deck, and the din of fighting was dreadful. The air was acrid with smoke and the odd, metallic scent of blood, which Phoebe was learning to recognize only too well.

"Phoebe!" Margaret gasped from behind her. "Come back!"

"Are you mad?" Phillippa added.

Phoebe groped for a weapon and found a heavy drinking ladle in a bucket of water. Grabbing that, ignoring Duncan's mother and sister, she flung herself up onto the deck.

A sword blade whistled past her and lodged in one of the masts, and Phoebe, fueled only by adrenaline, wielded the ladle with a force born of desperation. After that, she lost herself in the fray, swinging and dodging, coughing and squinting as she searched for Duncan. She had no time to ponder the question of what she would do when she found him.

Presently, Phoebe's head cleared a little, and she realized the futility of fighting pirates with a dipper. She crouched behind a barrel and waited, holding her breath.

Men screamed both in pain and in fury, and intermittently there were loud splashes as one unfortunate or another plunged over the side. On shore, a great fire blazed and roared against the dark sky, consuming Duncan's house.

Closing the passageway to the future forever.

And the battle continued, finally distilling, after what seemed like hours, to two men, swords clanging in the flickering light of a single lantern. The combatants were Duncan and the British captain, Lawrence.

From the surrounding silence, Phoebe deduced that, for everyone else aboard the *Phoebe Anne*, the fight was over. She couldn't guess which side had won, wouldn't look away from Duncan once she had found him again.

Lawrence was a formidable swordsman and almost forced Duncan to his knees at one point, but Duncan rallied in a burst of strength and, in a shower of bluish sparks from their upraised blades, drove the other man back into the ship's rail. Phoebe saw her husband stop, weigh the situation, and then thrust his sword through Lawrence's heart.

Duncan stared down at the man he'd killed for a long moment, but spared only the briefest glance for the fire on shore. After wrenching the sword blade free, he flung the weapon down onto the bloody deck and turned.

"Phoebe?" he rasped the name, and all his hopes and fears were audible in those two syllables.

She ran to him, flung herself into his arms.

They had met destiny, together, and they had altered it.

"It's gone," she said. "The house—the elevator . . ."

"It doesn't matter," Duncan said raggedly, holding her very close.

And he was right. Nothing mattered, except that they were together and, for the moment at least, safe.

The *Phoebe Anne* was a small vessel, and since there was no privacy to be had, some of the more eagerly anticipated aspects of Phoebe and Duncan's reunion had to be postponed. After the prisoners had been bound and the wounded attended to, they sat in the galley, across a table from each other, through all that remained of the night, saying nothing, palms touching, fingers interlocked. Souls joined.

When they dropped anchor, just after sunrise, in a cove off a rugged, unpopulated island, Phoebe did not recognize the landscape. It wasn't among those she had visited on the canoe trip from Paradise Island to Queen's Town, when she'd left Duncan to begin her brief career as a tavern wench.

"What is this place?" she asked, standing beside her husband on the deck.

Duncan grinned, leaning against the rail and surveying the white beach and thick foliage like a patriarch looking out over his kingdom. "I'm surprised you don't recognize it, Mistress Rourke," he said. "This is the Garden of Eden."

Phoebe looked back, taking in the population of the ship with a pointed glance. "It seems we have an abundance of Adams and even a few extra Eves," she said.

"It's a big island," Duncan replied.

And it was.

While the ship danced on sheltered, sparkling waters, Duncan and Phoebe went ashore in one small boat, Phillippa and Alex in another. The two couples parted from each other on the beach, traveling in opposite directions. The moment they'd rounded the first bend, Phoebe turned and planted herself in front of Duncan, slipping her arms around his neck.

"Not another step," she said. "I've waited as long as I can, Duncan Rourke."

He threw back his magnificent head and laughed, and the sound echoed over the waters that had been his home and his mistress for so long. "What a brazen chit you are," he said and kissed her hard.

She caught his hand and led him into the shade, where the sand made a bed of sugar and the foliage provided a bright green canopy, scented and moist.

He kissed her again, and they dropped to their knees, never breaking the contact, trying to remove each other's sooty, dirty clothes with gentle, awkward movements of their hands. They had been apart for what seemed like an eternity and had expected the separation to last forever, and now they found themselves together, in Eden. Patience was beyond them both.

Duncan lowered Phoebe to the sand and raised his mouth from hers only when he opened her bodice and spread the fabric wide, to reveal her full breasts. "I love you, Mistress Rourke," he said. "Will you make your home here with me and start the world all over again?"

Phoebe clasped his head in her hands and brought him to her nipple, giving a strangled cry of ecstasy when he closed his mouth upon her and drew greedily. "I love you as well, Mr. Rourke," she replied. "And yes—yes—I want this to be the beginning—of everything . . ."

He raised her skirts and tore her pantaloons away in desperation, entering her in a single long, deep stroke.

The first climax racked Phoebe the instant Duncan claimed her, and he compounded the pleasure, made it nearly unendurable, in fact, by moving with deliberation against that secret nerve center deep inside her, a place he had found and mastered during other, earlier sessions of love-making. After the initial explosion, there was another, and still another, until Phoebe was dazed and whimpering, dissolving into the hot sand. Only then did Duncan unleash the full force of his lovemaking and take her in earnest, and the result was cataclysmic.

When it was over, at long last, and they could move again, and breathe, they bathed each other in the warm, clear water. Then they came together again, in the ebbing tide, like two creatures of the sea, their strong young bodies flexing in graceful union.

They were a long time in satisfying each other, were Duncan and Phoebe, but it didn't matter. After all, this was Eden. The world was fresh and new, and they had forever.

Epilogue

Somewhere in Present-day America . . .

The book, offered for twenty-five cents at a church rummage sale, was old and musty, and there were probably only a handful of copies left anywhere in the world. Pleased, the collector held it close against her chest for a moment and smiled. Then, after paying the price, she carried her volume outside, into the parish garden, which was bright with flowers and spring sunshine. Taking a seat on a stone bench, she opened the little tome to its title page.

Duncan Rourke, Pirate or Patriot?

The woman flipped slowly through the pages, skimming a paragraph here and there and examining the lovely old engraved illustrations one by one. Finally, she turned to the last page, for she was overly curious and liked to know in advance how things were going to turn out, whenever the opportunity presented itself.

"The British called him 'pirate,' " she read, *"but every American must acknowledge Duncan Rourke as a true patriot. With the help of the mysterious Phoebe, his wife and partner, he continued to plague the English navy until the Revolution had ended in victory. After the war, the Rourkes returned to Troy,*

431

the family plantation near what is now Charleston, South Carolina, there to live long and happy lives, raising four sons and two daughters. They, and others like them, had fought for the dream, with hands and hearts and wits, and prevailed. And from their passion, a great, imperfect, and promising nation was born."

IF YOU HAVE ENJOYED READING THIS
LARGE PRINT BOOK AND YOU
WOULD LIKE MORE INFORMATION
ON HOW TO ORDER A WHEELER
LARGE PRINT BOOK, PLEASE WRITE
TO:

WHEELER PUBLISHING, INC.
P.O. BOX 531
ACCORD, MA 02018-0531